Alison Fell was born in Dumfries, Scotland, raised in villages in the Highlands and the Borders, and trained as a sculptor in Edinburgh. She became involved with the Women's Liberation Movement in 1969 in Leeds, where she was in the radical theatre group, Welfare State. In 1970 she moved to London to work in the Women's Street Theatre Group, and then on underground and left-wing newspapers and magazines. She was a member of the *Spare Rib* collective for several years and edited its anthology of fiction, *Hard Feelings*. Since then she has been Writer-in-Residence in two London boroughs and has also taught creative writing in an art college and in adult education. Her poetry has been published in several collections, amongst them *Licking the Bed Clean*, *Smile Smile Smile Smile*, *One Foot on the Mountain* and *Bread and Roses* (Virago), and she has read widely at events and art centres throughout the United Kingdom. In 1981 her children's novel, *The Grey Dancer*, was published. *Every Move You Make* is her first work of fiction for adults. Alison Fell lives in north London with her sixteen-year-old son.

Every Move You Make

Alison Fell

While I was writing this book, a number of friends helped greatly by reading the manuscript, criticising, listening, encouraging, buying me dinners and otherwise keeping my nerve up. Among them are Marsha Rowe, Ann Oosthuizen, Tina Reid, Michèle Roberts, Nigel Fountain, Liz Heron, Rosie Parker and Pete Ayrton. My thanks also to Stef Pixner, Jenny Uglow and Ruthie Petrie for their excellent editorial advice, and to Joan Curtis, for her generosity of mind.

for the urban nomads

Published by VIRAGO PRESS Limited 1984
41 William IV Street, London WC2N 4DB

British Library Cataloguing in Publication Data

Fell, Alison,
Every move you make
I. Title
823'.914[F] PR6056.E/

ISBN 0-86068-580-2
ISBN 0-86068-585-3 Pbk

Typeset by Clerkenwell Graphics Ltd.,
and printed in Great Britain by litho
at The Anchor Press, Tiptree, Essex

1

A light frost is melting on the grass in front of the cottage. Matt stands by the rainbarrel, scooping scum off the water. He is stripped to the waist and shivering.

'Is this water okay?' he asks unhappily.

'The well water's better for washing,' I answer, friendly. I have made up my mind; there is no longer any need for antagonism.

He gives me a wary look. 'Feeling better?'

'Yes. Weak, but mending.'

'Glad to hear it.' He dries his hands on his jeans.

A bird whirrs in the bushes, startling him. I smile. 'I had a very Zen shit in the autumn leaves.' I point to the beech wood across the track.

'You're a real country lass, aren't you.'

The words jar, but I nod, humouring him.

'Want me to hit you with my haiku?'

'Sure thing.' With his hands on his hips, he waits for me to recite.

With its dark brown smell
the shit curls
glossy as beech leaves;
a blossom falls on it.

Matt bursts out laughing.

'Well, give or take a syllable.'

'Impressive,' he says, 'I suppose you can operate the well too?'

Beside the cottage the grass is long, wet and dangerous with nettles. The exterior of the well is built of long trestles, nailed at one corner to the low thick branch of a sycamore tree. I grip the iron handle and begin to wind the bucket up.

'It's heavy,' I warn, as Matt takes over. 'If you let it slip it could break your arm.'

The pulley creaks as the rope winds in. I open the trapdoor and lean out over the black hole to catch the bucket, without once looking down. Drops splash from the full bucket and run back down into the darkness. I set it down at Matt's feet.

He lets the water run through his fingers. 'Mm, incredible. All suave and silvery.' Toothbrush in hand, he peers over the edge of the well, leaning a long way out.

My stomach turns over. The flat of my hand between his shoulderblades: he wouldn't have a chance.

'How deep is it?'

'Oh, fifty feet, maybe.'

Without turning, he beckons. 'Have you seen this stonework? They really knew how to build in those days. These walls are perfection.'

'I don't like to look.' My mouth is dry. I leave the glade and go back inside. Last night's dishes wait on the kitchen table; I begin to stack them in the sink. A bee which must be the very last of the season cruises loudly across the open door and nuzzles among the late roses. When Matt has had his wash, I will go back and sit by the mouth of the well, for I have unfinished business there.

There are white patches on the ground where Matt has spat toothpaste. I tip the bucket over them to flush them away.

The first glance brings vertigo. *I will drop like a stone*. I look away from the dark hole. I am empty, dry and empty.

When I look again, this time holding firmly to the trestle, I see at the bottom my own reflection, very small. I see it only for a moment before a drip from the seeping walls whistles down and stirs the surface into ripples, circular, intersecting ripples.

All I do is build walls. Walls of stone. Who goes there, friend or foe? Walls around my territory. Perhaps Matt is right to batter at them.

I put my head in my hands. If I leave him, it will be so lonely.

My body will fight for him.

Smoke rises from the cottage chimney. I can hear the thud of an axe, wood splintering; between the strokes I hear Matt crooning to himself. The sound carries across the clearing, it's Dylan, I could not mistake it. 'Are you willing to risk it all,' he is singing, full-throated now,' or is your love in vain?'

I think of London. Of Vi, narrowing her eyes at her easel, scraping off a muddy colour, squeezing a clean new one from the tube. Of Andrew, puzzling over the price of goalie's gloves and whether I can afford to buy them for him. Of last winter, and the beginning.

2

At the end of February, Andrew had an operation. The information they had given me at the hospital was wrong, so that when I arrived in the morning I found a space where his bed should have been. He went to theatre ten minutes ago, Sister said.

The bed gave him small electric shocks. He had complained about them the night before and, embarrassed, I'd gone to consult the nurses. I was afraid that he was having anxiety attacks again, and that the nurses at the desk would see through my composed face and think, Oh God, anxious parent: anxious child. However, they sighed and said yes, it's static, it collects – something to do with the metal bed frames. Shocks are an occupational hazard. They came through to the small ward and tested the bed by running their scissors along the edge of the frame. They said that sometimes they earthed the static by kicking the bed with their rubber-soled shoes. One said that she had touched the wedding ring of an old woman while taking her pulse and the sparks fairly leapt. They looked annoyed at the whole business.

But now Andrew was downstairs somewhere deep in anaesthesia, and I was stranded high on the sixth floor, in the white, white ward, with nothing to do but wait. I leaned on the window sill and stared out at the sun on Hampstead Heath, at track-suited runners, at kite-flyers. Straining, I could just see the Magdala Arms, where Jed and I had sometimes sat drinking on summer Sundays. Jed had told me that the last woman to be hanged in Britain was apprehended there. It happened in the fifties. Hers was a crime of passion: she shot her lover.

I turned back to the white room. It was empty of beds, and contained only some arrangements of plastic tubing, electrical sockets of various sizes, and a tray of steel containers, kidney-shaped. In the silence my mind hummed with morbid questions. About blindfolds, and whether she had refused them. About whether she was aware, at the end, of a deep brown well engulfing her, or only of a white flash of wall above a trap-door. Yes. She did what she had to do, and paid the price. In 1950 things were clear cut, symmetrical as melodrama. In 1978, on the other hand, you let your lover escape unscathed and choked not on a rope, but on your own bitterness. Jed had slithered away like this, so easily. I hadn't even had the heart to threaten him. Couldn't bring myself to deny the freedom he laid claim to. Oh, certainly I was bitter, but pointlessly, for what did it all add up to in the end but absence?

And then suddenly Andrew was wheeled in, high up in a bed with cot bars, and I was limp with relief, for at least I was here for him, a presence, in the flesh and in the heart (even if it had been necessary to dress the part, put on a mum costume of neat jacket, skirt, high boots, to reassure myself that, alone, I was sufficient. Solid enough, nurturing enough, for this child I've reared for ten years).

The nurse shook him to say, 'Mum's here', and I pressed his hand, whispering: 'It's me, it's June,' before he slumped back into infant sleep again; I hoped that he had seen me, had recorded that he was not abandoned in that darkness.

I bent over him. His face was so young, peaceful. The anaesthetic had taken years off. He was sleeping in the vulnerable way I remembered from years ago, with his arms flung back behind his head, wide open to the light or the dark or the scalpel. His right hand wore a criss-cross of lint from an injection.

The night before he had sat on a chair by the bed and refused to get back in. He simply turned his mouth down and went on strike, because of the shocks. The nurse remade the bed, I cajoled, but still he wouldn't move. Visiting hours ended, and I had to leave him there waiting for the nurse to wheel his old bed out and a new one in. Still he wasn't happy with it, they said: he complained of tingling feelings.

Opposite the Magdala Arms a red car slowed and parked, and I peered at the man who got out and loped across the road, convinced that it was Jed. Distance blurred the figure, and my obsession supplied the details: the denim jacket with sleeves too short, the skinny, poking shoulder blades, the flying brown hair.

When a nurse came to pull the blinds down, blotting out the red car and the green mounds of the park, I felt rebuked. Perhaps it's regulations, I thought. She lifted Andrew's coverlet to check for bleeding, and I got my first glimpse of the scar. There were several small sutures around his penis, and the end looked very naked without its foreskin, swollen and purpling. I was sure it would frighten him when he woke and saw it.

In the dimness he turned on to his side, restless. I looked at the dark crescent of one lash against his cheek. All around him was a sprawl of earphones, coiled wires, alarm systems. At the bottom of the bed lay a teddy borrowed from the ward playroom. I watched him travel slowly, slowly, back from early childhood, until at last he slept more normally, more like his ten-year-old self.

They say you don't dream under anaesthetic; they say it's a time which eludes memory, or which memory simply refuses. A time others must fill in for you, like the murk of infancy. I remembered Andrew's questions: how hard he tried to fill in those gaps. What was I like, mummy, when I balanced on daddy's hand? What happened when you dropped my cot downstairs? Did I yell, did I fall on my head? What happened when I was born out of you feet first? He asked those questions still.

His face was reddening. From time to time he stirred. I wondered what was filling his head. Football scores, perhaps, or Monster Fun Annuals. When the nurse moved him to change the plastic under-sheet he jerked his head up and clapped his hands wildly once, shouted 'Very well done!' and tottered confusedly back down into sleep.

Watching him wrestle with oblivion, I thought of the rape. I remembered nothing, only what it felt like to be seventeen and full of whisky, and what the moon looked like on the sea just before I passed out. For the real story, I had to rely on Rona and Jim, and the culprit himself. He pulled my knickers from his pocket like you would a handkerchief, they said; he was shamed to tears when he saw the way they looked at him.

All this is hearsay. There was little trace next day, hardly a soreness. Perhaps unconsciousness had made me deeply relaxed, or perhaps he moistened me with spittle; whatever the truth, he did no physical harm when he penetrated that rag doll on the sand.

In the hospital the technology of healing was silent; the nurses scurried softly, keeping watch at regular intervals over drips, temperatures, pulses. I sneaked the blind aside and looked out in time to see the red car make a three-point turn in the road. Had Jed heard, I wondered, did he know that Andrew was in hospital, and that I was up here, one of London's nurturers at one of London's windows?

No. The car was a new model, too long in the chassis to be Jed's. Of course he didn't know, and even if he had, what difference would it make? It was too late for him to share the anxieties and comedies of these hours of caring and soothing and inventing games and distractions.

Time for Andrew's pulse to be taken again. As the nurse approached she gave me a curious look, and I squirmed with self-consciousness. Where's the husband? – I could almost hear her thinking it.

'He seems hot,' I said quickly, and she slid a thermometer under his arm. Watching her hands flutter lightly over him, I wanted her to lift my wrist too, to hold it gently and confidently between her finger and thumb, to feel for my rhythms. I wanted her to brush my hair, I wanted a white muslin gown and blankets to snuggle in: oh, it was endless, what I wanted.

Andrew woke up. Seeing me, he smiled wanly. I put my hand out and he slipped his into it, groping for my fingers.

'I thought you were crying,' he mumbled.

'No.' I shook my head. 'I was watching you, and dreaming.'

Then he jerked upright, remembering, and threw the sheets aside to inspect his cock. He fell back, and tears welled up in his eyes. And then the needs and queries came tumbling. Did they put stitches in? Will I have to come back and have them out? Will it hurt to piss? When can I have a drink? The nurses were volunteering nothing, so that I had to go trotting to the desk each time, hearing even my whispered questions ring out in the quiet. I began to feel panicky. They're leaving all the calming to me, I thought; they are letting me judge and mediate his needs in the belief that I have a mother's expertise.

Dear mother, there are a few questions I would like to ask.

'Yes,' I told Andrew, 'you can have orange juice now, the nurse is bringing it.'

I watched the brisk women move through the ward.

'No,' I told Andrew, 'the nurse says you can't have any food yet, it'll make you sick.'

I half-sat, half-lay on the bed and put my arm round his shoulders. We pored over the Guinness Book of Records together, goggling at the tallest man in recorded history who died aged twenty-two at a height of eight feet eleven inches. Andrew complained of hunger again, so I fetched the nurse. Well, perhaps he could try a cup of tea and a dry biscuit, she decided. I glowed. My pestering had worked. Perhaps it doesn't matter so much, I thought. As long as I can piece together something that will pass as the real thing, then how are they to know that all the time I'm thinking: what if? What if my knees give way in the hospital corridor, what if Andrew leans on me and I cave in like a cardboard doll's house?

Andrew smiled as he tackled his tea and said yes, he felt less dopey now. Normality was returning. I watched biscuit crumbs roll off his lips and scatter on the bed; he chewed open-mouthed – squelch, crunch, mash, like a comic strip; the racket went on and on and little dribbles ran out of the corner of his mouth, I could hardly stand the din.

A trolley lady came up and asked if Andrew would be having lunch. She was Asian, Malayan, perhaps. Yes, tea, thank-you, I wanted to say, and two sugars please; my stomach rumbled mournfully. Pointing to the 'Nil by Mouth' sign over Andrew's bed, I told her that I didn't think he was allowed anything else, and she made a sympathetic face at him and padded away.

Hey, I wanted to yell, don't mothers get fed?

Andrew licked the last crumbs from his plate and settled back on his pillows. Like a Mogul, I thought irritably, like a little Mogul. After a couple of minutes he sighed and fretted about sicky feelings in his stomach. But he kept the food down: a good sign.

3

When Andrew was told that he wouldn't be discharged until Sunday, he took it with good grace, for in the meantime he had found himself a friend. A boy had been admitted to the small ward with an impacted wisdom tooth, and Andrew, with his operation safely behind him, had perked up, and was revelling now in the role of veteran.

On Saturday afternoon I left him explaining anaesthetic procedures to the frightened new inmate, and set off for

Brixton, where there was to be a demonstration for Women's Day. I went out of duty, came home with a mouth dry from cigarettes and too many disjointed conversations, and got straight into the bath. The phone rang immediately. Cursing, I wrapped myself in a towel and stumbled downstairs.

It was Vi, as I had thought. Her voice was high and taut. 'You *are* coming, aren't you?' she said, panting a little, and I heard a jingling sound. I could tell that she was tossing her head. I knew the gesture well: it was jerky and aimless and set all her long hair and her jewellery flying. 'I wanted to make sure you weren't too . . . freaked out, or anything.'

'Am I an invalid or something?' My voice was sharp. As usual, she was prejudging, pinning me down into an old pattern.

'Just making sure you were coming...' There was a muttered conversation on the end of the line, and Vi's voice came back. 'Sorry, Matt's making me jumpy. He's flapping around getting the chicken in the oven.'

I had a quick vision of him there beside her listening, and I felt exposed. At a loss for words, I stared into the receiver. Did she want everyone to know? Solicitude was all very well, but she should have realised by now that some areas of the past were better left alone. Or at least she could give me the benefit of the doubt for once. 'I'll be there at eight,' I said, and my voice sounded stiff, ungracious.

The draught from the front door raised goose-pimples on my shoulders. I got back into the bath and let myself slip deep into the water. Try as I might, I couldn't convince myself that dinner with Vi and her new flame was a tolerable way of negotiating the empty reaches of a wet Saturday night. It didn't even approximate to what I needed, so why deceive myself? I sank deeper, until the water tickled my upper lip. I was convulsed with discontent. All I did with my life was work on the magazine, see to Andrew, visit women friends. Living at the minimum: it felt like a disease.

Outside on the windy street rain and dusk mingled. In the bath the water turned cool and scummy, and I chastised myself.

I was ungenerous. Vi had been good to me, had been loyal and kind, had looked after me. So why did I still feel, sometimes, that she didn't really *like* me? In one way or another, I'd been puzzling over this all the time we had known each other. For those five years, something had held us together, but for the life of me, I didn't know what it was.

Drying myself, I noticed a faint billow effect of loose skin on my stomach. It wasn't a weakening of muscle, for when I pulled in my stomach it remained. It was ironic, really, how Vi, who used to envy my skinniness, fat tearful Vi, the compulsive eater, had suddenly become as slender as a string. Whereas here was I, with the casing of me beginning to slip out of control.

Bitchy, I thought, and towelled the soft belly energetically. I was not pleased with myself.

'We should have June over to dinner.' I could hear Vi saying it. The duty of the coupled woman to the single one. In the mirror my eyes looked back at me, greyish and bleak, and my lower lip jutted stubbornly. These days, with her awkward new love affair, Vi was always beautiful. She never ceased to surprise me. My mind returned to the first time I had seen her with Matt. It was a Sunday before Christmas. I had been in bed all day, sweating out the 'flu, when she burst into my bedroom and more or less shouted:

'Matt thought it was time we met each other's friends.'

My ears rang and I sank down in the bed. Vi led in a tall unwilling figure in a long trenchcoat.

'...So I thought I'd introduce you...' She managed to make it sound both grudging and graceless.

'Hi,' said the figure, without enthusiasm. He slumped down on one of the green floor-cushions and regarded me owl-like over the end of the bed. Vi perched on my desk, pottering with notebooks and felt-tips, disordering a manuscript I'd brought home from the magazine; she sat swinging her legs in bright red tights and fluorescent green socks, back and forth, back and forth, and the alarm on her face made me talk and talk until I felt my temperature soaring. Matt, meanwhile wasn't rising to the occasion. He stayed in a heap by the window and rolled a great many cigarettes. His head was sunk in the shoulders of his coat, which he hadn't taken off (perhaps he was expecting Vi to whisk him off as abruptly as she had brought him in?) and all I could see of him was a fall of American-looking blond hair and a small triangle of scowl tissue.

Vi had told me he was an actor, and so I asked him polite questions about his work, which were rebuffed. Annoyed, I decided that he was too passive by half. He was merely tolerating Vi, tolerating the situation. And as for the beauty Vi had spoken of, it was lost on me. Looking back, I could remember rubbery features, a rather pock-marked skin. As far as I could see, Vi was in love with a narcissist, and a sulky one at that.

The rain had turned to sleet by the time I reached Matt's house. It was an expensive address for an unemployed actor; it was so near Hampstead Heath that I could see the tall tower of the hospital, and even pick out the windows of Andrew's ward.

I pulled my shoulders back, held up my bottle of wine, and knocked. The door was large and solid, and the door-knocker was cast iron, in the shape of two coiled snakes. When it opened I jumped back, embarrassed, for Matt stood there looking down at me. He was wearing an apron and seemed enormously tall. As he guided me past a tangle of bicycles in the hall, I realised that his hair was different, shorter.

'Vi's like a cat on hot bricks about the cooking,' he said casually. 'I asked her who is this June, is she a big perfectionist or something?'

'You *are* American, then?' There was just the trace of an accent.

'Yes. Some, anyway – a mongrel.' He switched a light on, and paused on the stairs, barring my way. '*Are* you, though? A perfectionist?'

His tone took me by surprise. It didn't sound like an idle question, it sounded as if he really wanted to know. I had an uncanny flash of the sort of childhood games which had a password you could never be sure of knowing. One day you could be right, but the next day the word would change, and you'd be barred. I made myself say: 'A bit, perhaps. But Vi does have a terrible inferiority complex about cooking.' It sounded shy, shy and prim. I looked past him. Through the open door of the flat I could just see Vi. She had her back to me, and she was holding a tea-towel.

Matt stood aside to let me pass. 'She certainly seems to have a heavy number going for you,' he said, looking hard at me. His hair had been cropped roughly, so that more of the damaged skin showed. Under heavy, rather beetling brows, two dark blue eyes sized me up. I walked past him into the flat. The kitchen was narrow and white with a french window in the end wall. On another wall there was a cork board with a Rock Against Racism poster pinned on it, a few flyers for fringe theatre productions, and a Colour Supplement photo of Jane Fonda in *Julia.* Vi was crouching by the open oven door. Her straight black hair had fallen around her breasts and a strand of it was dangling in the fat of the roasting pan. I offered to help, but she shook her head. The smile she gave me was brief and harassed.

'Why don't you get Matt to play you a record in the living-room?' she said, formally, like a hostess. She looked so displaced that I felt concerned for her. She had been so adamant that living with Matt was hardly more than a convenience. 'It's a halfway house,' she'd said, 'and it's only till my flat is re-wired, no longer.' I had believed her then, but seeing her now, straining to accommodate herself to Matt's kitchen, I was more inclined to be sceptical.

Matt lounged easily in the doorway, watching us. He took the bottle from my hand and asked if he could take my coat. He grinned as he folded it over his arm, and gave an ironic bow.

I touched Vi's shoulder. 'You've dressed.' It was a statement of affection. She was wearing a red shirt and black satin pants with sequins at the waist. Her face relaxed a little, and she did a brief pirouette. Her hands went to her waist, to stroke the sequins.

'I sewed them on myself. You can get any colour you want in the market.' Her eyebrows flew up and down as she spoke. Her face was longish, pale, pointed, with the flat cheekbones and slanting eyes of an Egyptian sculpture. Behind me Matt coughed, and Vi became alert. He looked anxious, eager to please. I smiled, suddenly touched. They were making such a fuss of me.

'You've cut your hair.'

His hand went up to feel it. 'Vi slashed away at it.'

'I think the ex-hippy hanging around in the doorway is trying to tell you something,' Vi said. 'I believe he wants you to admire his living-room.' She nudged me. 'Go on, make his day.'

In the living-room there was another french window with brown shutters. Elsewhere, magnolia colours, and a fresh paint smell. There were bookshelves on either side of the fireplace, and a stereo gleaming under an anglepoise lamp in the corner. I thought of my own room, where work and sleep and recreation all competed for the same space, where the carpet was worn thin, and the shelves sagged. How dingy he must have considered it. I looked around. Here, the floor was sanded and varnished. Afghan rugs, cinnamon and black, were carefully placed.

Matt hovered. 'I have a balcony, too,' he said proudly.

'Nice room. Harmonious. You must have put a lot of work in.' Money too, I thought. The stereo – that spoke of certain priorities. No tinny tape recorders here.

Matt sat down in a rocking chair by the fireplace, cautioning me about the blue sofa I settled myself on. It made rude noises, he said, it was a monster, he would have to get rid of it.

We sipped wine.

'I like to decorate,' he said, watching me over his glass. 'But then, I live alone. As a rule. And time has to be filled.' Again that keen look. He dipped a finger in his wine and sucked it. 'Of course, you have kids and everything, don't you.'

Well, I replied, I only had Andrew, although sometimes the

other boy in the house seemed as good as mine.

Matt nodded thoughtfully. 'So. You're a busy person. And hasn't he been in hospital, your boy? That must've been pretty rough, wasn't it?'

I don't think Matt noticed how much his remark startled me. Shrinking away from the question and from the surge of gratitude it had aroused, I bent to search in my bag for a cigarette. When I lit it, I found my hands were trembling. The temptation to confess the strain of the last few days was so strong, unnerving. For once the floodgates were open, who could tell what other messes might spill out? I thought of the nurses at the hospital, and managed to say crisply: 'He's much better now. It was only a minor operation. A kind of circumcision.' And then I sat and smoked and wished to be invisible, until the precarious feelings receded.

'Quite a trauma, though,' Matt said. 'Poor kid.' He had crooked one leg over the arm of the rocking chair and the other was thrust out in front of him, the knee bending as he rocked himself gently. I watched a black cat cross the room and jump on to his lap, and thought suddenly how entirely comfortable he looked there in the chair, with his feet in soft moccasins, and the apron still tied round his middle, and the curled cat: entirely comfortable, and, in contrast to what I had thought before, entirely kind.

His fingers slid across the cat's fur. 'You must have married pretty young, to have such a big boy. What is he, ten or something?'

'Yes he is, and yes I did.' The wine was beginning to relax me, I was recovering. I laughed. 'Probably to please my mother. Certainly out of stupidity. I knew deep down it was a big mistake, but I wasn't strong minded enough to back out. In Scotland, living together just wasn't on. So I was a college bride. There were a lot of us in the sixties.'

'And then Andrew happened along?'

I nodded. 'Bad luck, and no Abortion Act – and I'm a coward.' Matt raised his eyebrows slightly at this, and, not wanting to appear hard, I hurried to say that of course I didn't regret him now, how could I? A note of apology had crept into my voice.

Matt went on rocking himself, nodding slowly. 'So you didn't fancy being a young mother,' he said. 'That's cool, the way I see it.'

Again I found myself faltering under his scrutiny. 'No. I never saw myself in that role. Nothing so mundane... A great artist, yes, or a great poet.' I tried to inject a redeeming irony into the words.

'Why aim at the fence post if you can go for the moon, you mean? I'll buy that!' He grinned widely, just as Vi, who must have overheard, shouted from the kitchen: 'My God, birds of a bloody feather.'

Suddenly Matt scooped the cat off his knee. 'Come,' he said, jumping up, 'You must see the bed I'm building.'

'Might the reality principle intrude for long enough to get the table set?' Vi called, 'Naming no names, of course.'

This time when Matt moved I couldn't help being aware of his grace. The soul-brother sway was studied, of course, it had to be: actors learned these kinds of tricks. I followed him into the next room, which was yellow, and contained a large platform bed.

'Very nice,' I said feebly, as he showed me the storage space under the bed, and drew my attention to counter-sunk screws and cunningly-fashioned dovetail joints, 'Very nice.' Stacked under the bed were some primed canvasses, and a painting which I knew must be Vi's, although the colours were uncommonly repellent, and the forms were more distorted than usual. A feeling of distress emanated from it. The painting showed a man, boldly nude, seated spider-like at the centre of a web of green telephone wires. It appeared to be a portrait of Matt.

'Neat, isn't it?' Matt was saying. 'And it all came out of a pile of old floorboards and packing-cases.' He was leaning against the bed with one hip jutting, striking an attitude. Just as I realised that I was staring, Vi's head came round the door.

'You must praise the bed, it's obligatory,' she said brightly, and I felt the first twinge of the guilt that was later to become so familiar. Trying for lightness, I said that actually I hated platform beds, they made me think of Indian burials with vultures circling. Matt pretended to be insulted, and Vi laughed.

With every minute that passed, Matt was opening, blossoming. Conscious of that small warning vibration from Vi, I told myself that the man who had come to slump at the end of my sickbed was the offstage Matt, whereas what I saw now was the actor warming up, and so the performance, presumably, was about to begin. Even so, it was hard not to respond to him.

Throughout dinner he went on plying me with questions. About the poetry book I'd had published, about the magazine I worked on, and the kind of feminist line it put across. He even asked me how I felt about Jed, whom he'd met briefly through Vi, and whom he dismissed as a 'duppy'.

'That's Rasta talk for a man with no soul,' he said, watching for my reaction.

His eagerness to take my side appealed to me, but the invitation to slander Jed was much too obvious. I played with the food on my plate and refused to be drawn. Hardly pausing for breath, Matt changed tack.

'So what about all the political stuff?' he demanded. 'Ms Fawcett here tells me you two were big buddies on the barricades.'

Dazed with attention, I glanced at Vi. She had hardly touched her food, and she was staring at Matt. It struck me that she had said practically nothing throughout the meal.

I tried to laugh. 'Well, I never expected the Spanish Inquisition!'

'Give her a break, Matt,' Vi said.

'Oh, it's okay,' I said, making an effort to include her. 'There isn't much to say, anyway. I mean, in 1972 you could hardly sit around cultivating your own artistic garden, could you? It was mostly a question of when in Rome . . .'

Vi said nothing and looked stubborn. I lined up my knife and fork neatly on my plate. My first feeling was remorse, for neglecting her. But then a familiar irritation overcame me.

How difficult it was to know when I was doing right or wrong by her, to know when she would smile, or when her face would cloud over and the tears rise to her long brown eyes. Certainly, Matt had been monopolising me, but he was doing no more than entertain, and surely Vi had asked me here to be entertained?

My head was floating. I put my hands up to my hot cheeks. 'I've drunk too much.'

I was relieved when Matt pushed his chair back from the table and cleared away the dishes, leaving Vi and me alone.

On the blue sofa, we moved closer, and began to talk about the group. Not so many years ago Vi and I had been activists together, had breathed the same hot-house air of libertarianism, but lately she had joined the Communist Party, and had begun to refer to these fervent times as a phase one had to go through, like thumb-sucking or nail-biting. So nowadays, when we talked about the era of the group, we tended to refer to the people, and hedge around the politics.

Vi had news of Phil. He had at last made up his mind to dig in, she said, and was emerging as a heavy in the local Labour Party. Jed, on the other hand, was adrift politically (like me, I thought, would she say the same of me?) He was disillusioned with the Printshop, she said, and with collective work, and he was thinking of trying for a place at college.

Although the mention of Jed hurt, I listened and smiled and exchanged snippets, and waited for the ritual gossip to draw us nearer. I wondered again how she saw me now. Or how, for that matter, I saw myself. Feminist, socialist, romantic idealist? In the old days it had been crucial to have a clear-cut political position, sharp and shiny as a new car, whereas now I shrank from definitions, and felt vulnerable to all the reproachful labels the left can pin. Individualist, fuzzy-minded, utopian. Oh, I still saw what was wrong with the world, there was no going back on that, but once upon a time I thought I also saw how to put it right.

Vi seemed, if anything, more cynical about politics than before, and when I mentioned that I had been on the

Women's March she tossed her head defensively. 'After last year's fiasco, how could anyone face it?' she retorted.

I stared at her. She had such a knack of changing position and then throwing the full force of her personality behind each reversal: I found it quite alarming. I had a picture of her on last year's march, bawling slogans into a megaphone, bracing her legs to keep her balance on top of a decorated float, exhilarated to the point of tears.

Surely she had to admit that the local march was successful, I said.

A bitter look came over her face, and she shrugged.

'Maybe. But what good could a mob of white feminists charging through black Brixton do? Waving placards with Free Castration on Demand, I suppose? Christ.'

Next door in the kitchen Matt crooned energetically:

If it's love that you're runnin' from,
There ain't no hi iiiii din' place

Vi smiled wryly, as if to say: what a handful. I could feel her attention drifting away, and annoyance made me persist. No, I said, the lunatic fringe was small, and anyway there were no placards, because of the police ban on marches.

Vi spread her hands. 'So what was the point?'

Her negativity was seeping through, dulling my brain. Women had signed the abortion petition, I said; they had smiled, waved, bought copies of the magazine. I couldn't accept that we'd had no impact. 'I mean, someone's got to do *something*, haven't they?' I found myself beginning to yawn.

Dishes crashed in the kitchen. Leaning closer to me, Vi said in a low voice: 'Talk to old fish-face about his writing, will you?'

'His writing?' I said grumpily, 'I thought he was supposed to be an actor.' I listened unwillingly as Vi told me how Matt really wanted to write, plays, mostly, and for television.

'I've seen a sort of story of his and I *think* it's good. But I'm not much of a judge of those things.' She glanced at the door and whispered: 'He's ever so quick to criticise other writers and theatre groups, but I just wish he'd get it together himself . . . I know he *could*,' she added hastily. 'He's had all that experience in fringe theatre and, well, he has that sort of demon, if you get me? She looked at me eagerly. 'I mean, if he's in the mood, he can make you *die* . . .'

'I expect he's just isolated,' I cut in. 'Writers need contact.'

'Isolated and crazy.' Vi rolled her eyes. 'Sometimes he drives me bananas.'

Matt padded back into the room carrying a tray of coffee cups and a percolator. His moccasins made a swishing sound on the polished wood of the floor.

'Ach so,' he said, pouring the coffee, 'Am I hearing the ultra-leftist conversations while being the hausfrau, nein?'

I couldn't help smiling at this, but Vi, inexplicably, rounded on him.

'So what are *you*, tell us, if not ultra-left? What's Rock Against Racism? And the Anti-Nazi League?'

Matt shielded his face with his hands, a pantomime defence.

'All richt, *darling*,' he laughed. 'What I mean is, you can hardly compare Rock Against Racism to your old bunch of urban nomads – the libertines, wasn't it? The loose knitting groups?' He blew her a kiss. 'Oh no. We're a United Front.' He grinned across at me. 'Vi knows all about *them*, of course.'

I took this to be some sort of dig at the Communist Party, and so I expected Vi to jump to the defence. Instead, she said something equally abstruse about middle-class Trotskyists in the Anti-Nazi League, and then Matt came back with another retort, and so it went on, while I listened, feeling rather excluded.

'Don't mind us,' said Vi. It's a routine we do now and again.' Her face was animated.

Matt sighed dramatically. 'Ah, politics. It's all bloody cock-pol anyway. Stiff zips and burly egos.'

This was no less mystifying but at least it was expressive. I found myself looking on entranced, as he began to turn his face inside out, mimicking male activists in general, and leading Anti-Nazi League worthies in particular. Nor, it turned out, was the women's movement to be spared. As he sent up varieties of feminism I hardly knew existed, he made terrible faces. Prudish ones, sly ones, lascivious ones. He even parodied – for my benefit, presumably – a typical *Womanright* editorial. It was a good parody, and it hurt. He aimed close to home, and had a keen instinct for the vulnerable spots. I could have pointed out that there were institutions more deserving of attack, and that he was letting them off scot free, but there was such brazen cheek in his performance, and such art, that laughter won out over disapproval, and I simply sat there and took the punishment he meted out.

'But *you*,' he said, perching for a moment on the edge of the sofa, 'You're a poet, right?' His hand brushed my knee. 'So why waste time pissing around with the middle-class sisters? They'll only wet their knickers at anything with a bit of guts to it.' His face twisted into a mask of primness, of moral outrage.

This time he'd really gone too far. How wonderful for him, I thought, to have me for an audience. I never could resist the charms of the mime or the clown, and here I was again, letting him get away with murder. But before I could retaliate, Vi stepped in.

'Leave it out, Matt.' She didn't sound shocked, but rather weary, as if she had heard this routine before.

Matt's eyes sparkled with malice. Ignoring her, he pointed a finger at me. 'What *you* need is a bigger audience. Exposure, yeah? Expansion.'

'Like what, exactly? Show business?'

'Come on, June. Surely you've heard about the Anti-Nazi League carnival. We've got a mass of kids coming to that, thousands of ordinary kids – that's who we address ourselves to, unlike some people and parties I could name. There's your audience. Maybe a hundred thousand. All you have to do is come along and read . . .'

'You take my breath away,' I said coldly.

Vi looked from Matt to me. The off-licence would be closing soon, she said; that is, if we wanted anything else to drink? She revolved an empty wine glass in her hands. 'You *could* read, June,' she said. 'He's been phoning round for days trying to rope in extra performers.' She sounded peevish.

'Yeah. Bring the sisters. Let your hair down . . . Oops!' Matt clapped a hand over his mouth. Then taking Vi's purse, he danced out of the room.

Vi drew a hand across her forehead. 'See what I mean? Always dreaming and scheming. The latest thing is that he's going to work up a comic duo with his loony mate Marshall . . . but it never goes further than talk, as far as I can see.' She pressed my arm. 'I mean, you work so hard, don't you. If *you* encouraged him . . .'

I wondered why we were talking about Matt again. If the opportunity arose, I said, I would try, but I couldn't make any promises. 'He certainly seems to have a lot of energy going spare,' I admitted grudgingly. After a longish silence, I asked: 'How's the Party?'

She made a face. 'Oh, the Party,' she said, without interest.

Later, the dope came out and Matt's face filled with tenderness as he talked of India. He had travelled its length and breadth; he had shared beds with spice-smugglers in Kerala and gun-runners in Afghanistan; he had starved, sickened, and nearly died. I sprawled beside Vi on the sofa listening to his adventures, captivated, resentful.

'And the women,' he said, in a soft, reverent voice which made Vi look up sharply, 'Such a silence they carry with them.'

'You're stoned senseless,' Vi snorted.

4

Andrew came out of hospital and spent the next few days watching television and taking a great many salt baths; the scar was still tender so he was fretful and demanding. Finally, he went back to school, and that day the first real snow of the winter came whirling in under my window sashes, so that I had to block the gaps with strips of toilet paper, prodding them into the cracks with a palette knife. The windows were high and broad and set askew in their frames. The floor slanted, too, and there was an odd join where the skirting board had been replaced at an angle to compensate for the list. It was a far cry from the warm, enclosing space of Matt's flat. Security of tenure . . . I'd forgotten what that was like. Looking back, a long line of squats extended into the past, a muddle of memories, a super-imposition of walls and halls and half-papered rooms. I thought of the efforts I'd put in, to make these transient spaces my own: such patchwork and invention and making-do. Time after time, until the next eviction.

And now this house, a tall, crooked house which sucked in draughts. It stood on the corner of a street lined thickly with sycamores which in summer hid the tower blocks to the east, where Hackney began and trees were scarce. A wall surrounded it, and a dense wild undergrowth of lime trees and privet overhung the steps which led up to the front door. It would have taken money, care, commitment, to put it all to rights. Permanence. None of us had ever been too sure of that. People passed through. Few of them stayed longer than a year. They left to buy houses, or to have babies, or to live alone. And so now there were only five of us left to fill a space meant for a sprawling Victorian family and several pantry maids: there was Marie, who darted around the borough on political errands, Tom, her taciturn lover of many years, and Zac, her nine year old son; and then Andrew and me. In the speed and flurry of life, the house, unrepaired, decayed slowly. And I dreamed more and more often of rooms, empty rooms, and dim corridors along which I inched, searching for light switches.

Outside, snow was gathering on the unpruned branches of the lime trees. I walked from window to window, checking the sills again and again until I was satisfied that they were secure, that there would be no more infiltration of those white flakes which looked so eerie when they drove in gusts through the cracks and spun in the corners of the room. Then I picked up my mending things.

With Andrew in hospital I'd had time to do repair work. The seams of his gloves had unravelled from fingertip to knuckle. With Vi's Christmas present, I altered trousers, hemmed cuffs, stitched buttons. She had given me a work-basket found in a junk shop, full of packets of rusty needles, fine embroidery silks, and dress patterns from the forties; the lid was lined with yellow silk, padded and ruched. It was more of an art object than a workaday thing, the sort of pretty treasure trove that Vi loved. Watching me unwrap it, she had flashed me an ironic smile, because of the silk and the frills, the very femininity of it. It was a gentle enough jibe at my puritan streak, but all the same, I was nettled, and there was a certain stiffness in my thank-yous.

Lately, though, I'd found that sewing could be soothing, could be a meditation of sorts. The dust of Jed's departure had hardly settled, and so any calm was welcome. There was so much clearing to be done inside my head; spaces he had occupied were still tousled and chaotic and had to be reclaimed; some kind of order had to be restored to what was left.

I thought of the weeks after he walked out, and the awful crying. I'd cried at most times and in most places, until one day I saw myself in the mirror, ash-faced, mascara-dribbled, and I swore grimly that it was enough, that pride must be preserved. Even if the inner flimsiness remained for a while, at least the containing shell could be patched up. Each to her own strategy.

Last Hallowe'en, after the turnip lantern had been put out and the children had taken themselves off to bed with the remains of the treacle toffee, Jed sat me down and told me. The smoky smell of singed turnip filled the house as I cried, hysterically, then softly, the whole night through.

Worse, though, than the crying, was what threatened to break through from underneath: being abandoned was more than enough to set the past straining at the leash.

For weeks I waited for Jed to return. He'll change his mind, I thought, he needs me. I kept the ghosts of the past away with routine. I worked. I observed birthdays and festivals. I even wrote poetry. He didn't come back.

Nights were still the hardest. At night I wore pyjamas, brushed my hair fifty times, and put off writing to my mother who sent me calendars of gum-tree panoramas and always knew how to keep her man.

A door banged on the landing, signalling that Andrew and Zac were making their nightly procession to shit. Always after the cocoa had been drunk and the goodnight kisses exchanged, their bare feet would pad across the landing, and the toilet door would bang. Usually Andrew sat on the toilet first with a comic spread over his knees, while Zac crouched on the stairs, holding the door open, so that he could see him. Afterwards, Andrew would wait for Zac to finish, and then they'd go back to bed together, forgetting to flush the pan.

I put my head round the door. Zac was on the toilet, concentrating. His bare feet were very dirty. 'You're like an old married couple,' I teased.

'Will you cut my hair?' he said.

'The colour of those feet!' I pointed. 'You're not going to bed like that.'

Zac looked down and shrugged. 'Okay. Will you cut it Elvis-style?'

I smiled. Nine-years-old and already so vain about his good looks. 'Yes, if it'll go.'

'Go where?' He frowned at me from under his fringe.

'Into Elvis-style, dummy.'

'Oh.' He drummed his fingers against the wall. Zac was rarely still; he turned somersaults and half-formed cartwheels in the living-room whenever he got the chance; he played noisy percussion with the forks and knives on the dinner table every night, and he suffered from nervous tics.

I supervised the foot-washing, bore the complaints, and then went back to my room. I didn't like always being the nag, but the only way out of that would mean galvanising Marie and Tom, which wasn't easy, since they were already so over-stretched. Marie, up to her neck in local politics, exuded urgency. She worked on the same community paper that Jed and Phil had founded back at the beginning of the seventies; I'd done the same myself, and understood the pressures all too well. There was always this or that council meeting one had to keep an eye on, or a new split in the Labour Party to investigate, or such and such a shop-steward to interview. I couldn't bring myself to carp at her just because she let the domestic side of things slide.

As for Tom, Tom was willing enough, and kind to the boys, but so absent-minded. Halfway through babysitting he'd wander off to fall asleep in his basement room, leaving the boys to stay up late and scoff all the fruit in the bowl. Marie apologised for him. It was because he worked too hard, she said – seven days a week at the Printshop, so no wonder if all he wanted to do when he came home was to slump on his bed with his banjo and his collection of penny whistles.

Andrew blundered in to say his third good-night. His little pink mouth swam in his moon face as he bent over me. Proudly he pulled on his cock and said: 'I pulled another stitch out.'

Zac called from the bedroom, querulous: where was Andrew, what was he doing?

'Better go,' said Andrew.

Next door, mattress springs creaked. Gradually the whisperings and rustlings stopped. Zac was asleep. I listened. After a few minutes, a book thudded to the floor. Andrew was asleep.

Remembering that I had to take him back to the hospital next week, I searched my desk for his Outpatient card. The drawers were hopelessly crammed. Crumpled letters, birth certificates, Social Security documents crawled out through the gaps at the backs of the ramshackle drawers and spilled down between the desk and the wall. And leaflets, too, and minutes of meetings: a whole straggling history of groups and collectives, actions and alternatives. The loose-knitting groups, as Matt had said. He was funny, I had to give him that.

When I came across the photographs, I forgot about the

Appointment card. The photos were summery and strangely bright, looked at on such a bitter night.

There was Vi, eating watermelon in Lisbon a few months after the revolution.

Jed and June, duplicating a newsletter at Windsor Free Festival.

A honeymoon photograph of my parents, an old favourite. Arm in arm in front of Marble Arch, they beamed for the camera. My father in RAF uniform, my mother in a square-shouldered suit and a hat set at a rakish slant.

And Phil, of course. Phil posing outside the cottage with a air-rifle. He was aiming the rifle at a red balloon which hung from the wooden trestle of the well. He was smiling with some irony. Behind him old-fashioned pink roses arched over the door of the cottage, and sunlight penetrating an open upstairs window glimmered on a white interior.

I looked at that one only for a second. Then I turned it upside down and thrust it to the back of the drawer.

5

I sit by the well with the October sun in my eyes. The sun gleams on the flints embedded in the stone walls of the cottage, and on the window of that same white room. The window is closed, furred with dust.

We haven't used the room. As soon as we arrived, I made sure of that. It was easy enough – since the room was freezing and I was ill with a cold – not to tell Matt that the locked cupboard in the kitchen contained paraffin heaters, nor that I knew where the key was kept; even with his instinct for nosing out lies and cover-ups he appeared to suspect nothing, and so now we sleep downstairs on a mattress beside the wood fire.

Matt is hacking at a log which even from here looks too green. He misses, and swears; the axe thuds into ground layered thickly with sawdust and wood-shavings.

I stretch my hand out over the mouth of the well. Coolness rises from the water fifty feet below.

I am empty.

Go deeper.

I had only been in London a year when I met Phil, but I'd already found most of what I had come for.

The life of a faculty wife in Edinburgh had never suited me. I had far too big a chip on my shoulder to slide easily upwards into the professional classes, and I was both too self-absorbed and too energetic to enjoy playing second fiddle to my husband at University functions. Oh, I tried to occupy myself as the other young wives did, with Le Creuset cooking pans and *Larousse Gastronomique* and being better mothers than our own had been. Like them, I bought suits at Wallis and wore my hair up and didn't toilet-train. Most of the time I was quietly, dully miserable. But every now and again, to revenge myself, I gave way to fits of surly exhibitionism.

Decked out in a red mini-dress and a three-foot-long cigarette-holder, I prowled the Faculty wine-and-cheese parties looking for someone to flirt with, or better still, to insult.

At first my husband found this unruliness amusing, and made light of it, but when I progressed from smaller academic fry to his Head of Department, who bred grouse and owned, I'd heard, half of Perthshire, it became clear that something had to give.

London seemed the obvious way out. In London, we told each other, there would be more room for manoeuvre. In London I could join all the women's groups I wanted, could run silkscreen workshops or do street theatre or turn the whole house into a commune; in London we could both spread our wings. And so we moved, and so we did, but in the doing of it, as might have been predicted, our marriage fell apart.

It was in 1972, during the final stages of the break-up, that I first met Phil. He was standing at the top of the Town Hall steps, propping himself up on a placard. His purple bell-bottoms were very dirty. He was on the fifth day of a seven-day fast, and heroically pale. Andrew drew back in alarm from this apparition with the gaunt face and the eyes which hunger had made bright with visions.

Later, as we lay on his bed, Phil watched me drink tea and eat digestive biscuits and his eyes filled with tears.

No, do go on, he protested, when, taking pity on him, I hid the biscuits under the pillow. Hunger sharpened sexual desire, he said with a grin.

We argued, I remember, about whether or not a public fast was a useful tactic. 'In prison, okay, I can see the sense of it,' I said, 'When there's no other way of acting effectively, and control of your body is all you have left . . . But not outside.'

We squabbled amiably. I was enjoying myself. Phil hurried to point out that he and his friends had also raised barricades to keep the bailiffs out of their street, and leafletted, and lobbied: this time, he said, they'd show up the scandal of empty houses once and for all. 'You wait,' he said, sticking his chin out, 'This is only the beginning.'

In the bath his red hair turned to seaweed tails, and he washed my back with a kind of starved reverence, as if he'd been celibate for many months. (Not true, never true of Phil, I was to learn later.)

For a few weeks we met sporadically, and perhaps the affair would have tailed off naturally enough, had it not been for two major upheavals. My husband, who had already decamped from the house, announced suddenly that he had found a buyer: the buyer wanted to tie up the deal immediately, and so did he – so could I give him any reason why he should hang around? He said this so bitterly that all my instincts for self-preservation fled. No, I couldn't, I mumbled back guiltily, and even when he went on to tell me that I had three weeks to get out, I still couldn't bring myself to argue. It was his house, after all, and I had never felt any particular rights to it.

At first, faced with fending for myself and Andrew, I wept with worry. Days passed, and builders came to scar the garden with cement piles and tear at the partition walls, and still I'd made no plans. And then, later that same week, bulldozers drove a splintered path through the barricades at the end of Phil's street, and the squatting campaign crumbled around him.

Homeless, we camped out in sleeping bags in the one room which the builders hadn't penetrated. A smell of Cuprinol hung about the house, and the room was shrouded in a fine plaster dust which rose up from the ground floor. For days we picnicked on sliced white bread and canned beans, and comforted Andrew, and were paralysed, until finally Phil roused himself. For single people, he said, squatting was still the only option; therefore, it was only sensible for us to team up. The important thing was to act without delay. 'The details,' he added with an embarrassed cough, 'can always be worked out later.'

I argued. For quite a few days I argued, and only at the last moment, with the new owners virtually on the doorstep, did I give in. 'I really can't see an alternative,' I said, to conceal how moved I was by this offer of rescue. I did lay down one rule, however. 'Separate rooms,' I said, telling him that I'd fought too long and hard against the tyranny of the marriage bed to forfeit what I'd won.

'Of course,' he said stiffly, 'I'm surprised you felt you had to mention it.'

On our squatting forays we wore black. There was excitement in the role of cat-burglar. Night after night we scrambled over pigeon huts and walls topped with shards of glass, swung from the branches of ash trees, balanced on first-floor window sills. I learned how to crack window panes with a hammer muffled in a sock, and then to undo the catch inside. Most houses were uninhabitable, for they had already been disembowelled by the Council. The gas and electricity were disconnected, the toilets smashed. The floors were strewn with an ugly ceramic litter.

Finally we found a house near Kings Cross. It was a disused laundry, rather cramped and with a shopfront window, but quite intact. Phil flicked a switch and the lights went on, startling us. In the back yard there was a jasmine bush, and a toilet which flushed. That night, we changed the lock. Next day, we moved in.

In the weeks that followed, other derelict houses came to life as squatting spread. All the way up the Caledonian Road, corrugated iron was stripped from doors and windows; fresh paint appeared, and cats, flowerpots, and bicycles; roughly printed posters offered housing advice and free pregnancy testing.

Phil was not the only militant among the new squatters. Jed, for instance, skinny Jed with the country accent, had been a union organiser for years, but had thrown up his job to start a Printshop further up the Caledonian Road; and there was Tom too, whom Phil had known at Cambridge, and who, like Vi, was a Claimants' Union activist. Tom moved into the laundry with us, and Vi, too, camped there for a time while she searched for her own squat nearby. Tom had an eerie wing of white hair, and struggled with a bad stutter, fighting to say things which were bitter and wild even then, but which were met with respect because they were uncompromising. Vi was as intense as Tom, but in a quarrelsome, Cockney, commonsensical way which I found more intimidating. She had dark, watchful eyes in a pale face, and dressed always in black to conceal her bulky figure.

Gradually, the laundry was taking shape. Tom, discovering a flair for electrics, rewired the whole house, and Jed came down from the Printshop to show us how to fit up an ancient Ascot water heater in the kitchen; in return, Phil and I helped Jed out with the squatters' handbook he was producing on his basement press.

Phil delighted in the ferment around us. His prophesies of political upheaval, meanwhile, were coming true: almost every week brought a new piece of Tory legislation, and a new campaign against it; day by day the climate in the inner city grew angrier and more demanding. 'Only at street level,' he crowed, 'does one see things as they really are.' Certainly I could see that there was much to be done. And in the laundry, whose doors were open to all comers, there was no question of opting out. At nights we sat up late under the poster of Rosa Luxemburg which I had pinned above my bed, discussing, discussing; in Phil's flat-featured, rather bland face, the eyes burned. Am I enough of a militant for him? I asked myself.

Phil was an old hand at spray-painting. 'Strike a Body Blow to Capitalism' we wrote big as a whale one night on the soot-grimed wall of Kings Cross. It was the least we could do. The Tories, out to test the muscle of the Industrial Relations Act, had thrown three shop-stewards in jail; the unions would respond, yes, but we too would do our bit.

Next day six thousand men marched on Pentonville prison, and Vi, distributing leaflets about social security for strikers' families, talked excitedly about a General Strike. 'This'll show the Tories who's boss!' she yelled to the march, and the men smiled indulgently back at her. It was a burning July day, and the younger men were in vests or shirt-sleeves, and sun-glasses; the older ones sweated in their good suits. I watched them file past our huge slogan, those dockers, printers, engineers, and, remembering my father, I clenched my fist. How proud he would have been, I thought fiercely.

Increasingly often that autumn, Jed came to visit, Jed with his dandyish long hair and his unlikely gold earring. One night he lounged on the bed with his restless feet corkscrewing the blankets and let off steam about the Printshop.

'We've got to get ourselves organised,' he exhorted from the bed, ticking off priorities on his fingers. 'We need a rota for manning the Printshop office, dealing with squatters and claimants advice, for a kick-off . . . Then we *definitely* need volunteers to teach tenants and so on how to print their own material. Otherwise all I'm doing up there is running a commercial press at rock-bottom prices, and frankly, I can think of better things to do with my time. And what we need most of all, in my view, is something that Phil and I've been mulling over.' He glanced at Phil, who nodded sagely. 'A community paper. Not one of your wishy-washy jobs with no class analysis,' he added, 'but a thorough-going socialist one.'

The rest of us were impressed, and grappled earnestly with the whys and wherefores of such a paper, but while we argued about the funding and distribution, and who the paper should be aimed at, it became apparent that Jed's attention was wandering, for he had rolled up a sizeable joint and was quietly applying himself to getting stoned. Absorbed in the flare of a match or the flutter of a straggled long cobweb on the ceiling, he seemed unable to keep up with us, and once or twice he giggled suddenly at himself, or, as suddenly, snapped back at one of us who had challenged or misrepresented a strategy he'd put forward. As if to compensate for Jed's fickleness, Phil's concentration intensified as the hours passed. Sitting on the edge of my desk, alert as a bird, he turned his face sharply towards whoever was speaking, and listened with his head on one side, gathering in the threads of possibility, giving form to things. Caught for a moment in the beam of Phil's attention, Tom, who was talking about one of the anarchist small presses which could give us some hints on newspaper production, stuttered terribly, and when it was Vi's turn she took quick breaths and talked very fast, like a child who can't predict when the interest of its parent will be withdrawn.

As I lay on the carpet straining to encompass everything that was happening in the room, I smoked cigarette after cigarette and wished for a tidier mind, a clearer perspective; I wanted to contribute, but it was hard, while my mind wriggled with unruly thoughts and dim amoebic sensings. When at last I did speak I heard my father's voice come from my mouth. 'No class analysis can be complete without including the emergence of women as a revolutionary force' it said, in his deliberately-phrased, dogmatic, very Scottish way, 'and if this paper doesn't take that into account, I can't be part of it.'

Phil looked round the room. 'Can we agree, then, that the paper would be committed to a deeper analysis of sexism and its relationship to capitalism?'

'Racism too,' Vi chipped in, nodding hard.

It was around this time that the five of us began, almost without noticing it, to use the word 'we'. Later, we were to worry and chew at the word, trying to define it, but in the wet and dismal extremities of that winter it was still a generous pronoun, and a heady one, which embraced all manner of mavericks and urgent dreamers – feminists and radical philosophers, commune-dwellers and LSD visionaries, squatters and anti-Stalinists.

'Has anyone seen the Parliamentary Road to Socialism?' Phil wrote one night on a poster of the Jarrow Hunger March, so that it looked as if one of the marchers was asking the way. He pinned it up next to Rosa Luxemburg, and we laughed then, with a particular zest and relief as we always did when the elusive we-feeling coalesced in a new slogan.

When we had moved into the laundry, Phil had chosen the ground-floor room with the shopfront window, but from the first he'd neglected it, preferring to bring his socks, his Moroccan rugs and his graffiti upstairs to share with me. I was surprised to find that I didn't feel encroached upon. The relationship, it seemed, was much less demanding than marriage; in contrast, it felt comradely, streamlined, as if pared down for action.

One night after the others had left and Phil and I were alone in the smoky bare room, I took it into my head to ask why he never expressed what he felt about me, or, for that matter, about anyone else in the group. I hadn't meant to accuse, merely to explore, but the question seemed to make him angry. Phil's father had been career Army, and there was something of the parade-ground disciplinarian on Phil's face, too, as he stiffened beside me, preparing to scourge incorrect ideas. His gingery eyebrows slanted upwards, and his nose grew longer and more pointed. 'You can really open a can of worms if you're not careful,' he said, in a restrained, chilly voice. 'I mean, once you start concentrating on personal feelings, there's no end to it, is there?'

Wasn't he over-reacting a little? I suggested, but he would have none of it.

'I've seen it all,' he said darkly, 'I know what happens to political collectives when they start wallowing in that morass . . .'

'Methinks the gentleman doth protest too much,' I teased.

Phil ignored me. 'They fall apart,' he persisted, frowning at the wall opposite the bed, 'they become ineffective.'

'Who?' I demanded, 'Like who?'

I should have known that Phil would have the facts at his fingertips. The examples came thick and fast. His last household, for instance, once so effective, now locked into some lugubrious interpersonal geometry; at least three political theatre groups, torn apart by sexual politics; a poster collective, decamped to the far reaches of Donegal to take up primal screaming . . .

There was a fire-and-brimstone flavour to his speech which reminded me of Scotland. I thought of dry-eyed grim funerals and joyless, maudlin weddings, and of my grandmother, who laughed only behind her hand. I thought of the narrow bounds of the permissible.

'I could go on,' Phil said, 'if you really want to hear more.'

'I think I've already heard it,' I said dourly. 'They didn't exactly encourage demonstrations of feeling where I come from, either. I just thought *we* were supposed to be in the liberation business.'

I intended to sting, but Phil didn't seem to take offence. Slipping a hand under the bedcovers, he tweaked my nipple. 'And not such a bad thing either,' he laughed. 'They don't sit around examining their navels up there.'

While the flickering reflection of the traffic lights outside the window turned the room red and gold and ghostly green, I went on arguing, and Phil went on bantering. Eventually, for the sake of sleep, I gave in. Yes, I said, I was as reticent as he; no, I didn't like self-indulgence any more than he did; yes, we were really quite well suited. By that time I could hardly remember what the issue was. Was it personal bickering, or political principle? I didn't care. I sank into sleep.

Something that made me brood more that winter, I remember, was Phil's resistance to innovations in bed. I suppose I'd imagined that he would read the signs of discontent for himself, and take steps. Far from it. I tried tactful hints. He appeared to be immune, even wilfully deaf. I became obsessed. For weeks – in supermarket queues, on picket lines, on the bus to Andrew's nursery – I argued with myself. I must be honest. I can't. I must. The city was full of women to speculate about. I watched them and I wondered. Would *she* say it? Or just fake it? And that one, how much would she risk?

Finally, telling myself that Phil, of all men, appreciated frankness, I plucked up my courage. What about fingers and tongues? I whispered into the pillow, hating him for having forced me out into the open.

He was hurt, there was no doubt about that. He was silent for a while, and then he gave a miserable little laugh.

'Don't you feel that mechanics . . . intrude on the mystery?' he muttered, which made me feel like dying, mainly because I agreed with it so much.

'Never mind,' I said quickly, 'Forget it.'

But he did not forget. Nights of effort followed. Watching him burrow around in the bed, I grew rigid with embarrassment.

'Like this,' I instructed, 'and now this,' and 'a little to the left,' suspecting all the time that the role of guide might be less disagreeable if the pupil were more enthusiastic.

Oh well, it's all struggle, I told myself, as the blood froze within me.

It was Phil who gave up first. 'I feel I'm doing something *to* you, not *with* you,' he complained, and although everything I'd heard in women's groups pointed to a flaw in his reasoning, I was hardly in a mood to protest. Already I'd ventured well beyond my boundaries and I felt displaced, and raw, and unprotected. It was a relief to retreat, to conciliate, to feel Phil's hand idling in my hair, to lie side by side again, and tranquil, like friends. Once or twice after that, I steeled myself to ask for more, but each time, the memory of that phrase tugged me back.

One misty Sunday afternoon when Andrew had been whisked off to the zoo by his father, Vi came visiting. The doorbell rang just as I was settling down to work on a cartoon strip for *Hard Times*, and I swore at the interruption, imagining the worst. A family newly-evicted, or just about to be (the parents trying to stay calm, talking non-stop, clinging to children who cringed away from their unfamiliar fussing). Or else, young Scots straight off the Glasgow train, searching for crash-pads and jobs and street-wisdom. The kind of people who trooped in almost daily to the Printshop advice centre. The kind of needs which were impossible to ignore.

I opened the door reluctantly, and there was Vi, a sad monochrome in the January mist. She wore a dark duffle-coat with a pointed hood and toggles which wouldn't meet. Underneath, a black smock stretched across her breasts. I took her into the kitchen, where it was warm.

'You look a bit low,' I said cautiously. She gave a shrug. To divert her, I showed her the cartoon strip, which Phil and I had spent a week on, and were ridiculously, childishly pleased with. She bent over the drawings, and I stood by nervously as she assessed them with the hyper-critical eye of the art student who has deserted painting for activism.

Vi has no one, I thought suddenly, fearing her envy.

She sat down at the kitchen table, and her fingers moved to her throat and fluttered there, as if to loosen some constriction. She had not said a word about the cartoons. Watching her, I smoked a cigarette I didn't want, and wondered what it was that she wanted of me. Comradeship, after all, we already had. I could hardly see that there was time for more.

Embarrassed by the silence, I cast around for common ground, and managed to mumble a few words about the

Women's Centre. It was an idea Vi and I had been mulling over for only a few weeks, but it had already – thanks to the fractious response of the men in the group – become 'our' project, to be nurtured and defended and endlessly justified.

'Phil seems to have a real bee in his bonnet about separatism,' I said.

Vi forced a smile. 'They're all scared the women's thing will take over, really. Jed says as much. Maybe he's frightened that if we split, he'll have to learn to get along with men.'

Reassured by her bitchiness, I laughed, and started to tell her about several empty shops that the council might let us use for premises, if we approached the right committee at the right time. Vi listened, and nodded, and seemed for a few moments quite excited, but then all of a sudden her mouth contorted, and she let out a sob.

'Look at me!' she cried. She stabbed a finger at herself accusingly. Look at me. I'm eleven stone, and I used to be a *wraith*.' In the cramped kitchen, she tore at her clothes.

'Oh Vi,' I said helplessly, as she plunged on.

'My mother used to say, Vi, with a face like that, there's nothing you can't have. You're the beauty, she said.' Vi glared at me. 'Can you believe that? And my mother's a *feminist*, or thinks she is. Men are so spineless, she says, they're so weak, with looks like yours you can lead them by the nose.'

Her brown eyes glistened with tears. Answers, I thought, she wants answers. But I would have to watch my words. 'Funny kind of feminism,' I muttered, held fast by the look in those eyes. I watched her catch a pouch of flesh under her chin and twist it, leaving weals. The fingers plucked and pinched, plucked and pinched. I stepped forward, protesting.

'You mustn't!'

Why not? the eyes challenged.

'You'll hurt yourself.'

Vi put her head in her hands and wept. The surface of the table buoyed up her heavy breasts. The weight, the ponderous softness of them disturbed me. I folded my arms across my chest. Why should she save up all this self-exposure for me? I thought with sudden resentment.

I offered her tea and stood by the cooker waiting for the kettle to boil. Action, I thought, tapping my foot. I had to intervene somehow, before things escalated. (I have no idea what cataclysms I feared, I only know that I saw no end to the crying and raging which boiled up from the depths of this woman.) For a second I thought of suggesting she see a psychiatrist, or at least someone with training in these areas, someone insightful. I gazed at her wide white face. No, I thought, she'll be insulted.

After a little while Vi drank her tea and seemed to pull herself together. Sniffing, crumpling her tears into the centre of a tissue, she told me how desperately she tried to control her eating, and how despicably she failed. Since I had never dieted in my life, I had no advice to give, and I listened uncomfortably. Patting her shoulder, I tried to tell her that people in the group valued her for what she was, for what she contributed, rather than for her looks. But then I caught the gleam of scepticism in her eye, and I stopped, realising that I didn't really believe it myself.

When at last Vi got up to go, I hovered uncertainly, wondering whether I should invite her to stay for supper.

'When we get the Centre open, we'll be working together more,' I said, to soften the separation.

Later that afternoon Andrew arrived back on the doorstep like a small red-coated parcel. His father had dropped him off and waited in the car until I opened the door; then he drove away. Andrew had chilly pink cheeks and new gloves attached to his sleeves with tape.

'I rode a camel,' he said, flapping his arms to make the gloves dance.

After tea I took him up to the Printshop with me, for I had to deliver the cartoon to Jed for printing. Phil and Tom were drinking canned beer at the oilcloth-covered table in the office, and arguing about our role in the community. They looked up briefly when I came in, nodded hallo, and went on talking. Phil seemed to be pressing for some kind of public forum which could draw in other local activists.

'I don't just mean the friendship network,' he said, 'but tenants' leaders, and the people from the hospital campaign, for instance . . .' His forehead wrinkled with concentration. 'I mean something more coherent. A place where we can discuss . . . well, how to relate to the Public Sector strike, for example, or the GLC elections. How to intervene, basically.'

Tom took a quick gulp of beer and pinged the empty can once or twice with his fingernail. 'Honestly, I think we're way off the mark if we see ourselves as . . . well, professional revolutionaries, leninist cadres, if you like . . . attempting to motivate or organise something we call the working class.'

Jed, who had gone out to the kitchen and returned with a cup of orange squash for Andrew, caught the end of this remark and scowled.

'Who said anything about leninism? Why can't we just recognise that *we* have an objective interest in revolutionary class change!' He bent down and gave the cup of squash to Andrew, making sure that Andrew had got a firm grasp on the handle before he let it go. When he straightened up and spoke again, his voice had lost some of its stridency. 'I'm not fundamentally interested in change for other people's sake – or in middle-class guilt complexes.'

Tom peered at Jed through his spectacles. 'My interest isn't *objective*.'

'What?' said Jed irritably.

Tom's eyes gleamed. 'Look, say we go on a picket line to stop hospital closures, or what have you – well, part of it is wanting to change the whole society, but it's also a matter of not wanting to . . . to have your leg cut off . . . You start it because of a *personal* thing . . .' He tilted his chair back. 'I worry about some of the words I hear used around here,' he added. "Class war", "objective" – that sort of Marxist shorthand blurs things, I think.'

I stood at the end of the table, listening, feeling invisible. I'd delivered the cartoon, and there was really no reason to stay. On the table there was a fan-shaped spread of collated issues of *Hard Times*. I picked up the staple-gun and began to staple. 'What worries me,' I said, 'is that so many of the people we meet expect us to solve their individual problem, and that's it. If you suggest they might have common cause with others – could organise for themselves – they get shifty, or abusive, even.'

'Bloody right,' Jed agreed, 'It's a pain.'

'Sometimes I feel more like a social worker than a revolutionary . . . when surely there ought to be a difference!'

Andrew finished his drink, and looked pensively around the room. Seeing no toys, no Lego, nothing of interest, he began to edge towards the door.

'I'm not cut out for the caring professions either,' Phil said tersely, as I got up to go. 'None of us are. But when the lid's been on these people so long, what else do you expect?'

In the spring, when the crunch came with Phil, it would have been easier for me if I had taken comfort from Vi, for certainly it was offered. But I could not.

For almost a year, Phil had been as faithful as I. And then one night he came banging home in the small hours. I heard him knock over a bicycle in the hall; then there was a woman's voice, whispering.

Hearing them enter the disused room downstairs, I sat bolt upright in bed. My mind whirled. Lately at some of the public meetings there had been a woman who had caught Phil's eye. She was tall, German, and unhappy.

It's her, I thought, he's taking advantage of her.

I decided to go down. I got out of bed and put on my dressing-gown. But when I got to the door something held me back. I could not open it. The four walls of my room confined me.

I began to pace. Phil's papers were everywhere. Phil's scrawls, and mine, on the walls. Above my desk I had pinned up a quote from Sartre, an old snipe at Phil.

> Reading today's Marxists one would believe that we are born at the age when we earn our first wages. They have forgotten their own childhoods.

Underneath Phil had replied: 'Are we to communicate

with each other only by writing on walls?'

I went on pacing. There were loose floorboards here and there, and I trod heavily on them. When he hears me, he'll stop, I thought.

I paused to listen. Downstairs the whisperings went on, and the creak of chairs or mattress springs. This time I forced myself to open the door and look down the stairwell. There was a chink of light in the hall, and a faint smell of dope. I rattled the banisters. Still no door opened and no head poked out. I might as well have been a mouse scratching at the skirting-board.

There were others that same week. Acquaintances, friends, even. It was an explosion outwards, away from me.

One morning, when he arrived back from the warm bed of one of his new lovers, I confronted him. We argued in the narrow hall, without touching each other.

'You forget that other people have a say in whether I stay or go,' he said frigidly.

'Bullshit!' I cried, 'It's either you or me, and you don't have a kid, so it's you.'

Slowly, bitterly, Phil packed his few clothes and strode off up the street with a rucksack on his back and his drawing board under his arm. Watching him go, I did not cry.

Later that day, when I walked into the Women's Centre and told Vi what had happened, she took a step towards me, raising her hands. I went over to the desk and took the Day Book from the drawer, and stared at it. 'After all,' I said, 'what else could I do, when he behaved like that?'

'Well!' she exclaimed, 'Let's hope that teaches the bastard.' She began to bustle round the room, straightening books in the window display, letting off little snorts of outrage.

I was thankful when people began to filter in. Some of them looked like students, and they scanned the information board for details of squats or study groups, or turned books over in their hands, examining the prices. Others had more urgent queries. Vi sat down for a long time with a very young girl and her boyfriend. The boy talked about abortion in a voice that was barely audible, and the girl hardly said a word.

Meanwhile, I bent over the Day Book. Several days had not been entered. There was a lot to catch up with. I wrote fast, trying to ignore a soft, persistent roaring sound in my ears. When my right eye began to twitch my mind conjured up scenes from a Polish film I'd seen with Phil.

A Party militant of upper-class origins had returned home to visit his ailing father. The father was alcoholic, had facial tics, was unrepentantly decadent. The militant went unwillingly, determined to make a final break with his background. But on the train back to the city, I remembered, his face had suddenly been assailed by a stubborn tic, like a badge of degeneracy.

I stopped writing to cross out a word. 'To take it gradually,' was what I'd intended to write, but instead of 'gradually', I had written 'grudgingly'.

At three o'clock Vi put a cup of tea on the desk beside my elbow. At 3.30 I drew a line under my report and closed the book. At four, Andrew had to be collected from nursery. Then he had to be brought back with me to the centre, where there was a meeting of the new health group, and after that an Ordinary General Meeting at which half a dozen new women might turn up. They would have questions. They'd have to be told how the centre was organised. And – depending on the type of woman – they'd want to know either what it could offer them, or else what part they could play in running it.

That day, I told myself that it was the end of my relationship with Phil, and so, perhaps, it should have been – but it was not.

Phil set up home at the Printshop with Jed, and for three weeks the cold war between us continued. And then, one morning just after Easter, a letter arrived. It was written neatly, even elegantly, on a large sheet of flimsy layout paper.

Dear June,
The fact that it is difficult to talk together at the moment is cutting me up.

With you it has always seemed possible to carry a dialogue into the most difficult zones. That was almost a definition of the relationship: one in which, whatever happened, communication would always be possible. At its best, this meant articulating whole new areas of experience.
Today I read stuff from the Claimants' Union Conference, and wrote up the minutes of the *Hard Times* meeting you missed. At the meeting we discussed the need to raise the organisational level of the paper. Most simply, this means supplying contact addresses of groups – women's, tenants', Blacks, etc., etc. – below each article. We need our politics to become clear not only in our statements, but also in the community struggles we involve ourselves in and link together locally.
Talked to some tenants on the phone about their rent strike. To Tom. To Vi. To a Tooting Situationist(!) To Jed, who wants me to take over more of the printing.
Last night at 2am saw Nixon's address to the nation about Watergate. Dreamed about Claudia Cardinale. She was giving me a piggy-back through a bombsite. Passing a policeman, I wondered if he would consider it unusual enough to stop us.
(Comrades from Newcastle just arrived wanting advice on how to start a community paper!)
Feel wounded by your accusations of my insensitivity and inability to respond to other people's needs.
Feel as if you recoil from me as though I had kicked you, betrayed a trust.
Hating the inflexibility of our staunch postures of rejection.
Feeling the need to be bewildered myself, to not know what I want. The freedom to find that out?
Know I have been brutal.

There was no signature.

Shortly afterwards, Phil began to wander down to the laundry again. He wouldn't say a great deal, just play with Andrew a little, and stay the night. I never knew when to expect him, but I knew by now what the risks were in trying to pin him down, so I opted for a strategic silence and tried not to listen for his key in the lock every night.

As spring wore on, I began to slide in and out of depressions which were deep, tearless, and corrosive. I said nothing of this, and only worked all the more feverishly. After all, there was no shortage of activities. Every day there were demands to be met, duties to be done. In my diary, every hour was accounted for.

All around me here, things move at their necessary pace. Frost melts. Water runs. Bees move slower as the cold of autumn sharpens. The leaves on the sycamore above me dry and fall at a gradually accelerating rate. Today, a hundred. Tomorrow, twice that, and then a thousand, until the yellow is all on the ground and the branches between me and the sky are black and bare.

Yes, it's possible, looking back, to see myself as a country girl out-distanced by the momentum of the city. But that would only be part of the picture. I was also a Scot, and Phil's coat of revolutionary moralism fitted my Calvinist shoulders nicely. I hardly felt the seams.

But that speed, that relentlessness. I find it inconceivable. The dislocation of it. Oh, it's easy to say now: if only. If only I had listened earlier to the part of me that sought my own pace. As it was, although the whispering became louder, became a warning shout, still I did not slow down, until the scream of brakes.

6

When I think of Jed I remember this story:

A young apprentice had Monday morning blues. He asked his mate Charlie to stab him with a flick-knife – a slight flesh wound was all that he needed, just enough to get off sick. Charlie agreed, and Charlie jabbed, but the knife slipped and went in deep, gashing an artery. The apprentice was in hospital with complications for six weeks. In court Charlie said: 'The boss kept giving him all the boring jobs, so he was fed up.' Both lads were fined.

The incident had happened in the aircraft factory where Jed had served his apprenticeship. He kept the newspaper cutting pinned on the wall of the office above the Printshop.

Throughout my troubles with Phil I had been spending several hours a day in the basement of the Printshop, where Jed was teaching me how to operate the process camera and the big off-set litho machine. As we bent together over the plate-maker, wiping the thin metal plates with image-developer and gum arabic, or shouted to each other across the clatter of the press, I found I was watching him with growing interest. There was an innocence about him which attracted me. I liked the smile lines which were etched from his nose to his chin, and the bony, weather-beaten face which changed with the expression in the deep-set luminous eyes. He was tall but small-boned, with arms which were stringily muscled and already tanned, because on fine days he would spend lunchtimes outside on the pavement. Parked on one of the rickety office chairs, with his eyes shut and his shirt open, he would take the slight spring sun. His hair was straight and fine, with a reddish glint. He was vain about it, and I liked that too. It made him seem approachable. He wore it very long, washed it three times a week, and treated it like a girl would, flicking it around, touching it a lot.

That hectic spring, it was Vi's idea to take a break. Unlike the rest of us, she had a regular, if part-time, job, and a worker's consciousness of the need for holidays. Once she'd persuaded us that with careful scheduling and a little help from one or two reliable people such a trip need not disrupt *Hard Times* or the Women's Centre at all, she set about organising it with a kind of wary determination, as if she still expected someone to turn round and denounce her on grounds of frivolity.

A newcomer to the Women's Centre, we discovered, owned a cottage in the country. She was a social worker called Michaela – a name which made me think of buck teeth and lionesses – who was known around the Centre as Mike. Vi and I had already been impressed with her commitment to the Centre, and if I had my private doubts about well-heeled feminists with good intentions, I could still see that she had sterling qualities. She was principled without being self-righteous, practical-minded yet also imaginative; as an organiser, Vi and I agreed, she was indispensable. When Mike, knowing next to nothing about the Group, shyly offered to lend us her cottage, I found myself wondering, rather unfairly, how much guilt there was in her generosity. All the same, we accepted, and so, on a weekend in May, we came to the cottage for the first time.

At the last moment, numbers dwindled. Tom blushed and confessed that he had muddled his dates. He had to go to a national Claimants' Union conference, he said, which I didn't believe for a moment, having noticed him the night before holding hands with a Cambridge student called Marie. Phil, characteristically, made no excuses, but simply changed his mind.

We were standing on the pavement outside the Printshop waiting for Jed to finish fixing the van, when suddenly Phil shook his head, turned on his heel, and went back inside.

I suspected that it was Jed's outburst which had decided things. Phil never had approved of tantrums.

Jed had been working on the engine mountings. I felt obliged to help, or at least to hold the torch for him, but Jed assured me that he could manage alone, and so I contented myself with looking on. When he came to tighten the last nut he threw the whole weight of his arm and shoulder behind the heavy spanner, which then slewed round, jamming his finger against the engine casing and chewing into his fingernail. He jumped back, banged his head on the bonnet, and yelled out.

'Enough, I've had enough!' With a bellow of pain and temper he hurled the spanner at the van, where it bounced with an alarming clang, scarring the paintwork. Blood welled up and covered the end of his forefinger. He stood shaking, nursing the greasy, wounded hand. Cautiously, for I was rather afraid of Jed's tempers, I offered him a handkerchief.

It was not I, however, but Phil, who took the brunt. While

Jed mopped at the wound, I watched Phil sidle over to the open bonnet of the van. He peered into the engine, poking ineffectually. He pursed his lips, and sighed. He looked so inept that when, a moment later, Jed finally lost control, I couldn't blame him for it.

'Me, me, always ME,' he shouted. 'Collective responsibility for vehicles, YEAH? Who does it? ME. Bloody intellectuals don't know their arse from their tit when it comes to mechanics!' Then, putting his head in his hands, he let out a sob.

Phil looked down his long nose at the ground.

'It's fucked,' Jed muttered, looking ashamed of himself. 'It's a filthy old wreck. It'll never go as far as the North Circular, let along a hundred and fifty miles.'

The weather, meanwhile, was thundering up: pea-green sky in the east, and the pavements turning an eerie yellow. The windows of the tower block opposite reflected a steely brightness. It didn't take long to agree that hitching was out of the question.

Phil turned then, and vanished into the Printshop, and Jed seemed to make an effort of will. Taking up the spanner again, he wriggled back under the van, while Vi and I crossed our fingers. After half an hour of anxiety, the nuts held, and the engine fired. Jed was jubilant, and patted the bonnet affectionately.

When it became obvious that Phil wasn't coming after all, I found that I was relieved. I'd been imagining that he would ration the nights we slept together at the cottage in the same way that he rationed his visits to the laundry, and I wasn't relishing the prospect. I was beginning to think that I preferred no expectations at all to hopes which were raised only to be disappointed.

On the Cambridge road, the thunderclouds blew away. Jed began to sing old Beatles songs, and Vi and I joined in, until the three of us were roaring out 'Hey Jude' and 'Help' and 'All You Need is Love', and drowning out the din of the engine. In the fields, young turnips were coming up bluish-green, and there was brisk yellow-green corn too, no more than four inches high. I gazed at it all with a thirsty astonishment, like a soldier coming home from the war.

Jed, too, said that he found it all quite miraculous. He was country-bred like me, but from Dorset, of farming stock, and the warm earthy accent was still in his voice. He confessed that he was glad to escape from London: from his wrestling matches with the printing press, and from the meetings, and the newspaper, and the sight of Phil's messy bedclothes cluttering up the office.

'I just hope,' he said with a scowl, 'I just hope I don't go back to a sinkful of dirty cups, and soggy teabags all over the place, and the cat's box going rancid.' Then he stopped, looked guiltily at me, and said: 'Pity Phil didn't come, though.'

I nodded insincerely.

The first evening at the cottage was interminable. Jed's dope made me tongue-tied, and the effort of concealing my feelings made me paranoid. Towards midnight, I decided that I must have been crazy to imagine that he might make a proposition.

After he had gone upstairs, I hid my disappointment and helped Vi to make up a bed for the two of us on the sitting-room floor. I was cleaning my teeth at the kitchen sink when he reappeared and said aggressively that there seemed to be a shortage of beds so if I felt like sharing with him, it would be cool. I stared at him for a moment, wondering what he meant. He was wearing only a pair of yellow Y-fronts with a white trim. His stomach was shallowly rounded but muscly, pitched between two narrow hip-bones.

'Okay?' he said, frowning at me.

Since my mouth was full of toothpaste, I just nodded; a few minutes later I climbed the stairs to the white attic room and got into bed with him.

He had lit a candle, which brought fat moths thumping against the uncurtained window; he looked anxious. I still didn't trust myself to say anything, and so we made love in silence. His long hair fell down and tickled my nose. He was very light above me, but strong and slithery, and his touch was firm. I didn't come, of course, because it was the first time and missionary position as well, but there was a physical harmony between us which I hadn't felt with Phil. Afterwards, surprised by the ease of it, I said as much, and we lay sweatily on top of the bedclothes, giggling.

'I like your cock,' I said. It was smooth and dun-coloured, and reminded me of a horse's, because of its curve and angle. I told him that he must have an affinity with horses, since so many parts of him resembled them. I touched them one by one – his nose, his thighs, the delicate arched bones of his feet.

He looked down at his cock, and then at me. 'Well!' he said, grinning, and took it in his hand with a milking movement, squeezing and stretching it.

We slept. In the morning Jed told me that he had dreamed of the West Country. He had been standing with his brothers in a Bible Tent, with his little boy's face pressed into his mother's thigh. Everyone was singing 'Jesus Loves Me This I Know, For the Bible Tells Me So', and in the row behind I was singing too, all the time rubbing a photograph of him against my crotch.

To me it seemed so obvious that Jed and I would go on being together, and I felt so little guilt about it, that I was genuinely shocked by Phil's reaction. The day after I arrived back he came to visit. He was wearing new white jeans, very clean, and he had cut his hair and trimmed his beard. He sat on the bed underneath the Rosa Luxemburg poster and smiled at me with a warmth I'd grown not to expect.

'Welcome,' he said.

Of course, I thought, Jed has told him: this is his way of giving consent. I started to laugh. 'I see you've heard.'

Phil's eyebrows lifted a quarter of an inch.

'Heard?' he said, for, of course, he had not. Jed had said nothing, had left the explanations to me. Pulling myself together, I told him quickly what had happened. When I had finished, Phil put his hand over his eyes and went pale. Then, with agonising politeness, he excused himself, and walked out of the room.

I lay back on the bed, astonished. For three hours I lay there and stared at Phil's graffiti and thought about sexual freedom.

On the wall above the door there was a circle of doves, with the insignia: We carry a new world in our hearts. Over the fireplace, for reasons which were more obscure, Phil had painted an Arthurian sword emerging from a lake. I lay there puzzling, trying to piece together the two halves of Phil. For if he insisted on following his own desires, how could he object when I did the same? How could he possibly justify such a double standard?

When Phil returned there were oil stains on his jeans and he was angry. He told me that he had spent the afternoon cycling in circles, and had met the same Labour councillor three times. The first time, he stopped and exchanged obligatory political gossip, the second time, he blushed and passed on, and the third time, he was quite unable to account for himself, and the Councillor stared, and he felt utterly humiliated.

Listening, I found him ridiculous, and I decided that if he were to make an end of it there and then, I wouldn't be particularly distraught. Folding my hands in my lap, I waited for his announcement, and my punishment.

Phil, however, did not punish, at least not then, and not in the way I had expected. Within a few days he had rallied, and things carried on more or less as before, except that Jed was with me on the nights Phil wasn't, and I felt that for the first time some kind of equality – or, at least, balance of power – had been achieved between us.

To this day I don't know how Phil and Jed organised these visits. They may have lived in the same house, but I know they never talked about them. I can only assume that they developed some kind of code to deal with the situation. Taking a bath, perhaps, or putting on a clean shirt, or parting their hair on a slant.

I can laugh now. I can see the absurd side. This must be Matt's influence. What Jed and Phil and I saw as the abolition of old structures, as roads to freedom, Matt sees as adolescent contortions. He believes that the real, the burning issue is one man, one woman, and that all else is evasion.

7

The day before the Rock Against Racism carnival was a rainy Saturday, and two things happened. First, my mother wrote from the other side of the world, and second, Matt phoned.

Confiding in my mother is something I do rarely, and with trepidation. I'm always afraid that she will disappoint me, and so she does, yet some intractable yearning propels me to try and try again to be comforted or borne up, or whatever else is in that bundle of deep and stubborn expectations we carry for our mothers.

It had taken me weeks to muster the courage to write to her about Jed, and so there was a chilling time-lag between the events and her response to them. She wrote:

My dear, it all sounds very complicated and sordid – you don't have any luck picking your men, do you? I don't know what opinion to give about your break-up with Jed because you never told me a lot about him. I do wish you had sent a photograph when I asked you. I'm always hoping you'll meet someone who has no strings attached or hang-ups or hang-outs or whatever you call them, who will take care of you and Andrew. It's no good, I always think of Andrew's dad and how he adored you and spoiled you from the first, it nearly broke my heart when you got divorced. It's always been a great sorrow to me that you two didn't settle down and specially with Andrew. Your kind of life isn't easy for bringing up a child – passing Andrew here and there and from one to the other. I know you'll say – oh mother, she's old hat – but am I? I've been lucky with the men in my life. I always knew your dad adored me, there was no one like me for him, and I knew he was my own man because he was my husband and your dad. Perhaps you'll find this a load of blethers but it's worked fine for me – and I've needed patience, all men are selfish, even the best of them.

I read this, and the shock of disappointment made me

shrink. My insides shrank. I narrowed my knees and shoulders and let my chest cave in. Outside the kitchen windows England was turning grey. Grey rain, grey grass, grey roses budding at the bottom of the garden. My fingers holding the airmail letter looked crinkled and colourless, as if they'd been in the bath for hours. I sat there for a long time, staring out at the garden. There was gluey mud on the path, and weeding to be done, and empty plots to be planted. Marie and Tom came and went and made toast and morning conversation which made no inroads on my dejection. They said they were going leafletting for the carnival and would take Andrew and Zac with them.

The phone had been ringing all morning for Tom and Marie, political business mainly, so when it rang again I left it for a while, hoping it would stop. But it persisted, and when I picked it up I heard a little laugh, and then Matt's voice said: 'Oh, there you are.' He sounded relieved. He began to talk very fast. He had a toothache, he said, a shocker; he was reeking of tincture of cloves. He had been up half the night reading *Womanright*, and really just wanted to tell me what a good writer I was.

'Congratulations,' he said, 'you're the real thing, aren't you?'

I laughed uncomfortably.

'You don't believe me? I wouldn't bullshit you about that, June.'

'Thank you kindly. No really, I appreciate it.'

'You'll come to the carnival, then?'

'I won't be able to read,' I said, and groped for excuses.

'Look, no hassle. Explanations unnecessary. As long as you come, for it's going to be *a–mazing*.'

It was only after I hung up that the warmth in his voice affected me. Praise. Enthusiasm. *Recognition*. All over, I was thawing, expanding, filling my proper space again. I ran upstairs to wash my face and decided to go and help with the leafletting after all.

8

In Trafalgar Square, everyone was looking for someone. It was a glaring day, and I put on sun-glasses to search the crowds for Mike. Meanwhile, the tail ends of my dreams whispered of Matt. All night, in rooms, in dim corridors, his long shadow had played hide and seek with me.

I had arranged to meet Mike at the foot of Nelson's column, but the police, as it turned out, had erected a barrier there to cordon off the speakers on the plinth, so I wandered around for a while, peering, listening to the PA system booming and echoing around the National Gallery. At last I caught sight of her in a clearing by a peanut stall, where a family of tourists were doggedly feeding pigeons. She was standing with her back very straight and her chin high; one of her hands played with the strap of an expensive suede handbag, the other was flattened protectively over the fastener. On her face there was a supercilious look which might have been interpreted as English sang-froid, but which was really no more than a veneer, for the essence of Mike was discomfiture. She was an aristocrat, it's true, schooled at Benenden and polished at Somerville, but her glittering privileges had failed to provide any of the self-assurance you might expect. She'd been uneasy about her background long before she ever tangled with politics, and drifting so far to the left had exacerbated this feeling of blemish, of handicap. It had taken her years to reveal the full extent of her pedigree to me, she'd been so afraid – and with reason, I admit – that I would reject her for it. Nowadays, though, she knew my curiosity was stronger than my prejudice. Nowadays she talked of escaping debdom in the way Americans talk of draft-dodging, and listening, I glimpsed another world.

At *Womanright* we complemented each other, sparked each other off. Any uneasiness could always be defused by jokes.

'One brought up to maintain the Empire,' she'd say, 'the other to tear it down – and whose upper lip is the stiffer?' We made a good team, we agreed, laughing.

As I approached her, she peered short-sightedly at me. Her face was tanned from a skiing trip – one indulgence she still allowed herself – and there were white marks around her eyes where the line of her goggles had been. Recognising me at last, she clasped her long white hands together.

'*Just* in time,' she said, 'We're moving off, and I've lost the *Womanright* bunch already.' At her feet was a pile of magazines tied with string. We divided it in half and held the magazines flat against our chests, cover side out, so that we were walking advertisements. 'Ready,' said Mike, with her cool public face.

'Hallo there.' I kissed her lightly on the cheek.

Her face relaxed a little. 'Yes,' she smiled, '*Aren't* we business-like?'

Around us marchers jumped down from steps and fountains and tried to line up behind the banners of Trade Unions and political parties. The circling movement became a whirlpool out of which Mike and I were cast, and carried on a wave of teenagers, and borne out of the square.

Mike spoke close to my ear. 'I promised a friend I'd meet her when we get to Victoria Park. I'm really sorry. I hope you won't feel abandoned.'

'Don't be silly,' I said quickly, 'The whole house will be there, and Vi, and endless other mobs from Phil's house, I expect.' It was true, though, I was disappointed. I had wanted her to myself.

On all sides youth of both sexes surged, leaping, jigging, waving Anti-Nazi League placards and multi-coloured balloons. In doorways tourists stood well back and clicked their cameras, for the Sunday streets were full of spectacle: fake leopardskin; hair in Mohican cuts, hair shaved or dyed pink or bristling with knitting needles; lurex pants and silver studs, chain-mail mini-skirts and Dracula cloaks.

'But June, they're so *young*,' Mike said as we bowled along, 'D'you think they're really here for the *politics?*' She had a fluting voice which carried; in front of us a girl with yellow glitter on her eyelids turned and stared, and Mike gave an embarrassed smile. Surrounded by chants, we walked in silence for a while, two seasoned campaigners and a little apologetic about it. We were leaving the City with its marble-faced banks and office blocks, entering narrower lanes of warehouses and railway sidings, when in front of us several lines of marchers linked arms and broke into a trot. Out of an old instinct to close ranks, Mike and I ran too. She was wearing espadrilles with wedge heels, and as we caught up with the line in front she staggered and I put my arm out to support her.

'When will I learn to leave these ridiculous high heels at home?' she said ruefully. 'I tell you, it doesn't matter where the struggle is, I'll always be limping along behind the lines.'

I teased her. 'All this fresh-faced youth must be making you jumpy.'

Mike fussed with a lock of hair which had fallen into her eyes. She pulled the fair, rather lacklustre hair back from her forehead and stabbed a slide into it. In profile her nose was sharp, her mouth small and pink, her chin pronounced. 'Perhaps. Perhaps I'm just stating the facts, though. That I've had my day. Or missed it, rather.' She made a mock-sulky pout.

'What *is* this? Missed it? Do I detect uncertainties about the centrality of your role in progressive movements past and present?'

She shrugged, smiling reluctantly. 'Well. You haven't exactly seen me in the vanguard of things, have you?'

'Oh, spare us,' I laughed, 'Whereas I, of course, was?' I shook my head, determined not to take her mood seriously. 'Are we still straining for purity of ideology and action, then?' Throughout the rigorous years of the group, it was Mike who'd been the repository of my doubts. Had she forgotten that? In her tidy house with its geranium-filled window boxes I wolfed down the brownies which her husband baked and let off steam about the pressures of transforming not only society but yourself as well. She'd been fascinated by our ideas, had listened avidly – but I was glad she'd stopped short of living them. I groaned. 'Whence cometh this angst all of a sudden?'

Instead of answering, she flicked distractedly through one of the magazines. 'I edit these damn articles about *relationships*,' she muttered, 'and all the time I'm only too conscious that the sexual revolution flowed past my life without disturbing one flowerpot . . . not a trace,' she added as I laughed. ' "Changing relationships" ,' she read. 'So what changes?' Her light blue eyes fixed on me. 'That last article was so smug, don't you think?'

I smiled. 'It had a certain lack of irony, I grant you.'

'She's just saying, isn't she – look, heterosexual relationships are perfectly unproblematic really, if you get them taped. Well, bully for her.' She looked sourly at the grey stains of printing ink which had rubbed off on her fingers. 'Myself, I was always too bogged down in the security of marriage to risk any changes – any real ones, I mean. But at least I never deceived myself that it was a particularly good solution to anything – or that I was wildly contented.'

'But it's a tricky area for journalism, the confessional. And these women aren't professional writers or psychologists or anything. We can't *force* them to be honest. We can't very well say: "We don't believe you, please examine your marriage more carefully and serve us up with the deeper contradictions." . . . Can we?'

The march turned a corner into the sun. Mike shielded her eyes with her hand. 'Perhaps we're just a couple of old cynics . . . contesting our readers' happiness with their men.'

'Not just with men. We've printed a couple of pretty starry-eyed lesbian ones too, in my opinion.'

Mike stared straight ahead. Her chin was up. 'At least that's presenting an alternative of a kind,' she said, in a stilted voice.

I looked at her tense face. It wasn't like Mike to take such a correct line, and I was rattled. 'For a minority, perhaps. But I don't see why we should romanticise it . . .' Mike, I remembered, had always been singularly unromantic, or at least about her marriage. One night after a meeting at her house, the two of us had lolled on the carpet together, smoking. Mike was nervous, worn out with acting host to the women's group. She sat hunched over the ashtray, tapping non-existent ash off her cigarette; suddenly she announced: 'Mel and I have homosexualised our relationship.' The briskness of the delivery made me splutter, until I realised that she was half in earnest. Whatever did she mean, I asked. 'I mean,' she replied, 'that Mel is a very practical person. When he reads *The Myth of the Vaginal Orgasm*, he doesn't just absorb it as theory, he believes in acting on it.'

'Well,' I said, thinking of Phil, 'Consider yourself lucky.'

'He's such a democrat,' she went on, with a smothered laugh. 'He insisted on equal shares of housework long before I ever wrote a word about women's domestic labour or any of that stuff.' She lifted her shoulders. 'So what can you do, when you can't think of any real gripes?'

Later, seeing me out, she said: 'I do consider myself lucky, of course. Sickening, isn't it?' I realised then that whenever she was in that house, even if Mel was out, she talked under her breath, as if he could hear.

Up ahead, the noise of chanting swelled to a roar. 'But you've never been one for over-simplifications,' I pressed her. 'I mean, sisterhood as a bed of roses, and all that.'

Mike opened her mouth as if to reply, and then seemed to change her mind. The march was slowing down, stopping under a railway bridge, and a helicopter came swinging low overhead to investigate the bottleneck. The clatter of its blades merged with the shouts of the marchers and the rumble of trains, and Mike dropped the magazines at her feet and put her hands over her ears. Nervousness came off her in waves. Feeling protective, I scanned the flats which overlooked the street. There was a Union Jack painted on one of the blocks – probably a relic of Jubilee Year rather than anything more sinister, but all the same, these streets were National Front territory, and I eyed the concrete balconies apprehensively. Evidently there were others who felt the same. Behind us was a Gay Liberation banner, and under it an exquisite young man intoned:

'Into the valley of death rode the six hundred.'

There was a ripple of laughter. 'Sixty thousand this time, ducky,' another voice piped up. 'Fascists to the left of them, fascists to the right of them...'

Mike had turned quite pale. 'Take it easy,' I said.

She uncovered her ears and grimaced. 'It's just the crowds and the noise. You know me, I don't really like people at all, I prefer cats.' She tried to smile. I steered her out to the edge of the march. On the pavement, we both breathed more easily. We sat down on the kerb with our feet in the gutter among empty Coke tins and the limp rags of discarded balloons. Mike stared at the ground between her feet. 'But I did miss it all, didn't I? When I was so busy propping up my little security structures . . .'

'So?' Again I wondered what she was getting at. She had never pretended to be other than cautious, so it seemed rather late in the day for breast-beating about it. 'So what if you defended some corners of private life against the wilder excesses of sexual politics? So you were just sensible.' I nudged her and laughed. 'Think of all the energy you saved for the wider struggle . . .'

She looked at me through narrowed eyes. 'That's exactly it. Sensible. No risks.'

'Starting a magazine like *Womanright* was really sticking to the straight and narrow, wasn't it?' I said sarcastically. 'Honestly, I thought we'd passed the stage when we had to be more-revolutionary-than-thou.'

Mike poked with her foot at a shrunken balloon, Then, abruptly, she said: 'Remember Sherry?' I watched her espadrille kick sideways; the balloon bounced, fell, bounced again, and deflated a little more. I searched my memory.

'Sherry who used to come to the Women's Centre? Your old...client?'

'My old client, yes,' she said, with irony.

Just then a woman stepped out of the crowd and came towards us. 'I *thought* it must be the new issue.' Around her neck keys jingled on a leather thong. Mike went about the small ritual of selling, of finding change, of sisterly chat, while I tried to piece together my recollections of Sherry. What came to mind first was an image of an eighteen-year-old with a frizz of red hair and a Pink Floyd album under her arm, a sullen face in the back row of a Women's Centre meeting. Other details I could reconstruct from what Mike had told me at the time. The same girl, but with cropped hair and electrodes clamped to her head. Ditto with headscarf, stuffing brightly-coloured felt animals with Kapok.

'Sherry didn't exactly take to the Women's Centre, did she?'

Mike smiled grimly, and shook her head. She began to pick at the varnish on her thumbnail, peeling it off in transparent strips. She seemed unwilling to look at me.

'What's up?' I said, feeling dense, but still she said nothing. And then light began to dawn. 'Is this an . . . involvement?' Incredulity made my voice quaver.

In response she hugged the magazines to her chest and gave the faintest of nods. A strange expression crossed her face. It was protective, almost brutally so, like a dog guarding a bone. She rested her chin on the magazines. 'I haven't felt what I feel now. Not ever.' Her voice was a bare whisper, but the words reverberated.

'Ah.' I felt a pit open in my stomach. We were sitting close together, with our shoulders almost touching; Mike sat neatly, knees together, ladylike as ever; only her face was in disorder.

'Mel knows nothing,' she said urgently, 'so please, please, not a word.'

'Of course not!' I was shocked. She should have taken that for granted.

Her eyes went blank, and she chewed absently at the spines of the magazines. Her teeth looked small and sharp. 'It's some kind of obsession,' she muttered, as if to herself. By the railway bridge there was movement; the congestion was easing.

'Onward,' I said, pulling her to her feet.

She gave herself a shake and looked round cautiously.

'Still, it's all very good-humoured, isn't it? Quite a lively lot . . . I'm sorry to moan on, but as you can see, I'm a bit all over the place.' Her face was still strained, but at least the vacant, lost look had receded.

'Apologies unnecessary.' I pointed to the magazines. 'And by the way, it's only comrades from the *Worker's Press* who have to eat the copies they don't sell.'

Mike glanced down at the chewed spines of the magazines and laughed.

At the entrance to the park the long column of the march dissolved into a swarm of bodies hurrying across the grass towards the oblong of the stage. By the park gates I caught a glimpse of the green *Womanright* banner among the red ones propped against the railings. Catherine and Andrea stood underneath it; they had their arms round each other and they were eating ice-cream cones. Catherine's short brown hair was brushed up into peaks and streaked with green vegetable dye.

Andrea saw us and waved. 'Vi Fawcett was looking for you,' she cried, pointing her ice-cream towards the stage.

We drifted on the dense stream through the gates. The tint of my sun-glasses intensified the green of the grass and the yellow of leaves just unfurling from buds. Beside me Mike scanned the landscape of moving figures, seeking Sherry, openly excited now, and watching her, I felt lonely. We stopped at last near the crush barrier at the foot of the stage, where the crowd thickened. At the back of the stage a dozen denim-clad men busied with coiled cables and mixers and speaker-banks; their expressions were haughty, and they swore a lot, and none of them was Matt. On the front of the stage a compère in an orange jumpsuit with the yellow flash of the Anti-Nazi League took up a mike.

'Sixty-eight thousand, can you hear me?' he screamed, pointing out across the park. 'Sixty-eight thousand, and we are still pouring through these gates!' The compère pranced triumphantly. The TV cameras panned. The crowd let out a roar which made Mike tremble. Then a plump girl danced on to the stage; she wore lime green socks and an acrilan suit which wouldn't have looked out of place in the Churchwomen's Guild. A hush. Murmurs. Could it be Polystyrene already? So early? The compère's voice was temporarily inaudible. Distorted by feedback, the amplification was fragmenting against the trees two hundred yards away across the park. And then the music began, gathering the rags of sound together. The crowd made a rush forward.

I clutched at Mike. 'Move out!' Surrounded by tall youths, we were too short, we could see nothing but the highest landmarks. 'Head for the trees.' Holding hands, we pushed firmly through a mass which heaved and panted and pushed as firmly in the opposite direction. Here and there other tightly-clasped hands of lovers, of parents and children, barred the way like fences. I smelled sweat, I smelled perfume, I smelled the stale wind of hundreds of stomachs which had marched on no breakfast.

A quarter of a mile from the stage, where the ground was higher and the crowd sparser, we found a vantage point under a beech tree. The music was fainter from here, the stage a distant matchbox construction. In front of it heads bobbed up from a moving sea, dyed heads, the many colours of boiled sweets. Perched high in the branches of the tree above our heads, a black girl swayed to the staccato music, and the trunk of the tree trembled. The beat was infectious. 'Come on,' I said to Mike. I moved my arms, shook out my hair, and felt my body loosen.

The fantasy slipped uninvited, as fantasies do, through the door opened by the dance. I imagined Matt and me together on the stage. Above us, helicopters and the spiralling seagulls. All around us, the multi-layered, sinuous music. We danced quicksteps, we danced tangos, we danced tap routines worthy of Fred Astaire. We circled each other, and closed, and broke away, and closed again to dance hip to hip like rubber dolls, heat-sealed, while from below the crowd yelled at us, applauding what the body said, what the music underlined.

Beside me Mike gyrated self-consciously. I sang along under my breath: it was a song about bondage, very brash, very bitter. Down in the crowd a blue light flashed, and the blare of a siren entered the song.

'Someone was bound to faint in that crush,' said Mike.

I stopped dancing, suddenly alert. 'Keep an eye open for the kids. They're here with Phil. Or they're supposed to be.'

'You have to meet them?'

'No, no, they'll be fine with Phil. Whatever else I might feel about him, I can't fault him on childcare!'

Mike looked at me curiously. 'Do they still stay with him every Saturday?'

'Not always. Sometimes.' I shrugged. 'Odd, isn't it? But Andrew's very fond of Phil.'

Mike glanced at her watch. 'What's he like with you these days?'

'A monster of reserve. We haven't talked for years. Apart from the occasional constipated political interchange.'

Mike's hand reached over to take the cigarette I was smoking. It was a languid gesture, graceful, as if she was extending her hand for a kiss. 'Just one puff. I must go soon.' She inhaled deeply, swaying a little, and her voice came faintly. 'I don't know what it could do to Mel.'

'I take it you aren't going to tell him?'

'Since when was honesty my strong point?'

I hesitated, fearful of prying. 'It's hard to take in. You and Mel. After all these years.'

She smiled bitterly. 'Don't I know it. The worked-out movement couple. While all around you freedom-fighters were following the . . . the multiple permutations of your desires!'

I laughed. 'And falling apart!'

'Yes, but bravely. "A society based on needs and desires." You can't imagine how admiring I felt . . . from a safe distance, of course.' Her lip curled, and she bent down, crouching over the pile of magazines. I watched her count the remaining ones carefully and make a note of the number in a tiny book with an embroidered cover.

'Aren't you being very hard on yourself? After all, you've enough trouble on your plate without all this self-reproach.'

She glanced up at me. 'Trouble? Yes. Christ!' In her eyes I saw, fleetingly, an expression which made me catch my breath, for what it hinted at was something quite rapturous. Then it was quickly veiled. 'I'm in deep, June,' she said, 'very deep.'

The movie language sounded strange on her lips. Understanding nothing, I nodded knowingly. I felt very shy. 'So stop idealising all that stuff from the past,' I said gruffly. 'It bothers me, the way you set me up as some sort of sexual revolutionary.'

Mike gave a puzzled frown. 'But don't you see it as heroic? The way all of you lived your principles, and never kow-towed to anything, or took the comfortable option?'

'Look, sometimes I reckon there wasn't a lot of difference between the Group and your marriage, say. In terms of what was *repressed*. . .What I'm saying is. . .perhaps you shied away from any experience which might disrupt your marriage too much – but didn't we also avoid coming to grips with anything which threatened our brave new theories?'

'Like what? Like dependency, you mean?'

'Oh yes. And romantic love was another no-go area. And passion – well, passion was altogether too chaotic!' Remembering Matt's droll parodies, I chuckled. For once I didn't feel like worrying about the injustices I might be doing to the past. 'Frankly, I'm not quite sure what *was* permissible – apart from sexual permissiveness.'

Mike stretched and smiled obliquely. 'I can't really believe that everyone was as repressed as you make out. . .But then, I never can accept that anyone else could be as uptight as me.'

'Well, you're staring straight at her.'

We grinned at each other.

'I suppose it all goes to show that you can't legislate for emotions,' said Mike.

'Unfortunately!'

A hand came from behind, lifting my sun-glasses, covering my eyes. A bracelet grazed my cheek.

'Garbo, I presume?'

It was Vi, in a shabby black coat and a wide skirt the colour of buttercups. She tossed her hair back and nodded to Mike. 'Watcher. Quite a scene, eh? Everyone I meet I lose again in two seconds flat.'

'Weren't you with Matt?' I asked, in the most normal of voices.

'No chance. I was with Phil and Co. a minute ago but I made the mistake of looking the other way and they vanished.'

'Were the kids all right?'

'What? Oh sure,' she said breathlessly. 'Look, if I know you're going to be parked here, then I'll go and brave the tea queue. I must have said hallo to the entire libertarian left, not to mention the Communist Party, and I'm *dry*.' She dragged her coat off and dropped it at my feet. 'It's so bloody hot. I dress for winter and it comes over all spring-like.' She rolled her eyes sardonically. 'Speaking of which, if Matt wanders past lonely as a cloud, grab him, okay? Not that I expect him. Tea?'

'Yes, two sugars please . . .'

Vi's yellow skirt vanished into the crowd. The band launched into another number, and the girl in the tree waved her arms recklessly. Mike checked her watch. 'I really must be off.' A shadow passed over her face. 'Wish me luck.' As I watched her ramrod back move away through the crowd, I felt again that creaking emptiness which had entered before when we sat together in the gutter.

Vi appeared in the distance. She held three paper cups and she was walking too fast, spilling tea down her skirt. 'Well, three teas for two, then.' When she sat down on the grass her skirt billowed out around her like a crinoline. She looked at me quizzically. 'No Matt?'

'Not a sign. Isn't he occupied on the stage somewhere?'

'Not him. He was supposed to be dealing with the Press, but he went off in a huff. You know him.'

No, I don't.

'It was the telly types he objected to. Called them a bunch

of parasites.' She spread her coat out and invited me to share it. 'Maybe he's right; what do I know about it?'

I was disturbed. 'But weren't they relying on him?'

Vi sniffed. 'Probably.'

Families, communes, groups of friends, had camped down on the grass all around us, hemming us in. Blankets were unfolded, and plastic picnic boxes opened, and bottles of wine produced from Sainsbury's carrier bags. The smell of dope was strong. I sat close to Vi, glad of her presence, and when she offered me a small joint, I refused it. 'Then I'd definitely get lost,' I said regretfully.

Vi smoothed her skirt over her knees and stretched out. Her feet in small black sandals stuck up awkwardly as she lay flat, smoking, gazing up at the beech tree. After a while she said: 'Temperamental bugger!' and smoke came out of her mouth vertically, in a rush. 'I'm not hanging around for him.' The lie pinched her face.

It was Andrew, as it turned out, who got lost. As soon as I saw Phil shambling across the grass I knew something had gone wrong. His sandshoes were muddy and a loose lace trailed on the ground behind him. His face searched. I jumped up, ready for bad news.

'Have you seen Andrew, by any chance?' he said, and laughed, as if trying to make light of it, but his face was chalky under the red hair. When I said no he put his head on one side and said, 'Ah.'

I tried not to be angry. After all, it could have happened to anyone. We stood there looking at each other, not touching, two grown-ups confronting a crisis. We talked in clipped, business-like voices about probabilities, and then we split up and started tracking.

Near the Information Tent was a small pennanted enclave marked 'Lost Children', but Andrew was not there. No, they said, no child answering that description had come by. For more than an hour I searched, criss-crossing the park, asking picnickers and policemen and badge-sellers if they had spotted a small stocky boy in a blue anorak. Ages ago, Vi had gone to put an announcement out on the tannoy, but if Andrew heard it, he didn't respond.

He's a dreamer, I thought angrily, he should know better.

In the end it was Phil who found him: sitting, he said, in a patch of grass which thousands of feet had worn to mud, digging glumly with a stick. For two hours, realising that he was lost, he had sat there in silence, approaching no one.

'I thought if I didn't move, I'd get found,' said Andrew, miserable but dry-eyed.

Phil's hand hovered just above Andrew's shoulder. 'He didn't cry once, not in all that time,' he said, with surprise or admiration, I wasn't sure which. Somehow this detail was the unbearable one. I stared at Andrew's small set face and exploded. He shouldn't try to be so tough and masculine, he should have gone to the Information Tent, he should seek help when he needed it, instead of trying to go it alone. Phil put his hands in the pockets of his big tweed coat and shuffled his feet.

'I couldn't see the Information Tent,' Andrew protested, huddling into the hood of his parka.

'That's just what I *mean*,' I persisted. 'You should have asked an adult to take you there.'

He started to cry then, and kicked at a discarded beer bottle in a burst of anger.

9

Insects are busy in the dry leaves under the bushes. The sycamores creak overhead. It is peaceful. Down in the dark circle of water a smaller circle of blue sky shines, and within that, the reflection of my head: a ragged, curly silhouette, peering, inquisitive.

Matt drops the axe and comes towards me brushing wood-shavings off his jeans. His hands are stained green from lichens.

'Ready for the market?' he says. His voice is loud and stirs a bird in the thicket.

'Not yet. Soon, though,'

'Such rosy cheeks. Been having a wank, have we?'

Stop interfering with me.

'Well, *I'm* ready now.'

'Soon,' I repeat.

'Cussed, aren't you?'

Sometimes in the middle of our arguments Phil would stop dead and look at me comically.

'Toughie,' he'd say, wagging his finger; then he would add wisely: 'Main strength: main weakness,' and although I asked him to explain himself, I never did quite understand what he meant. I began to think it was just a ploy to steal an advantage over me, or else some kind of veiled protest. More than once he'd hinted that my resistance to him was based on an empty and misplaced principle of independence, but as far as I could see, I was already too influenced by him, in danger, even, of being annexed by him. When I questioned, when I argued, when I relied on no intelligence but my own, I was simply safeguarding my autonomy – or what remained of it.

If Phil's aphorisms – he had an inexhaustible store of them, and they generally came from books I hadn't read – failed to clinch the argument, he often went on to do something idiotic.

For instance, on the night before we were to occupy the Electricity Board offices, Phil was exasperated with me. I had told him that I didn't like the odds. A handful of squatters versus the whole bureaucratic apparatus of the GLC and the Electricity Board . . .it would be a head-on collision, I said, and with everyone else on the left rushing about doing things for the miners' strike, who'd give a damn whether *we* won or lost? 'It seems so problematic,' I went on, 'particularly at the moment. It doesn't feel very *central*, somehow.'

Phil looked at me as if I had forgotten my times table. 'If our politics are supposed to be about fighting for control of our own lives . . .' He paused to let this sink in. ' . . . then really, as an issue, I don't see that you can get much closer to home than this one.'

I was irked by his patronising tone. 'I mean in relation to what's happening in the country. Perhaps I'm suffering from a failure of imagination, but I don't see that we can actually *win* this one.'

Phil jumped up from his chair and moved restlessly around the room. Defeatist, his frown accused. Turning his back on me, he stared out of the window. 'Every new age is unbelievable beforehand,' he quoted, 'and afterwards, inevitable.'

'But people are working a three-day week. They're having to cope with all the power black-outs. The Tories are screaming about bringing the troops in to shift the coal . . . I just feel we're way out on a limb.'

Phil swung round to face me. 'We'll rely on our wits,' he said, 'and on the element of surprise.' His voice trembled slightly with excitement. 'Wait till tomorrow. You'll see, we'll be a damned sight more than a handful.' Sitting down at the desk again, he picked up my cigarette lighter and began to flick it nervously.

'But there *are* so few of us. Don't you ever feel like a Jesuit or something?'

Phil threw the lighter down and raised his eyes to heaven. 'Lord luv a duck,' he spluttered. Then, grabbing a pair of my knickers off the back of the chair, he put them on his head. He pulled them down over his nose and sniffed gleefully. 'Speak for yourself,' his muffled voice said. And of course then there was nothing to do but laugh, and leave it at that.

Later that night, after Phil had drifted off and before Jed, as mysteriously, appeared, I wondered about those stubborn parts of me which wouldn't consent to Phil's position. Or to Phil's enthusiasm. I decided to find out if any of the others had similar reservations. If they did, perhaps I would feel easier about my own.

When Jed came in, I canvassed him. He was drunk: not quite at the staggering stage, but full of bombastic good humour.

'It's our own needs,' he said gaily, '*our* fight, and about bloody time!' He let himself fall on to the bed, and bounced. He sat up and began to tug at the heels of his high leather boots. The boots were too tight, and he flopped back on the bed, laughing, calling for help.

I hauled the boots off, while he lay on the bed in his thick coat, chattering happily about the action, and how he'd always said we had to make demands about housing, and well, now was the time . . . There was no division in the ranks here, that was obvious. Listening to him, I envied his certainty, and longed to be carried away by it, like driftwood on top of a wave. Compared to this, my equivocations seemed mean-spirited and pettish. I looked at his bright eyes and told myself that I would be loyal, even if that loyalty felt like a steel plate in my spine.

The next morning was bitterly cold, and overcast. The lights of shop windows were half-doused because of the emergency regulations, so that the goods on show – the wigs or eye-shadow palettes or rhinestone-encrusted dresses – looked as tawdry as they would in the cold grey light of winter streets.

'It makes you realise what London must have been like in the war,' Vi said, as we crossed the city.

There were already a hundred squatters in Kensington Gardens when we arrived, and more were filtering in all the time. They came warily, in twos and threes, in accordance with the briefing, and kept their banners furled until they were safely behind the tall privet hedge which encircled the park. The banners said:

'We demand the light to live' and 'All power to the people'.

The official banner was more explicit. Vi had designed the lettering and Phil had invented a logo of a clenched fist holding a bolt of lightning. It said:

NO COLLABORATION WITH THE GLC TO CUT OFF ELECTRICITY SUPPLIES TO SQUATTERS!

Jed and Phil strode off to liaise with other area groups, leaving Vi and me to guard the banner, I watched Jed pause beside a theatrical-looking couple in black cloaks and face-paint, and then he vanished behind the sheepskin jackets and red headbands of the Elgin Avenue contingent. My hand was still warm from holding his in the depths of his coat pocket, but the rest of me was cold. It was a grey chill not wholly attributable to the frost of the morning. The symptoms had come, like a virus, out of thin air. Shivers, as if from a sudden draught. The body rock-heavy, obdurate. The will suspended. I stood rooted to the spot and waited for the attack to pass, as I knew it would, and wondered – not for the first time – if I had a special allergy to partings. Specifically, to partings from Jed.

I was tempted to see the root of the trouble in the pleasures – deep, fluid, almost childlike – which we shared in the night. They were binding me to him, these pleasures, and the bonds had a will of their own. They protested at limits, at schedules, at those inescapable morning separations. At eight o'clock without fail, Jed would jump out of bed and stand at the mirror examining his teeth and his tongue, alert for lumps or inconsistencies or variations in colour. Then, when he had put on his pants he'd go to the window and stand there smoothing his waist and stomach with a tender, solicitous gesture, and say 'Fine day,' or 'It's pissing down.' And I would lie in bed watching him, with a tightness gripping my chest, and a dull, morbid apprehension spreading through me.

After he had kissed me goodbye, I'd tell myself to hurry out of bed, make Andrew's breakfast, set out clean clothes . . . and eventually I would do all of that, but with such a struggle, with my voice fading forgetfully and my movements clumsy and asymmetrical as a stunned fish. And as I walked Andrew up the hill to the bus stop the memory of the night's sex would stay crouched in my belly.

I watched for Jed's green army coat to reappear from the crowd. If he was unnerved by these transitions from love to life, he didn't say so. But at least, unlike Phil, he did let some of his needs show. If I came late into a meeting I'd see his face wrinkle up in smiles, and his hand pat the empty chair he had reserved for me beside him. Often his arm edged along the chairback and his fingers, touching my hair or tickling the nape of my neck, punctuated the stern work of the discussion with a dozen comforting and wordless conversations.

I shivered again. A few feet away, a group of women were dressed as if for summer: their bare toes poked out of sandals, their flimsy Indian skirts trailed on the frozen grass. Beside me, Vi jogged on the spot. Under her thin coat her heavy breasts bounced. She wore two long striped scarves and her old school hockey boots; her skin shone with Nivea cream.

Jed ran back towards us with his long hair swinging. 'We're off,' he said. 'Left outside the gates and straight down to Notting Hill showrooms.'

'That was a well-kept secret!' someone behind me said tartly.

Jed was brusque. 'Better security that way.' He turned to Vi and me. 'You two stick with me.' Vi and I looked at each other. We already knew from the briefing what to do.

'Sir!' Vi saluted. In the interests of unity, I looked at my feet and kept quiet. Grumbling about the rule of patriarchy, Vi stripped off her hooped earrings and prepared for action.

We were just in sight of Notting Hill Gate when a police Zephyr cruised past. The driver started radioing immediately.

'Bugger, let's get a move on,' cried Jed.

We broke into a run, close on two hundred of us strung out along the pavement, dodging prams and bus queues and traffic bollards, taking the road as well. We covered the last fifty yards in a flat-out sprint which sent coins spinning from pockets and clinking into the road behind, and skidded headlong through the doors of the Electricity Board.

'Bolt the doors,' someone cried. 'There's enough of us in now.'

Jed climbed on top of a washing machine and snapped the top bolts shut seconds before a spray of gravel tinkled against the plate glass windows, and three police vans screeched to a halt on the pavement.

The police pushed their way through the other squatters. 'Open up,' they shouted. Two of them rattled the glass door, but finding it locked, stepped back. Their faces were flushed and vengeful.

'They'd love to break our heads in,' Jed observed grimly, 'but they won't attack property.'

The three of us made our way through the displays of fridges and spin-driers, heading for the back door, which was our assignment. Phil was already at the reception desk, talking gravely to a bald man in a three-piece suit.

Behind the reception desk was a partition, and to the left of it, a staircase which led up to another showroom on the first floor. On the other side of the partition there was a small lobby full of fuse-boxes, and an emergency exit. Jed secured the crush bars with a chain he had brought, and Vi and I were hauling two heavy metal step-ladders across the door when someone pulled at my elbow. I looked over my shoulder. The face was young and acned, and underneath it a white carnation bloomed next to a matching tie-and-handkerchief set.

'Go away,' I said. The salesman blushed, and flicked invisible hairs off his jacket sleeve.

'We're occupying this place,' Jed said firmly. 'Better get used to it.' The effort of authority deepened the wrinkles which went from his nose to his chin, giving him a resolute look, but the same effort stiffened his jaw, so that the words came out jerky and catarrhal. But the salesman didn't read that faltering in Jed. He stood for a moment, uncertain, with his finger stealing up to scratch at a pimple on his cheek, and then he retired, out-ranked.

When the phone on the reception desk trilled it was neither the young salesman nor the bald manager who picked it up, but Phil.

'Yes indeed, this is the London Electricity Board,' he said pleasantly. 'These noises? In fact, what you're hearing is an occupation . . . yes . . . because some families have had their power disconnected . . . no, no, they paid their bills. Back-door evictions, we call it, and that's what we intend to put a stop to . . . Certainly we're staying put, until the Area Manager comes down here to discuss our demands . . .' Phil held up the receiver. A cheerful gurgling noise came from it. My spirits rose quite disproportionately. One member of the public, at any rate, was amused. Phil put the phone down on the desk, leaving it off the hook. He had put on a neat grey corduroy jacket for his role as negotiator, and the line of his lips was precise and calm. It was obvious that the manager was impressed.

Vi was examining a switchboard on the wall. Next to it, the Emergency Power order was posted. Half the ground-floor switches and all the ones for upstairs had been taped over.

She looked at me. 'What d'you reckon?'

I was still deliberating when a man with a painted face appeared in the lobby and, seeing the switchboard, chuckled with delight. His black cloak spread out like bats' wings as he stripped the tape off and flicked down every switch on the board.

'We refuse to help the Tories wear down the miners!' he boomed, in a theatrical voice. In the sudden dazzle he posed with his fist in the air, while behind his back Vi stuck her tongue out.

The combined light of fancy lampstands, hanging Chinese lanterns, television lights, three-pronged mock candelabra and cut-glass chandeliers blazed through the showroom and out into the street.

'That's done it,' I said to Vi.

In the centre of a city shadowed by blackouts, the showroom was golden, vulgar, shimmering.

Outside, the squatters who were picketing on the pavement cheered wildly.

'Up the miners, smash the Tories!'

'It doesn't look good,' I told Jed, waving my hand towards the invisible world beyond the window and the lit faces of the picketers. Jed shrugged. I looked over at Phil. He was bending over the manager, explaining, persuading; if he disapproved of the illuminations he gave no sign of it. All around the big room, which already smelled faintly of marijuana, people looked amiable and unconcerned. Clusters and knots of men and women squatted on the floor, or on the shiny white tops of fridges; they clapped and laughed and crocheted and rolled cigarettes in the spread laps of their skirts. In front of the window the man with the painted face swirled his cloak and whipped up support from the crowd outside.

When at last someone turned the lights down, I was relieved, and so, judging by his face, was the manager. He was leaning towards Phil, he was listening hard; now he was reaching for the phone. As he spoke into it his fingers pinched the bridge of his nose, warding off sneezes.

Phil rocked back on his heels and smiled. Word spread through the room and was shouted through a megaphone to the crowd on the pavement.

'The Area Manager is coming to negotiate.'

Phil led the small man to the front of the showroom, clearing a path for him courteously, even tenderly, and put the megaphone into his hands. He was prompting him: 'Make the police agree not to intervene when the officials arrive.'

They came within fifteen minutes: the Area Manager and a deputy. The police, keeping their promise, it seemed, drew back from the door and allowed the men to come in. The deputy unpacked papers from a black leather briefcase and spectacles from a black leather spectacle case. With Phil and the manager, they formed an earnest group around the reception desk.

Jed and I stayed near the back door, smoking and talking. Once or twice I noticed Jed glance across at Phil's bent head, and there was something like envy on his face.

A commotion erupted on the floor above. There was the urgent clop of Vi's hockey boots on the landing, then she was running down the stairs with her scarves flying behind her like streamers.

'They're on the bloody balcony! They're coming along from the next shop.'

Phil's upturned face showed complete surprise.

'Get the bigwigs up here,' Vi shouted, 'Get more people up!'

The burliest men from the Elgin Avenue group headed the surge towards the stairs. Within seconds the ground floor had emptied.

Jed looked torn. 'We should stay here,' he said. 'They could still try something from that back alley.' As Phil hurried past with the two officials in tow, Jed snarled at them. 'So that's how much your word was worth!'

The deputy looked over his spectacles. 'None of our doing, I assure you. Not what we had in mind at all.'

'We should have known,' Jed muttered. 'Nothing the Special Patrol Group like better than a spot of autonomous action. Fucking cowboys.'

Overhead the noise swelled. Feet shuffled and stamped and slid. Heavy objects were dragged across linoleum. And then came shots, and the sound of glass breaking. Jed and I dashed for the stairs.

Along twenty feet of windows, there was no daylight; instead, only navy-blue shoulders and arms, and pink faces, and tumbling police helmets. Most of the fighting was happening a few feet inside the windows; the police were coming in fast, vaulting down from the window-ledges, forcing the squatters back. The man in the black cloak, although bleeding into his face-paint, was among the last to stop battling. A yard away from him Vi was crying and shaking her fists. Her duffle coat was torn across the back and one of her scarves lay coiled at her feet.

'Who's the senior officer here?' Jed demanded.

A grey-haired officer stepped forward, brushing powdered glass from his uniform with a gloved hand. 'Inspector

Claybourne,' he said suavely.

'There's absolutely no cause for this!' Phil's voice was outraged. 'These gentlemen have already agreed to our proposals.'

'Absolutely none,' the Area Manager echoed, with a stunned glance at the shattered windows.

The men moved together. The red head, the grey heads, the bald head.

'Summit talks,' Jed said sourly, as we turned to go downstairs. 'Ever felt like a wooden leg?'

Ten minutes later Phil was on the landing, waving a sheet of paper at us. 'We have it in writing,' he said wearily. 'The squats will be reconnected. So we can all start leaving now. 'Behind him a blue uniform appeared, and then another. The police began to file slowly down the stairs.

Beside me Jed went rigid. 'Wait a minute! Have they agreed to no arrests? No heavy stuff?'

The Inspector leaned over the banisters. 'Yes, yes, you can all move along home now.' His smile was bored, tolerant. 'You've had a good innings, so the sooner you leave, the quicker we'll all get home.'

The police had reached the front door now. They were dismantling the barricade of cookers and washing machines, unbolting the door. They were forming themselves into a narrow corridor down which we would have to pass.

'I don't trust this,' Jed said in my ear.

Jed and I were almost the last to leave. Ahead, I saw Vi make it into the street, and then I was breathing cold air and exhaust fumes, and Jed was hauling at my wrist, saying, 'Don't turn, they're jumping people.'

The police cordon outside the showroom had turned on the picket line. On the fringes, the scuffle looked fierce. Placards flew out of the crowd and skidded in all directions. Women screamed. Banner poles cracked like kindling sticks.

'They've got Phil!' Vi shouted.

Shaking Jed off, I ran for the transit van. There were two of them holding Phil down, pinning his arms. With a relief that was almost joy, at the simplicity of the thing, I leapt on to a broad back, pummelled fleshy shoulders. Crooked an arm round the thick neck, trying to throttle. I hung there, flailing with my legs, shouting at Phil to run for it. In the corner of my eye I saw Jed appear beside the police van; he was all eyes, scanning; he was aiming a kick at one headlight, then another. It was neatly done, the glass cracked and caved inward, crystallising. Two policemen who had been heading for me or Phil dithered, and turned to chase Jed. Then I felt the arm-lock, and the hand on the back of my neck, forcing my head down, and I was thrown into the van.

Once inside, I began to shake.

'Well, you made it as a martyr,' the driver said cheerfully.

Half a dozen officers climbed into the van, wiping their faces and necks with handkerchiefs. A couple of them stared lewdly at my breasts and whispered to each other.

'Pigs,' I said under my breath.

I was grabbed and pushed against the window. There was a red face within an inch of mine, and a fist flattening the skin across my cheekbone. The raised stitching of the glove rasped and burned, and the leather smelled of school, and punishment.

'One word, and you'll need a cosmetic surgeon.' His breath smelled of fruit-gums. It's all an act, I thought: television thuggery. Soon there would be the laughing disclaimer: had you scared for a minute, didn't we?

The man with his fist in my face turned to the others. 'I get the feeling the bitch doesn't believe me, lads. How can I convince the bitch?'

I heard chuckles.

'They share their tarts, that lot, didn't you know?'

'Whose whore are you, then, blondie?'

I looked around for protection. There was one who was older, who had more stripes on his shoulder. 'Is this how the British police ...' I began, but I got no further than that, for the slap hit me then, jolting my head sideways.

'Stubborn, you Women's Lib bitches. Don't learn,

do you?'

Faces peered in at me through the condensation on the window. Hands banged against the side of the van in protest. Inside the van, the men were leering openly. A fog crept over my mind. What have I done, I thought, to set off such savagery?

At the police station the Duty Officer, filling out my charge sheet, said that he knew my address well. 'Brothel, isn't it? I'll put down "Frequents Kings Cross area".'

I asked for a complaints form, and the men who had arrested me laughed out loud.

'Just you go ahead and fill it in, love, and we'll get you, some dark night, you bet your life on it.'

The cells were too hot, heat pumping out of radiators which smelled of scorched paint, but I couldn't stop shivering. I wanted badly to pee but to get to the toilet meant running the gauntlet of men who sneered and spat and hissed obscenely. I sat in the tiled cell with my body swelling around me, soft, pulsating, indecent.

Outside the police station, there was a hero's welcome, but I hid behind Jed and spoke to no one. Later the story came out, but haltingly. I could not make Jed understand how hateful I felt. 'Don't be silly,' he kept saying: 'Look at it politically. The SPG are hand-picked sadists, they'd do the same thing to anyone.'

There were thirty of us in the Magistrate's Court on Monday morning. We were variously charged: obstruction, insulting behaviour, breach of the peace. The man in the black cloak was charged with attempted assault, and Phil, of all people, Phil the diplomat, with Actual Bodily Harm. He had broken an officer's arm by slamming a window on it, the police said.

Vi suggested that it could be mistaken identity, for she had seen someone wearing a jacket like Phil's; Jed, however, was certain that it was a trumped-up charge.

'Sub-poena the Electricity Board guys as witnesses,' he said, 'they'll have to admit they were with you the whole time.'

Phil let out a long sigh. 'Actual Bodily Harm, though. You can go down for a year on that one.'

More than once Matt has asked why, if I had so many reservations about the Group, did I go on? I'm never quite sure how to answer him. Sometimes I say that for me it was never possible to be anything but a socialist, there was no question of reneging. Or sometimes a hint of cynicism creeps in, and I say: Oh, I was always daddy's girl. But always I say that the Group was kith, kin, family, tribe, and I was afraid of leaving it, just as – but this part I do not tell him – I am now afraid of leaving him.

10

The day after the carnival was May Day, a day of muttering rain and forlorn collars of drips around the chimney pots. Zac and Andrew squabbled and had to be pacified with a game of Scrabble, which Andrew won hands down. For a while Andrew sat close beside me on the bedroom carpet drawing space satellites, ringed planets, and several varieties of robot. After what had happened in the park, I was careful with him, cuddling him a lot, praising his housework robot with its dozen jointed skinny arms, each of which held a different implement – a vacuum cleaner, a mop, an iron, a dustpan. Its belly was a washing machine into which it scooped clothes.

'You forgot the thing for washing Zac's feet.'

He grinned and held his nose. 'This one's going to Jupiter.' He pointed. The drawing was spiky with ray-guns and mid-air collisions. The spaceship was erupting from its launching pad and veering north-east, towards the top corner of the page. All around it were cosmic explosions, space debris, laser artillery. The violence in it was disturbing; all the same, his eyes asked for appreciation, and so I looked dutifully, and searched for something to say. I remembered a radio programme I'd loved when I was his age; it was before there was TV, I explained.

Andrew sneered a high-tech sneer. 'How long ago, then?'

I stuck out my tongue. 'You'd have liked it, It was called 'The Lost World'. It was about a group of children who go off to search for a new planet. None of the grown-ups believe them when they say it's there, but they go anyway – some professor helps them, and they sneak off . . . '

Andrew listened politely. 'And they find it?'

'They find it.'

'But how do they *know* it's there?'

'How? Oh, they heard little messages from it, little bleeps or something.'

When the doorbell rang around four I sensed it was Matt and Vi. Andrew watched me with surprise as I flew round the room straightening bed-covers, pushing the hot water bottle under the pillow, filing papers in the wrong drawers.

Vi's mouth was sullen. 'Are we interrupting you? We were bored and quarrelling, so he dragged us round here.'

Matt bared his teeth at her, but when he looked at me his expression changed, which made me very nervous indeed. I gushed about the carnival, and how massive it had been, and so terrific to see all those youth on the streets for the sake of anti-racism, and wasn't he proud of himself? What a fool he must think me, I thought; but I could not stop talking.

'Do you fancy coming to the movies?' he interrupted. 'We thought we'd take a look at *Mr Goodbar*. It's only up the road.' He smiled. 'Why not come with us?'

'Yes, why not?' I said quickly, 'Bank Holidays are such dreary days.'

'Well, *that's* settled, then,' said Vi sarcastically.

I recoiled. 'Don't you want to?' My voice sounded small and defensive.

'Oh, it's fine by me. Me, I'll just make the coffee, if that's all right.'

'Let me.'

'No, I insist. Old what's 'is name wants to pick your brains about a minor masterpiece, I believe.'

Matt waited pointedly for her to go out. He shook himself quickly before he spoke, like a dog shaking off water. 'I meant to bring a story . . . I wanted you to . . . but I forgot . . . ' He coughed, and seemed to grope desperately for words. 'And how's *your* writing going?' he said after a moment.

'All right, I suppose. The biggest problem is time . . . I would like to see your work some time, though.' Bland, but encouraging, that was the right tone.

'Really?' he said, and his face shone.

Shit, I thought: what if I hate it?

'In fact, I might have left my story in the van somewhere . . . '

I hid my amusement. 'You could go and look.'

Matt went out and returned within seconds carrying a blue folder. 'Guess what?' He seemed unembarrassed by the transparency of his behaviour. The folder was extremely thick.

'Aha. More of a novel than a story?'

'It's long,' he admitted, 'Do you mind?'

'No, I said I'd look at it.'

'Thank you,' he said with fervour, 'thank you.' He sat down on the bed again, bouncing slightly on the mattress. His eyes were on me, full of expectations.

'But I won't look at it right now.'

'No, of course not.'

I put the folder on the desk and knelt by the electric fire, warming my hands. Next door someone tried to flush the toilet, pumping the handle several times. Matt was still watching me, I could sense his gaze.

'Nice room,' he said, in a hollow voice. 'What's it like living here?'

My tidying had not been thorough. Two pairs of jeans were draped over the chair, a towel lay in a heap on the dressing table. There was a dusty pile of paperbacks by the bed, with a full ashtray on top. Intending to make a joke about the squalor, I smiled at him, and for the first time that day my flickering spy's gaze held his. And I stared. He had woven his fingers together and was pressing them hard against his forehead. A fierce curiosity stared back at me. His face was convulsed with it.

I felt the colour rush to my face. His mouth had fallen open, and a broken filling showed jaggedly. The beginnings of a cold-sore blurred one corner of his lower lip. He looked stunned, guilty, yet the blue eyes held mine, and opened wider.

No words came. The everyday part of my mind, the part which responds to banal questions and puts friends and visitors at their ease, had flown away, and in its place something else was rising in me, like a cloud of birds or bats fluttering, responding to the absolute unprotectedness of that look. It was like watching a child wave from a racing train: you have no choice, you must rid yourself of everything you carry and wave both arms back like a mad thing. Frightened, I looked at my hands. They trembled, they glowed red from the fire. Holding them to the heat, turning them this way and that, I saw in the workings of bone and tendon and the pads of flesh at the base of the thumbs the frantic wrigglings of a pink and powdered baby who squirmed with all its strength towards this gawky stranger. I am a coward, I thought.

Matt shifted on the mattress then, which I felt rather than saw, so blurred had the boundaries become between looking and touching. Longing and antagonism flowed in the current between us.

I broke the contact with an effort, turned to gaze out of the window. How to explain this away? Already my mind was busy at it, sorting, listing, searching for a vantage point. Outside, the lime trees were in bud, the chestnuts in leaf, and the lilacs just preparing to flower. The season progressed, everything was as it should be.

Blood started to flow again. My hands settled and resumed their normal business. I lit a cigarette and tried to dismiss the thought that I had robbed Vi most scandalously. I split a match and used the point to clean under my fingernails. The sooner everyday channels were reopened, the better. I had done nothing, after all; I hadn't moved a muscle. One glance. The rest was imagination. Without looking directly at Matt, I told him how Andrew had got lost. He dug in the dirt with a stick, I thought, with a sharp stick.

Matt consented to the distance. 'Christ! Poor lad. How did you find him?' He sounded breathless.

'I didn't. Phil did, in the end.'

Matt curled a short strand of blond hair round his finger. Round and round the finger moved against the scalp, in a toddler's soothing magic. He frowned. 'Phil? Who's Phil?' he demanded.

I looked at him warningly. 'You don't know him. Someone I used to live with.'

Matt was simply too tall. Even at the wheel of the delivery van he'd borrowed from work he had to stoop, and in the Circle seats at the cinema his knees, jackknifed, were up around his chin. When he took off his donkey jacket I smelled him: wood shavings, turpentine. I remembered being thirteen, and drunk with power. Sitting beside a boyfriend in the matinee, I squeezed his knee in the dark. All through the film the smell of his feet seeped through his tennis shoes; it was a sweet-and-sour smell, like silage, the scent of the petrified male. This time, though, the desire and the fear were in me.

Conscious of Vi on my other side, I sat very still and forced myself to watch the ads. On the screen pretty girls carolled: 'You can't hide it when it happens to you, you can't hide the natural in you', and hat after hat flipped off, and their long shining hair was loosed and swished in slow motion, like theatre curtains, around their shoulders. Vi and I hissed in unison.

I was short of breath, anxious. Cramps were spreading up my thighs like growing pains. 'Can we change seats?' I whispered to Vi.

'Claustrophobic?' she said, with a look of concern, and got up to give me her seat.

I stretched my legs in the aisle and nodded gratefully. 'I'm fine now. There's more space here. Don't worry.'

But the film alarmed me more than I cared to admit. I watched it mainly through my fingers, ninety minutes of footage in which the heroine fucked constantly and compulsively, and then died bloodily.

As we filed out, a man and a woman were arguing behind us. 'She only got what she asked for,' the man was saying. I shuddered under my raincoat.

In the pub next door, on television, there was a documentary on blood sports: more red meat, flesh everywhere, but I had to look at something, for Vi's glance flurried constantly from me to Matt. Luckily, someone changed the channel to a Bette Davis film. Her hair was tucked under a severe black hat; she stood framed in a doorway, spoke arrogantly, slammed out. Her silk dress swung in the draught. 'Such a devastating hat,' I cried, as Vi performed a tremulous little dance in the high voltage area between us. Matt gave me a fleeting smile.

Vi leaned back against the bar, and her elbow, careless, spilled an ashtray brimming with KP nut packets. With a look of exasperation, Matt bent to pick them up. I'd die if he looked at me like that, I thought. The collar of his donkey jacket framed his rough blond head; under the hollow cheeks a muscle in his jaw worked angrily. Next door in the public bar a band struck up an emigré lament, and my sense of dislocation grew. 'Must we stay? I can't bear this noise.'

Matt looked as if I had slapped his face. 'We could go somewhere else,' I suggested quickly, 'we could always watch TV.' I turned to Vi, addressing her particularly: 'May '68 anniversary is on, did you know?' With one apprehensive look at Matt she dodged the invitation by referring it to him. How could she bear to be on such tenterhooks all the time? I thought: she was almost asking to be crushed. She would go where Matt decided, and then hold it against him: I knew that particular stalemate as intimately as the lines on my face.

I shrugged. 'After all, I wouldn't like to miss my hero.'

Matt looked at me curiously. 'Cohn-Bendit? No kidding? I thought heroes were out these days.'

'Maybe so. But he ranks high in my gallery of greats.' I smiled wryly at Vi. 'I have been teased about it.'

Back at the house Vi sat in an armchair firmly clasping her handbag while I persuaded the television into life with the flat of my hand. Zac and Andrew were already in bed, and Tom and Marie had vanished to their rooms: downstairs Tom was playing a Scots medley on the penny whistle, and from Marie's room came reggae sounds.

Cohn-Bendit's kind freckled face solidified on the screen. Matt squatted on the carpet, hunched over, attentive. 'They almost didn't let him in,' he said. 'The BBC had quite a wrangle with Immigration.'

'Ten years after?'

'You bet your life.'

Wobbly footage of stones flying, a young face streaming from tear-gas, a girl retching in a gutter. When Matt offered a joint I accepted, and inhaled it deeply. Vi smoked too, but the line of her mouth promised repercussions. My head swam.

In the clouds of white gas a boy in a leather jacket was clubbed to the ground. Police cars, beached on pavements, burned furiously. As I watched, a tear ran down my nose.

From high up in her chair Vi tutted at the children on the carpet. 'But it's such a *bad* programme,' she said sharply. 'It gives no analysis of May '68, it just encourages you to nostalgia or outrage, depending which side you're on already. I'm telling you, it's a media wank, that's all.'

Matt and I exchanged guilty looks. The dope made Vi's comments reverberate in my head. I tried to work out how what she was saying did and did not fit in with my own experience, but the meaning swirled away in a pattern of sounds, leaving me only with the conviction that Vi disapproved of me: always had, and always would.

'. . . that capitalism has not yet satisfied . . .' Cohn-Bendit was saying, '. . . cannot satisfy the demands which exploded ten years ago.' Matt was holding out the joint, smiling with painful eagerness, but I shook my head, for paranoia was hovering, thick, insidious, full of echoes. '. . . control over our lives, our environment, education . . .' the voice went on.

The interviewer smirked. This was all so terribly old-hat. 'And so, the struggle continues, as you would have it?'

'Of course.' Cohn-Bendit answered seriously. 'The events, the thinking of '68 have entered political life. There's no going back.'

'Too short,' I said, as the credits came up.

'Good. He was pretty good,' Matt said.

Vi tugged at the neck of her coat, searching for buttons where there were none. It was that same gesture she'd used years ago, when she first came seeking friendship: that clawing movement, searching for flesh to punish. But now the slender Vi was standing up, saying aggressively that she really didn't see how Cohn-Bendit helped us to figure out where we were now, or what we ought to be doing.

I got up too, trying to argue that '68 represented part of our history, after all, but what came out of my mouth soon degenerated into a ragged string of 'yes' and 'well' and hums and haws. I could feel her determination to win pressing on me. The dope was dredging up echoes of family. I was smothering again in rooms full of garrulous aunts and their sharp-beaked opinions; I was shrinking in the blast of my mother's vivacity, my father's jovial dogmatism. How can she talk so fast, how can she be so certain, I thought. I looked helplessly from her to Matt. He was lying with his head cradled on his arms, gazing humbly up at me. Between Vi's pugnaciousness and this besotted sheepdog gaze there was little to choose. There was no comfort in either of them. I stood staring at my two guests, while their separate strong tides of emotion battered at me, and I could hardly wait to be rid of them.

After the door had closed behind them I sat down in the armchair and stared at the blank television screen. If only I'd had the courage to slash through all the dissembling, I thought angrily. To tell Vi to have more respect for herself, to tell Matt to stop pouting and peering. My skin still prickled with the after-effects.

That night I dreamed my mother was getting married on the dusty, splintered stage of the Kirk Hall. She was a pretty bride, and greedy for affection and praise. I was matron-of-honour, sober in grey silk; I had many organisational responsibilities. When I mismanaged the flower arrangements and forgot to trim the sandwiches into triangles, the bride threw a tantrum. Then Matt appeared, heading straight across the stage towards me. In the middle of the minister's speech he stuck his hand up my skirt; it was my crisp shell that he prised open, and inside I was soft, like oysters. 'It's not *my* wedding,' I hissed at him, but with a lewd grin, he persisted. The minister, faintly disturbed, patted his top pocket where the pipe tobacco was, and continued with the ceremony.

11

I tip the last drops from the bucket into the well, and my reflection at the bottom quivers, breaks into segments.

It was a morning soon after the LEB affair. Jed and I had walked down to Kings Cross together, where he was to catch a bus to the East End, and I was to take the tube to Notting Hill. We said goodbye at the bus stop, and I hurried into the entrance of the Underground. Halfway down the steps the first blast of warm sooty wind hit me, and I began to sweat in my thick coat. There were crowds ahead of me, and crowds behind me, all hurrying, sweeping me on down to the long tiled tunnel. At the bottom of the steps, without knowing why, I stopped dead. 'Excuse me,' I said, and turned, and fought my way back up to the open street. As I looked around for Jed, the noise of London rose and echoed around me. The din of a passing juggernaut, of a transistor held to someone's ear. The splatter of leaking drainpipes. A newspaper seller's harsh cry. At last I glimpsed him on the platform of a bus. The bus was moving off. I called out to him, but he didn't hear.

On the tube, snatches of night came back at me. Counting stations, I shivered.

Jed's tenderness boring holes, leaching away at the bedrock.

'Wider. I can't see it,' he demanded, with his long tongue ready.

Image of a chestnut, shiny-new, rolling in its bed of white pith.

Disregard.

Rounding a bend in the tunnel, the carriage rocked. Baker Street, with its warrens of sidings and shrill whistles. I looked at my watch. The meeting with the Notting Hill defendants was set for ten o'clock. It was already 9.30. Far too late to make it by bus. Fighting for breath, I watched the doors close.

Sit tight. Read the headlines on the newspapers. 'Miners force Election'. 'Tories to go to the Country'. 'Polls forecast landslide for Labour'. Smile. Light a cigarette. Go where the tube goes, where the other passengers go, with their newspapers and their cigarettes and their destinations. My day, like theirs, was mapped out. My role every bit as clear. All I had to do was settle into it. As Jed was doing right now in Hackney. Co-ordinating defence. What could be more purposeful?

(What defence?)

Disregard.

The Notting Hill group lived in a row of crumbling terraces underneath a flyover. Demolition had already begun, and some of the houses were no more than facades.

A freckled woman in dungarees led me upstairs to meet the others. 'We call it Death Gulch,' she said, 'because it's so like a set in a cowboy movie.'

On the kitchen table, mice had left feather footprints in the butter. I went through my list of questions and notes, ticking some, adding others, not smoking too much, because of the business of holding the match steady. The house, unquestionably, trembled, but I wasn't sure that this would stand up as an excuse. Each time a lorry passed the coffee cups jiggled towards the edge of the table, and each time, someone reached out to save them with an automatic movement which didn't even interrupt the flow of talk. Yesterday, the freckled woman said, they had lost a pint of milk this way.

Away from the flyover, on the wide roads leading back to the West End, the houses were tall and tailored, and magnolia trees stretched curved branches across the gardens. I sat on top of a bus with my hands clasped, watching this strange country.

Loss. To be lost. To lose yourself. Something was draining out of me, leaking away like spilt milk.

I got off the bus on the corner of Oxford Street, and waited for a connection. Pigeons wheeling over Marble Arch cried out and dropped white splodges. The wind of the traffic sucked at my skin as I leaned out into the road, watching for buses. There were so many 8s, 15s, 12s: all kinds of buses with destinations which had no place on any of my maps. Mile End. Tottenham. Palmers Green. Places to get lost in. It was a 73 I needed, a 73 back to Kings Cross.

I had forgotten about the January sales. Oxford Street was jammed with cars along its length, and a mile of pavement was choked with shoppers; the tops of thousands of heads bobbed sickeningly. There was no escape on foot, and hardly a chance by road. And the Tube, this time, was out of the question.

Clenching my hands in my coat pockets, I concentrated on the shop windows.

Focus. Eliminate the non-essential.

The window display was stuffed with paper roses in anticipation of spring – pink and white roses, sprays, bowers of them; behind them the clothes fought for space. There was no form, no order at all. I began to feel quite furious with the window dresser whose sloppiness had made it so hard to distinguish one dress from another. With those conditions, it impossible to decide what you wanted, and what you did not want.

In the next window a red dress shimmered, a dress with a skirt like a knife. The plaster mannequin was six feet tall, with copper hair like fusewire and a face with sharp bright features, like a painted egg. In the mirror behind her I saw myself reflected: a shadowy child, a schoolgirlish coat, an irresolute white face.

Another window, more mirrors. But this time, an irreproachable outfit. Fairisle sweater, cream silk shirt, calf-length skirt in corduroy. And bangles, the outfit included bangles. The career woman, down to the dictation pad in the model's plaster hand. Nothing could have been less provocative, more purposeful.

In bed Jed looked up at me, pink and blurred and shiny with sweat. I could have done what I wanted with him. (What did I want to do?)

Teeth chattering. (So many lovers, so many eyes and mouths and perilous choices.)

Can you see the real me? That's how the song goes.

I looked down at myself. Coat, jersey, jeans: everything was black and in place. But the eyes of the copper-haired mannequin drilled through to the dampness, and the dimpled flesh, and the bones, bleached and knobbly against a dark X-ray plate.

Out in the homing traffic, there were only two dimensions now; everything was flattening, losing body: the buses looked like cardboard cutouts, painted fairground flats. It was all quite wrong, going very wrong. Something bad was beginning in me, eating away like lime. And the colours of the buses were . . . Oh, too bright, unaccountably sparkling, like laser light, with auras.

In front of me in the queue was a woman's broad, tweed-coated back. It frightened me, this trusting, vulnerable back, and I drew back, giving it distance. For there was no telling what I might do, now, on the cold street where colours pierced, and I was unrecognisable.

Check. Check what you feel, are, have been. Look behind, check in the driving mirror, it will inform you as to direction and speed. Unless the mirror has been fogged or misplaced or vandalised.

A passing shopper jostled; lumpy, clumsy, hands full of plastic bags. Oxford Street was under occupation by a graceless, unco-ordinated people. If I hit out at them, the sound would be like jellyfish smashing against rocks. Their bags would spill tangerines and brand new tights and nests of saucepans.

I lit a cigarette. It was okay. The fingers still performed. Around me white faces wobbled, but seemed to suspect nothing. Faces who knew who they were, and where, and where next, who could point to their names in telephone directories, who could stand up in any witness box and say whom they had married, and what they had come here to buy.

I stretched my surface tight. My feet on the pavement gripped; there was still weight enough in them to keep me upright.

A goal. From standing, proceed to walking. A goal was crucial. To wait was no longer viable, among strange sights and sounds and bodies impinging on me. Strange bodies of passers-by, strange bodies of lovers.

Disregard.

Home is where the heart is. I started walking fast towards where Jed and Phil would know me, and Vi, and Andrew. Where the streets and bus routes led to familiar landmarks, my very own geography. Keeping my head well down, I fled on, tackling, using my elbows.

12

On the day of the LEB trial, I took one of the tranquillisers which the doctor had prescribed.

He was there in the witness box, the one who had tormented me. He stood with his chest puffed out and his black gloves tucked under his arm, and read stilted evidence from a notepad.

'Yes, your Honour', he was saying, 'No, your Honour', 'Only for the purposes of restraining the accused, your Honour.' The face he turned to the magistrate was ingenuous, appealing, but when he glanced across at the dock the insinuations in his eyes forced me deep down inside the cushioning layers of the drug. I was glad that I'd prepared myself. It meant that in the battle of eyes and wills, I stared back. At that moment, I would have done anything rather than show weakness. To cheat him of that triumph, I would have sealed myself in a tomb, if necessary.

We were tried hurriedly, in batches of six, and despatched with ten pound fines. The anti-climax took my breath away. In the public gallery, Phil, who had opted for trial by jury and could count on no such leniency, smiled feebly.

Mostly I walked in underwater dreams, clinging close to those who would tolerate it. At those times I was meek, and the word 'apron-strings' rang in my head, and all around the colours were luminous. At other times a bitter and angular greyness descended which sent me into the corners of rooms. From this exile I observed how the others laughed and chattered and planned actions and celebrations quite shamelessly, as if I did not exist. And then I would berate them, and when they turned on me I would wring my hands and weep, having got no more than I deserved. Afterwards I would sit penitently for a while, enjoying the calm, until the next storm broke inside me.

In the days, in the evenings, I surrounded myself with people, for otherwise I would have been left to the mercies of the unpredictable inner events. At first Vi and the others were mystified by this sudden lust for company, but I explained to them that only dire emergency could have persuaded me to make such demands on them. I spoke of panic, but not of the terrible darkness which had opened at the heart of me, and into which I would fall like a stone if they did not hold me back. Grouped around me, they were mirrors, partial and imperfect, but in them I could still glimpse the familiar and nameable.

In dreams, though, I had no choice, and journeyed alone.

During this time, I dreamed of napalm. I spread it across the stubble fields around the village where I was born; it seeped like water or petrol across the narrow grit roads and the banks of new heather. Although I knew it was hazardous to my health, it was my job, and so I did it. Fragments of my teeth came off in the fumes, and bit by bit my jaw broke up, until the lower half hung only by a small metal dowel, and I was horrified at the prospect of going out on a date with such a disfigurement.

Granted, it was not a country into which anyone else could easily follow me. But Phil, for one, didn't even seem inclined to try. When he stopped sleeping with me, I did not protest. When, soon afterwards, his visits stopped altogether, my imagination supplied the reasons he had failed to give. It was just as well, I thought. There were dreams I could cite in evidence. My womb was meat, gaping, as if after vast childbirth. It could retain nothing; if I stood up, everything emptied from it.

With what was left of me, I clung on. As long as I persisted in sitting around at the Printshop, Phil treated me more or less normally, which I found bizarre. Sometimes he even asked me to transcribe an interview or edit an article for *Hard Times*. Sometimes I even tried, but then the headaches came and blinded me, and the words jammed up stubbornly in my mind, losing all meaning. Neither Phil nor the others criticised me for these lapses, but I was sure it was only a matter of time before their patience ran out. They were already burdened enough, so how long would they tolerate someone who did not pull her weight?

I pottered desperately, without achieving much. The smallest task exhausted me. And always there was Phil in the background, typing, collating, cranking the Gestetner, producing, producing. Sometimes, watching him out of the corner of my eye, I was filled with a feeling that there was something he knew which he wasn't telling. But since I knew that I was only there on sufferance, I didn't dare ask him what it was.

After a few weeks I decided that bowing out gracefully was

preferable to being ejected, and I began to withdraw. But the less I saw of Phil, the more I craved for answers.

One night I ate with him and Jed in a Greek café near the Printshop. Or rather, they ate, and I watched them. Beside me, Jed chewed listlessly and pushed his plate away without finishing his kebab. Phil sat facing me, well-placed for conversation, and although he kept his eyes averted, I knew that mere politeness would make him speak eventually. The noise of his chewing was very loud and jarred my nerves, but I waited patiently. Over his shoulder I could see a glass-fronted counter in which trays of papery cakes dripped honey, and a notice which said 'Please do not ask for credit as a refusal sometimes offends'. After Phil had finished off a dish of houmous and a plate of stewed lamb, he patted his stomach, and looked round the table for something else to eat. Finding nothing, he pulled Jed's plate towards him and picked at the left-overs with an absent-minded air.

'I've chewed that,' said Jed with a shudder, looking at a piece of pork fat which Phil had speared.

With every mouthful, Phil's face seemed to grow more rotund, boneless, as if disappearing under layers of camouflage. Suddenly, looking neither at me nor at Jed, he launched into conversation.

'I think this sexual . . . running around . . . ' he began, 'I mean, this satyrism we go in for . . . ' He nibbled thoughtfully at a tomato, leaving me holding my breath.

'This *what?*' Jed said. His foot began to tap angrily under the table. Phil bypassed the interruption.

'I've found that I've felt very displaced . . . in periods of sleeping with a lot of people, that is.' He looked briefly at Jed. 'Like tripping, in a way, you know?' His eyes travelled on round the room, over the gold-flocked wallpaper, the blown-up photograph of the Trossachs, the table by the cash desk where the proprietor's brothers were playing dominoes. He cleared his throat. 'I remember once just drifting about for days on end, hardly knowing where I was. My head was floating with . . . well, rather strange feelings.' He swallowed nervously and looked down at his plate. 'Omnipotent sort of feelings. Rather *odd*, it was. None too pleasant, either.' He glanced at me, and then away. This time the message was definitely for me, then. Eagerly, I leaned towards him.

'So what did you do?'

'Do?'

'If you had these anxieties?'

'I tolerated them,' he said evenly, 'What else?' Excusing himself, he got up and went to the Gents.

'It beats me,' Jed complained, 'why you have to hang on to his words of wisdom. Blood out of a stone, that's what I reckon. Besides, the poor bugger's got enough on his mind with his defence case. He can't think straight.'

Although I'd felt it coming, the scolding brought tears of humiliation to my eyes. 'I wasn't,' I lied, unable to justify myself.

'Oh,' said Jed helplessly. 'Don't cry, for God's sake. Can't you leave it alone for a bit? And look, why don't you eat something . . . a cake, even.' He pointed to the trays in the glass case. 'These shredded wheat ones are nice.'

I wiped my eyes. 'I can't eat, you know that.'

Phil came back and sat down. His fingers daintily scored a table napkin into creases, edges lined up, corners sharp. He waited for me to finish blowing my nose. When he spoke again, his voice was kinder, but what he said was no more comforting.

'I do think these anxieties are a concomitant of living in new ways, you see, and of breaking down structures which oppress us.'

Brave words, missionary words. I tilted them this way and that in my mind, but whichever way I looked at them they filled me with the same feeling of doom.

'We made certain choices,' Phil went on. 'We try to change things . . . so how *can* we expect to feel secure all the time? I'm not even sure that all these people who lead "normal" lives feel as snug as they make out, anyway.' He waved his hand towards the window, and the street, and the world of normality. 'No. Anxiety is intrinsic to our lives, I'm sure of it. An aspect of life which should even be . . . well, welcomed, if you see what I mean.' He brushed his red hair back from his forehead, and scanned the room again with a swift, shifty look. 'I mean, I feel anxious before a demo. I feel anxious selling *Hard Times* on the street, or arguing with councillors about housing policy, or signing on every week and wondering when someone's going to challenge me and stop my dole money . . . You can't avoid it, wherever you turn.'

The sheer common sense of it was crushing. Beside me, Jed, who had been sighing now and again, and fidgeting with his fork and knife, was suddenly still, listening hard, and nodding agreement.

'But surely there are levels of anxiety which aren't tolerable?' I whispered.

Phil's answering silence was like a blow. My skin itched with shame, for the plea, and the refusal. I remembered a brass bowl on the sideboard at home, which had contained my grandmother's hairpins, and keys to forgotten doors. How it shivered and sang at the vibration of voices, so that a *no*, said sharply, resounded there long after it had been uttered.

When I looked up, the proprietor was standing at the table holding out a plate. There were three pieces of Turkish Delight on it, with cocktail sticks in them. Pointing at the plate, and then at me, he smiled broadly, and made eating motions with his fingers. 'Thank you,' I said automatically, and pushed the plate over to Phil. Phil put a piece in his mouth and chewed self-consciously, wiping the powdery sugar from his chin with a napkin.

'You're sure you won't?'

I shook my head. 'The doctor gave me tranquillisers,' I said, watching for his reaction. 'He told me to take three weeks holiday.' The confession seemed to embarrass Phil. He glanced quickly at the door, as if seeking an escape route. I tried to laugh, to redeem myself. 'Doctors seem to think life is so straightforward, don't they?'

Suddenly Jed spoke, in a brash, stubborn voice. 'Maybe they're not so far off the mark,' he said. 'Doesn't sound like such bad advice to me.'

Phil gave him a disapproving look. 'Tranquillisers don't help. They only suppress things.'

'I haven't taken them regularly,' I said hastily.

Jed glared. 'Right, are we finished, then?' He stood up and pushed his chair back.

I leaned towards Phil. The question was too urgent to be postponed. 'Do you think I should see a therapist?'

'You mean a psychiatrist,' Jed corrected sourly from behind me.

'Oh!' Phil exclaimed, 'I really *don't* believe in therapy.'

I sat still, with the strength draining out of me. I sat still, for there was no place else to go. When Jed held out my coat, I allowed him to drape it round my shoulders. I am nothing but a parcel, I thought.

Outside, the night was orange and starry and smelled of carbon monoxide. Phil said that he had to meet someone, and hurried off towards Kings Cross, leaving Jed and me alone. At the end of the block, where the road to the Printshop turned off, my arm crept through his, and he read its question.

'You want to come back?' His breath steamed in the cold air. 'Am I right?'

I hesitated, trying to remember what I ought to take into account.

'Well? You're free, aren't you, with Andrew away?'

I nodded shiftily. It was true. Without Phil, there were no limits on how often we kissed or clung or fucked. Yet I couldn't help remembering what Jed had said after Phil's withdrawal. He had seemed so worried about dependence, and losing his freedom. Shreds of conversations came back to me. We had agreed to be vigilant, to mark out our boundaries, to ration our meetings. I could remember the imperatives, if not the exact reasoning behind them. I knew that there were prohibitions, whatever Jed said.

'Well?' he urged, 'are you coming, before we freeze to death?'

The attic above the Printshop was painted in colours which

jarred. Black, orange, lime green. The slanting gable over the head of the bed had been papered with silver cooking-foil, but roughly, so that in draughts the foil shivered, and the colours of the walls, reflected in the creases, darted here and there, and merged, and separated again, like a light show.

Jed had thrown off his clothes quickly and was sitting up in bed with a sweater round his shoulders, smoking a joint.

'Want some?'

I shook my head and wondered about sleeping pills. Jed would certainly have something hidden away, because when he was on a binge he took anything. He might start out on beer and dope, then drop a tab of acid, and wash it all down with a handful of barbiturates. Once, after a weekend of excesses, he'd blacked out in the toilet and tumbled down the stairs on to the landing, where Vi and I had found him; his trousers were round his ankles and there was a puzzled smile on his unconscious face. Between these binges, he hoarded his drugs, stockpiled as conscientiously as any wartime housewife.

'Do you have any sleeping pills?' I asked, as casually as I could.

Jed frowned. '*Barbs?*'

'Anything.'

'But you lecture *me* about them . . .' Staring, he shook his head. 'Well, it's your funeral. They're in the top drawer of the dresser, unless Phil's been at them.'

I rummaged in the drawer among neat piles of ironed shirts. I held the small tube up to the light and rattled it. It was almost half full. 'We started out on Burgundy and then we hit the harder stuff,' I said, to make light of it.

'Don't remind me,' Jed said ruefully.

Inside the envelope of blankets he held me tight, curving himself against me. His hand ran along my ribs. 'You could be quite a solid little person, if you'd only let yourself.'

My body was stiff and full of small twitches. Holding hands, we lay in silence with the light blazing and the garish reflections moving on the silver wall above us. Like amoebas, the blobs of orange and green slithered and merged. When

Jed laid the tangle of our hands over my pubic hair I quivered, not knowing whether to encourage or repulse.

After a moment, Jed pulled his hand away and said crossly: 'Where the hell are you?' and I realised that I'd been twisting his signet ring round and round on his finger. 'Sorry,' I said, as above me two green pools swam towards each other, collided, bounced back, and dissolved into one.

Jed put his arms round me roughly. 'I just wish you'd stop staring at the wall, that's all.' He began to stroke my hair. 'Your pupils are really dilated,' he said, more gently.

'It's because . . . I feel no control over any of it. Can't you see that?' I started to cry.

Jed sat up. 'You know what? All I see is that you're fucking exhausted, and I'm going to turn the bloody light off.'

'Not yet,' I begged, 'Not till I'm asleep. I can't bear it.' Ashamed by the admission, I cried harder.

Grumbling, Jed wriggled back down into the bed. Gratefully, I rolled in close and burrowed my head into his lap. The muscles of his thighs were tense, resisting.

'It's *me*, you know,' he said. 'Doesn't that help?' he gave an uncertain laugh. 'A big hunk of a man like me?'

He sounded so miserable that I hated myself. Selfishly, I had forgotten how much he had to put up with: surely he deserved whatever moments of happiness I could still bring him.

'It does, it does,' I assured him, wiping my eyes on the sheet, and then bringing my hand down to ring his penis familiarly. I heard him let out a long sigh, and felt him begin to relax. He drew me up beside him, and pulled the covers around us, tucking us both in. His chin was rough and warm against my forehead.

'You're on too much of a head trip,' he said equably. 'You just need to take things very easy.'

He spat on his finger and began to explore. Remember, I thought, opening my legs, it is easy.

There was a moment of crisis when I flattened out and gripped him with thighs suddenly rigid as a bicycle fork, and I begged him to hold me, later, until the pills put me out, but he was patient, and promised, and stroked me on beyond the fear until we both, separately, came.

Afterwards, I took one barbiturate and then, automatically, my contraceptive pill. Before I put it in my mouth I looked at it resentfully. Even in the depths of the night, I thought, I am wide open.

13

I was soon to learn that Matt's humble, soulful look was not the whole picture. Oh no. Matt has always moved fast, straight for his target.

'Phone for you,' Marie yelled much louder than was necessary, as she does when she thinks it is far too early in the morning for any phone calls at all. I hurried out of bed.

'Sorry, did I wake you?' Matt's voice said huskily.

'No, no,' I mumbled.

'Ah. Well. Have you read my story yet?'

I looked at my watch sleepily. It was 9.15. 'Yes. Actually I did. And made some notes.'

On the other end of the line I heard a grunt.

'What?'

'Efficient. I said, you're very efficient, aren't you?' It wasn't a question. The tingling started in my thighs again, and I had just enough time to feel the honeyed flush of a woman desired before the brakes went on. Be careful, I thought.

'Can I come and talk to you about it, then?' The sentence ended in a little gasp.

I forced the fuzz of sleep from my head. 'When, though?'

'Today?'

'Look, I don't think so.'

'Oh, are you working at the magazine today?' He sounded surprised. I admitted that I wasn't. Where was he getting his information from?

'Tomorrow, then?'

I stared into the void of the black mouthpiece, calculating. I didn't want to seem heartless, but I had to think of the consequences. I wavered. Was I simply inventing difficulties, shying away from purely imaginary risks? 'Oh *you*,' my mother had said so often, 'you're frightened of the day you'll never see!'

'Has Vi been at you? Has she?' The question was abrupt, startling.

'I *beg* your pardon? I haven't got a clue what you're talking about.'

Matt let out a small explosion of irritation. 'Don't bullshit, June. Please don't bullshit me.'

'She hasn't been in touch with me, if that's what you mean.'

'What, no sisterly pacts?'

'Jesus!' A hole was opening under me. I clutched the edges of my dressing-gown, hugging it to me.

Matt chuckled. 'Oops! Awfully sorry.'

I fought a powerful sensation of sinking. 'Look I'll ignore that remark.'

'Good. I can come, then?' He sounded gleeful. I had a strong image of a baneful, sly imp jigging on the other end of the line, and I blocked.

'Aren't you driving today?'

'No way. I didn't feel like work. I'm chucking it in, anyway. I don't have the temperament of a delivery boy. Not obliging enough.' There was a silence. 'Listen to this . . .' From the receiver came a seductive drone which sounded like Dylan. 'You like?' he said, chuckling with delight. 'It's the new album.'

'Yes,' I said sourly. He was inveigling his way into my day, infiltrating my house with his music.

'I won't take up much of your time . . .' He was wheedling now; I pictured him with his feet up on the table, grinning, playing with the cord of the telephone. The music flowed on. Despite myself, I started to smile.

'I give up. Come this afternoon, then.'

'Thank you. Thank you very much.' Suddenly he was meek, ingratiating.

I put the phone down. Idiot, I thought, and thumped the hallstand with my fist.

A week passed before Vi contacted me. The phone trilled faintly when I was on top of a ladder pruning lime trees much too late in the season. Even before Andrew called out I knew who it was. I dropped my saw and climbed down.

'It's me, Vi,' she said, in a small voice which boded ill. 'How are you?'

'Rather sunburned, actually,' I said, and started to prattle nervously about how hot it was for May, and how Tom and Marie said that the lime trees would never recover from the lopping I was giving them . . . 'And you?' I asked politely.

'Surviving, I suppose. I hear you were very helpful about the story.' Her voice was non-committal. 'June, do you think he's good?' She sounded so anxious, suddenly, that I warmed to her. 'I need to know what you think, you see.'

'I'll tell you the same as I told him. He's prodigiously talented and utterly undisciplined. His feel for words is great, enviable, in fact, but he refuses structure completely.' I laughed. 'Verdict delivered.'

'I'm so relieved. I lose all perspective, you see. I mean, he could be a con man or a bloody genius, and I wouldn't be able to tell . . . It's so confusing, June.'

I stiffened. 'What is?'

'Who to trust. What to trust. He says such awful things about other people's work.'

'It's isolation,' I said with emphasis. I didn't want to hear exactly what sort of things he said. 'I told him that he needs to find his peer group, he really must have *contact* . . . '

There was a gulping sound, as if Vi was going to erupt into sobs. The drowning sensation began again. Gathering my strength, I swam for the surface. 'Vi. I feel solidarity with him. I can't help feeling it if he's struggling to be an artist . . .' My words drained away into the silence. Something was very wrong, I could tell.

At last Vi said, in a muffled voice, 'What about me, then? Where do *I* fit in? In your gallery of artists and writers and *sensitive*, sensitive people . . .'

'Oh *Vi* . . .'

'Yes, *Vi*. Vi just jollies along, didn't you know, she doesn't have the *heavy* responsibilities we have, to our feminist magazines and our new wave cultural vanguards and our *art*, you see . . .'

I tried to interrupt. 'Look, is it Matt you've got it in for, or me, or what?'

'Well, aren't you just the same? Does either of you *see* me?'

'This is craziness,' I said weakly.

'Do you think I *like* being a clerk?' she demanded. 'Do you?'

'I thought . . . well, I thought you did it for political reasons, more than anything. Your union work, and so on?'

'Oh yes, to be with "ordinary people",' she said with sarcasm. 'Party instructions. Vi, the red-hot cadre . . .' Her voice broke. 'Well, let me tell you there's more kindness among the women in that office than I've seen in the whole damn left put together . . .'

'What's *happening*, Vi?' I waited as she blew her nose, wondering what was to come next. I felt a stab of self-pity: what had I done to deserve this?

'Why ever do you think I moved in with him in the first place? It meant something, don't you see? He may be crazy but he is . . . an artist . . . It meant I was changing, needing to paint again, after all these years and years of politicking . . .' She drew a quick breath. 'But did *you* see that?'

I was silent, affronted. How was I supposed to have known? And how long had Vi been sitting on this resentment?

'But you obviously don't think my work merits attention . . .'

This was too unfair. 'I've always tried to support you in your work, but you hardly ever mention it.'

'You didn't say a word about my painting of Matt. I mean,

it's pretty difficult to ignore. You must have seen it in the bedroom.'

With a jolt I remembered the portrait against the wall: the ugly, elongated face, the huge green telephone. Not the sort of painting one could overlook. 'Oh, God, of course. I meant to ask you about it that night, but I forgot . . . '

'That's what I mean,' Vi muttered. 'Who sees *me*?'

'Oh, stop it, Vi.'

'It's true,' she said, with a sob. 'Not everyone swans around the trendy end of the movement, you know . . . at least you could admit that you like the prestige. Just *once*, if you'd only be human for *once*!' She began to cry in earnest.

There was something else going on here, I was sure, and if Vi wasn't going to get to the heart of it, then I would have to. Numbly, I decided a confession was called for.

'Forget it,' Vi wept, 'forget I said that. I'm such a bitch.'

'Look, about Matt's visit . . .. '

'Don't tell me! Don't say a word. You must do what you want, both of you.' She hiccupped suddenly, and then said in a voice barely above a whisper, 'Who am I to stand in your way?'

I stared at the receiver in dismay.

'I know I need to get out. I know it. I'm just too fucking weak.'

'Jesus, Vi.'

'Yes I am. I hate myself.'

I took a deep breath. She had me upside down and inside out, I was losing my bearings completely. Okay. If she wanted it, she could have it. 'All right, all right,' I said. 'I fancy him. June fancies Matt. I can't help it. There it is.' A chestnut tree in a wood, a heart and an arrow: I could see the penknife carving it. 'But I've no intention of acting on it. Right?'

Vi was silent, digesting this.

'And that's quite separate from any difficulties you might have with him yourself,' I added firmly, as if mere firmness would make it come true.

'I don't know who to trust,' she sniffed.

I waited for her to come round. How many more assurances does she want, I thought. In the silence I stroked the blond hairs on my arm. The skin was warm, smooth, freckled. When the words came, they burned.

'He tortures me, the shit. He says, "What if I'm really in love with June?" And then he denies it all and . . . tangles me up, till I feel so *crazed* . . .' She let out a wild sob. 'Just so's you know what you're getting.'

'He can't do that.' I leaned my forehead against the cool surface of the wall. 'You don't know what you're saying.' I tried to think of some way of stemming the corrosive flow of secrets. Short of slamming the phone down, I had no answers; it was going to flow on, whatever I did. The receiver seemed to have attached itself to my ear, like the sucker of some noxious plant.

'But maybe you *are* the right one, and I'm just in your way,' Vi continued stubbornly.

'Listen to me, Vi, you're tearing yourself apart over nothing.'

' . . . Or in his way, I can't bear that either . . .'

'Get a grip on yourself.' I tried to laugh. 'I'm not going to take him on, am I? He's too much of a bloody handful!'

'That didn't stop me.'

'I'm not blind and deaf and I notice that he hasn't done you too much good.' Insults, I thought. She needs me to insult him, then she will believe me.

'But maybe *I'm* just too difficult, as the bastard says. I don't know what to think any more . . .'

'Leave it alone for a bit, Vi.' But she won't, I thought: she'll stampede on, sowing doubt and confusion.

Vi coughed harshly and blew her nose again. 'I'm exhausted,' she said, after a long moment. There was a hint of gratitude in her voice. 'I don't know what gets into me.'

Relief made me more sympathetic. 'Are you sleeping?'

'Hardly,' she said, and then she added: 'I'm sorry, I've got to think.' And abruptly, she rang off.

Upstairs, I fell on the bed.

To think that Matt would say such things.

Heat teased at my skin voluptuously, and a cold voice inside reminded me of that incautious glance at Matt, and the havoc it had already unleashed. I had to watch out. It was simply a question of being aware of your own weaknesses. For didn't I know how sex could tear you from kin and country and toss you out to fend for yourself? Could send you running from bed to bed and in the end leave you stranded in a room white with moonlight?

Punishment by exile.

Enough.

The front door banged, and the house vibrated. Feet hammered up the stairs and into the toilet. I threw open the bedroom door. Andrew was aiming a stream at the toilet bowl and missing. 'That door!' I shouted, 'You'll have the bloody house down round our ears one day.'

14

After that phone call I retreated into work, burrowing into the piles of manuscripts on my office desk like a badger going to earth; for once, I thanked my lucky stars for *Womanright*. The magazine was a co-operative, and a place of daily quarrels and struggle, but compared to the combined effects of Matt and Vi it seemed like a haven. Even the desk itself was reassuring. On and around the other desks there were Busy Lizzies and birthday cards and frilly Valentines sent in a spirit of high camp, whereas my space was ascetic, like the cell of a novice. Free of feminine clutter, it spoke only of the security of work done and work to do. There was a typewriter on it, and three wire trays labelled Current Features, Fiction, and Futures, and sheaves of paper belonging to different stages in the life of the magazine. On one pile, riddles of pencil marks represented editing done, meanings clarified, academic convolutions straightened out. On another, pages of rough notes starred with doodles would, by the end of the editorial meeting, be transformed into next issue's cover headlines. And then, laid out carefully at one side of the desk, there was the meat of it all: the long shining proofs notated in blue pencil, with the typesetter's corrections on separate sheets clipped on to the edge, all of it ready to be pasted down on the layout boards over the next few days.

In the middle of the editorial meeting, I put my feet up on the desk and let the words wash over me. At the next desk Jude sneezed and swore and pulled toilet paper off a roll. Opposite her, Mike's head bobbed over the agenda book as she tapped with a pencil, calling for attention. Beside Mike, at a desk at right angles to hers, Andrea ate tangerines and got on with the accounts, raising her head to interject only occasionally, when items of finance or distribution came up. On the floor in front of Mike's desk Catherine squatted silently with her layout plans spread out on the carpet around her, waiting to discuss the design. And completing the circle, there was Clara, who was on phone duty and hating it. Each time she picked up the phone her voice went reedy with annoyance, since even to say: 'We're in a meeting at the moment, can I take a message?' meant that she might miss a vital exchange in whatever argument was currently in progress, and of all of us, Clara had the most insatiable appetite for the political controversies of the movement.

Tipping my chair back, I gazed at the ceiling. The girders which held up the roof were a vivid scarlet. I had painted them four years ago, when I first joined the magazine, and still they glowed. It was the sort of job I liked: you knew where you were with it, because the results were so tangible. When I had finished I was triumphant, and stood at the top of the ladder surveying it all. I'd looked down at Mike, who was steadying the ladder with her foot on the bottom rung. Didn't she ever marvel, I said, didn't she ever marvel at where she was now? I waved my paint-brush, and the ladder wobbled. 'Don't you ever think what a long way you've come?' Mike's smile was willing, but puzzled. Not really, she said – perhaps she should? Feeling a little ridiculous, I climbed down, and hurried to explain that where I came from it was another country altogether: so different, such a long way to the north – although that was hardly what I'd meant. But for Mike's help, the mechanic's daughter might never have come so far; I knew it, but I couldn't bring myself to say it.

Surrounded by rustlings of paper and the smell of Andrea's tangerines, it was pleasant to daydream, to take stock. Four years of *Womanright*. Of course I'd known that it would be no idyll; I had been around the left long enough to know what to expect. At *Womanright* there were countless irritations – some petty, some not so petty. The derisory pay. The personal/political crises followed by sudden, tight-lipped resignations. The winters when both radiators failed and we huddled ill-temperedly around one small electric fire. And sometimes worst of all, the attitude of visitors who believed that we made a virtue of poverty. There had been one of those last week, an American from the National Organisation of Women, who exclaimed in shocked, admiring tones that she just didn't know *how* we did it. Staring at her crocodile-skin shoes, I had felt poor, and proud, and patronised. Certainly, there was plenty to bitch about, if bitching was on the agenda . . . but right now, looking around me at the others, I was really quite satisfied. Four years of shared effort, four years of constructing something: after all, it wasn't to be sniffed at. I glanced up at the girders, and again there was that small thrill of content. See, once they were bare iron: I changed that.

There was a lull in the meeting. Clara was arguing with a caller, and the others were listening. 'She's in a meeting right now, will you call back?' She covered the receiver with her hand and scowled at Mike. 'Won't take no for an answer. Someone called Sherry?'

The effect on Mike was startling. She jerked upright and brought her knees together sharply, so that the agenda book slid off her lap and fell to the floor, emptying letters and press releases all over the carpet. I took over the chairing while she took the call on an extension at the far end of the office. By the time she came back we had worded a job description for an advertisement, and agreed a proposal for a special issue to mark the magazine's anniversary.

'I told her not to phone in meetings,' she muttered. Her face was composed again, but a rash of red blotches had appeared in the open neck of her plaid shirt.

There was only one more item on the agenda. Keeping a straight face, I held up my hand. 'And lastly, do we want a feature on Carmelite nuns?'

'Mm, lovely. Just the job,' said Jude, drooping her eyelids. There was a shout of laughter, in which even Clara joined, and a loud chorus of 'No'. Beside me, Mike laughed gratefully, covering her mouth with her hand.

The days slipped past, hot and sultry and busy. Within a fortnight, intelligence began to filter back via Marie that Matt and Vi were breaking up. Marie had run into Vi at a Trades Council social: she had been very high, very made-up. Marie related this like any other casual gossip, unaware of its effect on me. At least my conscience is clear, I thought, at least I acted correctly. I tried to put it out of my mind, and went on spending long hours at the magazine. June came, and the heat intensified. In the office, I washed my hands repeatedly, for the sweat on my fingers made the typewriter keys slippery and stained the clean white proofs.

Coming home from work one afternoon I ambled through the park, where the swimming pool had at last opened for the season. Walking under an avenue of plane trees, I drew up an agenda. 1. Shopping (leeks potatoes cheese fruit milk). 2. Swimming (kids bikini sun-glasses, hurry before the sun sinks). 3. Cooking. 4. Work/poetry (decide later).

I was so involved that I didn't notice the two men until they drew level with me.

'Hey gorgeous,' said one, 'your bra's showing.'

Surprise made me turn on them. I'd felt so unassailable, in the loose, rather masculine shirt, with my breasts tucked tidily away inside my bra. I could hardly be accused of being provocative. 'And what's so bloody fascinating about bras these days?' I cried, 'Haven't you seen enough tits on page three?'

There was a moment's silence, in which we glared at each other. I began to walk on, and they followed. My heart thudded. Now I've provoked them, I thought.

Then one of them shouted: 'Hey! Scragbag!'

Hugging my manuscript file to my chest, I hurried across the road.

'They'd have to pay me a bonus to rape that!' On the other side of the road the two men walked on under the dappled shade of the plane trees, kicking at the ground, laughing now and again in angry bursts.

When I got home I was shaky, and my skin felt dirty, as if they had fingered it. I thirsted to be in the water. I shouted upstairs several times before Andrew and Zac appeared with their bathing costumes; their teeth were black with liquorice, and there was a fine powdering of sherbet around their mouths. Zac twitched with excitement. 'Go, go, go,' he muttered under his breath on the way up the road, and when we came in sight of the pool he charged on ahead, leaving a trail of bathing trunks and goggles on the path.

The crowd at the pool had thinned out, leaving some late sunbathers who lay with their heads diligently propped against the doors of the changing cubicles, soaking up the last slanting rays. The boys ran off to change, and I spread my towel and lay down. A lazy murmur of voices surrounded me: the usual swimming pool small talk. In the shallow end, children were smashing the water with the flat of their hands, splashing each other, leap-frogging, hurling themselves in off the edge with their knees clasped tight to their chests so that they hit the water like cannonballs.

The voices of neighbouring sunbathers drifted across. There were three of them, a married couple and a woman. The woman wore a bright yellow bikini, and was already tanned; she was telling her friends how she kept chucking in her jobs all the time, she just never could seem to settle, not with men either. Under cover of sun-glasses, I watched. She was about forty, with a short, tailored hairstyle and a firm body, unlike her friend, who was softer, more puddingy. Her legs were good, shaved smooth, and she wore a gold bracelet on one ankle. She was leaning towards the married one, speaking gaily. 'I said to Terry, "Don't you have *any* mates who aren't married?" And he says, "Oh no, you're not up to *that* again . . ."' Hugging her bare knees, she laughed a throaty laugh. 'I reckon I'll settle for an ugly bod that treats me nice. But then again, I don't *like* ugly men.'

Her voice carried. Her companions smiled at her, but I could see that they were embarrassed. There was something so uninhibited about her laugh, about the way she looked over the men lounging on the steps of the diving board. She was single, the message said; she was available. Evidently she saw no perils in this. I felt vulnerable on her behalf, and wondered if I was giving off similar signals without being aware of it. I thought of the two men, and shivered; it was a hateful idea, not being in charge.

Down at the deep end, the pool was empty. Dead wasps floated on the surface. I held my nose and jumped, feeling the pressure in my ears, the rush of air bubbles.Then I swam back to the five feet six mark, where I felt safer, and floated on my back in the slightly greasy water, staring up at the sky. The water was cool and neutral, the opposite of a lover's touch. I floated, letting it define my boundaries.

Vi had moved out of Matt's house, or so Marie said. The idea filled me with a traitorous excitement. I had cautioned Marie and Tom about the phone: if it's Matt, I'm not in.

In the shallow end, Andrew and Zac were commuting noisily from one side to the other, shouting : 'Three widths!', 'Four!', 'Five!' 'Watch us, June, watch us!' the streaming faces cried. I swam underwater for a few strokes and surfaced beside them. Their eyes were pink from the sting of the chlorine.

'Watch me dive.' Andrew clambered out and executed a cheerful belly-flop which hurt to watch. Zac followed, shivering. A clean dive.

'Better?' he demanded. Better than Andrew, he meant.

'Better than ever,' I said, 'Point the toes, though, and keep the legs together.'

The two boys listened eagerly. I watched their faces shine as they showed me their prowess in breaststroke and crawl and underwater somersaults. They were such zealous, unashamed exhibitionists that I could only laugh, and spoil them with praise, and wish that somewhere there was someone who would watch me, too.

According to Marie, Matt had phoned three times in as many days. When she told me this, I dreamed of my hand being severed, my head, Andrew's leg.

At the edge of the pool, the lifeguard fingered the loose sleeves of his white T-shirt, rolling them back, displaying his bronzed shoulders. He was staring at the yellow bikini woman as she swayed past on high-heeled mules. 'Out of the pool, ladies and gents,' he cried, blowing his silver whistle.

I got out obediently and persuaded the boys to follow. I couldn't quite put a name to what I was feeling. It wasn't really loneliness, I thought – more a sort of aching boredom.

15

On a hot Sunday a week or so later, Vi and I sat on the kitchen steps talking about holidays. She looked better than I had expected, less drawn, now that she and Matt had called a halt. She was dressed seductively, in a low-necked black vest and the wide yellow skirt she had worn at the carnival. Her eyes were rimmed with kohl, and she had divided her hair into a dozen snaky plaits each of which was woven through with coloured ribbons and finished off with a red or green bead. She'd come to say goodbye before she left for Italy: she was going alone on a package tour and she was angry about it.

'It's brave of you,' I said.

'No option, have I?' She bit into the rough skin on the side of her forefinger. 'Got to take my three weeks, like everyone else.'

At the bottom of the garden Andrew and Zac, ignoring a pile of grass cuttings which I had left for them to rake up, swung from the lower branches of the ash tree. They were taking turns, timing each other to see who could hang on longer. It was beginning to look quarrelsome.

'Will you be going away?' Vi's voice was rather too polite.

'Oh, perhaps – when Andrew goes off to his father.' I wasn't very organised this year, I added quickly. Past summers with Jed hovered in my mind, but mournful reminiscences seemed inappropriate. I reached out to touch Vi's bare arm. 'I must say, you look blooming, considering . . .'

'No thanks to fish-face,' Vi said with feeling. She gave me a quick, bitter look which I tried not to take personally. No thanks to you either, it seemed to say. Yet in these last weeks, hadn't I listened to her patiently enough, as she wept and grieved into the phone, denouncing the duplicity of all men and the monstrous cruelty of one? There had been mistrustful asides for me too, and I hadn't challenged them, had made allowances for her – but would she make allowances for me? I was still waiting to find that out.

Vi spoke again, in a girlish, piping voice. 'Marshall's been good to me, that's all. We get on.'

It came quite out of the blue. I sat still and thought hard. At the bottom of the garden Zac managed to hook his knees over the branch and lowered himself gingerly, swinging upside down. 'Marshall?' I echoed. There was no end to her tangents and surprises. 'What does he have to do with it?'

'God knows what Matt's told you,' Vi said angrily. 'God knows what he's twisted it to mean.'

I stared at my bare knees. They were dirty and scratched from the thorns on the rosebush I'd been tangling with. 'I have no contact with Matt. I thought I had made you understand that.'

The disbelief in Vi's glance was positively insulting. I held on to myself. Someone had to stay in charge, and it obviously wasn't going to be Vi. 'I thought Marshall was Matt's friend?'

'Friend?' Vi scoffed. 'Have you seen them together. They hate each other. I told you, all they do is act out these lunatic schoolboy jokes.'

'Are you saying that you got off with him?' I tried to control my voice.

'Oh *well*!' Beside me the beads swung abruptly as Vi tossed her head. 'It's all right for *you*. One flash of the mysterious Guthrie eyes and so on. You just have to sit quiet and they fall at your feet . . . don't think I haven't noticed.' Her chin trembled, and she took a handkerchief from her bag and held it to her mouth. Here we go, I thought.

'How long ago was this?'

'A while.' She gave an angry shrug. 'Is it surprising?'

'Before you and Matt split?'

'I expect so,' she said, and tears began to fall. 'I had to do *something*.'

I watched the tears drip off her chin and splash on the yellow skirt and the mossy stone steps. I wouldn't have let her get away with it, of course. If she'd told me at the time, I would never have allowed her to cast Matt as the ultimate villain, and she knew it. It simply suited her better to play the victim. I was appalled at such trickery. 'It's just a bit odd,' I said, 'your not telling me till now.'

Then Vi exploded. '*Some* people,' she cried, 'some of us have to go out and *look* for it!' The two boys turned startled faces towards us. Vi clasped the crumpled handkerchief to her mouth and looked at me beseechingly, but too late, for the words were out. I pulled at a honeysuckle trailer, stripping off the flowers, shredding the petals in my hands. I should just hit her, I thought, she's asking for it.

'You talk as if I were a *femme fatale*!' I took her arm and shook it. Blind, I thought, she is blind and deaf. 'Haven't you ever considered that I might just be *shy*?' Vi rubbed her arm and squinted suspiciously at me. It's not worth it, I thought;

however I defend myself, she'll always have something in reserve, some irrefutable and crushing complaint.

'The hat,' she said. 'He got you the hat.'

'Hat?' I repeated dully.

'You said you wanted a black hat, remember . . . like Bette Davis.'

I felt the blood rush to my face. 'Christ, how ridiculous.'

'He stole it when he was delivering to Theatre Supplies.' Vi's voice was regretful and accusing.

I held up my hand. 'Wait, now, that's not my responsibility.'

'. . . so you see how hard it is for me to believe you? Shy?' She shook her head. 'It won't sink in.' The beads on her plaits rattled musically, and a spiteful choir took up the refrain inside my head. It *won't* sink in, it *won't* sink in. Meanwhile, a vision of the hat was taking shape, and I couldn't stop it. It was made of black felt, it was brimmed, it had a diagonal slant; it was an alluring, intriguing, impossibly idiotic hat. Whoever does he think he's dealing with? I thought incredulously.

Beside me, Vi's face was woebegone. I shook my head, trying to smile at her. 'You'll end up convincing me that I'm in possession of a deadly charm, if you carry on like that.' Vi didn't respond to the clumsy joke. Surrounded by smears of mascara and kohl, her eyes looked enormous. 'I've no intention of seeing him, and I've no intention of getting together with him. So what else do I have to do to convince you?'

She shook her head fiercely. 'It's done now, isn't it?'

'Don't you believe me?'

She smoothed her skirt over her knees and stared out across the garden. Zac and Andrew, with their sixth sense for an audience, swung farther and higher and louder, and each time they jumped down they grinned towards us. Finally Vi gave a grudging nod. 'Anyway, it's over. I suppose I should apologise for dragging you into the dying convulsions.'

It was half-hearted, but it was still a step forward. I picked a fresh honeysuckle and dropped it in her lap.

'At least Matt and I aren't driving each other mad any

longer,' she said.

'Or me,' I retorted, 'or me.'

Vi tucked the honeysuckle into the waistband of her skirt and smiled reluctantly.

After the gate had clicked shut behind Vi the boys came squeaking at me babyishly, demanding cocoa. Their faces were grubby and mischievous, and there was a six inch rip in the seat of Andrew's jeans. I began to scold, but he held up his hand to stop me. 'I know, I know,' he said, nodding.

I turned my back on them and put a pan of milk on the stove. Fair's fair, I thought, and burst into tears.

'Sorry,' said Andrew, realising, 'sorry about the trousers.' His arm headed for my shoulders, to console, but he was too short for that, so he settled for my waist, and patted it energetically.

'Not the trousers,' I sniffed.

'What's wrong, then?'

'Tissue, please.'

'Zac, get the bog roll,' Andrew ordered. Zac glanced uncertainly at him, and then at me. 'Go on.' He steered me over to the kitchen table and made me sit down. 'I'll make you a nice cup of tea,' he said brightly. It was such a good imitation of adulthood that I had to laugh, which made me sob harder. The tea, when it came, was white, just hot water with milk; the teabag still floated in the cup. He pushed the sugar bowl towards me. 'Now. Why are you upset?' It was the sight of the tea that made me pull myself together. And Zac too, picking at a mauve toilet roll, tearing the ends into fringes.

'Oh, I don't know. Just lonely, I suppose. Not worth worrying about.' I tried to smile at Zac. 'Don't worry.'

'I'm not!' He looked startled.

Andrew patted my back with nurse-like briskness. 'I get lonely too. I understand. But we'll look after you, won't we, Zac?'

A frown of incomprehension settled on Zac's thin face, but he nodded. 'We'll put ourselves to bed, really we will.'

'See?' said Andrew. 'So why don't you go and have a *nice rest*.'

Upstairs, I set the thin tea down on my desk beside a pile of unread manuscripts.

As for Vi, Vi had simply attended to her face and, polished again, she had set off to meet Marshall. Just like that. Her hair regained its shine. Just like that. The look of a woman with something to look forward to.

Outside the evening which Vi inhabited was pale violet and haunting. Noises carried on the clear air: small sounds of birds in the lime trees, the click of roller-skate wheels on the paving stones, the clink of cutlery through open windows. The scent of honeysuckle drifted up from the garden. It was a night for softness, for pleasure, a night when pain was all the sharper for being somehow reprehensible, a waste of resources.

I began to sort through the manuscripts, spreading them out in front of me like cards in a game of patience. I thought of the women who had written them: their hopes, their expectations, all there, spread on the desk in front of me. But it was useless. The bitter comparisons choked me – those scenarios in which Vi laughed and flirted and grabbed for what she wanted, and I sat alone with the summer stretching before me.

A sweep of my hand sent the papers flying to the floor. Paper-clips glinted across the carpet. No. Not this time. I wouldn't pick up the first page. Wouldn't read.

Why didn't I let her have it? I stamped my foot hard down on the pages.

My mind wheeled. There was a toddler somewhere, and a garden; she trod the garden path, pulling behind her a toy lorry which her father had made. The lorry cab was yellow, and inside the blue tailboard something wriggled. The wheels went click-click over the paving stones, and then the child – too furtive for her age – emptied the load of caterpillars on to the concrete and hammered them flat with a toy spade. The carnage was terrible. The girl's hands and dress were smeared with brown and green slime. With gritted teeth she stamped and stamped on the wobbling pretty green bodies.

The image drifted, out of time. The girl licked her lips and smiled, a broad smile of cruelty and delight, and suddenly I knew, first, that she had picked the caterpillars one by one, delicately, from the gooseberry leaves, and second, that her mother's breasts were wobbly and soft, and her stomach, and her sex.

Sit down. Find that roll of flesh again above the waist of my shorts – formless, ugly, unmanageable. Think of Vi somewhere across London sleeping the smug sleep of those whose legs tangle amiably among the thighs of this or that lover; grip the folded flesh as if to strangle it. The anger swells, the room will not contain it. Jealous. You're only jealous.

Pressure from above. Displaced, slipping from the chair, sinking down. Knees on the floor now, but even so the weight is too much, gravity is winning; the only solution is to allow the force-field its way, give in, lie flattened and spread among the papers on the carpet.

Wide eyes. The horizon is limited. Torn pages, two hairpins, a crescent of nail-clipping. Exile without appeal, here, where the colours are so very beautiful.

A speck in the growing dark, I watch my fat bare feet wave as the moon rises.

16

Mixed Bathing
Pond, Hampstead
Saturday, July 8

June. Now look here. This whole thing is frustrating me utterly.

Not only does Vi read the Sisters Act (solidarity support validation) to you to exclude me from you, but your whole house seems involved in keeping me in my place,until I'm blinded with blood-eye. You make me feel I know nothing about sexual politics, women, or indeed sexuality and that I am truly a bull in yr. china shop (I'm not!!). I actually thought we were friends and there is no need for this non-communication but it seems you don't trust me. If you categorise me and so forth without *listening* to me and without explaining yr. side it only leaves me assuming that Vi (who I don't trust) is shit-spreading about me.

I think Vi's reaction to our attraction was more to do with you and her, and not me, and coupled with this was her obsession with the sexual element in our relationship which, while undoubtedly there, she distorted and exaggerated the budding relationship I held dear and which demanded (demands) honesty and clarity and an integrity I really have to grope for these days.

I really wish you would talk to me so that we can clear the air, which is my main concern at the moment. I think the truth is that you're a last puritan romantic who, punishing herself for pleasure and joy with man offers help and love to loveless women by way of redemption! Eh? It has been known . . .

If we can talk then I can be *me* again with you, and no longer suffer this feeling of unfair rejection, this feeling that you and Vi (and possibly the whole sisterhood?) are plotting against me in some conspiracy aimed at undermining my identity and infuriating my sense of self into a caricature of ego, hungry for gratification at the submissive spread-eagle of your good self below, gasping for more punishment while grovelling for mercy!!!! *(What?)*

Look, I think you were sensationally sensitive about my work, and the carnival and all.

I'm not asking for much. Just give me something. Anything will do, if it's true.

There is vitality and fertility between us, and you're wrong to feel guilty about it. There is an inevitability about us which will not leave me alone. Once when Vi was there but not in the room, there was a feeling which came between us and, I think, united us, and a flowing sensation flooded down into me that was not so much affection or sexuality – tho' it was both – it was essentially calm and complete, a tingling sense of completeness with myself that was inseparable from a sense of empathy, harmony and fulfilment with you. It expanded to the infinite. I *know* you know what I mean. This is what matters, you can disregard all my other madnesses . . .

Can't we talk, let it flow?
You are never far from my thoughts.
Trust me.
P.S. You have the only copy of my story, and I have the only copy of your hat!

I held the letter gingerly between finger and thumb, like a daddy-long-legs. Dear Matt, I appreciate your distress, but . . . Dear Matt, please don't be so paranoid . . . I didn't know where to start.

Dear Matt,
Remember that Vi is one of my oldest friends and is still trying to recover from the relationship with you. I, too, need space to recover. If our friendship is as inevitable as you say – then what's the rush? We move in the same circles, after all, we can hardly avoid meeting. Please, let it rest at that for the moment.

I flew up the street to the Post Office with the letter inside my jacket to protect it from the July rain. Holding action accomplished.

17

Matt has disappeared inside the cottage. Around me, the woods rattle with wind, and the handle of the well sways and creaks. In the corner of my eye a sudden movement startles me: a shadow, brushing past behind the window of the white room. I look again, and of course it's only Matt, prowling. His finger traces a heart and an arrow in the dust of the window pane, then his face appears in it, glowering.

It was May, once again, when Jed brought me to the cottage. He had staked so much on the trip, hoped so hard for a cure, that my heart ached for him. He had looked for a lover in me, but had found only an invalid, and I swore to myself that I would set this straight.

I tried so hard to be calm. I wanted so much to be absorbed in the ordinariness of eating and drinking, to sit in the garden and watch the evening grow iridescent over the spiked pines, to sink companionably into the tender, cold-nosed sleep of the country. I wanted so much to be quiet and loving. But in bed that night, when Jed busied along me with his lips sucking and smacking, saying Get into your body, for Christ's sake, everything jarred again, and my mind raced, and the words tripped out into the white room and froze there like sharp frost needles. Eventually Jed turned over in exasperation at my ramblings, and I was abandoned to the terrible chirpings inside my head, an uproar of accusations. For what Jed didn't know was that I had almost, almost bitten down on his tongue as it pushed and slithered like a snake's strong head in the cavities of my mouth. And he hadn't even sensed the danger, didn't seem to realise that in pushing him away I was only protecting him.

As Jed slept his innocent sleep, I got out of bed and went to the window. Outside, everything was still. The lilacs in the garden, the rope hanging from the trestle, the massed dark forest. I tested the stillness with a down feather held in the air and it froze like a fossil.

'Tomorrow,' he'd said, 'Tomorrow we'll drive somewhere – to the river, perhaps, or to the seaside.' He had used the word so lightly, so effortlessly, and left it hissing in my ear like an obscene thing. For in that stillness of time and leaf and air, it was I who must thrash and churn and move the wheels of the night, to journey to the other side. No such courage was demanded of him, who could still slip through the hours like an eel across a pond.

The cube of the room enclosed me like a cold womb. Immobile, expectant, the waiting walls dared me to embark.

In the morning, when the grey light came in to dim the candle flame, I knew beyond doubt that I had passed the point where Jed could recognise me, or I myself in him. I knelt on the edge of the bed for a moment to watch him sleep, but did not touch him, for I was afraid for him and wished to preserve him from the cold sear of my fingers; he would be far, far safer without me.

Clear in the knowledge that everything was over for me, I became calm. I looked out at the lilacs in the garden and they were ghostly. I looked at the spring woods and they were in tatters.

There will be no more damage, I thought. And I ran. Jed slept, and I ran through the woods, and only there did the tears begin their hot river through my head, and burst on my face like the breaking of the waters when a birth is due: that humiliating, inevitable flooding.

I came to the village station, where a smell of new wood drifted up from the sawmill. The guard gave me a ticket with an irritable snap of his ticket-punch. In the wood yard, a circular saw whined. I looked east along the track, into the sun, to the gash in the forest where the train would emerge, and west, towards London, where Phil waited.

Like the I Ching, I would probe him for answers. For he, more than anyone, had lived the flux of events for so long that sheer centripetal force had turned him solid in the midst of all the swirlings.

And then I was swaying in the box of the train lavatory, steadying myself against the sink with one hand, and up-ending a bottle of Bell's with the other. *Now*, if my friends could see me *now*, I crooned to the mirror, toasting the woman I had tried so hard to love. That one, she was a high-flyer, a regular parachute woman. True or false, I asked the mirror. In my head, or on their lips?

The blonde in the mirror tilted back her head and sucked whisky.

I would pick up a taxi at Liverpool Street. I would be at Phil's by lunchtime at the latest. He would be printing in the basement in his green apron which reeked of acetone, that familiar pear-drop smell. When I rang he would answer the door, pushing his hair back with fingers which smeared ink across his forehead forlornly: a rumpled, Ghandhiesque figure.

I thought you were in the country with Jed, he would say, and his lip would flap open like the sole of his left shoe.

I heard the shriek of a whistle as the train entered a deep cleft between houses. For I am the baby borne at speed through the streets in the shrieking ambulance, I thought, and oh, what love I have to spill and what needs to eat him with.

I found him stooped over a makeshift drawing board, lettering a leaflet with a fine black pen. On the wall above his head there was a new poster, a SWAPO poster of a girl militant. Watching his industry, I thought: how he will hate his sturdy comrade now she has come to a full stop.

When I started to sob he spun round, blotting the leaflet.

'It's you,' he said, and took a step back. 'I haven't seen you for weeks.'

I hid my face in my hands.

'People said you weren't at all . . . well.'

I shook my head wildly in protest at the lot of them.

Coming closer, he asked me if I was all right. I touched his hand and felt him flinch. Weeks had gone by since we had touched each other.

He moved past me to shut the door of that familiar waiting room where political people talked and hovered and passed on, and asked where Jed was, and wasn't I supposed to be on holiday?

I forced myself to examine the leaflet.

'Cohabitation Rule,' Phil said. 'A demo at the DHSS.' His eyebrows were raised, the flat Scandinavian forehead wrinkled. He offered me a paint-stained handkerchief.

'I ran away,' I said, 'because I had to see you.'

'Ah.' With the pen Phil made a careful circle of dots on the ball of his thumb.

I wiped my eyes and waited and thought: if only he knew the places I'd been.

'Are you cold? You're shaking.'

'I'm cold.' I thought of the icy journeys of the night.

'Come by the fire.'

'I need to talk to you.' The request frightened me. I heard my voice rise and thin.

Phil swallowed. 'Steady on.' Taking my elbow, he led me to the fire, and moved a cardboard box to make space near the small heat of the one bar. There were kittens in the box, blind and mewing.

'Get warm first.'

I sat down on a cushion on the hearth. Phil installed himself in an armchair beside me, straddling his legs like a grandfather; his belly showed over his trousers. The heaviness in him was new, and it startled me. I clutched at his knee and tried to speak.

In the silence, Phil began to hum a tune.

When the feelings came, they spurted. Desperately I threw words after them, like turves on a dam, to close gaps, fight floods. 'Family,' I cried, appalled at the effort of stemming the flow, and 'rock' and 'love' and 'father'. I shouted them again and again, but still the meanings escaped; I watched them tossed and carried on the current like so much flotsam. Phil patted my shoulder when I told him it was him I loved. He did not say – What about Jed? – but I knew he was thinking it.

'It's like next of kin, don't you see? You get to see them in the cells, before the end.' I saw my tears splash on the dusty tiles of the fireplace, among the brown rings of coffee cups. And heard the useless mouselike scratching of words.

Phil cleared his throat. He was speaking. 'I rather thought it was I who was on trial,' he was chiding, with a faint smile, 'but somehow I don't think they'll hang me for it.'

I shook my head impatiently. There was so little time left, and in any case, weren't Phil's ears quite closed?

Fury entered the room as a murderous weight, thickening the air. I saw the flesh of Phil's cheeks flatten against the bones. I will protect him, I thought, burying my face in his lap. The springs of the armchair made a grinding sound. I heard his slow breathing, and the ticking of the clock on the mantlepiece. I waited, terrified, but he did not die.

And then everything began to happen too fast. Somewhere a liquefaction was going on; a personality was melting.

I heard a woman's voice shout out in protest, and felt a hand on my head. But then all structures slipped away and the journey began.

It was a journey of erratic speed, rainbow-coloured, through shifting spirals of seashells and whorled molluscs and silver-frilled, undulating starfish. A journey without words, of image, sound, sense – a roller-coaster dash down into the waters of a bay, down into phosphorescence. I came up with a splash, blinking, from the radiant spray, a mere baby who knew no better than to stare and adore, but then away up I was tossed, sickeningly high, a scandal: the sky turned red with rage. And then down again lurching through a feeling which lived in a sound like a squeal of axles; then, just after, a grey straight ride through sandbanks which was despair, until, once again, the exhilarating soaked brilliance, in which I tried to stay, crouching, through which I looked up at Phil, dazzled.

'So that is the meaning,' I said, believing I had died.

'What is the meaning?' Phil asked, and I stared blankly at him.

Doors opened and shut, militants and acquaintances came and went, but I was past caring.

'Primroses,' said Phil, and touched the wilted flowers on my lapel. How fastidiously his lips moved.

'Exactly what is it you fear will happen to you?'

'Sliding,' I whispered, holding to the last iridescence. 'Farther in.' There was the room, farther than the web of words could reach. There were events intrinsic only to white rooms. Mad, madder, maddest. I was slipping through his fingers, and still he did not realise how little time was left. My hand pinning his was already skeletal.

'Beyond recognition.'

Phil leaned forward to catch the whisper. I looked at him beseechingly. If he only wanted to, he could blow away the terrors with his strong laugh.

His eyes flitted restlessly; his teeth nibbled at matchsticks, at fingernails. Yes, I thought, he is keeping something from me.

He hoisted himself up out of the armchair and loomed above me. If I were big enough, I thought, I would turn him upside down and shake him till the truth dropped out like a hidden ring. I looked up at him resentfully. Big, bigger, biggest.

'I used to know a good massage. Perhaps that would relax you?' He took a doubtful step towards the door. 'But I really ought to write up some minutes first.'

I was astonished. 'But you can't leave now.'

He stopped. His mouth was trying to smile. 'I wasn't intending to go farther than the toilet.'

On the landing the noise of the printing press drifted up, an everyday clatter. There were three linoleum-covered steps up to the toilet. I sat on the top one and waited. Holding the door open, I listened to the click of his belt as he unclasped it.

'I'm having a shit,' he said. His peevish expression told me that he still did not realise that these were exceptional times.

'I don't mind.' I smiled tolerantly at him.

He shrugged, and his patched jeans sank around his knees.

'You need that shoe mended,' I reminded him. When he squeezed, his face went red and I grinned my encouragement; when the smell filled the toilet I savoured it. The richness was a comfort to me.

Afterwards I followed him back to the room hung with stencils, where his hands stripped me, laid me out on the floor, strongly kneaded me. When I tried to explain exactly why I had needed to stick close to his warmth and fur, his solids and substance, he ordered me not to talk, and I felt his weight bear down hard on my back. My legs flopped and rolled as he lifted and dropped them gently.

The front door slammed and quick footsteps started up

the stairs. Alarmed, I crawled under the meagre blankets on Phil's mattress, scattering cats.

Phil whispered at the door, explaining something. He returned with a girl I had seen on the fringes of meetings, a very young girl with full cheeks and an eager, fluttering smile.

They would sleep upstairs in Jed's bed, Phil said, but they would stay until I fell asleep. They dimmed the lights and stroked the kittens. I dozed gratefully, with the murmur of their voices in the background.

I woke when a body slid into bed beside me and shunted me over to make space for itself. A change of plan, I thought. Still, the warmth of the body was consoling.

The room was empty and peaceful. Downstairs all comings and goings had ceased, and the printing press was silent. On the hearth rug the kittens tucked their heads into their mother and purred softly. I watched them until Phil flicked the light off, and then they were gone. He moved on top of me in the dark, lifted me like a limp lamb, pushed into me.

Two days later, Mike and Vi took me to Reuben.

18

I have never been able fully to explain to Matt (who suffers from no loyalties) the nature of my obligation to Vi. My solution to this has been to ban Vi as a subject of conversation. Otherwise it would be too easy for him to lead me into more betrayals.

'It's a healing regression, not a madness one,' Reuben said, as the weeks passed and I grew worse. 'Feel your feelings,' he said smoothly, 'indulge your childhood fantasies. Don't work, don't study, don't organise.' I drew back in fright from this mandate for aimlessness.

'And what will contain me then, if I do nothing?' I whispered, holding my hands wide. Reuben's response was to write his telephone number on a piece of paper and hand it to me. 'Call me,' he said, 'whenever you need to.' Then he came and stood behind my chair and grasped my shoulders firmly.

'You're in my hands now . . . remember that.' He grinned down at me. 'You won't disappear, you know. Just do the things that please you. Follow your desires . . . on your own, yes, but also with people. 'Yes, and sex too,' he added, seeing my shudder. 'There's nothing to be afraid of. You can drift away in it, but you always come back.'

With a courtesy that came from other worlds and other eras, Reuben escorted me to the door. 'You'll thank your lucky stars you had this breakdown,' he said, holding it open for me. 'You'll become more feminine,' he added, 'you might want to dress differently.' In the walnut-framed mirror in his hall I saw myself, whippet-thin, in my rough grey army sweater, and all the warnings I'd ever had from Phil and the others flashed in my head. Brainwashing, they would say: that's what it amounted to. Reuben's hands hovered over his chest, sculpting breast shapes in the air. 'You never know, your breasts might even develop.'

'I'm not a thirteen year old!' I cried, and slammed the heavy door behind me.

The day of the next session arrived, but I found that when I thought of crossing the city and re-entering the anachronistic wax and blotting paper smell of that room where every emotion was permitted, a diaphanous mist drew down across my window, and thickened there, becoming perilous. I knew then that street names and the number of buses would be the first to be blotted out, and that I must not even try to find my way to Reuben's, for the risk of getting lost was simply too great.

Hours later, Vi found me at the window.

'I'm calling a taxi,' she said at once, 'we're going together.'

When Reuben told Vi that it would be necessary to find a safe place for me and Andrew, if mental hospital was to be avoided, she only hesitated for a moment. She was about to move into a flat above the Women's Centre, she told him, while the woman who owned it was away: she could arrange with Melanie for me to use the spare room, at least for the summer.

Reuben commended her with such warmth that she danced from foot to foot with discomfiture. Her eyes darted uneasily around the drab opulence of the consulting room.

Reuben rubbed his hands and looked pleased. 'My feeling is that you'll be fine, June, with your friend here. You can let loose. Do what you like. The trick, you see, is to keep it off the streets.' There was a gleam of mischief in his smile. He turned again to Vi. 'And now I want to ask you to do something for me. May I?' He took Vi's hands and placed them on my waist. 'Can you lift her? Can you take her weight? She'll be demanding, remember.'

Vi flushed red and looked frightened, but she did not rebel. I pitied her, having to lift this great gawk that was me, but before I could apologise for the whole embarrassing pantomime of it she had bent backwards, swinging my feet off the floor. I was carried up on her breasts; they yielded under me, so spongy and vulnerable that I cringed with the fear of crushing them against some tougher underlay of bone and gristle. Yet there seemed to be no such resistance; I was suspended in something as soggy as marsh or cloud. She was taking my weight easily. Her hair brushed my face like a brown feather. I lay upon her, smelling the intimate moist warmth of her breath, for a moment entranced, yet in the same moment beginning to panic, straining to draw back from what was both sumptuous and treacherous, and could open below me an immensity of deprivation. I opened my mouth to cry out that I was too big for this, much too big, and heard Reuben say with ringing cheerfulness:

'You see what a good mother she'll be? I'm confident of that.'

When Vi set me down, we did not look at each other.

Reuben had high hopes that once I was safely installed in the Women's Centre, things would take a turn for the better. And so did I, at first, but having successfully wormed my way in, I began to see a divergence between his notions of safety and mine, and I felt like a fraud. For when Vi came into my room with cups of cocoa, like a ghost in her white Victorian nightdress, was that safe? At least when Jed came to stay, bringing string bags full of vegetables to make sure that I ate, I knew what he wanted of me. But I did not know what Vi expected, or why she should go to such lengths to help me with Andrew, or take me on canal-bank walks and bicycle rides and raids on antique clothes shops. No, even in the enclosed world of the flat above the Women's Centre, this safety which Reuben had promised was elusive. To find sanctuary from the dance of knives, I saw that I would have to become smaller still, to shrink away like Alice, to burrow farther underground.

'This conflict you feel between me and your colleagues,' Reuben said, 'you mustn't let it tear you apart. It's an inner dynamic, rather than an external one.' He leaned forward in his leather armchair, and picked up two pencils from the desk. He held one in each hand and moved them up and down like scales. 'Either or, either or . . . the reality isn't like that.' He brought the two pencils together. 'The reality is that you don't have to deprive yourself, you can have both.'

Seeing that I was unconvinced, he frowned slightly. 'Look, I can prove it to you. If you're agreeable, I can spend an evening with your group.'

I looked at him, quite amazed. 'I don't think you know what you're letting yourself in for.'

Reuben pretended to shiver. 'Will they tear me to pieces, then, these dangerous revolutionaries?' He shook his head.

'I think not. For, you know, no matter how way out their ideas are, people are not so very different from each other underneath.'

I didn't like the smugness in his smile.

The sitting-room in the flat above the Women's Centre was, by the standards of the group, far too luxurious. Melanie had furnished it in a kind of alternative bordello style, with lush red pile carpets, heaped velvet cushions, and thick curtains with bobbly fringes. The ceiling was disguised by a draped canopy of Indian muslin,and there were a great many mirrors on the walls among the left-wing posters. In a corner by the fireplace stood a black and red lacquered screen hung with chiffon scarves and long strings of beads, and dotted around the room were low tables of cane and glass, and lamps with dimming switches and art nouveau shades.

Reuben arrived late for the communal dinner which Vi had cooked, so I offered him the remains of the blancmange, which he refused. In the kitchen I brewed real coffee for him, procrastinating, while next door the group waited. Eventually, though, the moment of confrontation could be postponed no longer, and I was obliged to take him through to the sitting-room.

When I introduced him, he seemed smaller than before, less rock-like. He delved his hands deeper into the pockets of his cable-knit cardigan and nodded gravely to everyone. His face was masked by a professional blandness, and showed none of its usual irony. This insipid look bothered me. I wondered if he was making a special effort to look humble in the presence of all these socialists, and whether he believed that by flying democratic colours he would somehow evade attack.

After the introductions the group went on talking amongst themselves, which struck me as unnecessarily rude, but I was hardly in a position to take them to task, and so I sat down on a beaded cushion and waited for something to happen. Reuben sat down next to me, straight-backed and alert in a half-lotus, silent in the murmur of political gossip. I watched him covertly for signs of fear. Across the room, Jed's face was half hidden behind the stained glass shade of a low hanging lamp, and lit in lozenges of pink and green; he was saying something to Vi about Melanie, and Vi was arguing. Beside him Phil made a note in a diary and put it in his jacket pocket; then he sat with his hands folded. I watched him not watching me and worried once again about the trouble I was causing: the juggling of appointments, the meetings they must have neglected in order to be here.

As the conversation died away, eyes focused on Reuben. 'Who's the top man and top woman in this group?' he asked into the silence, with awful innocence.

Above my head the muslin canopy whispered. It was, of course, the worst possible beginning, and would be taken as a calculated provocation. It was obvious that all my warnings had falled on deaf ears. With an artless expression, Reuben waited for his answer. I knew that Phil would be the one to reply, and watched him battle with himself about whether Reuben's question was malicious, or simply naive. In the end he must have decided to give Reuben the benefit of the doubt, for when he spoke it was in the patient, schoolmasterish voice which he reserved for the politically illiterate. 'You see,' he said carefully, 'we don't have leaders here. We work collectively.'

True, I thought; liar, I thought: it's you, and it was me, before I toppled right through the bottom of everything.

Reuben blinked and stroked his beard. 'Don't misunderstand me. I respect your politics. I have no intention of attacking your politics.' His voice was mild. 'It's what goes on between people . . . the underlying dynamics are what I'm after.'

Tom leaned forward, rocking slightly. He was squatting on a cushion on the other side of the fireplace from Phil, and his head was framed against an Angry Brigade poster which said that an army of lovers could not lose. His lips moved for a moment before words came. 'Give us one good reason why we should trust you.' He smoothed his white wing of hair and looked round the room challengingly. 'Shouldn't we know more about where he's coming from? I mean, we don't know what we're getting into here.'

'You want to know my qualifications, perhaps?' said Reuben helpfully.

There were nods from everyone except Vi, who, with a disgusted look at Tom, said she would make tea, and left the room.

Reuben gave a faint shrug, and began to list his credentials. Clinical psychology, group dynamics consultant to several consortiums, Harley Street practice.

'Ah!' said Tom, and sat back, with a satisfied look. Behind the stained glass lamp Jed's back slid a little lower down the wall, and his sharp knees poked up, hiding his face completely. Reuben was smiling, unperturbed, quite unaware that Tom had just blown his cover. I shrank smaller on my cushion, and blushed for him.

Vi came back into the room with a tea-tray. Her earrings, which were made from clusters of miniature bells, tinkled when she moved; her eyes were panda eyes, black-ringed, anxiously peering. When Reuben crooked his arms as if cradling a child and asked if anyone knew anything about caring and nurturing, the huge eyes filled with tears. I strained to see how the others were taking this, but the room seemed suddenly dark, as if someone had dimmed the lights; now, of all times, when it was so vital to get to the truth of the matter.

The child, though, I could see clearly enough. It was wrapped in shawls and Paddipads: a baby burden, clinging, crying, shitting yellow runnels down Reuben's white cardigan.

In whose hands was I?

Phil coughed. Phil spoke. His face was not right. It was long and stiff and straight as a door. 'We all want to help June through it . . . whatever "it" is. But June doesn't seem to think that the care being offered is adequate for her.'

I hung my head and saw my outlandish expectations, and

my ravenous demands, and my mother's long-suffering face, and didn't know how to atone for any of it.

When I risked looking up again, Vi seemed to be opening her mouth to say something, but then Phil waved his hand – order, comrades, order – and returned to the issue of leadership.

'Everyone in the group plays an equal part,' he told Reuben, with a smile of surprising charm, 'just different parts, that's all.' With a sweep of his arm he enclosed all of us in a communal enterprise. He looked to Jed, he explained, when it came to any kind of direct action – 'Which you may not see as necessary,' he added, 'but we see it differently.' He paused, as if waiting for Jed to comment, but Jed said nothing. 'Tom,' he went on, 'Tom's the practical organiser. And June, the theorist – on feminism, and things like that.'

'Socialism too, I would have said,' Vi said tartly.

'And Vi, of course.' Phil eyed her, 'I'd rely on Vi to stand up and, for instance, say the right thing . . .' he smiled faintly, '. . . shout the right thing, at Council meetings, and . . . occasions when spontaneity is called for?'

The rest of us were sipping the tea Vi had brought, and Phil was going on and on, distributing roles like favours at a Christmas party. In normal times, I thought bitterly, I would take the floor from him.

Reuben listened with every appearance of interest to Phil's speech, and then resumed his questions, wanting to know, this time, about the sexual side of things.

Once again I froze, waiting for Reuben to disgrace himself. I'd already tried to prepare him, to explain that sexual relationships were as much a matter for political struggle as anything else, but after hearing me out with the driest of smiles he professed himself quite flummoxed. He had no line on such things, he said, and was more than content to be old-fashioned. Angry at his complacency, I countered with: 'I wonder how content your wife is,' but it turned out that he had a girlfriend, not a wife, who wasn't, he added sweetly, a 'women's libber', but a very forceful person all the same.

Jed's head appeared from behind the coloured lampshade. He began to talk about freedom, and why he and everyone else in the group believed that the nuclear family was a bad thing. He started out in fine style, and spoke with passion, but in the middle of explaining how marriage and monogamy perpetuated women's oppression he suddenly stammered, and went red, and demanded: 'What about you, anyway? What's *your* sexual practice, since we're on the subject?'

Unfair, unfair, I thought. Jargon like that means nothing to Reuben.

'Frequent,' said Reuben, and grinned.

Vi let out a startled giggle, which she immediately stifled. Simultaneously, a tremor passed through the men in the room, a tensing for combat. Sexist, someone muttered. Reuben's smile remained, but his hand strayed nervously across the bald spot on the back of his head. Jed stared hard at me, and then at Reuben, and his expression was ugly. If he led the attack, I didn't think that I would be able to protect Reuben. For Jed had my interests at heart, I was certain of it; he was only trying to make sure that Reuben was worthy of my trust. He was the one I had told about the brainwashing incident, and so naturally he was suspicious, naturally he wanted to protect me. He might be angry and do violence, but his motives were pure. I, on the other hand, plunged deeper into betrayal with every step I took.

The night before, I had dreamed luminously. There was a room divided by a makeshift partition; one half was a printshop, the other half a garage. It seemed to be my father's garage, for it had the same grease-puddled floor and stacked boxes containing screwdrivers and wire brushes and spark-plugs. The group was there, on the printshop side, and in the garage half were half a dozen women from the Women's Centre. When I tried to talk to the women about Reuben they fell silent and eyes flickered away. At last one of the women spoke.

Why do you call him The Shrink, she asked, when presumably you're intensely involved with him? There was a glint of envy in her eye.

Exactly, said another voice, it's so depersonalising.

I searched for the correct answer, the answer which would also satisfy those on the other side of the partition, but before I found it, four or five other people arrived and asked me if I wanted to go for a drive. They had kind faces, so I agreed gladly, and followed them up the rickety stairs out of the basement. But as I climbed towards the light I felt an unfamiliar bulge chafing between my legs. It seemed to be a disposable nappy of some kind, and it was patterned with blue flowers, like the sanitary towels I'd worn after Andrew was born. Stealthily I loosened my jeans and pulled it out, and threw it into the dark cavity under the stairs.

As we emerged into the sunshine, I saw a woman with a pram pass by. She wore only a transparent plastic raincoat, and underneath, damply sagging and unmistakable, was that very same blue-sprigged bundle. Agonised with embarrassment, I began talking loudly and dogmatically, to distract the attention of my new companions.

In the room above the Women's Centre, Vi's earrings tinkled as pleasantly as bells on a pram, and the skirmish had not broken out after all. Instead, character witnesses were talking about June. I turned my head from side to side, listening to one conduct report after another.

In whose hands was I?

I opened my mouth, once, to intervene on my own behalf, but at the last moment a delicious spite overtook me, and I lay back luxuriously on the velvet cushion and vowed to say nothing. After all, hadn't I taken enough initiatives these last few years?

'For now,' Reuben had said, 'you will move best by standing still. Leave the future to its own devices for once.'

So now, if it pleased me, I would turn away. The speeches of a lunatic would in any case carry little weight.

I looked round the dim room with a vague smile which

included everyone. Crossing my fingers behind my back, I hoped that Reuben in his wisdom was instructing them all to be gentle.

19

On the first morning of the school holidays Marie looked at my set face and asked if I minded Andrew going away for such a long time. But passing Andrew, 'here and there and from one to another', as my mother put it, wasn't something I felt like discussing. I didn't feel like talking about the flurry of washing and mending and packing, or about the tactful way Andrew was trying, as usual, to hide his excitement about crossing the frontier in the cold war. And certainly I couldn't confide in her how, at times like this, the past rose up with a grim face and arraigned me for my failures: for all the games I hadn't played, stories I hadn't told, stability I hadn't provided; for all the months (years?) in which Andrew had had a mother only in name. And so I replied curtly that it was routine, I'd got used to it. 'Plenty of mothers would envy my freedom,' I added, 'so I can hardly complain, can I?'

Rebuffed, Marie said that she supposed so, and sighed, and wandered out of the kitchen. And I turned back to the cooker, and to Andrew's scrambled egg. He'd already said that he wasn't hungry, but I knew that if I didn't persuade him to eat before the train he would spend pounds in the buffet on pork pies and Seven Up. At the kitchen table he was turning the pages of a comic, pretending to read. I piled the scrambled egg on to a plate of toast, poured orange squash, and set it down in front of him. He leaned his head on one hand, slumped forward over the plate, and sucked the butter-soaked toast up like ice-cream.

Behind him the roses tapped their heavy yellow heads against the window, and a wind bent the long grass of the lawn. I thought of the flat country where he was bound, a country of marsh and silt, without windbreaks, and as I watched him eat I could see by his absent-mindedness that he had already departed, was already rushing headlong on the blue and yellow train across fens and latticed ditches towards his father's arms. I couldn't stop the explosion. 'Use a fork, can't you? And for God's sake, blow your nose. *Then* you can breathe. *Then* you can eat with your mouth closed.' I threw a Kleenex on the table, disliking myself.

He sighed. 'All *right*.' He screwed the tissue around his nostrils and let out a tiny snort.

Already he's comparing us. Already Daddy wins hands down. I wondered suddenly if his father watched him as jealously for signs of preferring me. It didn't seem likely.

Andrew was swallowing the last mouthful, thrusting the plate away, getting up from the table. 'Pack something to read,' I said, 'in case it rains a lot.'

He stopped in the doorway, with a guarded expression on his face. 'I'll have comics waiting for me. My dad orders them now – three a week.' He counted on his fingers. 'Since the Easter holidays . . . that makes . . . thirty-six.' A smile slipped through. I looked at him, storing him up. By September he would be hardly recognisable. The spurt of growth, the thickening of the shoulders. Each time he went away he came back looking more like his father. An extra height to the arch of the eyebrows, a fast blink to express surprise. The mannerisms stuck.

It was getting late. 'Brush your hair now, and fetch your coat.' With a long-suffering look, he vanished upstairs. And if I didn't order you about, I thought, if I didn't send you off brushed and sleeked and full to bursting, I'd soon hear about it, wouldn't I? I put on my jacket and checked my purse for fare money, for keys, for his ticket. Hurry, I thought, straining towards the moment in the echoing station when we would wave rather too cheerfully, and it would all be over and done with; only speed, I knew, would smother the diffuse ache.

'Move it!' I called, 'We're walking to the Tube.'

'*Walking?*'

'Lazy sod.'

'Coming.'

His feet thumped on the stairs. He'll break his neck, I thought; he's already broken that wrist and the other arm and he's only ten.

We were trying to squeeze his anorak into the packed holdall when the phone rang. I cursed and went to answer it.

On the other end of the line a voice drawled: 'Hiya, Ms Guthrie. It's me, Matt.'

'Oh.' It was a small, foolish sound, like a hamster surprised out of sleep.

'Oh what? Can't you do better than that?'

'I'm rushing for a train.' He, of course, has all the time in the world, I thought.

'A likely story.'

Fuck you.

'Where are you running to?'

'*Andrew* is going to his *father's*.'

'You don't say.' He hesitated. 'Can we meet, then?'

At the door Andrew hopped up and down, pointing at his watch. 'I think not,' I said hastily, 'You read my letter, I presume?'

Matt let out a hoot. 'I sure did. And you read mine – I *presume*.'

'I've got to go right now.'

'Okay, you win . . . but remember . . . '

'Right *now*.'

' . . . I'm going to get you, June Guthrie.'

He laughed again, triumphantly. When I put the phone down that laughter echoed in my ears, rampant, fanatical, and I felt my nipples sting.

20

Matt continued to ring, or so Marie said, and I continued to be out. Eventually she set off for Essex Folk Festival with Tom, Zac, and a carload of camping equipment; then, alone in the house, I tensed each time the phone rang. But it was never Matt. A moral victory, I said to myself, but my dreams told a different story, and as the summer hung heavy on the city and the first stale tinge crept into the green of the leaves, I began to feel cheated.

Mike and I had intended to spend a couple of weeks at the cottage while Mel was at a conference of micro-biologists in Frankfurt; thanks to *Womanright*, however, the plan fell through. The hitch was that we had put forward an idea for an arts supplement to the birthday issue, but when the deadline was nearing, we found that we were short-handed. One by one, having booked their holidays early, Jude and Clara and the others left for Scotland or Crete or the Pyrenees, leaving Mike and me sighing at our schedule, but, like all good martyrs, knuckling down to it.

Apart from this extra work, there were few demands on my time. Without cooking or babysitting to fret about, I felt all manner of stirrings and stretchings inside, as if somewhere in me, great freedoms were limbering up. For a few weeks I could come and go as I pleased, eat or not eat, seek out whatever pleasures the city offered. On the bus home from the office, the evening opened out before me, golden, promising. But somehow, when I'd eaten a makeshift meal of cheese or boiled eggs, and sat alone with the evening paper, trying to choose from a quite petrifying range of films and plays and lectures, the feeling of freedom faded to a dull anxiety. Memories of birthday teas floated back to me, of tables crowded with éclairs and fruitcake and meringues and winged angel cakes frilled with butter-cream. Trapped in the good manners of poverty, I had hung back, envying the other girls their happy appetites, certain that no greed of mine could ever be as innocent.

The past needled. The future accused. Coward, they said, as I pottered round the empty house, snipping dead heads off geraniums, yearning for bedtime stories to read and grey soapsuds to rinse out of childish hair.

I'd expected to spend a few evenings with Mike while Mel was away, but each time I suggested a date she would fuss and flurry in her handbag, and would have mislaid her diary. 'We'd better ring each other,' she would say with a skittish smile, but when I rang she would be heavily and apologetically tied up with old friends from Oxford, or with some bothersome piece of family legislation, or the recurrence of an old back complaint. If I hadn't felt so sure that Sherry loomed large in all of this, I might have challenged these hurtfully thin excuses. But something – more a fear of trespassing than a prejudice, exactly – made me keep my distance. And day by day as we worked together in the semi-deserted office, I waited for Mike to mend the rift between us. It was for her to confide, I thought in a fury of tolerance, not for me to pry; it was none of my business what she chose to do with her time while Mel was away. But date after date fell through, and still she didn't come clean.

One Monday morning Mike didn't turn up for work. I assumed that she was ill, but put off phoning in case she was not. That evening, while I was drying my hair in the kitchen, the doorbell rang. All evening I had been dreamy and slow, as if waiting for something new to enter me, something which the glint of the sun on the tangled deep green garden hinted at, and so, hearing the bell, I stood up, patted my hair like a sleepwalker, and thought calmly: Yes, it will be Matt, come to get me. The crazy lovely certainty carried me as far as the hall, where with my hand on the door I was suddenly back with myself, and wondering at my stupidity. For it was Mike, surely: how could I have imagined anyone else? I opened the door with a thankful smile, ready to forgive her everything now that she'd come to seek me out, and saw, instead of her, a young, thin, freckled face.

'You're June, aren't you?' the girl said. Her lips were chapped, her hair was red and cropped short. It took me a moment to realise that this modish person with the elegantly spiky hairstyle was, in fact, Sherry. 'I'm looking for Michaela,' she said quickly. 'She's a friend of yours, isn't she?'

I nodded enquiringly. Although it was a sultry night, she was wearing a leather motorcycle jacket, tight blue jeans, and suede boots. She held a rider's helmet upturned like a bowl; inside lay a pair of leather gauntlets. Her clear light eyes looked past me, searching.

'I wondered if she was here?'

'Sorry,' I said, still holding the door, 'I haven't seen her.'

'What's the matter with her these days?' Sherry edged closer. It was obvious that she wanted to come in, and equally obvious that I did not want her to. Abashed, I stood back. 'Why don't you come in for a minute?'

'I could do with a drink of water, if that's not too much trouble.' She put her helmet on the hallstand and followed me to the kitchen, while I wondered how to avoid offering her tea. She brought out a packet of ten Players and offered me one. 'Smoke?' Her eyes travelled indifferently over my face. I felt myself flush. To her I was no more than a fast passage to Mike, and she was making no attempt to hide it.

'No thanks,' I said curtly, and her chin came up. She ruffled her hair, so that it stood up around her head in a red brush.

'She's gone missing, did you know that?'

I was shaken, but determined not to show it, for her tone was proprietorial, and it rankled. 'Oh, but that's nonsense. I'm sure I'd know, if anything was wrong.' Would I, I thought, would I?

Sherry rose to the challenge. 'So do you know where she is, then?'

Hiding from you, most likely, I thought angrily.

'Or where else she hangs out?'

I fought off a wave of pure temper. If she wanted

information, she was certainly going about it the wrong way. 'No,' I lied, 'I don't.'

Suddenly the fight seemed to go out of her, and she dropped into a chair. 'I don't get it,' she said miserably, 'I just don't get it.' Her shoulders drooped, and her head rolled back, and her eyelids closed. Her neck was smooth, her mouth vulnerable; she looked very young. 'I have to see that girl,' she muttered.

She looked so defenceless that I felt ashamed. 'I'm sorry I can't help. All I know is that she didn't come to work. Perhaps she just went away for the weekend . . . but I do think it's too soon to start worrying about it.'

'Without telling me, though?' Sherry opened red-rimmed eyes. She shook her head. 'It's because I was shitty to her, I know it.' She turned to me. 'I've got to say sorry, see?'

'Probably she's at her parents. They're quite demanding, I think.' I looked away shiftily. I couldn't bring myself to say that Mike and I had fixed up a theatre date for Wednesday. But perhaps she wouldn't turn up now, anyway.

Sherry shook her head again, and stared gloomily at her hands, stretching them out so that I could see the scratches. 'I came off the bike,' she said. I sensed that I was to take this as proof of something, but whether of her need, her regret, or her sincerity, I couldn't tell. I was afraid that she was on the brink of confessions that I didn't want to hear, because loyalty to Mike forbade it, and also because I didn't know how long it would take. I edged towards the door.

Sherry took the hint, and stood up quickly. 'Can I use your loo?' she said, in a slightly huffy voice. I noticed her quick inquisitive glance through the open door of Marie's room, and fought off a sudden mean suspicion that upstairs she might feel free to roam about and peer through other doors, rummaging for traces of Mike.

When she came down, I handed her her helmet and gloves.

'I'll be off, then,' she said, with a hard little smile which only made her look more fragile. 'Ta, anyway.'

'Sorry I couldn't be more help. But if I see her I'll tell her you're looking for her.'

'Yeah. Ta.' She looked at me sideways, a wary, testing look. 'You don't think she'd give me the run around, do you? I mean, she's not the type, is she?' She revolved the upturned helmet in her hands, hesitating.

I leapt to Mike's defence. 'Oh no. I'm sure she wouldn't.' But after Sherry's motorbike had spluttered, started, and revved away, I found myself wondering just how sure I was.

Mike failed to appear at the office next day, and none of my phone calls succeeded in locating her, so by Wednesday night I was worrying, and I ate with my eye on my watch and images of Sherry and her clashing in my mind.

At seven-thirty sharp her car drew up outside, and she picked her way up the steps, smiling, swaying like a mannequin on her high-heeled sandals. She wore a navy silk dress, 'forties style, with a row of pearl buttons down the front. In wordless apology, she pressed her hands into a steeple. It was an awkward mime which she was too self-conscious to carry off.

'I know I'm becoming unreliable,' she said, 'but I wouldn't miss our date, would I?' She followed me into the kitchen, and stood by the window looking out at the garden. 'It's so peaceful, this room,' she sighed. Her arms and legs were unevenly tanned, and there were bleached streaks in her hair. I waited for her to tell me where she had been.

'You look thinner,' I said tentatively.

'Oh yes.' She swung round to face me. 'I have lost a little weight. One benefit of love traumas!' She smoothed her skirt over her hips and suddenly decisive, added: 'I owe you an apology. I have seen her. It was pretty awful of her to come barging in on you like that.'

I hesitated. 'You weren't really hiding?'

'I most certainly was.' She made a wry face. 'I scooted off to my little country shack . . . I *am* sorry, to have left you holding the baby.' She stood stiffly, with her stomach held in to accommodate the cut of the fashionably old-fashioned dress. Her chest rose and fell sharply. 'But in the end duty called, and all that.'

'Look, don't worry about it. It was only a day or two.'

Mike sat down at the table and took a cigarette from my packet. She lit one and gave a short laugh. 'Anyway, she was waiting outside the house when I got back. Perched on her motorbike, eating a bag of chips. Mel, luckily, is still away.' She shuddered briefly. 'So there we are. Wherever that is.'

I sat down beside her. 'Are you sure you're all right?'

'Not really. Brave face, you know. You know what a coward I am.'

'Sherry was in a bit of a state.'

Mike held her cigarette upside down and watched it burn. The smoke rose through her fingers. 'Yes, I'm sure she was. We've a lot to sort out.' Her voice was flat. 'It's a question of getting myself to face up to things . . . ' She looked at her watch and stood up abruptly, dangling car keys from her finger.

'Yes,' I said, 'We should go, if we're going.'

'Well, I'm keeping my minor resolutions, at least,' she said with a brittle animation. 'I've taken up early morning swimming.' She laughed. 'Every day is the aim, but needless to say the discipline isn't quite up to it yet.'

On the way to the theatre Mike drove fast and badly. She sat in a hunched position over the wheel, clutching it so tightly that her wedding ring dug into her finger. In heavy traffic at Highbury roundabout she glanced across at me. 'She thinks I'm playing with her, you see. "Bloody bisexuals" she says.'

We came up behind a large container lorry, and Mike braked just too close to the tail lights for comfort. I held on to my safety belt. Ahead of us air brakes hissed, and the lorry swayed on its suspension, speeding up. Mike accelerated. 'She says I've got to make a decision.'

'About Mel?' I looked at her anxiously.

She nodded. 'She's right!' she burst out, 'I mean, all this hole and corner stuff, it's ghastly. The way we have to sneak off to pubs miles away from anywhere, or these afternoons in her bedsit . . . ' She bit her lip. 'It has that awful wood-grained wallpaper, you know, and the gas ring's got burnt milk encrusted on it . . . just unutterably depressing . . . oh, I *know* I'm being bourgeois, but I just can't pretend to like it.'

I kept a wary eye on the road and tried to cope with a welter of thoughts. I wanted to ask if she had thought of helping Sherry financially but that was a tricky subject, for Mike's guilt often made her see attacks where there were none. It was a paranoia I felt impatient with, but I didn't want to put her on the defensive. 'I don't think it's bourgeois. I'm sure Sherry doesn't like it much either.' I was treading carefully, I thought, but I saw from the stiffening of Mike's back that I had blundered. '*Can* you choose, though?' I said quickly.

Mike's face was prim. 'I just want to do right by her.' The oddly formal words made me think of honourable marriages and property settlements. Mike took a sharp right hand bend at speed, and then we were climbing towards Hornsey, passing under a vertiginous metal bridge. She looked around helplessly. 'Where do we turn? Am I going the right way?'

'Here,' I ordered, 'turn here.' We drew up in a side road by a grey granite church which had been converted into a community centre. Mike parked neatly and turned the ignition off.

'So what does one do?' she said, flexing her fingers and opening them wide, as if to let sand trickle through.

I shook my head irresolutely. She had said so little about feelings, and so much about responsibilities, I had no idea what on earth I was supposed to offer her. Some ready-made ethics, perhaps? But ethics were out of style, and in any case I had none which could encompass a situation so far away from my own experience. 'But it depends on what *you* want, too, doesn't it?'

'Ha!' she exclaimed, 'Safety, of course – what else?'

This time I didn't even attempt to contradict her, but simply sat there, feeling more and more ignorant, and more and more vexed, wanting to say that I too had felt the tug of desire, that I too wanted always to do the right thing . . . but was the right thing always to be found in restraint, loyalty, principle, or did it live instead in the recklessness of wishes and the truths that only my dreams spoke of?

Mike gave me a rueful look. 'Disregard that little outburst. You're right. Self-punishment isn't really helpful, is it?'

I shook my head. 'Forget it. I'm a coward too.'

Mike made no move to get out of the car. A queue was forming by the entrance of the community centre, so after a moment I put my hand on the door. 'Shall we go in?'

As we climbed the steps I took her arm, and felt her yield and lean towards me a little. The evening air smelt of jasmine and melting tar. Overhead, plane tree branches hung motionless in the heat. I looked up through the pointed leaves and saw broken patches of a sky tinged now with apricot and ribboned with the easy drift of narrow clouds, and for a second I was wide open, and light, and sure. I turned to Mike. 'It's who you *love*,' I urged, 'who you *love*.' I was entranced with the simplicity, the energy of it. Not so Mike. Some kind of shame flared in her eyes, and she looked quickly away. 'No, no, I'm not saying that *I* live by it – only that it's what *matters*. It's what's *necessary*.'

Mike gently disengaged her arm, and made much of opening her handbag and getting her purse out, and suddenly I was neither sure nor soaring, but earthbound again, observing myself, worrying that I had offended her, worrying about that terrible naiveté of mine which could burst out so unexpectedly. 'Spoken like a true romantic,' I added, by way of apology. We shuffled forward with the queue, our elbows rubbing together awkwardly.

Suddenly Mike said: 'Did you see Sherry's wrists?'

'No, she had long sleeves . . .' I thought of the bruised knuckles, and then I understood what she meant. 'No!'

Mike nodded. Her face became masked, professional. 'She's tried pills too. Oh, not recently, and never *very* seriously. But still, you have to take anything like that seriously, don't you?' She set her lips together tidily.

Following the queue, we moved out of the sunshine and into the chillier shade of a rhododendron bush. The flowers had fallen, and the dark green leaves were silhouetted, razor-sharp, against the sunlit church wall. I shivered. 'But how much responsibility can you take?'

Mike poked with her toe at a heap of dry pink rhododendron flowers, stirring them. 'Oh June, it's so sickeningly *unequal.* I mean, what has she known, except institutions? And here I am with my privileges and my scruples . . . and yes, my needs for men, for that kind of identity. It's not so easy to dispense with that, it seems.'

'No, I'm sure it isn't,' I said with a secret stirring of relief.

'Anyway, I'm sorry for all the doom and gloom . . . one just has to hope that it will work out, I suppose.' She drew herself up and became businesslike. 'I was going to say, will you let me pay for the tickets . . . ?'

I shook my head, and said no, but she could go and buy me a whisky if she insisted.

When I reached the bar the diffident Mike had not yet been served. Stranded in a crowd of shirt-sleeved, sweaty men, she looked in need of care and protection.

'You've got to shove.' I demonstrated by wriggling my way in. 'Just watch the men do it.' I waved a pound note across the counter and smiled over my shoulder at her, enjoying the small display, when just then there was a resistance, an intransigent forearm in contact with mine and lodged there, not giving way. In the corner of my eye, a tartan shirt stirred. I planted my elbows on the bar and turned to glare at it.

'Hi there, June,' a cool voice said from on high. Six inches above me, blue eyes considered me over the rim of a beer glass.

'Well, Matt, what a surprise,' my voice chirped.

'Is it?' he said, as my hand opened, and the pound note fluttered down into the dark chasm between the bar counter and the packed, leaning bodies. Matt let out a snort of laughter, and crouched down to help in the search. We met face to face in a forest of knees. It was impossible not to be conscious of the half-unbuttoned shirt gaping open almost to his waist, and of the prickled rough jaw, and the tender hollow at the base of his throat. His cheeks sucked in, swallowing a smile, as he allowed the silence to take shape between us.

'Shall we?' he said at last, and crawled, groping, with his

nose to the ground and his bum in the air and the most earnest expression on his face. And as I watched him, down there in the glade hidden from the grown-ups, I sat back on my heels and trembled with laughter and fright.

Matt held up the note and pressed it into my palm. He closed my hand around it and winked, like a kind uncle giving secret pocket money. Then he released my hand, and we stood up, and conversation was necessary.

'Mike works with me at the magazine,' I told him. He inclined his head and, for some reason, looked amused. I introduced him to Mike without defining him – an actor? Vi's ex? The explanations could always be whispered later in the privacy of the darkened auditorium. Fixing him with a determinedly friendly smile, I asked if he had seen the theatre company before. No, he replied, but someone he knew in Berkeley said they were hot stuff. And how his writing was faring – No comment – and whether he had given up his driving job? – You bet! With each answer he retreated farther. His smile faltered, and finally faded. A pained, yearning expression took its place. With Mike right there beside us, I felt I had to cover up for him, and kept talking, until in the end he cut me off in mid-sentence.

'I'm with friends,' he said tightly, pointing to the far end of the room. Then he was moving away, weaving through the crowd with his beer glass held above their heads.

Beside me Mike was trying to hold her ground in the shifting and jostling. In my agitation, I had hardly said a word to her.

'He's attractive.' Her face was sad.

'Do you think so?' I said casually, while the joy rose in my throat.

All the players in the theatre group were women. The black-haired actress was mountainous in satin, her decolletage deep and sleazy, her lace soiled and trailing. A small cowboy in long johns sidled up to her, spinning pistols from his thumbs. In one jerk she had him by the scruff of the neck. His feet dangled, his mournful rat face registered helplessness, his thumb popped into his mouth.

Mike and I sat on our hard horsehair cushions and howled.

'It's so savage,' Mike said, 'It's magic.'

The actress dragged the macho baby to the back of the stage and hung him up on a hook like an old coat, and there he dangled, dolefully sucking his thumb. Then on the stage there was a princess, and a cross-eyed frog which crouched on her pillow, wanking most horribly. The cross-eyed frog became a cross-eyed prince who croaked dirty suggestions in the princess's ear. Bewildered about which suitor to choose, she consulted the audience.

'The frog,' we cried in unison, 'Go for the frog.' I put my head on Mike's shoulder and wept with laughter. Under the hot lights the actresses were baying, sweating, farting, flaying the audience; with every swagger and shout they were urging us to expand, to go at the world big and raw and unexpurgated. In the front row, a man complained loudly that he hadn't paid good money to see childish obscenities, and one or two people got up to leave. A cheer went up as they reached the exit. Yes, I thought, nothing could be more dreary than the barriers of the decent, the sensible. Matt knew it. Matt saw through it. The cramped spirit, the strategic lie, the exchange of words deadened by restraint. 'But you,' he'd said, 'you're a poet.' I glanced up at the tiered seats behind me, seeking out his face, needing to gauge his response, but I could not find him.

'One advantage of women's liberation', the fat actress was saying in a pious voice, 'it did help me to come out as a *bitch*.'

The audience whooped their gratitude.

After the encores, our hair lay flat and our arms shone with sweat.

'What a tonic,' Mike sighed, fanning herself with her programme.

While Mike queued for the Ladies, I watched for Matt. When the long figure emerged, blinking in the lights, it looked as if he might pass without a word or a glance, so with new found brazenness I asked him for a cigarette. He stopped beside me, patting the top pocket of his shirt. He looked distinctly uneasy.

'Weren't they terrific? Such energy, didn't you think so?'

He offered me a packet of Embassy speechlessly. His face

above me was all O's of eyes and cheeks and mouth, cherubic, slightly stupid; the few hairs on his chest were plastered flat with sweat.

'What was so marvellous,' I persisted, 'was the sheer sadism of it.' I smiled up at him, wondering why his telephone fluency had deserted him. When he did speak, his voice was scathing.

'They certainly knock shit out of the British groups. You feminists over here could learn a lot from them.'

I opened my mouth to argue, and, realising that I agreed with him, closed it again. Already he was looking over my head, searching for someone: evidently I was to understand that I was delaying him. Fair enough, I thought, he's entitled to play it cool too. Tit for tat. It would only make me more determined not to lose him again. I spread my hands. 'I wanted to apologise. I didn't mean to be as unfriendly as I was.'

And then he was fully engaged. He put his hand on the wall and leaned over me. 'You don't say.' His voice was grim.

I said hastily, 'It was the situation I couldn't deal with. Everything was so tangled.'

He shook his head at me. His face was changing, closing; now it was long and flat-planed under the heavy straggling eyebrows, long and thin and bitter. The hard stare went on and on, until I dropped my eyes and leaned weakly back against the wall. Now that I had come out into the open, he was going to reject whatever I offered, reject it out of hand. And that would be that.

'You hurt me,' he said flatly.

'I couldn't help it, believe me. It wasn't something I enjoyed.'

'Yeah?'

'You think I got a kick out of it?'

'How do I know? How do I know what you women get off on?'

I looked up sharply, ready for a fight, but there was a glint in his eye, a self-irony which took the edge off the words. He reached out and picked up my wrist. It was a light, experimental touch, as if the pulse rate or the temperature of the skin would supply him with all the information he needed.

'Don't call us, we'll call you,' I laughed, to conceal my

pleasure. He let go of my hand.

'Seriously, though. Can I ring you? I'd really like to sort it out, somehow.'

The red lips pouted. 'I don't know,' he said, slow and sour, 'I don't know if I should.'

I stared. Was he flirting? Playing hard to get?

'I don't know if I trust you.'

I could detect no irony in his face now. For an unsteady, bewitched moment I stood there in a trance, vulnerable and transparent, wondering what knowledge he was privy to. Suddenly there was no hiding place. It was as if he had spied on my dreams and gleaned information there that even I was ignorant of – something cruel I had done, perhaps, or some undisclosed wickedness deep within me.

'You really don't have a clue, do you?' he said.

I stood stock-still in the trap, searching my conscience.

'About what?' I said, 'About what?'

'About how you put me through it!'

'But you're exaggerating, surely.' I spoke with an effort. 'I'll ring you. We don't have to sort it out now . . .'

'When?' he rapped.

I was shaken by his fierceness, and wondered for a second if it wouldn't be wiser to drop the whole business and back out gracefully. But a perverse obstinacy drove me on. I would make him see my side. I would make him see sense. 'In a day or two,' I retorted.

Matt folded himself back against the wall, turning concave under my eyes. His fingers fumbled with his shirt buttons, modestly, even prudishly, doing them up. His force was weakening, his whole body signalling some kind of timidity. 'I don't know,' he muttered again.

I watched this unfamiliar Matt with the beginnings of exasperation. The wilting lily, I thought: quite a performance.

On the far side of the foyer Mike was craning, waving. I brushed Matt's arm lightly. 'I'll ring you, okay?' And before he could contradict I hurried off to usher Mike through the dawdling, chattering crowd and out into the freshness of the night.

21

On the ground beside the well, frail propellers of sycamore fruits. I gather a handful and toss them up, and they fall, spinning.

Good girl/bad girl. I only have to touch him, and everything is topsy-turvy.

Of course there never really was any question of resisting him. Anyone else could have seen that. Vi did see it, clearly. The only wonder is that I held out for so long.

Excuses.

But surely, after so many years of playing safe, even saints and martyrs would be susceptible to the unruly forces of malice and delight.

Excuses, excuses.

I stuck my head out of the office window. It had rained at last, and a sharp, singed smell drifted up from the streets. Across the road in the metal workshop a man on an arc welder was silhouetted against blue flashes. An ice-cream van trundled past, with its speakers grinding out a distorted version of 'The Bells of St. Mary's'.

In the editorial meeting a fight had broken out between Jude and Clara; it was about an article which Jude had promised to edit, and had promptly forgotten about. As a rule Jude was an easygoing woman, quick to laugh irreverently, and not given to defensivess. Clara was her polar opposite – tall and pale to Jude's dark sturdiness, pernickety to Jude's effervescence. But this time Jude had been roused to fury, had thrown the unedited article down on the desk, shouting that she was tired of taking on dud articles which no one else would touch with a bargepole.

'I never wanted to do it in the first place,' she said, glaring at Clara.

Clara began to fling books and papers into her bag; her hands were trembling and she was nearly in tears. 'Why should I always have to pick up the pieces for you?' Her voice rose shrilly. 'When you're always criticising *me* for not getting things in to deadline. It's typical of you!'

'Because it's *true*!' There was a silence in which Clara sniffed several times. Jude looked as if she was trying to bridle her anger. 'You were late for your office day again,' she said flatly, 'and I had to answer the phones for two hours – again. Okay?'

'Clara was at the hospital,' Mike interrupted. She looked upset. Already both of us had intervened without success and I was beginning to think that there were deeper antagonisms between them which, typically, were being left unsaid. Earlier I had overheard Jude muttering that anyone would think Clara was the only woman on earth with gynaecological problems. Mike thought that it was something to do with Jude trying to get pregnant, but if this was so, Jude wasn't admitting to it.

'Oh *shit*.' Jude sat up straight and looked around furiously, 'So I'm in the wrong again, am I?'

Andrea dragged a hand across her forehead, shook two codeines out of a tube, and washed them down with cold coffee. Jude and Clara confronted each other across the circle. The angry words tumbled out and blew around, confounding everyone. It didn't look as if either of them would yield. I was irritated. Self-criticism, I thought, that's what they forget. After all, we all have grievances: I could throw my head back and scream about a dozen annoyances, about the delays and the laxness and the sectarianism. And then we'd get nothing done, would we?

Mike looked helplessly at me.

'Let's keep a grip on ourselves, shall we?' I said.

'Can't we just drop this article?' Andrea suggested, with an anxious glance at the list of items still on the agenda.

Clara was on her feet ready to leave, wrapping a crocheted shawl round her thin shoulders. I picked up the dog-eared pile which Jude had dumped on the desk and leafed through it. 'We could farm it out, perhaps?'

Andrea leaned forward, clutching at straws. 'But who to?'

I tried to think. We can kick it about till we lose it, for all I care. 'Marie,' I said, 'Marie could do it. She's done a lot of work on Social Security legislation, so it is her field. And she writes well.'

Clara sat down again.

'When she gets back, I'll ask her.'

Lunch was a delicatessen picnic eaten in the park. Smoked mackerel, cheeses, Italian bread and plums from the market. Andrea was wearing a dress for once, a green sundress with halter straps, but she hadn't shaved her legs. They were pale, and the long dark hairs looked ugly to me.

'I've got used to them,' she said amiably.

'Not me.' I rolled up my jeans and showed her my freckled shins. She shuddered at the feel of the short bristles.

All around us on the park benches and on grass which was still damp and smelled faintly of dog shit, other women – clerks, salesgirls, workers from the Family Planning Clinic on the corner – sat in twos and threes, eating and talking. Most of them wore tights or stockings, and their clothes, compared to ours, were neat and close-fitting, sculptured with darts. Some of them had kicked off their sandals, and their stocking soles were soiled with dust and sweat. At ease now, our small group sprawled, barefoot, bare-armed, and chattering. Even Jude and Clara were calm again, although not sitting close to each other. I licked sticky plum juice from my palm, and watched them, and wondered why it was so hard, working with women. The smell of the smoked fish clung to my fingers.

As I walked to the station, violet clouds closed overhead. My trenchcoat, still damp from the morning's journey to work, hung in a bundle over my shoulder. The sky was darkening, lights were winking on all the way up the Post Office Tower. I had phoned Matt from the office after lunch. He had been full of hesitations, bashful. At first I was brisk, friendly, trying to allay his fears, but gradually he began to wear me down. Perhaps he was right. I thought, perhaps I was simply blinding myself to the dangers and so, ready to give up, I said: 'Let's leave it, then.'

'Oh what the hell,' he said then, rallying. 'Just come right over. We can have a jaw, at least.'

I could almost hear his mind working: afternoon, safe, non-sexual.

From the North London line you can see five miles of spiky urban skyline, and the silver tangle of railway lines which lead to Euston and Kings Cross, and the white worm of the canal. By Camden Lock the first huge drops of rain battered at the roof of the little train, and ripped the surface of the canal in a volley of small explosions. The faces at the train windows turned an unearthly green, and down below, in streets suddenly emptied of people, cars crawled bumper-deep in spray.

In the seat opposite mine a round woman jabbed her thumb at the carriage roof. 'He's got it in for us this time,' she chuckled. 'Wish he'd throw the lifebelts down while he's about it.'

Windows slammed up, and the carriage filled with smoke haze and murmurs.

'Shocking, isn't it?'

'See the size of these drops!'

'Must be all them nuclear explosions.'

Everyone leaned towards the windows. Dismay was what the voices expressed, but the faces wore enchantment.

I am going to see Matt.

Outside Gospel Oak station the big umbrella leaves of a sycamore tilted a cold avalanche of water down my neck. My soaked raincoat sagged around me as I paddled along the streaming pavement. My sandals squeaked with wet. When the rain got through to my T-shirt I shivered at first, and then I laughed and stripped off my headscarf. It was fitting, I thought, that the rain demanded absolute surrender.

Matt took one look at the spectacle on his doorstep and burst out laughing. 'I don't believe this. Is it really June Guthrie?'

'Whether it is or not, let me in, for pity's sake.'

He led me upstairs, looking over his shoulder every few steps to grin. My feet left a wet trail on the linoleum. 'You drowned old badger.' In the living-room he backed away to get a better look. 'We'd better get you dried off.' He fetched a towel from the bedroom, a pair of jeans, and the tartan shirt he'd worn at the theatre. He retired to the kitchen while I stripped.

'Socks, please,' I called.

He put his head round the door. 'Are odd ones okay?'

When I had dressed he sat down in the rocking chair facing me. 'I'll make tea shortly, but in the meantime, what have you got to say for yourself?' Weaving his fingers together, he perched his hands on his knee. His upper lip grew long and ecclesiastical. I started to giggle.

Immediately his expression changed. 'I mean it.'

'I can't keep up with you, Matt.'

'So you came to "sort things out", did you?' It was an accurate enough rendering of my accent, but he had added a hypocritical Jean Brodie ring to it, and I recoiled, feeling offended. Here it was again. The hot seat. The feeling that I'd wronged him. I eyed him silently, while the black cat sprang up on to the sofa, and lowered itself delicately into my lap.

Matt leaned forward. 'What is it you *want* from me?'

I answered reluctantly, 'To make peace, I suppose.' His look was piercing. 'Yes,' I insisted. 'To make friends.'

He got up and began to pace the room. Once, twice, hands in pockets, shooting glances at me. Dramatics, I thought. All the same, I couldn't take my eyes off him. He had switched on a standard lamp by the fireplace; the light flattered him, colouring his hair an ashy fawn, like the lightest part of a lion's mane. He came over to me and crouched down by the sofa. 'How do I know you won't hurt me again?'

'Come on,' I said, embarrassed, 'we hardly know each other.'

A heavy sigh. 'You really don't understand, do you?'

'Understand what?'

His knee joints cracked as he stood up. 'You still don't get it? Then you don't know how much of me has been going in your direction – for *months*, Ms Guthrie.' He shook his fist at me, a pretend threat.

I looked up at him, unwilling to admit that I had also thought of him, and far too often. 'But I've hardly seen you.'

'I, on the other hand, have seen you. Oh yes.' Again he crouched down beside me. 'You can't imagine how many times I drove past that great barn of a house you live in. But you never saw me, did you? You were there, though, by that upstairs window. Doing your thing at the typewriter. *Immensely* oblivious.' He took my hand and gave it a little shake, like a cat shaking a bird to make sure it's truly dead. 'Crazy in love, I was.' He laughed shortly. Outside the french windows a stream of water from a gutter drummed irregularly on the balcony. I was silenced. He had used the past tense, as if discussing a corpse. 'So you see,' he added, 'for me it's been a long time.'

His hand pressing mine was warm and dry. I touched the shallow grooves and smooth pads of his palm, and the tendons on the inside of his wrist, and the bones above which the blond hairs began. Suddenly he withdrew his hand and jumped up, smiling, saying that he'd forgotten just one thing. He returned from the bedroom hiding something behind his back. 'I'll only give it if you promise to wear it.'

'The hat,' I said at once, and laughed, glad of the diversion. As I reached out, he held the hat high above my head, swinging it by its elastic; I had to stand on tiptoe to catch it. At the mirror above the fireplace I manipulated the soft felt this way and that until the slant was just right. The glass reflected a handsome couple: a young woman with hair escaping under the brim of a forties' hat, a tall, beaming man at her elbow. I couldn't help comparing them to the honeymoon couple in that old snapshot, the one taken by a street photographer at Marble Arch.

'Let me see you.'

I turned, feeling infantile, and he clapped his hands. He tugged at the brim. 'That's *it*.' He turned me back to face the mirror. 'Absolutely the bees' knees.'

I was mesmerised. I had never thought that I looked at all like my mother, but now, the resemblance was marked. Matt made a frame with his fingers, and stared through it at me. 'And so you stole it?'

His smile was proud. 'For you – anything.' His eyes shone; little tremors of laughter shook his chest. 'Is this *rilly* happening?' he said, in a dreadful Hollywood drawl. He looked so happy that I was afraid for him, and stepped back. Because it wasn't as simple as that. It couldn't be. There was a postcard propped on the mantlepiece. Indigo sky, a white-hot courtyard. It transmitted perceptible waves, pricking at me.

Matt saw my glance stray. 'Venice. From Vi,' he said matter-of-factly. He tilted my chin up and then splayed his legs wildly so that the long grasshopper body lost height and the eyes came level with mine. 'Vi's just fine. Don't you worry your *head*.'

'Yes,' I said, and saw Vi striding the cobbled canal walks with their stink of fried fish and urinals. She would be walking in the shade, shielding her fair skin from the sun. Under her arm she would carry an empty sketchbook to lend her an air of purpose and fend off the young men; beneath her garish cotton dress her body would be taut with apprehension. I thought of the last time I'd seen her, setting off to meet Marshall. 'And now I'm going to have a good time,' she had said at the garden gate, in a desperate voice. No, she was far from fine, and persuading myself to believe anything else would be taking the easy way out.

I would go, then. Shake hands, turn away. I saw it all, saw the honourable June walking out of Matt's flat in her borrowed clothes. And did not move an inch. For a moment I felt quite light-hearted. The shirt on my back reeked of Matt, the cat on the sofa was his, and the jeans I wore; inches away, his forearm radiated warmth. Because of course it was really too late. I could agonise about Vi as much as I liked, but in the end, wouldn't mere proximity decide? Matt saw my expression change, and he understood, I could tell, that Vi had entered, and now Vi had left, and that his pull was the stronger. And he smiled. He knows he is going to have it all his own way, I thought with a surge of resentment, and I took off the foolish hat and threw it on the sofa.

He whispered, 'I feel as if I've come in from the cold.' Simultaneously his teeth set up an Arctic chattering. He looked terribly young and beleaguered, and when I reached for him he shook against me in small, childish spasms. After a few moments he drew away, leaving a cold draught.

'Something's wrong?'

He put his head on one side, watching me, and then he began to cry. He wept unselfconsciously, fluently, neither raising a hand to wipe away the tears, nor apologising for letting them run. 'What the *fuck* am I doing with you?' he said, and began to hiccup. I drew him to the sofa, fetched water, ordered him to swallow three times. He relaxed into my arms and allowed himself to be petted and stroked. His hair felt springy and tough in my fingers. And then he muttered: 'I wonder what's in it for you, though?' Again the sulky, mistrustful face.

I sighed. Without knowing exactly where we were going, I was beginning to find these stops and starts and changes of gear exasperating. 'Search me,' I said lightly.

'Kiss me, would you? Just hold me.'

His lips felt dry and rough, and entirely familiar. The close-up scent of his skin, too, was shockingly recognisable, as if a shared history had been hiding between us. My nose prodded his, and a cool part of my mind considered Vi, remembered why his mouth felt so forbidden, and wondered also whether I was now committed, and to what. Meanwhile, in the interior of his mouth, I was sinking, sliding back down the long tunnel to the sea where we all come from. My very bones were softening, betraying me. 'Jesus!' I broke away.

Matt scowled. 'How eloquent we are today.'

Through the open bedroom door I saw the platform bed, with a yellow duvet plumped on top of it. Jackets and shirts hung neatly in the storage space underneath.The room spoke of order and care. 'I'm thinking perhaps I should go.'

'You have to decide that for yourself.'

No sulks, I thought, no inducements?

'I've waited this long. I can wait longer.' His face was stolid, serious. He took my hand firmly in his. 'It's not just a screw for me, you know. Quick sex is easy enough to get . . . No, I'm not shooting a line. I've had that up to *here*.' His frown was puritanical.

I looked away, feeling shifty. Perhaps I was the chaotic one, after all? 'It's all so new. I feel uncertain.'

'Oh my,' he sighed, 'maybe it's time for tea.' He uncurled himself and stood up; it was an odd stance, almost provocative: shoulders thrust back, bum jutting unnaturally. I stared, quite ill with wanting.

'What?' he said, looking down at himself. 'Is that all you want?' His face hardened. 'That's what they all want.' I shook my head, but he ignored it, and snapped his fingers. 'Okay, okay. Will you come to bed, then? No strings, I promise.'

'You talk as though women came begging for it!'

'You could put it like that. It gets to be a drag, after a year or so.'

'Really!'

He put his hands on his hips. 'Yes, *really*. Have you led a sheltered life, or something?'

I stared, laughed, waited for his answering smile. 'You're outrageous,' I spluttered.

He joined in politely, and then added. 'Women exploit men too, you know. As sex objects. Or hadn't you heard?'

I shook my head, still laughing. 'As I said, I can't keep up with you. Not your moods, not your concepts.'

'Oho. So you don't believe me? Then you don't know your sisters like I know them . . . You'd be surprised,' he said darkly, 'at some of the tales I could tell . . . '

'Spare me, please.'

He pulled me to my feet. His thigh pressed against mine. 'So. Are you taking me to bed, Ms Guthrie?'

In the bathroom, I realised that I had no contraceptives. Luckily, it was a safe time, but I thought how unlike me it was, to leave things to chance. Not to make the decision in advance.

I lay in bed waiting for Matt to crawl spruce and chilly

between the sheets; I ran my hands over my stomach, over the rigid muscles. Cold as mutton, I thought, feeling the nervous goose pimple rash on my skin. First fuck. It would be bad. I would be useless. And then Matt was in bed beside me, unstrapping my watch with a grimace.

And then surprise, at the easy heat of our combined skin. A routing of apprehensions, as we rolled and hugged. Looseness. My head swam. Silly things bobbed in it. We are two jelly babies, I thought. Made in the same mould, melting at the same temperature. There was a pigeon watching us from the windowsill. I saw the gleam of its beak and thought how it could peck up our soft parts quick as winking.

Outside the rain eased, and a bright blue hole opened in the black sky. Inside, our skin was silk. Matt's hand moved somewhere between my legs, but I couldn't be sure whether it was inside lips or outside fur, for the surface of everything had become too liquid and undifferentiated. He was licking, too, elusive sensations round my breast. An unfamiliar bully in me grabbed his head and forced his mouth to my nipple. He raised his hips and mine, inched into me. Such a little at a time, I thought, does he want me to beg for it? I looked at his face, searching for a triumphant smile, for some flexing of will or power, but it was rapt, brimming, and when I shut my eyes that after-image remained, nudging slipstreams in me, in the blood, the skin, the roots of the hair.

To be lost.

'Open your eyes,' he said, 'Look at me.' His lips were drawn back, his eyes full of tears.

The streaming started with a vengeance, bolting up through me. Catching in sobs in my chest where the past rose to wrestle with it.

To be lost. To seek. To find. To seek clues, in the room with the dressing table on which lie crocheted mats clotted with face powder, and tarnished brushes choked with red hair. Under the bed, in suitcases, in cardboard boxes as enticing as Christmas Eve – oh rifled secrets of my mother. To be lost, to seek a breast to beat against. To find only a little girl, after all, and will no one tell her what's happening?

Staring into my eyes, Matt arched his back and howled out.

Afterwards he lay over me and his chest heaved. His face was wet. I wiped my own tears away on a corner of the duvet.

'You're crying,' he said, 'We're crying.' He touched my face with his finger. 'I'm sorry, I couldn't stop myself then, it was all too much . . . Did you come? Did you? No, I didn't think you had.'

'I did in a way. But emotionally, not physically . . . if you see what I mean.'

He nodded solemnly. 'Shall we go on?'

The question seemed irrelevant. In a sense, whatever happened next, it came to the same thing. Whatever we did, it would be going on.

'I'll have another bash at it later,' he said, with a shaky laugh. 'I will. But, my God, look at the freckles on your back. How will I ever get out of bed with you? How will I ever get any work done?'

Holding hands, we smoked. Our legs were glued together.

Sex in the afternoon, writing in the morning, running first thing – that was the way to live, he said. He waved his hands, sketching in the future. I listened to these reckless plans, every detail of which included me, and nodded, and giggled, and couldn't believe that this was me, allowing myself to be so quickly claimed. Eventually the talk turned to sex, and I found myself confessing how hard it was to come with some men, and how those were often the ones who put you down for it, and made you feel a failure.

'And you *believed* them?' he said angrily. 'You dolt. You're the best. I could drown in you.'

Outside the sun broke through to shine on the wet railings of the balcony and the iridescent feathers of the pigeon, and the silver ring on its wrinkled crimson leg. On the platform bed, I felt as if I were on stage, in full view of any neighbours who cared to peer up from their tree-shaded gardens. Petted and pampered, I exhibited myself.

'If music be the food of love,' said Matt, 'I'll put some Beethoven on.' Getting out of bed, he kicked his legs in a high can-can step, and disappeared into the living-room. The music started softly, and swelled, and Matt reappeared on a surge of cellos, conducting.

'I want to see you.' He advanced via the bottom of the bed, lifting my splayed legs at the knee. Obediently I opened my thighs wider, told myself not to tense. Again the choppy feelings came, disturbing my peace; his presence was watery, tumultuous. 'Look at you, aren't you lovely,' he crooned from below. He disentangled his head and looked up at me. 'I can't believe a baby came out of you.' His face glistened with juices; even his blond hair looked dark and sticky. 'And those thighs – such strong, strong thighs.'

The ardent words flowed around me. 'Guid broad hips for the childbearing,' I said, to cover my confusion. I had a vision of my desk with its smooth red top and its clear view. High and dry, a good vantage point.

Matt rolled on to his back. 'I must say, it's getting a bit powerful in this bed.' He wrinkled up his nose and laughed.

'Time to wash,' I said quickly, getting up.

'Don't move. Just lie there like a queen, while I run the bath.' He blew a kiss from the door, went out. Came back like lightning, with Buster Keaton slickness, and leaned on the doorpost with a soulful expression. 'I've just got so much to give you, June Guthrie, so much in store for you.' He clawed with his fingers at the doorjamb, trying to climb it. I watched in admiration, and with the slight distance that admiration gives, wondering what was heart and what was art? It was difficult to tell sometimes, with Matt. But the words aroused me, I'd never heard such promises. Momentarily I saw the gift in terms of sperm, an inexhaustible milky supply, and I was scandalised.

When Matt returned to the bedroom to fetch clean towels, the position of my hands gave me away. 'Wanking, is it?' he said immediately. 'You cheeky badger.' I laughed. We might have been married for years. He put his head under the covers to suck my toes and spy on me. 'But I've done it already,' I said into the yellow gloom.

He mumbled back indistinctly: 'You should have saved it

for me.'

'Imperialist,' I jibed, poking him with my toe, enjoying this new freedom of speech. With anyone else, I thought, how guilty I'd feel.

'Watch yer lip,' he retorted.

Later we dressed and went walking on Hampstead Heath, where waterlogged grass soaked my sandals and my borrowed socks. The day had been long, and I felt dull with tiredness. On a damp seat by a pond, under willows which shed drips, Matt took exception to my silence.

'What's so private all of a sudden?'

'I'm okay,' I said, startled by his belligerent tone.

'That wasn't what I asked.' In the half dark, two mallards rose from the water and fled away across the pond with a low beating of wings. Matt sighed. 'Why don't you trust me a little? I only want to know what you're worrying about.'

I shrugged. Mostly I wanted to go home, to spread myself luxuriously in my empty house, among my own dust and papers, to lie in a solitary bath, and love him from there. In my room, I could consider the day at a distance, hold it up like a kaleidoscope to the light, and marvel at its patterns.

'Well?'

Instinct told me not to mention separations. I squeezed his arm. 'Let's go back to the flat. I'm worn out, aren't you? It's all been so intense.'

He stiffened. 'But then, we're intense people, aren't we?'

I laughed. 'I suppose so, yes.' I stood up and rubbed my cold legs.

'You *suppose* so?' His voice was sharp with sarcasm. 'Don't you acknowledge an intense relationship even when it comes up and socks you in the jaw?'

I held up my hand. 'Hey, slow down a bit.'

'Or aren't you in it? Is that it?' His eyes probed my face in the dark.

I shook my head helplessly. 'Don't. It's not necessary, all this. Don't let's fight. I'm just having a bit of a mood. A reaction. Let's just head for home.'

Matt got up and put his hands on his hips. 'Oh, pardon

me,' he said cuttingly. 'I forgot. Vi told me about those. One has to watch out for them, I believe?'

I backed away from him. 'What's *wrong* with you?' I said, staring at him, remembering the fervent lover of the afternoon, chilled, disbelieving. I felt my feet sink and slither in the mud of the path, and caught at the park bench for balance. 'What did I say? Why are you hurting me?' I turned and stumbled away along the path, away from the sour, unmanageable face and the darkness. He caught up with me in one bound.

'You're so touchy.' He pulled me round to face him and pressed himself against me. 'Come here. Hold me.' I felt his warm thighs again, warm bony knees, furry warm sweater. 'Look, I didn't mean it. So what if you get depressed? *C'est normale*, eh?' He was murmuring in my ear, rocking me. 'Single mum, not enough money, no security . . . Oh, the reasons are legion . . . ' His voice was gentle again, and rich, and it enveloped me. All I had to do was listen, while it plucked out thorns, named causes, found excuses. We swayed together in the dark, and blood began to flow again, and warmth re-entered me.

He held me by the shoulders and gazed at me. 'Better?' he said, and his voice broke. 'Oh June, I'm sorry.' This time I watched him a little warily. The tears seemed to come so easily: could they really be sincere? 'I love you so much, you see. I get the big fear demons. Just feel me.' He shivered all over, knocking his knees together. 'Forgive me, will you? Forgive my tantrums? I'm not used to this love stuff. I've been alone too long, it's not good for a man.'

His voice resonated inside me. Speechless, I hugged him hard.

'Oh, I'm so glad,' he breathed. 'It's that bloody big mouth of mine, you've just got to be tough with me.' He kissed the top of my head. 'When I think of all the good things I want to give you, and then all that bad rubbish comes out instead . . . '

'It's all right,' I said, 'it's all right.' I laughed nervously. 'I think we need some time to get used to each other, that's all.'

'You could be right.' He untangled himself and took my

hand. 'Let's get out of this mire. Let's go home and be peaceful.'

'I feel like a drink, first,' I said, thinking with sudden longing of the public world, and ordinary things like buying gin-and-tonics, and holding hands, 'to calm down a bit.' I wondered if he had a local, with pool tables and artificial chrysanthemums, and a barman who called him by his first name, where we could settle down under the incurious yet accepting eyes of others, like normal couples did.

Matt seemed surprised. 'If you like.' No, he said, he didn't have a local, he found pubs a bit sordid on the whole. But there was one opposite the tennis courts if I really wanted.

With our arms twined awkwardly around each other's waists we walked towards the street lights. How little I know about him, I thought.

There were gay strings of coloured lights outside the pub, and red leather banquettes inside. I ordered whiskies while Matt hovered beside me. In the engraved mirror above the bar my face looked flushed and excited. By some trick of the light the eyes which looked back at me were bright blue – blue reflected from Matt's borrowed shirt, perhaps, but blue anyway, and eager, like my mother's. My hair was curly from the damp air, and shone more red than blond. The colours were vulgar, chocolate box; again the similarity was unsettling. Next to my reflection, I caught a glimpse of Matt, in profile. He was glancing around uneasily, looking self-conscious and stranded. Just then the whiskies arrived, and fumbling in my purse, I was suddenly full of doubts. Did he want to be ordering and buying? Did I want him to? Did he resent me for dragging him into the public eye? My hand shook as I handed the money to the barman.

'Do you want ice?' I asked Matt, and felt my smile falter. The tongs were hard to handle; they kept springing open and the slippery cubes escaped and dropped back into the bowl.

'I don't mind,' he replied, without helping. I handed the glasses to him and waited miserably at the counter for my change. When I risked a glance across the room I saw him sitting in a corner, staring into space. His nose was red, and he looked gangly, open-mouthed, not at all handsome. And then he saw me watching, and gave me a preposterously soupy smile, and the bad moment had passed. The corner seat was a good vantage point, but secure and contained as well. Matt seemed content to sit holding hands and murmuring nonsense things, not noticing what was around him, not seeing the elderly couple who smiled at us confirmingly, or the three men at the next table whose eyes kept straying towards us while they argued about cricket scores.

'We're meant for each other, of course,' he said suddenly. His voice was still low, but just then the sportsmen's conversation lapsed, and the words fell into a silence. 'You know that, don't you?' he went on seriously, oblivious, while I looked down at my hands and could not smile back at him, could not respond, was conscious only of the listening ears and the dangers of envy and ill-will.

There was a cough, a loud scratch of match against matchbox, and then the argument was resumed more enthusiastically than ever.

I moved closer to Matt, so that our thighs touched. 'There certainly is something of a highly electric nature going on,' I whispered. He laughed and kissed my nose.

Heads turned. At the end of the bar counter two women in tracksuits glanced at us and averted their eyes. They were sitting very straight and poised on high stools, a couple of feet apart, and there was a deliberateness in their not-touching which reminded me of something Mike had said.

'You learn to keep your hands to yourself.' Her crisp schoolteacher voice echoed in my ears. No one, she had said drily, no one looks on with indulgence when two women kiss and fawn, oh no. The two women went on talking quietly, their smiles inward-turned. At first, Mike said, she had been the rash one – rash with her eyes, rash with her words – until Sherry, the old hand, taught her the rules.

And yet what else had I come here for but that security, that complicity? Ashamed, I looked away.

Later in the high bed Matt's orgasm was long and loud and punctuated by shouts of laughter.

'The hysterical orgasm,' he said, 'that's a new one on me.' Before subsiding into sleep he murmured: 'You didn't, did you? I want you to so much.'

In the night, the darkness smothered me. I lay watching a chink of light under the living-room door, and I scratched furiously at a mysterious itch; eventually I could stand it no longer and went next door to search myself for fleas – the cat was responsible, I supposed. I checked ankles, waist, neck, the usual places, but there was not a mark, only the shifting itch. Wrapped in Matt's towelling robe, I sat in the rocking chair and watched shadows of leaves move on the varnished floor.

Itch of anger, itch of disappointment? Yes. But the shores which Matt had left me on when he had shrunk away and slept were quite familiar. Routine. This agitation went deeper, I knew it went deeper than that.

Weight of history, dark mazes. Gaps. There was so much that Matt would never be able to understand. No matter what tenderness was woven between us, no matter how much I wanted to share. 'Don't you trust me?' he'd said, but when he turned that piercing gaze on me I was afraid; it was as if he wouldn't rest until he burrowed through and reached places that even I had not excavated.

A wind rattled the french windows and lashed the shadow branches to and fro. I want to. I can't. My head hurt and hurt. A silly old song came back at me. 'Under my thumb, the girl who once had me down . . .' I was afraid, yes, I was afraid he would push and prod me down into that wordless darkness where countless invasions and penetrations were possible, where there were so few boundaries against the leakage of one into another.

Trust? Already my skin was becoming too thin. And where did I end and the world begin?

Morbid, I thought, moving my bare toes around on the smooth floor-boards. If I were to tell Matt that this recoil, this retreat, was an illness, would that satisfy him? Or would he pry further in?

I clutched the robe around me and rocked. My breasts were warm and soft under the towelling. But whose breasts, and for what? Breasts which itched and stung at the thought of Matt, unfamiliar breasts which would no longer be carried quietly but were alive with strange demands; my belly, also smooth under the robe, also in thrall, the tissues seeded with itchy spores.

Under my thumb, I sang, as I rocked in darkness, as my mind ranged in darkness. But who else does the body belong to, I thought, than the mother who rocks it, who guards it from harm, who regulates it with her own pace, who buries in the marrow of its bones her own apprehensions?

Among the shifting leaf patterns the shadow of the tree stood guard like a dark sentinel.

Ah, too easy. All too easy to blame the past, or to see Vi in the corners of a room. Shadow-boxing. Surely the answer, if there was an answer, was patience. If Matt had patience enough to wait, who knew what trust might grow and what barred doors loosen?

I left the room of moving shadows and climbed back into bed. Matt breathed into the pillows with his mouth open and his eyebrows arched as if in surprise. I watched him. He was beautiful. I watched him in the way I watch Andrew when he is ill or defenceless. Protectively, achingly. I did not know whether this primitive feeling should be called love. Love, after all, I knew nothing about. The word had never been mentioned, had never grown roots in me. All I knew was the flesh, and death was present in it, buried like a splinter, and would emerge.

22

In the morning I woke to find a pair of eyes fixed on me. Matt kissed me on the brow.

'Good morning, my queen bee.'

Through the drowsiness, the insect-like rustlings under the skin began all over again. A bulbous, drugged creature, I stretched, luxurious, under his hands. And the sharp little mind pecked: I shall lose this throne as easily as I gained it. Pay attention.

It was a bothersome notion, unworthy of the sun shining on the wall, and the two skinny sunflowers craning from their pot on the balcony, and in the kitchen next door the smell of bacon frying, and the radio playing 'You're the One That I Want . . .' Flapping my arm at it, I chased it away.

Hampstead Heath was Saturday-busy, the sky full of fighting-kites: dragons, coffin-shapes, mythical birds. With our eyes on the commotion above us, we strolled up the tarmac path which led to the top of the hill. At the back of my mind, like a dark ground on which the brightness of the day was mounted, was the memory of another Saturday. It was Reuben who had walked with me then, on the same path.

'Look around you,' he said, as we breasted the hill. 'The world is so full of riches, if you'll only allow them in!'

At his house he had pushed a fruit bowl towards me, and a vase of flowers, forcing me to choose gifts. Unwillingly I had accepted a peach, a yellow freesia.

On the crest of the hill, Reuben handed me a card. The picture showed a blue amphora, round and capacious. 'Learn to contain,' he'd written. Reading it, I tightened my mouth. When he saw this he quirked an eyebrow and said that there was a part of me which attacked anything good I had – such a very envious part, he said.

With my mind set so firmly on suicide, I hardly listened: if he imagined such mumbo-jumbo would dissuade me, I would prove him wrong. Arm in arm we walked, the stubby-bearded man and his sulky charge whose pockets were stuffed with his gifts and whose eyes were fixed on the ground, until, losing patience, he bullied me into looking up at the silver-green willows, and it felt like force-feeding, and the colours hurt my eyes.

And so I was grateful now, to need no one to force me to look at the kites or the treetops or the stretched blue city, to have eyerything, and thus have nothing left to envy.

I hung on to Matt's hand and watched a woman in a wheelchair manipulate a blue speck which was so high it seemed that it might tickle the bellies of the jets which periodically cruised overhead.

'Five thousand feet's our ceiling,' she said, 'Air Ministry regulations.' And she clicked her tongue with annoyance, for high above, a thin thread of tail had wrapped itself around the line, and the kite began to spin. 'It's my own fault for not keeping an eye on it. You've got to keep control every second, at that height.' Up in the sky the circling speck began to dive. 'Here we go. If it comes down over the flats, I've lost it.' Her hands flashed, winding in the reel; the ratchet crackled.

'It's like fishing, but in air,' I said to Matt, looking up. He responded with a blank smile, and then my feet were nipped out from under me, and all of a sudden I was flat on my back on the grassy slope, with the breath knocked out of my lungs. Shouting with laughter, Matt jumped on top of me, and hauled me over him, so that we started to roll down the hill. With hip-bones grinding, ribs grinding, we tumbled over and over; the sky wheeled and the gay dots of kites jumbled with the green of the grass and the white stars of daisies; until near the bottom of the hill we slowed, and came to rest in a patch of clover, with our feet higher than our heads.

Matt beat his fist on the ground. 'Swept you off your feet!' he cried triumphantly.

I lay spreadeagled, breathing in gasps. The sky teemed with mythical beasts, playful, aimless.

There was another memory from the era of the death wish.

It was after Reuben moved from Harley Street to a therapy centre in Kilburn, where we sat on cushions on the floor and the silences between us were punctuated by bioenergetic yells from the adjacent rooms.

When I walked into his room that day he turned his transistor radio off and set his face attentively. Seeing this small effort at accommodation, I was incensed.

'I'm nothing but a burden to you,' I accused, 'so why pretend otherwise?'

His luminous eyes looked back at me. 'What is it you want me to punish you for?' he countered, inscrutable.

'Don't change the subject,' I cried, wanting to shake and shake him, and I bit and worried at him with my words until he put his fists up and said – Come on, then, fight me – and so we did, feinting and butting, wrestling, heaving, rolling around on the carpet, until we were exhausted and lay still, eye to eye.

'I don't think you realise how much energy you really have!' he said. And then again we were sitting facing each other, and he was firing more disconcerting questions, until he came to the most irritating one of all.

'What do you really want to do with me?' he asked, and as I glowered back at his grinning gnome's face, the words came unbidden. 'Play,' I said, 'I want to play,' and I burst into tears for the life of purpose which lay in shards around me.

In the grass, I laughed out loud with relief. 'All I ever wanted,' I said, 'was a man to roll me down Parliament Hill.'

Matt inclined his head graciously.

'My pleasure, madam.' And then he added, with a slanting look, 'I know what you feminists like.'

I rolled on to my stomach. My fingers began to worry at the ground, and then I took a twig, and dug away at it. The hands busied themselves in the grass, feeling yesterday's dampness at the roots, raiding for dry stalks, plucking at yellow ears of rye. He gives it, he takes it away, I brooded, gathering, prevaricating. As the silence stretched, the small heap of grass ears grew. I picked them up and began to scatter them across Matt's chest, absently; little by little the sweep of hands took on a rhythm, and the scattering became somehow purposeful. The seeds fell in arcs, littering his red sweater.

'What's this?' Matt stuck his head up so that his chin tucked back into folds of neck. My mind caught up with my hands.

'I'm only marrying you,' I said.

He sat up. 'You're a case. Nutty as a fruitcake.'

'Fertility symbols,' I insisted, laughing, a little aghast at myself, 'it was a rite.'

Matt flapped a limp wrist.

'Gee, man,' he squeaked, 'Women's rites', and I threw the rest of the grass in his face. 'Peace,' he begged, shielding his eyes. 'Okay, I'll marry you back. If you're good.' He grabbed my hand and kissed it. 'Consider it done.'

We grinned foolishly at each other, and he struck his forehead with his hand. 'Oh *Gawd*.'

Again that feeling of certainty, the superstitious chill up the spine. He jumped to his feet and pulled me up.

'But then, we were anyway. So come on – now for the honeymoon. At the fair.' The long arms wound round mine, the legs laced through mine. 'And so now you can't leave me,' he said, matter-of-factly.

At South End Green, ringed by willows, the bank holiday fair was tawdry-bright against the soft blue day. Nearby, high up on the hospital tower, the windows were open, and white-clad patients sunned themselves on the balconies.

Matt was tugging at my arm. 'Come on, we're going to ride the Waltzers.'

Circles within circles. At the top of the steps I watched round carriages careen over rippling hills and valleys, and I hung back. The slatted boardwalks were constructed like ornamental bridges, with mock ramparts, frail balustrades made from fretworked hardboard, Chinoiserie, cherubs. Yellow paint, green paint, sugar-pink and silver paint. The mechanical skirt was slowing, settling, the brakes going on.

'Relax,' said Matt, steering me into a car. 'Night Fever'

roared from the P.A. Two attendants jingled change in their canvas aprons and went soliciting among the onlookers.

When the roundabout gathered speed and the pressure began to build, I forgot Matt's instructions and fought the pull and counter-pull which buffetted me. I tried to focus on the horizon, on the solid block of the hospital building, but the familiar tower lurched and bobbed and whipped past sickeningly, and the willow tops dissolved in a green froth.

The attendants rode the mechanical waves like surfers, picking out the pretty girls, slapping the flat of their hands against the cars to keep up the rate of spin, judging their success by the screams.

'Let's hear you, girls,' they commanded, 'scream for us!'

And then against the side of our car a slap like an explosion: we had been singled out. They were going, of course, for the ones with the terror plain on their faces. The carriage flew into a fierce whirl, and I felt the flesh on my face flatten against the bones; onlookers and balustrades raced at me and away, and up over the side of the car my hair rushed like streamers.

I saw Matt's stretched face loom at me, dazed and swooning. 'Don't tense up,' he gasped. 'This smartass has got it in for us . . .'

When I tried to breathe, a yell flew out. I let out another one: just testing, like a girl's first scream for Elvis. It felt better. I screamed again, and we hurtled into another figure of eight which was also the downward swoop of a kite, a roller-coaster, a bad skid, but I was moving with it now, not fighting, letting my bones turn to jelly, and all the soft parts wobble. But then, slithering along the thigh that was crushed against Matt's, a sneaking awful excitement came, stealing into my belly, melting it. Above, behind, in front, as the car spun, the glint of teeth said that one of the attendants was staring down at my splayed legs, and there was nothing I could do, no resources left for defence or retreat, just this thrill, and the blood rushing to my face. I shut my eyes tight and held on.

Gears ground, and the roundabout began to slow.

'Are you dizzy?' said Matt. 'I feel like a fucking corkscrew myself.'

I put my head on his shoulder and rested there for a moment, recovering. A trio of windswept girls got out of the next car and picked their way across the slatted boardwalk on high heels. Dizzy? Yes. Among other things. But the sexual ferment seemed too adolescent to confess. There was something so wayward about it, so autonomous . . . Instinctively, I kept it to myself, in case Matt took offence.

We stumbled out of the car and sat down on the steps. White-faced, Matt put his head between his knees and shook it like a dog shaking water from its coat. On the swingboats opposite, two girls were pretending to clutch at petticoats which ballooned up in the wind. I watched the familiar gesture: the knees clenched, the hand flattened between the thighs. The girls' heads tilted back as the folds of their skirts escaped from their hands, and they laughed, and hairslides fell from their hair.

When Matt, recovered, pronounced the ground solid enough to walk on, we went to buy toffee apples, and ate them on the Dodgems. I drove wildly with one hand, while Matt sat in the passenger seat, absurdly tall in the toy car, shouting instructions through mouthfuls of crimson toffee

In the centre of the circuit there was a bump and a shout, and a shower of sparks. A black turban rolled incongruously across the rubber floor. I had noticed the Sikh couple before – the man, statuesque in his white Sunday shirt, and the woman in a turquoise sari, young-looking and bashful. Now the man was leaping from his seat and braving the weaving cars. On top of his head his long hair was coiled in a red and white band. As everything banged and collided and stopped the woman sat quite still at the centre of it all, holding a white cardigan on her knee and giggling from time to time behind her hand.

Matt's eyes did not leave her until, smiling and abashed, the young husband retrieved the turban and climbed back into the car. 'These Indian women,' he murmured, covered my ear with kisses which were sticky with toffee.

'You told me,' I said, and spun the wheel hard.

Looking back, now, on that long and stolen afternoon, I

can scarcely believe the frenzy of it. Matt strutted around the stalls, cocksure, preening – how enchanted I was by such a prize, and how we dazzled each other, so that each time our eyes met we had to stop and kiss to shut out the brilliance for a moment, rationing it, making it bearable. The sheer alarm of such happiness, enclosed by the circular rim of the fair, with its sugared colours and spindly machinery and raucous blare of music.

I knew that somewhere in the crowded fairground there would be acquaintances, and so I wasn't surprised when Phil's red hair swam into view. His face – pink and sunburnt behind a white burst of candyfloss – showed surprise and a hint of pleasure, and then the suppression of it. His eyes moved from me to Matt, took in our clasped hands and rapt faces, dropped.

'How are you?' he mumbled, 'How's Andrew? I've been on the Big Wheel . . . '

'Andrew's on holiday,' I said, 'How's it going?'

'Ah yes.' He cleared his throat. I watched his face for signs of censure, but he merely glanced down at the candyfloss, licked his lips, and gave a slightly apologetic smile. He waved an arm towards the Big Wheel. 'The others are still on it . . . suckers for punishment, in my opinion.' And with a nod he ambled away towards the shooting gallery.

'That's done it,' I said, but Matt was annoyed. He sucked in his breath.

'You might at least introduce me to your friends.'

'But he isn't . . . not close, anyway.'

'So who *is* he? Or don't you want me to know?' He turned away, and began to walk fast, so that I had to hurry along beside him. His head was down and he was scowling.

'It was only Phil,' I said. 'What does it matter?'

He lengthened his stride. 'You're bloody rude, that's what I think.'

'How could I introduce you?' I panted, trotting along beside him. 'What would I have said?'

He stopped and stared at me. His face seemed to slip out of control; his lips flattened against his teeth, as they had under the dragging pressure of the Waltzers. 'Don't treat me as if I didn't *exist*,' he hissed.

I threw up my hands. 'Oh! I don't believe it. So we're going to have a stupid fight in the middle of the fair.'

'Chickenshit!' Hunching his shoulders, he walked away. I ran after him and put my hand through his arm. He was surly, but allowed it.

'Drop it,' I said, 'let's drop it.'

We walked towards the pond where the trees were thick and enclosing and the ground rolled with acorns. The green was dense, soothing. As we walked, Matt shook his head silently, as if shocked at himself.

Ahead of us in the trees I saw the Sikh couple. They were strolling close together, engrossed in each other, but not touching. Their future is secure, I thought, mapped out. I realised that I was trembling.

'Well,' Matt said at last, and his face lightened, 'lovers have tiffs, don't they?'

I nodded and held him more tightly. We had a week. Then Vi would be back, Andrew would be back.

23

'Market,' Matt has written, backwards, in the dust on the window pane.

The well is full of trickling sounds, drippings. The walls allow moisture through by seepage.

Learn to take in good things, Reuben said. Storing, I am storing up. Through seepage, perhaps, I'll fill. Absorb, like an unglazed pot.

One day in July a Crown Court jury ruled – as we had

feared – against Phil. We knew as much when Vi came out of the witness box shaking, and stood with us in the tiled corridor outside the court. 'I messed it up,' she said. 'It was the bloody *truth*, and the Prosecutor still tied me in knots.'

When the verdict came I leaned my head against the wall and cried for myself, and for Phil, and for all of us, until Jed led me away.

In August Jed and I went to the Windsor Free Festival. I came back to London a couple of days before he did, and that night on the nine o'clock news I saw the battle scenes and the burning of tents. Jed returned in a foul mood with a van full of abandoned sleeping bags and rucksacks which he had gathered up in the aftermath of the eviction. For several days he paced about dark-faced, kicking out at cats, until, one morning at the Printshop, when we were sorting through the salvage for owners' addresses, he confronted me.

'We could live together,' he said, smoking a joint far too early in the day. 'Do you want that?'

The offer was made so angrily that all I could do was apologise. Because I'd been irresponsible, because I'd neglected all thoughts of my future, of Andrew's future, and had left Jed to worry and brood and plan.

'I can't stay much longer at the Women's Centre,' I conceded.

'Obviously!' Jed flung himself down on Phil's bed. 'Look. Only if you *want* to. Don't tell me that you haven't thought about somewhere to go?'

'No. Yes. I've tried.' I started to cry.

'Don't dissolve on me now, June. Just think, will you?'

Through a drizzle of tears I looked at him obediently. He wants us to live together, I thought.

'We could get a squat,' he said. 'I've got my eye on something. If you *want* . . .'

In September we squatted a small house of odd angles, one of two sandwiched between stucco terraces on the corner of a tree-lined Barnsbury square. 'The other's for Phil,' Jed said proudly, 'when he gets out.' He counted on his fingers. 'Seven more months. Five, with remission. So that's February, if he keeps his nose clean.'

At first, Jed seemed happy. He swung around the little house full of songs and jokes, heaving cookers, tables, copper piping, bookshelves. I painted the living-room in shades of pale pink, so that it glowed when the sun set, and on the wide windowsills I set pots of lemon geranium and trailing ivy.

At the back of the house, beyond the garden wall, was a secret wood. Jed and I had heard of it, even seen it on maps of the borough but now here it was, like a surprise or a good omen, with its swaying ash trees and dark undergrowth in which curly-spouted kettles mouldered, and umbrella ribs, and spilled armchair stuffing. Andrew, too, was delighted with it.

For my bedroom I chose a back room which overlooked the wood. I painted it scarlet in a burst of optimism, thinking that soon I would resume normal life, soon I would be able to inhabit a room of my own.

Sunbeams. Colours of dawn. Jed's backbone knobbly and warm under the bedclothes. Small things, I remember, which held me the right way up to the light. Like a seedling, I absorbed. But slowly, very slowly. The rest was will-power. Every morning before I got up I recited to myself primary reasons for living. The first, Andrew, was above all a matter for pure will, because secretly I was quite sure that I was far, far too young to be a mother. But of course I knew that everyone else thought it came naturally, and so I didn't disabuse them. After all, how could I tell them about the natural in me? How could I tell them that I'd only ever beaten my dolls, starved them, painted their china-smooth faces and made them mince along catwalks, and put them to bed in their cold shoe-boxes without any supper? No, I couldn't risk it. Instead, I would keep quiet, do my duties and watch myself very carefully.

November brought the IRA bombing campaign to London. When I went out I walked the city streets shrinking from parked cars, avoiding Tube stations. The dark dreams which invaded my waking life absorbed the extra fear greedily, like thirsty plants. As the war inside escalated, I clung more closely to Jed. I will soon be better, I told myself, but the red room remained cold and empty.

That winter, I went out agency cleaning, to pay Reuben's therapy fees.

'That's good,' he commended, 'cleaning. That's repair work. Keep at it.'

I kept at it. It was a routine of sorts. I scrubbed pristine floors in Golders Green, mummified a cheeseplant with Wax Pledge in Hampstead, smiled and smiled till my face ached. In a penthouse overlooking the Chinese Legation, I broke a jade elephant the size of a thumbnail, and was fired on the spot. The owner screamed at the agency down the phone: the elephant was not insured, what a scandal, to employ such incompetents!

I escaped in tears and found myself in a mirrored hall which was large enough to house two families. I stopped beside a mirror to wipe my eyes, and then I saw the man in uniform. He held up his hand.

'You go ahead, my dear.' His uniform was braided and buttoned, like the ceremonial wear of some long-gone regiment, and it fitted badly. He came out from behind his desk.

'Apartment twenty, was it?' His accent was East European.

I nodded, still shaking. Then he took my arm and spoke again.

'You do not upset yourself over these animals.' His face was bitter. 'They treat the working classes as dirt under their feet.' He led me across a yard and into a room with a stone floor. A kettle steamed on a gas ring in the corner. He pointed to a sink with a cold water tap. 'Rest here until better. There is a towel, for washing.'

Afterwards, I hurried home to Jed with my tears and my stories and my gratitude heavy in me. Jed was still in bed, and I could tell from his face that he was in a black mood. Ever since the Free Festival, Jed's appetite for acid had been on the increase. I'd begun to keep track of how many times he took it, and to quarrel with him about it, for although the drug made him jubilant for hours on end, and gloriously kind to Andrew and me, afterwards he was drained, and would lapse into an ominous strained listlessness which sooner or later erupted in frightening tempers. And these moods were lasting longer all the time. It was a week, I knew, since he had taken any.

I told him the bare bones of what had happened, and crept cautiously under the covers beside him.

'Arseholes,' he said with a kind of abstract bitterness, watching me take off my sweater. Stripped, I lay silent, still as a winter mole. Jed reached out and prodded. *No*, my stomach muscles said. Before I could stop myself, my thighs had jerked together, closed tight. The brown arm retreated.

'You want me for security,' he accused, 'but no truck with sex.'

I shook my head miserably, wanting to accuse back, to say that it was his demands which had escalated, but I knew too well how long it was since I'd turned to him of my own accord, and even to defend myself I couldn't deny it. I thought of all the times I had said yes with my will only, despairing of my body's stubbornness and mysterious dreads. I was afraid that he would leave me, if he ever found out what resistance really lay coiled inside.

'True?' Jed demanded. He gave a long shuddering sigh. I turned over on my side and hoped against hope that the blow-up would not come.

The morning sun flickered on the curved windows on the other side of the square. By afternoon it would shine into the bedroom and reveal the stippled tracks of a paint-roller on the wall, and the rough patching of lining paper above the fireplace. Across the square the convex windows had a deep gleam. I had called at one of the houses once, to thank the owner for handing in a lost purse to the police. The house was tall, the colour of butter icing, and smooth to touch. There was no answer to my ring. When I pressed my nose against the window I saw fitted carpets, dishwashers, the copper-beech shine of antique furniture. It was a grown-up world, in which nothing was makeshift, in which toys never broke. It was the world I cleaned in; I breathed in its dust, my nose reddened with its sneezes.

Jed fished for a half-smoked joint in the ashtray beside the bed, lit up, and coughed. The pillowcase crumpled behind his head as he heaved himself up straight in the bed.

I lay still and stared at the curtains, hating them. They had been left by the previous tenants, and they were fawn, with a yellow trellis pattern over which pink flowers climbed with claustrophobic regularity. Jed could see nothing wrong with them, had insisted that they stay.

It's a doll's house we live in, I thought, a trap of cardboard walls furnished by dressmakers' scraps. I had an image of a tiny pink plastic lavatory pan, of serving tea in miniature cups from a sideboard the size of a matchbox.

I rolled over and put my nose against Jed's arm. I would apologise; somehow, I would make it all right. 'Look, I couldn't help it,' I said. Play with me, I thought, help me move the little bed the size of a beetle, help me glue the baby elephant together with Bostik.

'Yeah?' he said derisively, 'that's a real bloody comfort, isn't it.'

I drew back, folding my arms around myself. I watched him surround the joint with his lips, suck smoke in angrily through his teeth. His breath hissed out. He inhabits his sex like a baron his castle, I thought suddenly: washing my face or peeling vegetables at the sink, his eye will always be on me, a giant's eye big as a radar bowl filling the tiny window.

'You're not going to work, then?'

'Not today,' he muttered. He moved his leg away from its nest beside mine. I looked at him. His suffering hurt. Give in, I thought, give it, then he'll feel real.

'Let me play with you.' Reach for the cock I wouldn't take inside.

His face flushed. There were broken veins on his cheeks, and one or two dark hairs wisped from his nostrils. 'Just give up, will you?' He was offended. When he thrust my hand away it fell back impotently against my thigh. 'It's no good if you have to *try*.

You didn't always have to *try*.'

I looked at his shoulders, at the long bony chest, the lean lines of stomach; once upon a time I'd grasped for it all so eagerly. I felt the energy drain out of me. 'Maybe we both have to try, now . . . '

'Oh, bugger off!'

' . . . to work something out, that's what I meant.'

Jed pulled the bedclothes up around his neck.

His cock, I thought bitterly, *his* fingers clutching the blankets, *his* frustrated desires. An inalienable right. Evict him, fire him, take his union card, steal his stereo, he'll still have that left.

'I can't stand this.' Jed's elbow bruised me as he threw himself out of bed. The light bulb swung in the draught he made. I watched him fumble in the wickerwork basket where he kept his clothes.

'Filthy,' he was muttering, 'Filthy.' The hairs rose on the back of my neck. Suddenly he grabbed his hair and screamed. His eyes were red-rimmed with exhaustion. He's ill, I thought, cowering back; he's going over the edge. He needs help.

I reached out my hand. 'Jed, stop. I'm sorry. Come back to bed.'

A leather boot flew across the room, hit the electric fire. Overturned it. 'I'm going to the Baths!' Jed shouted. The fire crackled dangerously. I dived for the plug and wrenched it out of the socket, and heard myself scream out: 'You'll kill us both one day, you crazy bastard.' And then I was running at him with my head down, butting him in the stomach, yelling, clawing, beside myself. Greedy bastard, he was mad, intolerable, thought he had a right to *everything*. I threw the boot back at him. Naked, I pummelled him. 'The acid's driving you *crazy*.' His hands were over his face now, protecting it. 'See? See?' I shouted, 'You think I like living with your rages? See what it's like?' I took him by the shoulders and shook him. His hair caught in my fingers. 'I can't *bear* to be so scared!' He looked back at me through the tangle of his hair, incredulously, and when I let him go he sank to his knees.

'I know it,' he groaned, 'I know it.' His feet were blue with cold, his chilblains ugly red. He covered his eyes with his hands and rocked. The long curtain of hair moved from side to side. 'But I never mean to, I swear to you, I swear.'

I knelt down beside him and held his head, feeling his scalp warm under my cheek. Let's make up, I thought, let's patch it up. Live at the minimum; be good to each other, at least, if we can do no more.

'Why is everything so wrong?' I said into the soft hair. Jed's reply was inaudible. He leaned against me, trembling. He did not know, any more than I did, what to change or salvage; I saw that now, staring me in the face.

If there was to be change at the root, it would have to come from me. But how? I had already tried, with all the force of my will I had turned to face the strain; I had fought that night at the cottage to regain myself, fought in ways I hardly dared remember, and had fallen back, blinded, like a bat, into a territory that belonged not to me, but to others, and was ruled over by them; a place where I had no rights.

I don't know how, I thought. For a moment I saw myself, saw my roots clinging stubbornly to the thin soil of the plots behind the corrugated iron: my place was a cobwebbed house where boarding criss-crossed the windows like elastoplast, and I wouldn't be ousted from it.

And which was true? I looked at Jed, who had no answers. 'Oh Christ,' I said, and wrapped my arms around him.

24

If it was some rash new instinct for joy which tugged me to Matt, it was not disappointed. For after the fair, the miracle continued.

Even the hours at work passed in a haze of exhaustion and goodwill. I would have confided in Mike – for I longed to confide in someone – but she had gone to the cottage with Sherry to attempt some kind of reconciliation, and so I typed hard and kept my counsel, and when Jude, sensing, as she put it, 'a change in my aura', began to probe, I deflected her with a joke.

After work I returned to Matt, and to hypnosis. In the flat, we did nothing; it was as if the place had become a womb or an egg, cut off in time and space. We tried from time to time to behave normally, but even the simplest tasks – shopping at the grocer's on the corner, cooking an omelette, or setting a table – a child could have done more efficiently. Our movements were drowsy, attenuated, like people in a dope trance. Often we stopped in the middle of something and became tangled: once we forgot the leeks frizzling in the pan, and the cat crept on to the kitchen table and ate the chicken; afterwards we called each other hopeless incompetents, and laughed, to discharge the fear. By mutual consent, we didn't venture far afield. The world seemed too fast, too dry, unsympathetic. Like toddlers, we trailed each other round the flat, or else sat at opposite ends of the noisy blue sofa, staring at each other, while from far off came the busy hum of traffic. Over and over again, shaking our heads with astonishment, we explored our short, shared history. There on the blue sofa, each day was weighed and measured and added to the storehouse of memories which proved conclusively that we had been made for each other.

'Do you remember . . . ?' Matt would say on Tuesday, talking of Monday, 'Do you remember how we phoned each other at the very same moment?' Or, ancient history now, 'Do you remember our first quarrel beside the duck pond?' But Matt's obsession was strictly limited; he sifted only the recent past, and didn't seem inclined to venture further back. Questions about his work with theatre groups he turned aside impatiently, saying that my achievements might be worthy of discussion, but his were negligible, he had hardly started. 'Without a relationship,' he said seriously, 'I just mess around. Now, with any luck, I'll really be able to get down to it.' I remember the thrill of shock I felt then. There's so little caution in him, I thought: what other man would place the stakes so high?

One evening, when I pressed him, he produced a handful of family photographs to giggle over. Unbelievably, he had three ugly brothers. Their sad round eyes and long necks were similar to his, I had to admit, but only in the way that a caricature resembles its subject. 'Brilliant, all of them, but boring as budgies,' he said, and then, with an assurance that I found enviable, he added: 'I was my mother's favourite.'

I looked at her picture, and saw a stern-featured woman in a felt hat shaped like a snail. 'She's okay,' Matt said wistfully, 'she's the one who always takes my side.'

'And your dad?' I asked, for he appeared nowhere in the photographs. 'Is he as handsome as you?'

Matt's face darkened. His father managed a steel works, he said, and had never concealed his dislike of him. He would go no further than that.

One night, feeling slightly more adult than usual, we ventured over the Heath to Hampstead Village, where the streets smelled of ground coffee and ratatouille. Open blinds revealed brightly-lit interiors: fitted kitchens, parquet floors, bentwood chairs with paisley-patterned cushions. As we strolled and scoffed at the Colour Supplement perfection, Matt romanticised about his dream home. The Bay of Bengal, he said, or else Big Sur, where Henry Miller was. Grey stone in the mountains, I argued: bare boards, and two rowan trees outside the window.

'You're an ad-man's nightmare,' he laughed. 'You're supposed to enjoy all this. What you've got to learn is without a stripped pine dresser, you're deprived.'

I thought of Reuben, and smiled. 'My ex-therapist was hot on that. You should have seen me trying to explain class antagonism to him! As far as he was concerned you could boil down the entire Russian Revolution to a spot of oedipal envy.'

'Very comforting for him, I imagine.'

I stared at the shining kitchens. 'You'd wonder how on earth they keep them so clean.'

'Maids, darling. Maids and nannies.' He caught hold of my belt. 'Come here,' he said, 'Tell me about this psycho-*anal*-ist character.'

I scowled at the curtainless windows. 'Look at them. How smug they are. You'd think they had nothing to fear.'

'Now, now,' Matt's finger chastised. 'When you snuff it, they'll find Bolshevik carved on your heart, and that's for sure.' He chuckled. 'They're not worth worrying about. Harmless, they are. If you're an artist, you can have them eating out of your hand.'

We sat down on a bench under a Victorian street lamp. A wisteria bush hung over the weathered brick wall behind it, its purple flowers bleached by the white light. I was surprised to find, after all, an urge to confess. It felt like a pushing upwards, a need to loosen and lift a weight which had pressed down, dark and dense as stone. Matt was waiting, blowing smoke rings up at the starry flowers. I struggled for words. If I give him an outline, I thought, keep it schematic, perhaps he'll be satisfied.

Matt listened. Beyond an occasional shake of the head, and a shudder or two, he didn't seem unduly disturbed by what I told him, so far from it, in fact, that I began to wonder if he had heard me at all. All the same, his steady warmth was encouraging, and I talked on, feeling the weight begin to lift a little.

It grew late. Nearby someone played Mozart, liquid and perfect. 'A direct line to the gods,' I said, and Matt nodded. And then remorse jabbed at me. Because there was always the risk of misrepresenting, of indicting the innocent. I became silent.

Matt prompted. And then? And then?

He will delve and mine, I thought, until I have no defences. 'I've said too much already,' I protested. 'My memory is full of gaps, I don't trust it.' But for a little while my dead voice, obedient, continued to recite.

It was past midnight when we rose from the bench. As we walked back along the cobbled street, Matt stopped suddenly and said: 'But you're a powerful woman with a talent for *life*. You don't need to hang on to these inadequacies any longer.' He gripped my shoulders and pulled them back, which reminded me so much of my mother that for a second, I resisted. Too soon, I thought, I'm not big enough yet.

'Okay?' he said, peering, and I relented.

'Okay.'

Matt's eyes were bleary with tiredness, and his hair stuck up in wisps around his head. 'After all, it's not your fault that these wimps didn't know how to treat you, is it?'

'Is it really that simple?' I said, with a thrill of disloyalty.

'Yeah. Things are pretty simple, really.' He sounded almost irritated. 'Anyway, you've got me now, you don't need all that baggage from the past.'

To stand clean and clear and full to the brim. Yes. Of course. That's what I wanted. But as for the rest, I thought, am I to abandon it? Leave it on a doorstep, simply because it's messy?

25

Next day, encouraged by the Hampstead expedition, we went shopping in Camden Town. Camden High Street was swerves, nerves, buses with sidelights flashing, cyclists with shirts and skirts flapping. On the pavements, black youths roller-skated, and men mended cables in hazardous deep holes, and rush hour crowds racketed towards the sump of the Tube station.

We drifted, holding on to each other. From time to time people collided with us, and tutted at our lazy pace. Matt carried a string bag which was still empty, for we could not decide what to buy.

Whether we paused at a shop window or passed by was dictated by a minute consultation of wrists: what interested one, the other also stared at, as if seeking information about the looker. Outside an Indian shop, I suddenly wanted to buy something for Matt. I had no idea what. I had no idea what was good enough. I looked at the glass jars of coriander seeds, the gold-threaded sari lengths. There were sacks of red beans, and rows of thonged sandals, and a pyramid of Tide boxes which reached the ceiling. Staring at the unsuitable commodities, I felt dazed, and urgent. It would have to be something light, round, perfect. I would give him nothing flawed or uneasy which would weigh heavy on him.

'We don't know what we're looking for,' Matt observed, and I laughed. Smells of pomade and aniseed wafted from the shop door. I felt the secret trickle of sperm. I'll give him a baby, brand new, I thought, and my knees trembled.

Holding up the empty string bag, Matt put his thumb in his mouth and looked distraught. 'Help,' he said.

'My mind's blank too,' I laughed nervously.

He shrugged. 'So who needs to eat?'

We headed for the market. At the stalls, Matt had no opinion on peppers versus aubergines, or about how many pounds of potatoes we needed, and while I asked the price of things he stood back and looked on, chewing his lip.

Later, at the bus stop, he said suddenly: 'You're getting so speechless these days.' He looked disgruntled.

I was too startled to reply immediately. It had never entered my head that those silences between us – which to me were filled, abundant – might irk him. 'But I'm quiet by nature,' I stammered, 'you know that.'

Matt looked perplexed. 'I mean, I need you to put energy into me, too.'

Miserable, I defended myself, saying that words could trip you up, that deeds were what counted, in the end. Matt's face grew more morose. Finally he peered around angrily and said: 'Why are we hanging about here? The bloody bus isn't going to come, is it?'

A group of skinheads came along the pavement towards the bus stop, jostling each other, spitting noisily into the gutter. Perhaps Matt was right. Perhaps I was getting lazy. I put my arms round him, wanting to close the gap. He responded by going rigid. 'Jesus, you seem to think streets are as safe as a kindergarten.' He picked up the shopping bag. 'Come on. I'm walking. Didn't you *see* them?'

'I didn't think about it . . . '

'There are fascists about, and you don't *think* about it. That's great. You prefer Noddyland, do you?'

'But I feel safe with you, you idiot,' I cried at him.

'Well. I don't feel safe with *you*.'

'What could happen anyway, in broad daylight? I didn't even see any badges . . . ' I walked after him, arguing. He was so tall, husky in the thick leather jacket: whatever was he afraid of?

He walked faster. 'They've done Rock Against Racism members already, you know that, don't you?' He tucked in his chin and glanced round warily. 'Broad daylight or not, I still have a few survival instincts left.'

'Oh, I'm *sorry*,' I said resentfully. He was talking out of the side of his mouth, like Humphrey Bogart; in a moment, I thought, he would turn his collar up.

'You just walk so *slowly*!' he cried.

I stopped dead. Commuters hurried past. Pink, pale, black faces seemed to swivel and stare.

'Sometimes I think it's deliberate,' he said, and his mouth trembled.

On the pavement at my feet there were watermelon smears, crimson and pulpy, leaking streams of pink juice. My mind whirled. What had I done wrong? Had I been too clinging, too feminine? Crossing the road on the way to the market, I had faltered, held on to him – could it be that? My toe poked at a trail of black watermelon seeds. 'You make me feel I fall short,' I whispered. In a moment he'll melt, I thought, he'll repent, he can't mean it.

'Oh well,' he said, 'no one's perfect.'

I began to cry in earnest, and he dived for me. 'Oh *God*,' he said, trying to get his arms around me, and the shopping bag swung against my leg, and the first egg slithered from the carton and hit the ground. There was a small sound and a splatter of yellow. We fumbled hopelessly, while another rolled out, and another. I caught the bag and cradled it, while Matt closed the carton, and I waited for that cold look, the one he had flayed Vi with, waited him to call me clumsy, a clumsy girl . . .

Matt hung his head and looked as if he might cry too. 'What a mess. What a godawful mess.'

'Never mind,' I said quickly; not knowing which one of us I was trying to reassure. 'Never mind.'

'It's the responsibility,' he said miserably, 'I feel so responsible for you.'

Back at the flat, he gave a huge sigh and apologised for everything. It was the fear, he explained, he simply couldn't bear to feel so exposed. His face was clear again, the face he turned to me in the night, no longer the closed, brutal face he had worn on the street.

'I always saw the streets as men's territory,' I said, 'That's why you shook me.'

'Not true.' He took off his leather jacket and hung it up behind the door. 'It's just armour. They're all wimps underneath. Just like me.' He grimaced. 'And so now you know.'

I tried to laugh. 'If you must know, I thought that you were tired of having me round your neck.'

He looked at me in disbelief. 'Christ, no. How could I be? How could I ever?'

I started to cry then, big frantic sobs interspersed with giggles, at the absurdity of it all. Matt took a bound towards me, and then, pulling at our clothes, tripping, we stumbled through the bedroom door. When we began to make love my cap lay untouched in its white plastic box. Now I thought, thrashing. Now.

'Lovely June,' Matt breathed, 'I can feel all of you.'

'It's all yours,' I said, in a desperate bid for oblivion.

Matt stopped moving, and held his breath. 'Watch it,' he whispered, 'watch yourself.'

Soft mouth, cruelly gnawed at the downward bow of the upper lip. Flaring nostrils; plump, chilly lobe of ear. It was his decision now, to carry or drop. I lay waiting, dark and dispersed. I felt him struggle, and then, with a terrible groan, he withdrew, and my destination faded. 'Put your cap in, for Christ's sake.'

The cap was cold and too slippery. I wrestled with it under the bedclothes. See how well he takes care of me, I thought; but I felt more robbed than grateful. He grumbled, entering, at the touch of the thick rubber, but soon he was moving silkily again, undeterred, talking dirty, saying give it to me, and I was trying, saying nearly, not yet, but then he was already there, the neck jerking back, the fevered whimpering.

In the night, half asleep, I thought or dreamed of June. A hand was pushing her roughly through the bedroom door, and there were eggs, brown and white eggs still crusted with hen droppings: a whole tray of them on a chair inside the door. The door was slammed behind her, and in the dark she fell, and in the dark the eggs crushed sickeningly under her, she could not save them. She knew, too, that in times of rationing such hoards were precious, and therefore that her father's belt would come out, and that she would rather die than face it.

26

By Monday morning my hungry urges of the night were growing shadowy. At the office, where typewriters chattered and rang, where abortion posters stared down from the walls, I was back within myself, contained there, and any other way of being jarred was incongruous. With the telephone under her chin, Andrea was nodding, listening, adding up columns of figures on a notepad. Over at the layout desk Clara was sorting back issues, and a small Spanish student with long plaits was wrapping subscription copies on the carpet in the centre of the room. At the desk next to mine Jude was typing fast with two fingers, breaking off every now and then to prod at jammed keys and curse all man-made machines. I was conscious, suddenly, that I was the only mother among them; yet they'd always said that it was hard to see me in that role. You hardly mention it, they said, and never write about it. Perhaps because I never really wanted it, I'd replied: in these days accident played as big a part as choice.

Reuben, too, had interrogated me. How did I feel about Andrew? Did I want another child?

When I snapped back: Certainly not! he paused just long enough to let his disbelief enter me.

I sense you want a little girl, he said.

I folded my arms and seethed. How dared he be so free with his interpretations, how dared he try to plant seeds in my mind, to grow me in his own image. I watched him sit there, quiet, confident, waiting for me to capitulate, fully aware that I was vulnerable, suggestible. Have it yourself, I thought furiously, and waited in stony silence for the session to end.

Jude dabbed at her manuscript with Tippex. Her brow was furrowed, her nose shone. There were strands of white in her springy dark hair. If Mike's information was right, Jude's choice was made. Jude took her temperature every day, religiously. With her girlfriend's agreement, she visited a man friend every month at the right time, and agonised when her period continued to arrive. I watched her and wondered. What must it be like, to experience that crisp separation of means and ends? To know that need –

unmuddled by madnesses of the blood – so clearly that you would pledge half a life on it. To trust yourself to that extent.

I turned again to the work on my desk. Picked up a blue pencil, marked a paragraph indentation, struck out a limping phrase. Put the pencil down. Failing such trust, you flung yourself into fevers and hoped to be saved. As if the impossible lure of impregnation had anything in common with birth, and weaning, and teething, and the long haul up the years. I had already done that once, I'd done what was expected of me, and had it made me feel any more of a woman? Had it brought me any closer to some unassailably feminine essence?

No. My course was set. I could fantasise, certainly, but my fantasies wouldn't tempt me into action. Passion apart, I hadn't come so far merely to undermine myself.

When I returned to the flat that evening I found the street door ajar. Music floated down from upstairs. It was Bob Marley, pungent, throbbing, melancholy.

We'll be together, with the roof right over our head
We'll share a shelter . . .

The cat greeted me at the open door of the flat, rubbing itself against the door jamb. I decided that Matt must have run out to the corner shop. There was a pile of cups in the sink, and tea leaves in the drain. I threw away the newspaper in which last night's chops had been wrapped, while the cat stiffened with excitement and purred wildly.

Next door the record ended, and there was a small sound.

'Matt?' I pushed the door open. Matt lay on the sofa curled on his side, like a foetus. His feet were bare and his shirt hung loose outside his trousers. On the floor beside him was a small pile of used tissues and a very full ashtray. He was awake, but bleary.

'Did I wake you?'

He shook his head. 'Come here, perfection,' he said, and his eyes moistened.

I knelt beside the sofa and put my cheek against his. He had not shaved, his skin felt gnarled, prickly. 'What's up?

Tell me.' He shook his head, and muttered something. It sounded like 'ashamed'.

'You're so *upset.*' I sat back on my heels and looked at him tenderly. 'What's been happening?'

'Give me a cigarette.'

He let the cigarette hang from his lips until I lit it, and then he shut his eyes and inhaled as if his life depended on it. His hand was over his heart, the fingers spread very wide. 'Waves of feeling,' he whispered. 'You touch something so deep, it scares me rotten.' I watched his tears run. 'I'm good for nothing, you see.'

'Idiot.' I took his hand and squeezed it hard. 'You're good for *me*, at least.'

He shook his head. 'I'm telling you, it's no joke. When I think of you, it gets me *here* . . . ' He prodded his chest. 'I'm unmanned.'

'But you're my hero, stupid.'

His face took on an obstinate look. 'Well, now you see the real me. It's not what you expected, is it?' He waved his hand towards the telephone on the table. There was an address book beside it, and a limp banana skin which was browning at the edges. 'The things I had to do. People I had to call. Nothing. I couldn't do a bloody thing.'

I thought of my competent day at the office, and felt a sneaking gratitude for the bulwarks of routine. At least it meant that one of us had his head above water. 'It doesn't harm to have a day doing nothing when you feel shaky,' I said, as much to convince myself as brace him. 'It's hard to be disciplined all the time when you work on your own.' I leaned over to kiss him on the ear. 'After all, it's only one day in your life.'

'Oh, is it?' he said darkly. He looked at me. 'When you're *here*, it's all right . . . I would have called you at the office . . . I nearly did . . . '

'You should have.'

'Maybe,' he sniffed. 'But I thought the sisters might take offence or something.'

'How silly. Why should they?' All the same, I felt a twinge

of alarm. I picked up the overflowing ashtray and got up. 'I'm going to make you some tea.'

Matt smiled weakly. 'Thanks pal, you're a brick.'

In the kitchen, I brooded. There were no biscuits in the cupboard, and the bread bin was empty. Never had the flat seemed so cheerless, so unappetising: it was as if the heart had gone out of it. I couldn't help remembering that first dinner party, when the place had been full of the smell of roasting and new paint; how cosy it had seemed, after the white ward and the impersonal nurses. A sanctuary. With Matt at the centre of it all, a gleeful, engaging despot. And Vi shrivelling, Vi growing shadowy . . .

I stood by the cooker, hugging myself, watching the first wisps of steam escape from the kettle. I couldn't push the thought of her away indefinitely; underneath the smokescreen of anxiety, she lay in wait. All I wanted was a little more time. Soon enough the truth would be out, and she would come banging at the door to take her revenge; soon enough, it would all be over. But not yet. And there was no need for Matt to invite her in prematurely, to leave the way wide open for her.

When I gave him his tea he held the cup in both hands, like a child, and drained it greedily. Then he set it down on the floor beside the used tissues. His shoulders drooped, his whole body expressed defeat. I could see it was up to me to reconstitute him. I bent to pick up the cup. 'You'll be okay,' I said, discouraged.

He beckoned.'Come sit with me.'

When I squeezed on to the sofa beside him he leaned against me and shut his eyes. Now and again a mournful shudder passed through his body. He grew heavier against me, a dead weight. 'Don't go away,' I said, feeling him sinking out of reach. 'Tell me what you were trying to do today. Was it Rock Against Racism?'

I felt him stiffen. He opened his eyes. 'I've had it for RAR,' he said sullenly. 'I thought you knew that. What's the good of wasting my time with them when they don't listen to a word I say?'

'Oh, I'm sure they do.'

He shook his head impatiently. 'It's who you *are* that

counts with them ... Oh, not the women, the women are great. They just don't get a look in.' He sniffed. 'It's the knee-jerk boys I can't stand, the ones who're in it to make their names.'

I held his hand and listened to his complaints, although this time around, the invective was less amusing. 'I really can't believe you don't have an impact in the group,' I chided. 'You underestimate yourself. You should hang in there, give yourself a chance. Otherwise, won't you just feel like a failure?'

Matt scowled.

'I'm only speaking from my own experience,' I said hurriedly. 'I'm not trying to say there aren't frustrations in political groups, and all sorts of power struggles ... I know there are. I know what a strain it is ... '

'So why are you trying to argue me back into it?'

'Because what else is there? Because you have to feel effective, somehow. You need to have a focus.' Otherwise you drop like a stone, you fall right through the bottom of everything.

Matt let loose another string of abuse. They were wankers, elitists, sexist to the core, I had no business defending them. I protested that I wasn't defending anyone, but Matt's flow would not be stemmed. I lay back and let the words wash over me. At least he's letting off steam, I thought. Already his face was more animated, and the dead weariness had gone from his voice.

'No,' he said at last, with vigour. 'The nuke issue is the only one. People don't see it yet, but give them a couple of years and they will.' He sat up and crooked his arms behind his head. 'That's what I was supposed to be doing, all bloody day, instead of whingeing around. I was *supposed* to be ringing these two guys about fast-breeder reactors. It was research ... ' He swung his head round to look at me, testing my reaction. 'Research for my play. I had it all set up.'

I looked back at him in surprise. 'You haven't mentioned it before.'

'Superstition, I guess. It's so big, it scares me a bit. It could be a stunner, you see. I've got the contacts, I've got the ideas . . . and the crazy thing is, nobody else seems to have tumbled to the idea, it's like a clear field. And some of the material these guys have is shit-hot, I can smell that already . . . ' The sofa squeaked excitedly as he moved into top gear, plotting and planning, predicting pitfalls, inventing critics only to shoot them down in flames a moment later. 'I'm not just talking about breaches of safety regulations, you see, or waste-dumping, I'm talking about tie-ins between the Electricity Generating Board's nuclear reactors over here and the war machine in the States, real under-the-counter deals. Our excess plutonium – from so-called *civil* power stations, right? – for Uranium 235, gift-wrapped from the US of A, without which, of course, no warheads.' Matt shivered. 'You've got to go for the whole picture, because that's exactly what they don't want you to see.'

'You certainly think big,' I said uneasily.

'Well, you've got to, don't you? *They* do. While the left over here sit around bellyaching about wage claims, the Pentagon are busy getting their rocks off on sexy little feasibility studies about the European Theatre of War, and 'surgical strikes' and what have you – I tell you, even the language makes your hair stand on end.'

'What about translating all this into theatrical terms?' I shook my head, wondering how I could bring him down to earth. 'I simply wouldn't know where to start.'

Matt frowned. 'I don't see why. Not if it's television, and that's what I'm talking about, after all; that's what you've got to crack these days, if you're a writer with any politics at all. No, don't turn up your nose. It's the only medium, there's no point being snobby about it. You've got to learn to use it, turn it inside out. Take its codes and break them . . . Just you wait.' He sighed heavily. 'All I need is some time, time to get down to it. Time to let it flow.' He pointed to his chest. 'Here. That's where it all jams up, and you're stuck up shit creek, waiting. But once you get started, it comes in no time. I know it. I really feel it, this time.'

Perhaps I lack imagination, I thought. I made a face. 'Me,

I'm a plodder. If I waited for inspiration . . . I mean, I could hang around till the cows come home.'

Matt dug his elbow in my ribs. 'A plodder? Come off it. You're the muse herself.'

'Oh no you don't! I don't fancy that role one bit.'

He laughed. 'Oh, but I'll be your muse too. A reciprocal arrangement. Think of it. Me working in one room and you doing your poems and stuff in another . . . I wouldn't disturb you, cross my heart and hope to die.' He grinned shyly. 'I know how much you like your peace and quiet. Bliss, it would be. A blissful existence.'

I snorted. 'As long as I don't have to clean the cooker!'

Matt was silent for a moment. 'Seriously though,' he said, taking a deep breath, 'I do think it would be different if we lived together.' He pulled himself up and looked at me eagerly. 'I'm not such a wimp as I make out, not really. Or at least, with you here, I wouldn't be.'

I smiled. 'You wouldn't want to take me on, you know. I'm none too good at living with men.'

'Oh, bullshit. I know you better than they did. I'll take a chance on it, if you will.' His face was completely earnest; I wouldn't be able to slip out of this with a joke. Suddenly I was wary.

'But there's no room here. It's Andrew you're talking about too, remember. I'm not a free agent, you know.' Not like Vi, I thought, and turned cold.

'Think positively. Anything's possible if you want it enough.'

I stalled. 'I'm only trying to be practical. One of us has to be. Look at it – we've no money at all.'

'And I don't have a job.' He shrugged. 'So what? Fuck it, we'll work something out. Who knows, the flat upstairs might come vacant soon – or so the landlord tells me.'

He made it sound so easy; I wanted so badly to believe him, wanted to believe in all his visions, however insubstantial, all his promises. Tears of irritability rose to my eyes. 'Will it?' I said, throwing the words at him. Prove it to me, prove it.

His eyes widened. 'What a badger! Where's your optimism, girl? Here I am, thinking about our future, and you look at me like I just offered you a one-way ticket to Alcatraz.'

'I'm just trying to take it in,' I muttered.

'Come on.' He put his head on one side. 'Am I your hero or am I your hero?' His eyebrows shot up and down like Groucho Marx. His eyes rolled. His teeth flashed. I couldn't have wished for a more complete recovery. With that face shining at me, daring me to say no, I felt like a coward, a killjoy.

'I give in. Anything to put the roses back in your cheeks.'

Just then the telephone rang, and Matt grinned broadly. 'Excuse me,' he drawled, 'that'll be my agent.' He purred into the receiver: 'Marshall, *darling* . . .'

I listened, not so much to what he was saying, more to the remarkable acrobatics of the voice itself. It slithered through half a dozen tones in as many seconds, skimming up into a falsetto and then plunging again, and always there was that slight trill to it, a boisterous resonance which burst out in ungovernable laughter whenever Marshall – or so I supposed – said something particularly witty. But now Matt was looking at me, saying 'Yes she's here.' He winked at me. 'Oh yes, undoubtedly the big one. She's the queen.' He held his hand up, closing his finger and thumb in a circle. 'Supremo.' He laughed delightedly. 'Bye now, old chap. Must go.' Wiping imaginary sweat from his forehead, he put the phone down. 'That guy,' he said, still laughing, 'is *so* fucked up. He's just spent a fortnight being roadie for a bunch of really tough ladies, and he's still making his public school jokes about the beast in his trousers . . . I ask you!'

'I've just realised what your laugh reminds me of. Dundee cake. Dark brown and fruity, with nutty bits on top.'

'Oh yeah? Just watch it. Dinner later, I say. Fighting now.' Matt jumped up from the table and struck a fencing pose. 'Up, up, on guard! Shall I compare thee to a mince pie?' He dragged me to my feet, and made me stand opposite him. 'Your eyes, my darling, are greenfinches on the wing.' He lunged.

I parried. 'Your hair is barley in the pearl dawn.'

'Oh, touché. Poets' Corner, I get it. Let me just think now. Let me lean on my rapier and prepare my riposte . . . ' His face contorted into an agony of thought. 'Got it!:

'Describing my love for you,
Words fall on their backs
And stick their feet in the air
Like dead hedgehogs.'

I held my sides. 'Vanquished!'

Matt stretched himself up to his full height. 'Did I really say that?'

'What can I do but surrender?'

'Mm,' he said, approaching, 'say that word again, would you?'

27

On the floor beside the mattress a battered alarm clock said seven o'clock and was quite silent. I picked it up, shook it, searched for my watch.

Beside me Matt stirred and lazily opened one eye. 'I can't find your little bud sometimes, you know,' he mumbled.

I looked down at him. 'No.' The hostility in my voice surprised me and brought him wide awake.

'Right. So what's the trouble?'

'Oh, nothing. I'm late, that's the trouble.'

Matt sat up and combed his fingers through his hair. 'Come on. Let's get to the root of this.'

'Not *now*,' I said. Propped against the wall opposite the end of the bed was a mirror which Matt had taken down while decorating. The mirror recorded a tousled woman, owl-eyed from yesterday's mascara, who cupped a watch in her hand, whose face was startlingly surly. 'Look, it's really all right . . . it's great, as a matter of fact, you know it is.'

Matt stuck out his tongue.

'Yes,' I insisted, while the face in the mirror contradicted me. I dangled the watch from my fingers. Eleven o'clock. I was definitely late. 'So I get a bit frustrated... but it's early days yet.' I sighed. 'Give it time.' I moved to get up.

'So do I get frustrated, believe me.'

'Look, it isn't your fault, it isn't to do with technique or anything. I don't really know what it is...'

'Well, I'm willing to find out, if you are.'

I shook my head. Now Matt will grub away like a pig after acorns, I thought, and was immediately appalled at myself. 'It's late. I must meet Mike.'

'It's Sunday, for Christ's sake.'

'I told you, it's the supplement.'

Matt leaned over and plucked the watch out of my hand. 'Oh no you don't. I'm going to lick you with my honeyed tongue. Where the bee sucks, there suck I...' He grinned his most persuasive grin. 'Knees up! I'm going to have another go at this before I let you out of here. And that's a promise.'

'There's no time,' I protested, squirming. Across the room the mirror reflected a swell on the blue bedcover as Matt wormed his way down inside the bed.

His tongue slid. Sometimes skilful, sparking shivers of pleasure, sometimes numbing. I hold his rough head between my hands: it's too late, I can't do it. I wondered how to stop him, how to tell him without hurting. Already Mike would be in Bloomsbury, looking for a parking space, climbing the narrow wooden stairs to the typesetter's, talking to the woman about costs and corrections; in half an hour she would be waiting at the office.

A small glow spread between my thighs. I should be telling him what to do. He deserves guidance. Encourage his tongue and fingers this way and that. So elusive, the pleasure, like quicksilver – arriving, departing. And such a long time for him to wait, and such concentration needed; I'm doing my best, he is doing his best.

After a while Matt pulled the cover down and looked up at me inquiringly. 'Have we struck gold yet?' His face was soaked and shiny in the valley of my knees.

I shook my head and tried to smile. 'There's no mistaking it.

If I had, you'd hear about it.'

'You *could* try talking to me. Say when it's good. I get to feel lost down there.'

'So do I,' I said miserably.

Matt wiped his face on the sheet and crawled up the bed.

'You see, you touch one bit, and it's lovely, then the next minute I don't feel anything. Just a blank. Or a sort of irritation . . .'

Matt sighed. 'Well, it doesn't do much for my confidence.'

'Oh God . . . I could say the same, you know.' I reached for a cigarette. 'I knew we shouldn't have started this. Not this morning.'

Matt frowned. 'You smoke too much, you know that? The old fags come out, and you retreat. A mole in a hole.'

It was too near the truth. 'Why don't you just call me frigid and be done with it!' I scrambled out of the bedclothes and began to fling my clothes on. 'Piss off,' I muttered, 'piss off.'

'Oh, come off it. I don't believe in frigidity, remember? I just think you're a bit too fond of your ivory tower. What's wrong with saying that, if it's true? What worries me is that you don't want me enough.'

'You're crazy. You *know* I do.'

'Do I? Do I?' There was a strange expression on his face, a mixture of mischief and spite. 'So what's blocking you, then? What's stopping the old energy flow?'

I stood still and clenched my fists. 'Of course. It's all my problem. I forgot.'

'Anger, perhaps? Just a smidgeon?' In one bound he had jackknifed out of bed. 'Enough of this!' He put up his fists. 'Come on, let's have you.'

'Go to hell.'

He grabbed me. 'Not on my own, dearest. We're in it together . . . although you'd really rather poke at your own oyster, wouldn't you? Anything rather than really *be* with a man.' There was an expression of pure rejoicing on his face as I swung at him. 'Aha! Got you steamed up at last.' With his fists crooked up like a boxer's, he began to dance bent-kneed around the room. His cock flapped between his legs. 'Come on, get that anger out!'

'Don't come at me like some fifth-rate therapist!' I lashed out at his grinning face. He parried, and the blow struck his arm. A hook from his leg and I was on the ground, with him on top of me. I lay winded. In the corner of my eye the wooden legs of Matt's desk loomed, and the metal frame of the gas fire; somewhere out of sight the mirror leaned precariously against the wall. From this angle, the room was an assault course of sharp corners and cutting edges. I struggled under him. 'You're a control-freak. Power mad.'

He pinned my hands behind my head. 'Yes, dear.' He grinned. 'And you?'

I heaved, and we rolled, chafing each other red where we rubbed, and again he was astride me, a great bruiser of a man. His pectoral muscles stood out as he held me down.

Of course he would win. If this were serious, I would be mincemeat, flattened against the ropes in the first round. His penis rose against my stomach, and he laughed. I ground my teeth. I hated being a woman.

Fury at the odds made me buck, throwing him off. I twisted round and got him in a leg grip. Strong thighs, he had said? Then I'd show him just how well they could squeeze. I squeezed until I thought his ribs might crack, until he released my hands.

'Okay!' he gasped. 'One all.' He gave a salute.

'Patronising bastard.' He was laughing at me, and I was breathing heavily, coughing; I had fully expended my strength.

He sucked a bleeding graze on his wrist, and grinned. 'You know, for such a blond person, you've got a powerful stash of dark energy. Like a pulsar. Old Jung would love you.'

I pushed him off. 'Oh yes? What's a pulsar?'

'A neutron star. A star which has collapsed, with massive density. Gravity a million million times that of the earth.'

'Oh, terrific. Sure it's not yourself you're talking about?'

'Tsk, tsk.' He waggled his finger. 'They give off vast magnetic fields, and . . . oh yes, they spin faster than anything you can imagine. Pretty neat altogether, I'd say.'

As I zipped up my jeans I felt fluids trickle out of me, making an uncomfortable wet patch. I scowled. Thanks to Matt's antics, there was no question of wasting any more time, no time to wash or change or eat.

'I always did fancy myself at physics,' Matt said modestly. He wrapped a towel round his waist. 'Hey, sourpuss . . . I love you to distraction.'

Fight or no fight, the look on his face almost melted me, would have done, probably, if only he'd left it at that. But no, the manic teasing was not over.

He pulled me to him, rubbed himself against me. 'A little breakfast, perhaps? Sausage? Egg? Frosties?' His eyes rolled lewdly.

I struggled free. 'Oh,' I cried, in extremes of irritation, 'I'm going.'

The grin faded from his face. 'Grudging bugger, you are.'

On the way out, I had qualms, and called back: 'Pick me up for the cinema, okay?'

'Maybe,' he shouted after me.

The office was quiet and empty. The wastepaper bags had been put out, the worn carpet hoovered clean of the usual scatter of paper clips and rubber bands; even the mugs on the tea table had been washed up.

'It's not like you to be late,' Mike said, but it was more of a question than a criticism.

'I'll tell all,' I promised, 'as soon as I get my breath back.'

Mike was sitting at a high stool at the angled layout desk, with a sheaf of proofs in front of her. Her hair was hidden under a mauve chiffon scarf, and there was a blue pencil behind her ear. 'I brought lunch, by the way. Some salad, and houmous from my good Greek shop.' She made an apologetic face. 'I hadn't really started. I was waiting for you. Holidays make me even lazier than usual.'

I plugged in the kettle, and spooned Nescafe into two cups. 'How was it?' I asked, through a yawn.

Mike tinkered with the gold bracelet on her wrist. 'Actually, good. So much easier than London.' She looked at me. 'Sherry liked it.'

'No fights?'

'No fights.' She was frowning slightly.

I carried the coffee over and put it down carefully on the

flat ledge at the top of the desk. On the wall, where Catherine's layout sketch was pinned, a random series of images overlapped. There were photos of suffragette demonstrations, a cartoon of flying nuns, an etching of Virginia Woolf hawk-faced under a flower-trimmed hat, and two crinoline ladies with feminist symbols embroidered on their skirts. The juxtaposition was faintly unsettling.

'Right,' I said, and rolled up my sleeves. Mike had stacked the rough layout sheets in order, and had already cut up some of the typesetting, and so I began straight way on a finished paste-up. I worked fast with set-square and cowgum, pausing now and again to check the all-over design against the rough. Beside me Mike sliced off the dark edges of bromides with a scalpel; her rings clicked musically against the steel straight-edge. Since it was Sunday, no phones rang, and as we worked, the small sounds of the room took over. Flies buzzed. The cowgum spreader squeaked across the page. Mike's scarf whispered in a draught from the window. A foot away, the curve of her cheek, a slight smile in profile, gave off a gentle, neutral attention.

Bending over a sheet of proofs, I scored with the knife. The shorn edges parted cleanly and fell away in straight strips. 'There's this crazy man, you see, who makes me late . . .'

Mike stopped working and looked at me.

'. . . But I don't expect it'll last.' She'll laugh, I thought, I'll see the incredulity on her face. 'You met him once. At the theatre, remember?'

'Not the one who pestered you?'

I nodded sheepishly. 'The same.'

She laid down the steel rule.

'I gave in. It was a case of the will being weak and the flesh being strong – or something.' I waited for her gesture of recognition.

She looked thoughtful. 'Wasn't he Vi's *amour*?'

'They finished,' I said quickly, 'a good while ago.' I drew the scalpel blade along the edge of the desk, teasing the wood up, feathering it. 'She doesn't know yet,' I said, answering the question Mike had been too tactful to ask. 'She's been away.'

'Will she mind a lot?'

'Oh yes. She'll mind, all right.'

Mike nodded silently. She reached up to tie the headscarf more tightly over her hair. 'I've got purple streaks,' she said, with a shy laugh. 'Sherry was trying to up-date me with her hair dyes. 'With the movement of her arms the low neck of her T-shirt gaped and a dark channel appeared between her breasts. For a second the cleft reminded me of dress designs I had drawn as a child: dresses with nipped waists and bell skirts and cleavages which hinted at mysteries I scarcely dared aspire to. Thinking of Mike and Sherry together in play or in passion, I felt the same intimation of peril. I looked away quickly, and stared at the images on the wall; half-formed thoughts hovered, and tailed away guiltily in mid-air like garden gate gossip. The crinoline nagged: the wide skirt like an inverted goblet, the engulfing folds of it. What I would have done, as a girl, what crimes would I not have committed in order to own it. I shifted uncomfortably in my seat.

'But do you really think it's awful of me?'

'Hardly. I couldn't really, could I? The pot calling the kettle . . .'

I hesitated. 'Have *you* decided what to do yet?' The words came out with a challenging edge which I hadn't intended.

Mike pulled her shoulders back. 'I'm going to tell him.' She took a deep breath. 'There. I've said it. I keep hoping that if I say it often enough, I'll end up doing it.'

I could see that this time she meant it. 'Christ, I wish you luck.' I cast around for something to give her, a kiss, a cigarette, anything.

'Everything changes, doesn't it?' she went on breathlessly. 'I can barely keep up with myself. Half the time I just shake, and the other half . . . well . . . ' She smiled a small ironic smile. 'When I was trying to make up my mind, you know, I threw the I Ching so often that I got the hexagram which ticks you off for importuning the oracle!'

'But in fact you look relieved . . . in the middle of the panic, I mean.'

Mike shook her head. 'You're still talking to a weed,

remember. And the weed, superstitiously, says wait and see.' In a brisker voice, she added: 'But *you* ... this person makes you happy, does he?'

'Chaotic,' I said, 'he makes me bloody chaotic!'

Mike laughed. 'The Thunderclap, as the I Ching would say.'

'He does, though. For some reason, he does make me happy.'

'Then I'm glad for you,' she said simply.

Such permissiveness made me feel quite light-headed, even though I had wanted it so badly. On the wall, the embroidered face of the crinoline lady simpered, looked deceitful. I remembered the face of my mother as she came into my bedroom and kissed me on the brow. There was a lipstick rim on her front teeth and her smile was raddled by anxiety. 'Congratulations,' she said, 'you're a young lady now.' I hadn't trusted that permission, either: had rubbed the red mark from my forehead, pulled the covers over my head.

'You know,' Mike said pensively, 'I'm sure you'll laugh at this, but when I first started coming to the Women's Centre, I assumed that you were gay ... You had such a boyish, sinewy look – oh, I know I'm talking stereotypes, but that's how I thought, then.' She smiled. 'And the way you pronounced on things ... not often, but with such great *authority*.' She held up her hand to ward off my protests. 'No, it's true. There's my role-model for the future, I thought to myself.'

'This need for heroes,' I mocked, to cover my edginess, 'Are we all the same, d'you reckon?' I thought regretfully of that clear-cut self, that rebel: had she really vanished for ever?

'Oh yes.' Mike grinned. 'Reprehensible, I agree, but widespread ... and they're not always men these days, either. Shocking, isn't it?'

'As for being gay ...' I tailed off, losing my nerve. Mike gave me a cool scrutinising look, and I gathered my courage and spoke quickly. The whole subject gave me gooseflesh. 'Look, I know I've steered clear of talking about all that ...'

There was a slight pause. 'You have, haven't you?' The hint of reproach in her voice almost brought us to an impasse again.

'Misplaced tact, I suppose ... or fear of making an idiot of myself.' I stumbled on, trying to articulate the strangled, impossible thoughts before the impulse left me. 'But you're right, I *do* feel boyish. With women, I really do. But when I try to imagine . . . being with a woman, I freeze. It's a blank. I mean, who would I *be*?' I glanced anxiously at her. 'Am I making any sense? Whereas with men, at least I feel . . . *some* sort of certainty about it.' I thought of Matt: Matt who could look like a hero in his black leather jacket, Matt outspoken as the crinoline lady was devious. The truth, or just the trajectory of my wanting? Or were the two inseparable? I shook my head. 'Oh, I don't really know what I'm trying to say.'

Mike was examining her nails. 'You mean that you define who you are by opposition?' I'd only ever heard her use that incisive, emotionless voice for interviewing, and I flinched inwardly. She wasn't making it any easier for me.

'Something like that.' How unnatural it must sound to her, how frail and butterfly-like. 'Being with men makes me feel . . . feminine, I suppose. Or as near as makes no difference.' I thought briefly of the morning, and Matt's efforts, and I faltered. 'Mind you, the deeper I go the more problematic that gets, too.' I shrugged helplessly. 'So you see, how *could* I be gay? It's as if there's no basis in me for it. For making that choice, if you like.'

Mike frowned and lined up the steel rule with the edge of the desk. 'I see. At least I think I do. It would be just too confusing, being with a woman.'

'It's so complicated, isn't it? Whether it's a choice, as everyone says – lesbians, I mean – or whether it all comes down to mother stuff, in the end.'

'Yes . . . ' Mike said doubtfully. She bent over the desk and began to clean one of the finished boards with quick, delicate dabs of a cowgum rubber. For a while we worked in a silence broken only by a few murmured consultations. As soon as I completed a page I passed it to her, so that she, being defter, could strip in the tiny page numbers and corrections. I watched her spear a word the size of a matchstick and ease it into position with the tip of her scalpel. Her fingers hovered over the clean page, making no marks. When she had glued the word down she let out a long sigh. 'I'm always scared of sneezing, and blowing the corrections away.' She put her hands in the small of her back and stretched. 'But it doesn't *feel* complicated to me, you see. I mean, I don't feel feminine, with Sherry, and certainly not masculine, like you've described.' She wrinkled up her face, considering. 'Female, maybe? I think that's nearer it.'

I looked down at the blank sheet of layout paper in front of me. 'I don't think I've ever known the meaning of that word.'

'You sound so sad.' Mike was looking at me gravely. 'But you had that strong connection with your father, didn't you? I've envied you that, sometimes.'

'That's true. And I thank my lucky stars for it.'

Mike pulled a fresh sheet of corrections towards her, and began to cut them up. I remembered with a surge of warmth that I owed her a debt, too. 'It's nice, isn't it, just the two of us here?'

'One certainly gets more done,' Mike said amiably, 'and we've still got the whole afternoon.'

I picked up the cowgum rubber and moulded it between my fingers. At five o'clock, Matt was due to arrive. I pictured him coming through the door, stooping slightly, with his arms and legs everywhere, and a madcap face to make us laugh. 'He's coming to pick me up later. The man.'

Mike's smile broadened. 'So I'll get a look.'

'You will indeed. I hope he's on his best behaviour, that's all. He's such a headcase, you never can tell . . . '

'But you're compelled?'

'Oh yes, I simply can't help myself.'

Mike manoeuvered the strip of typesetting on the page, and pronounced: 'It's a passion, then.'

On her lips, the word didn't sound so out of place. A passion. It fitted, it had the right ring of fate, of the preordained. I realised how much I had wanted her to name it that.

28

Matt arrived at the office in an old corduroy jacket which sagged, and with his hair shorn almost to the scalp. The savage new haircut stole all his blondness and made his features look hooded and crow-like.

'I was sick of it,' he said aggressively. 'I felt like a change.' He stood in the doorway and peered round the office as if expecting an attack, his uneasiness displacing the delicate flow of confidences between Mike and me. I moved nervously to meet him, to draw him in; Mike, too, put every effort into welcoming him, rearranging chairs, offering cigarettes. She made him coffee and told him amusing snippets about the early days of the magazine; she would probably have recounted the entire history of it, if Matt had appeared at all interested. But Matt was not to be seduced. All the time Mike was talking to him, he hardly said a word and the look of boredom and suspicion never left his face. If Mike had been a man, I would have concluded that Matt was simply jealous, and might have made allowances for him, but as it was, I found his behaviour quite inexplicable. I watched him with growing fury as he gazed listlessly at the layout boards. When Mike asked his opinion of the cover design he shrugged with stark rudeness, and got up, and prowled down to the far end of the office, examining posters, whistling through his teeth, leaving me feeling foolish and stranded and responsible. I hardly dared look at Mike. My one thought was to get him out of there as fast as possible.

'Phew,' he said, as we went out into the street, 'the inner sanctum.'

I tried to keep my temper. 'Oh don't be silly. Men *are* admitted, you know.'

'On sufferance.'

'Oh yes, we really grilled you, didn't we? We really gave your credentials a going over . . . I wish you could hear yourself sometimes, it's quite ridiculous.'

Matt looked offended, but surprisingly, backed down. 'I gather it's too holy to have a joke about,' he grumbled.

'Come on.' I took his arm and steered him towards the cinema. 'Otherwise we'll miss the beginning.'

'Yes mommy,' he said pointedly, and a yoke of tension settled across my shoulder-blades.

After the show, when I told him that I wanted to sleep at home for once, he pulled a face. 'One night outside the palace walls won't kill you,' I said, trying to jolly him along. Uncomfortable, uncomfortable man, I thought. Dragging his feet, he followed me to the bus stop, and lapsed into a gloomy silence which I felt too dispirited to break. Somewhere nearby a church clock chimed, and a flock of starlings rose over the street in a chattering cloud.

Matt stared past me into the oncoming traffic. 'Vi knows, by the way.'

The hairs rose on the back of my neck.

'Don't look at me like that. I didn't tell her. I didn't have to.'

I watched the starlings circle and scatter, a black stampede of birds. The air filled with their high thin whistle.

'She knew because she got no answer when she phoned your house.' There was the shadow of a smile on his lips, a look of affection, but not for me, no: this time the appreciation was all for the memory of Vi. Shaking his head, he laughed. 'Quite a girl, our Vi. She's so full of the joys of spring after her package tour, you wouldn't believe it.' He bent over me and peered into my face. 'Look, it'll be all right. Don't flap.'

I stared back, disliking him. 'Did I say anything?'

He puffed out his cheeks. 'That's the trouble with you. The bottom lip goes out, the shutters come down. I *was* trying to make it easier for you.'

When the bus came, it was crowded, and we had to strap-hang on the lower deck. Matt stood crushed between me and a large woman in an imitation fur coat. His shorn head brushed the ceiling and there was a look of wounded dignity on his face. Evidently he considers public transport beneath him, I thought. Like pubs, like politeness, like all things ordinary.

Although the house was dusty and empty, there were signs that Tom and Marie had returned. Mail opened on the hallstand, and in the kitchen, a pot of red beans left to soak. Matt vanished upstairs, and when I carried the tea tray up I found him frowning at himself in the mirror.

'So you don't like my new look?'

I admitted that I didn't.

He put his hands on his hips. 'Sometimes I think you only want me to show off to your feminist friends.' He looked at me with mock belligerence 'Eh, eh, eh?'

I set the tray down with great care. 'I seem to remember that you were the one who wanted to meet Mike.'

Matt turned back to the mirror and flattened the bristle above his ears. 'Oh, her . . . ' he said, studying himself, 'Did I?'

'Yes, *her*. And with all that bloody charm at your disposal, you might at least have *tried*.'

He raised his eyebrows at the mirror. 'What's wrong? Didn't I make a good impression or something?'

Speechless, I watched him go to my desk, sit down, cross his legs, and calmly roll a cigarette. 'I mean, she's okay. I just don't find her very interesting, that's all.' His tongue came out, very red, to lick the rim of the cigarette paper. 'She's just a poppet, really, isn't she?'

'She's a *what?*'

'Oh, you know – the rosebud mouth and the big blue eyes gazing up at you . . . everything geared to men.'

I couldn't believe my ears. '*Men?*'

'What have I said?' he asked innocently. 'Is there something wrong with saying what I think?'

I sat down hard on the bed, rattling the teacups. A snow of white spots danced in front of my eyes.

'Hey, what's up?'

There was something very crazy going on here, I could feel it stirring around me, trying to enter. I fought against it. He couldn't mean it; it was a provocation, no more, no less.

'Do you really think you can slander Mike in front of me

and get away with it?'

Matt leaned back in his chair. 'Slander?' His sneer was ecstatic. 'Well, well, quite a protection racket you've got going. No criticism of the sisters while Mama June is around to shelter them under her big big wings, eh? Isn't it just a *bit* compulsive?'

My mind slewed, as I looked at this thing he had unearthed, and found it true, or at least not to be ruled out, and suddenly I was without balance or defence. 'Get out of here,' I said desperately.

'Oh, but it's true. Not a word about mimsy Mike, nor our mutual friend Vi, not even the gay girls who *woman* the office, eh?' He was still grinning, brazening it out, but his voice shook with rage. 'I mean, what have you got to hide?' He threw his tobacco tin into his bag and slung it over his shoulder. 'My heart bleeds for you all, it really does, to be in need of such *tender* care . . . Oh, and I'm going. No problem. I never intended to stay.' He waved his hand at the room. 'It's such a slum here, you're more than welcome to it, darling.' And then he stalked out and slammed the door behind him.

That night I floated in darkness loosely, and Matt's wings beat against me, and nothing was certain. I struggled to see the Mike I knew, but time and time again she slithered away, and another Mike rose before me and posed provocatively, and offered up a waxwork smile. I turned away from the dark, seeking a sliver of light under the door. Behind the door my mother was puffing out the layered white net of her skirt and pinning a tartan sash at her shoulder with a Cairngorm brooch. She was the most beautiful woman in the world, and she belonged to me, but when I stretched out my arms to make her mine they withered in their sockets, and when I tried to call out, my tongue swelled up and began to tick, like a time bomb.

29

On the Tube going to Vi's, I watched my reflection in the window. There were two of them: one sharp-edged, one blurred and waterlogged, and they overlapped. Adjacent to my twin selves, a middle-aged man wearing the maroon badge of the miners' union read Thomas Hardy's *Woodlanders* with close attention, never once raising his head. His shirt neck was open under his hot blue suit, and his brown shoes were scuffed and shabby. I felt shabby too. City grime, city pimples, shining nose, all reflected mercilessly by the window. I hated the Tube, most of all the constriction of it. The load of ground above, the weight of worms and sewage pipes, gasworks and office blocks. I would never stop hating it.

For several days running Vi had stalled, her voice on the phone clipped and punishing. Yes, she was seeing Marshall. Yes, she was painting. Of course, Italy with its angular light had inspired her.

A wait. The doors of the carriage wouldn't close. I thought of jumping off, walking the rest of the way. Outside, at least I could look around, take my mind off things. See real light on wet slate roofs, poplars blowing, women steering prams over zebra crossings. Instead of those strained faces, those arrangements of little rivets.

A woman entered and sat down next to the Hardy reader. Lustred nails, lustred cheeks. Cared for. She looked at her watch. The gold strap winked under the hard light; her shoes shone, too, like chrome. Her face was composed, but as the minutes passed and the doors still did not close her high heels clicked as she crossed and uncrossed her ankles. When the doors finally hissed and slid together she ran a fingertip along the curve of her eyebrow, and her mouth slackened ever so slightly. The rubber edges of the doors met and sealed. I thought of what was to come, and shivered.

Vi opened the front door without smiling. Her hips swayed in front of me as I followed her upstairs: narrow hips in tight corduroy pants. She wore an old grey sweater darned at the elbows in many colours, and the backs of her arms were streaked with paint. There were boxes of books on the landing, stacked canvasses.

'You've been working?'

'No.' She held the kitchen door open. 'You'll have to come in here. I'm decorating upstairs as well. It's to be my studio.' Her voice was expressionless.

'Good,' I said, nodding my approval.

'At least that's my story and I'm sticking to it.' She laughed shortly.

I threaded my way through a jumble of rolled carpets and upturned chairs. Under the superficial muddle, it was clear that the room was being transformed. A skeleton of brackets jutted from the wall above the sink, and a large patch in the centre of the floorboards showed the lighter marks of a sanding machine. Vi had put curtains up, too: parental cast-offs in acid colours, lime and brown and purple. It was all very disorientating.

'Sorry, can you find a seat among the junk?' Vi went to the cooker and fumbled with matches. The corners of her mouth were gathered into two neat tucks, like smocking stitch.

I moved a paper lampshade from a chair and sat down at the kitchen table. There was a collection of carpenter's tools on the table, and a pink birdcage with a hamster in it, some straw, and a small millwheel. Seeing me, the hamster bolted out of its straw nest and began to scurry from one side of the cage to the other. 'You're building shelves,' I said, paying tribute.

'Yes.' Vi opened the fridge and brought out a carton of milk. Apart from a butter dish and a small wedge of cheese the fridge was empty. Evidently she still believed in keeping a bare larder, as if stocking up on supplies would doom her to a lifetime of greed. 'I thought it was high time I got this place together,' she said, with her back to me. When she turned round her eyes were unnaturally bright.

Outside, a train rumbled north out of Kings Cross. I cleared a space on the table for the teapot, pushing aside Vi's rings, a saucer in which Polyfilla had hardened, scattered Rawlplugs, a Black and Decker drill. The rings at least were familiar; the other objects were as new and strange as the lines of determination around Vi's mouth. The self-control was unnerving, too.

In the birdcage, the treadmill began to click and turn. The hamster took several steps on the rungs and then stopped, with its tiny eyes alert and its beetle-black nose scenting the air. I watched Vi carry the teapot to the table. Perhaps we were going to sweep everything under the table, then. Perhaps she had already accepted it. Perhaps Matt was right, and her premonitions – so very far in advance of the event – had already armed her.

Vi began to pour out the tea. I watched the stream from the spout falter, waver, and finally cascade over the table as her control slipped. She set the teapot down with a bang and backed away. 'Actual bodily harm! That's what you make me think of.' She wiped her wet hands on her jeans once, twice, many times, staring at me without seeing. Her eyes without kohl were lighter, the colour of old bracken.

I rose from my chair. 'Sit down, Vi.'

Her hands, freed of objects, flew up into fists which shook in the air at either side of her head; for a moment her face was unrecognisable: seamed, crimped, compressed. Her eyes screwed shut and her lips folded in on themselves, wrinkling, like an old woman's. Two great tears rolled down her cheeks. 'I always *know*,' she wept. 'I knew you were going to do it. Months before Matt and I were over, I knew . . . but you went on denying it.'

'No,' I said, moving the electric drill away from the spreading puddle of tea. 'It wasn't like that . . . I warded him off, Vi, grant me that. If it's a question of loyalty, I did try.' Vi put both hands over her mouth and shook her head violently; her tears trickled over her spread fingers. I picked up one of her rings from the table, threaded it on to a loose Rawlplug, spun it. If you tied a ring to a hair and dangled it over your pregnant belly it could predict the sex of the child: straight lines for a boy, and for a girl, circles. I looked at Vi's streaming face and wished that there was some specified punishment that I could simply take, and then go, poker-faced, with some dignity. Reparations I could make. Otherwise, it was the same old trap. Accusations, denials. Pointless, inescapable; futile as the hamster on the wheel. Outside the window a light rain was falling, but beyond the rooftops on the other side of the street the sun still shone, and over the railway bridge the transparent arch of a rainbow curved. I thought of Matt. Not the ugly, petulant Matt, the one who since our quarrel had obstinately refused to phone, but the other, the man of blinding tenderness who laughed and laughed and scared both of us half to death with his transports.

'Surely I have a right to happiness too?' I had to force the words out. To me the appeal sounded hollow, rhetorical, but perhaps for Vi it would have some resonance. After a moment her sobbing quietened, and she wiped her eyes on the sleeve of her jersey.

'It was the silence. I come back from holiday and I don't hear anything . . . and you just let me find out. You didn't even tell me *yourself* . . . '

'Because I didn't think it would last.' Well, it was almost true. And becoming truer, perhaps, as the days passed and Matt did not phone. 'I kept thinking it would burn itself out.'

'Bullshit!' she cried. 'Why didn't you just tell me, it wouldn't have been so bad if you'd *told* me?'

I threw the ring on the table and watched it spin. 'What difference would it have made? It's awful, whichever way you look at it. I'm not pretending it isn't awful.' I hadn't come here to put up a defence, for there was none, after all. Tears came to my eyes. 'We're not exactly having an idyllic time, if it helps.' As soon as it was out of my mouth I regretted it. Vi looked at me, through me: a soaked, insulted stare. I was as transparent as glass. I laid my hands palms down on the table: an offering. She is seeing him talking to my cunt, I thought, she is hearing him name me the real woman to her counterfeit. But mostly she is hearing him turning me against her, demanding my acquiescence in his casual slanders, tossed out and then gone as fast as cigarette ends thrown in a stream, you'd hardly believe they'd happened.

They used to cut off the hands of thieves. My fingers trembled. Vi's white face floated above me. She was so close I could smell sweat, patchouli oil. 'Do you want me to go?'

She looked at me for a second, biting her lip hard. 'Suit yourself.'

I stood up. Suit yourself, she said, after all the difficult years. And so I would do just that. I stumbled through the avenue of chairs. I had my hand on the door when she exploded.

'All these years I spent admiring you,' she shouted, 'and you're just a *bitch*. Like anyone else . . . ' She sat down and started to cry again, a grating, painful, lost sound. I turned back, hopeful. Her dark hair hung over her face, hiding it; all I could see was the handkerchief which came and went. I listened to the small girlish snuffles which came from underneath her hair, and wondered if it would be hypocritical to comfort her. Then she said something in a tiny voice which I had to strain to hear. ' . . . And I thought I'd failed you.' She threw her hair back and glared at me through her tears. 'I never could make you feel any better, could I? No, I was the dumb cluck, the insensitive one, wasn't I?'

I stared back, hypnotised. It was as if all of a sudden I saw myself through her tears, and I was a blur, like the reflection in the Tube window. Stations flashed past, and lights shone on me more and more brightly, and in the centre of the bombardment I was moist, permeable, a small slug of indefinite shape. I shivered, trying to obliterate the memory. The emptiness, the salt on the tail, the skin dissolving.

Vi's gold eyes held me. I ached, watching her. I ached all over with the familiar cold. I had been chilled that year, chilled to the bone, like a long 'flu. I must set the record straight, I thought: at least I can do that. 'Nobody could have done more than you did,' I said.

She looked at me intently for a moment, and her upper lip quivered. 'They thought I was being hysterical, you know. "Oh, Vi's going over the top again." But all the time I was so scared that you'd . . . ' She stopped short, picked at a dry patch of paint on the inside of her wrist. 'I know that's what they thought of me. Phil more or less admitted it.' She blew her nose and tucked her handkerchief into her sleeve, like a schoolgirl; then she continued in a low voice. I remember one day we went cycling – a sunny day, it was in June. It was a better day for you. You smiled, you *looked* at things... I was so happy about that...' She paused, and her face set with resolve. 'And then later when Jed came round and asked how you'd been, you said –' her throat worked nervously '– you said, "Terrible." Just that. You wrote me off completely.'

I searched my memory. Nothing.

'I didn't say anything about it – I didn't think I ought, because you weren't strong enough. I just walked out of the room.' She glanced at me and added bitterly: 'I don't expect you noticed.'

'I'm sorry, but what can I say?'

Vi got up and began to move around restlessly, picking up screwdrivers, putting teacups in the sink. She picked up the saucer in which Polyfilla had solidified, and began to chip at it savagely with a chisel. 'Of course you don't remember,' she muttered, 'because it was always Jed for you, or Phil. Oh yes. It's the men who have the magic, isn't it?' She jabbed hard at the centre of the saucer. She'll break it, I thought; she should approach it from the edges, coaxing it off.

Vi stiffened her shoulders. 'Would you mind going, because I have to work now.'

I turned away. 'As you like.' What gives her the right to be so harsh? I thought. What irreproachable virtue? Once again I headed for the door. Then on a spiteful impulse I turned back. 'I think we should talk about our competitiveness some time,' I said.

Vi shrugged.

On the down escalator, images slid by, rushing up and over my shoulder like planes taking off, an ugly offensive. The blonde in the ad unzipped her boiler suit to show her bra. 'Underneath, they're all lovable.'

The soft belly exposed, I thought, then the punch below the belt: underneath, they're all monsters. Expansion, contraction, expansion. Was it worth it? Was it even worth trying, with Vi?

The forecourt of the station was rain-drenched, people fleeing. All the way back to the house I saw Vi standing there with her toes turned in, awkward and steeled in the centre of the disordered room. She has finally found a charge which will stick, I thought. After all these years.

Head down against the rain, I longed only for something to ease the defeat. The cosy blankness of valium. Matt's arms. Whatever the cost. I remembered what my mother had written. 'All men are selfish, June, you've got to use a lot of patience.'

30

Andrew was due to return next day, so that afternoon I began on the usual preparations – dusting and hoovering the children's room, checking the cupboards for clothes that were too small, or needed patching. There were several boxes of old toys I wanted to sort, too, the detritus of two sets of birthdays and Christmases which I'd rummaged through already without much success. Zac had agreed to help with this, but only because I insisted that otherwise I would have no idea what to save and what to discard, and as it turned out, when the time came to begin, he was nowhere to be seen.

'Oh dear,' said Marie vaguely, 'I think he said something about football.'

I emptied the boxes onto sheets of newspaper and gazed dejectedly at the dusty heap. All around me the floor rolled with marbles, and ball-bearings, and rubber wheels the size of thumb-nails. There were drawing pads, scribbled and dog-eared, odd sections of track for racing cars, crumpled comics, debris of plastic aeroplane components. And cars: I had never seen so many different Matchbox cars. There were woolly bears and broken puppets and tiny parachutes with tangled strings. There wasn't much worth saving. I sat back on my heels and felt cross, for once again it was surface tidying, make-do and mend, when only a complete renovation could really solve the problem. More bookshelves for the walls. A carpet which covered the whole floor rather than petering out three quarters of the way across it. Wall cupboards. New window frames. It is a slum, I thought: Matt was only stating the obvious.

I had come back from Vi's to find the telephone pad covered with messages and exclamation marks. 'Matt phoned.' 'Matt phoned again.' 'Matt will phone later!!' 'Ring Matt this evening!!!' Finally, at the bottom of the page Marie had scrawled: 'I wish you'd tell me your secret!' When I rang back his voice shook with relief.

'I don't know what got into me,' he breathed, 'you're so precious to me, but it's so hard to handle.' Pause. Sound of kisses on Matt's end of the line. 'I swear I didn't mean it – what I said about Mike. You should have punched my face in . . . will you forgive and forget? I mean, can you?' Sound of scrabbling. 'I'm on my knees now . . . '

'You were awful.'

'I was awful,' he agreed. 'Never again.'

I crossed my fingers and wished for it to be true.

'I'm still down on my knees . . . '

I giggled.

'Oh!' He let out a small gasp.

'What's wrong?'

'Instant erections, you are.'

'Lunatic!'

'It's true, the beast is straining at the pants, as Marshall would say.'

'Can you save it?'

'It's meant for no other.'

I had laughed out loud, with relief. I beamed among the rubbish, remembering. Like it or not, we were as twins, teamed beyond choice or compatibility: so said Matt, sweeping aside all obstacles. Trust me, he said, speaking of nothing less than total transformation; leave home, live with me. Make a fresh start. The extremism was irresistible.

Lying upside down on top of the heap was an Action Man, rubbery-pink in khaki, with no genitals under his fatigues. At one time there had been half a dozen, until one day Andrew and Zac had equipped them with toy parachutes and sent them flying out of the attic window. Writing at my desk, I'd seen a miniature invasion force float past my window, and midget paratroopers veer off course to lodge in the upper branches of the lime trees. This one was the sole survivor. I picked him off the pile and tried to make him stand to attention, as he was meant to do, but just as I succeeded the dust made me sneeze, and he keeled over, and one of his legs fell off.

Once upon a time I was courageous, I thought: before I turned into a drudge.

At Kings Cross I leaned against a pillar and smoked, standing where I could keep an eye on Platform One and Three, for Grantham trains were due in at both, and I had missed Andrew this way before. Overhead the arched glass roof was speckled and brown with bird droppings and diesel fumes, and pigeons fluttered among rusty metal girders. At last the train nosed in under the great arch and the platform barriers swung open.

Butterflies. I showed my platform ticket and walked through. Quickly Andrew's face was there, one of many sticking out of the train windows, beaming, mouthing things, *so pleased* to see me. My heart filled up.

'I've got a racer bike!' he shouted over the noise. 'It's got no gears yet, though.' He accepted my kiss absent-mindedly and tugged me towards the guard's van. Together we manoeuvred the large blue bike on to the platform.

'It's second-hand. We're going to do it up.'

I admired. 'Did you trade in your little one?'

'Mm, sure . . . I changed trains, you know. All on me own.' His face was pink with pride.

'Weren't you nervous?' I asked, as I tried to help him with the bike and his holdall and two bulky plastic bags.

'It's okay, I can wheel it . . . I wasn't *really* nervous . . . ' He slipped a hand expertly into his back pocket and waved his ticket at the collector. 'Wait till Zac sees my bike! Albert had ten babies, too . . . Albert's the pig,' he added.

I laughed. 'Albert's a man's name.'

He laughed too. 'Oh, I didn't think of that. She's a lady, though. They all feed off her, all at once.'

I looked at the burly figure beside me, marvelling. 'How big you always seem when you come back.' His father's face grinned back at me. Was that *all* adults could ever say?

'Yeah. I did building work too, on the roof.'

'You look good on it.' Sunburned arms, hair going blond, freckles on his nose. 'Did you get any sun on that lily-white chest, like I said?'

'Nope. On me arms, I did. Two *hundred* tiles. That's what I carried up the ladder. Maybe more.'

'You mean slates, or the old red ones?'

'Yeah, the heavy ones. They *weigh*, they do,' he said, glowing. 'About six or seven pounds each.'

At the exit I stopped short, wondering what to do with the new bike.

'Where's Marie's car?'

'She's out somewhere, she couldn't come.'

'Zac too?' He sounded disappointed, and I looked at him anxiously. 'Oh well,' he said after a moment, 'we'll just have to walk, then. I'll ride alongside.'

Cars, bikes, piglets. One day, I vowed, I would provide them all.

31

Pencil in hand, I stared at the typescript of *The Popular Book of Statistics*. It was as bad as Andrea had said it would be, but at £4.00 an hour I couldn't afford to turn it down. With Andrew back, my expenses were soaring. New shoes, trousers for school, cinema outings, gears for the racer bike: *Womanright* wages simply wouldn't stretch that far.

'In these bra-burning days of Women's Lib,' I read, 'Canada's ladies lead the field in lingerie. Three out of four women there let the men wear the pants and stick to their uplifts.' I turned the page and leafed through the other chapters, searching for something more neutral. In the middle of 'Alcohol consumption per Capita' a commotion at the front gate disturbed me. I opened the window and leaned out, and saw Andrew and Zac at the bottom of the front steps, with a spilled dustbin rolling on the ground beside them.

'We'll clean it up,' they cried in unison, 'but can we have money for chips?'

'What about your dinner?'

'It's not for *ages*.'

'Oh, all right,' I said, waving them upstairs. They dashed into the room with their hands outstretched.

'I've got a letter for you.' Dancing from foot to foot, Andrew searched his pockets. 'It's about the school campaign to save a teacher.'

'Go to the *toilet*.'

'It must be in my schoolbag. But I said you'd go.'

'Is it something to do with cuts?'

'Mm, something like that. Miss Anderson says we need all the parents in it so I said my mum will definitely go . . .'

'Oh, did you?'

'Sorry,' he gasped, 'got to go toilet,' and he shot out with Zac at his heel. Their draught swirled through the room, blowing papers off my desk. From next door came the sound of loud pissing, like a cow in a stall.

When they had gone I sat down to work again, but my concentration was broken. Outside on the street which led up from the school, streams of children passed. Dawdling girls, shouting girls, girls on skateboards. Boys on bikes, boys swinging sports bags, boys carrying squarish cellophane-covered cakes home from cookery class. The term had hardly started, but already my desk had gathered its usual autumn store of paperwork. There was notification of a Parents' Evening (smell of chalk dust and schoolbooks and Old Spice from spruced-up dads), a permission slip for a day-trip to a farm (please provide packed lunch, no glass bottles), an Education Authority questionnaire asking for my first, second, and third choice of secondary schools, and a form to fill in for free school lunches. And now, presumably, a whole string of meetings about this cuts campaign business. As if the days weren't full enough already. Too full. Sighing, I began to fill in the means test for free dinners.

At five o'clock, just as I was beginning to think about Matt, the doorbell rang, and he stood there in person.

'We're going for a drive,' he said mysteriously, swinging car keys. A white Mini was parked at the gate.

'At this time?'

'I thought I'd surprise you.'

'Whose?' I pointed to the car, 'And where?'

'Marshall's, and I'm not telling.'

'But it's rush hour.'

'So?'

'What about the boys?'

'So leave a note.'

My protests were overruled, and I was whisked away. Euston, Marble Arch, High Street Kensington, Hammersmith. Pale stucco houses in a frill of green. I was intrigued. Where were we going?

Matt shook his head. 'Wait and see, badger.' He wore a new white shirt, loose and slightly transparent, and his mood was jaunty. As the car edged along in the traffic, he leaned an elbow on the open window and whistled.

Chiswick flyover. The rumble of traffic was deafening. I stretched and yawned.

'Tired mother?' Matt asked fondly, 'Or tired worker?'

'God, both, I suppose . . .'

'Sometimes I forget you have a great big son.'

'Likewise – but not for long.'

Uxbridge Road, and the whine of jets gathering power for takeoff. 'Pack up your troubles in your old kit bag,' Matt sang, whistling when he forgot the words.

'Windsor. That's it, isn't it?'

In answer Matt whipped the Mini into the inside lane and the car came to a sudden halt on the verge, its wheels scattering the grit.

'So where are we?'

'You'll see. Out you get.'

The wind from the traffic blew my hair everywhere, so that for a moment I was blinded. Then, on the other side of a red and white striped fence, I saw a runway, miles of it, and parched grass, and, hazy in the distance, the control towers of Heathrow.

'We're rather near, aren't we? Is it allowed?'

Above the noise of the traffic a new sound was distinguishable: the deep rumble of a large, low-flying plane. 'Let's go!' I said, panicking, 'Let's get back in and get out of here.'

Matt grinned wickedly. 'Now look!' He took my shoulders and spun me round. 'This is the good bit.'

I heard myself scream. Bearing down on us in a shimmer of fumes was the underbelly of a DC10, its landing carriage dangling, its flaps shuddering. I clawed at Matt, trying to get away, trying to duck, but his arms clamped tight around me, and he forced my head into his chest. I heard his heart thump with terror. Above me the tons of straining metal poised at stalling speed, and I died, and the monster lurched on, howling. A smell of scorching rubber filled the air. For a brief second I pictured my own flesh on the tarmac, a jellied smear in the rainbow sheen of petrol.

'You bloody sadist!'

Matt threw his head back, bursting with laughter. 'But isn't it FAR OUT,' he yelled. 'It's so good for me, it's a tonic!' His upturned face was blissful.

'Oh yes, good for Andrew too,' I cried, 'Bloody marvellous, being orphaned!' I got back into the car and slammed the door. Matt stood for a moment with his arms flung out and his face worshipping the sky; then he climbed in after me.

'I thought it would loosen you up, break the old work routine.'

He chucked me under the chin. 'You know. Thrills and spills.'

'Get off!' I huddled back against the window, glaring at him.

'Come on, don't be such a spoilsport.'

I lit a cigarette with trembling hands, and sat staring straight ahead. Cars passed alongside. In the slipstream of each one, the Mini shuddered. Without a word, Matt put the car into gear and drove off. When at last I looked at Matt all the radiance had left his face. 'You just shouldn't scare me like that,' I said, weakening.

'Oh, forget it,' he said, in a resigned voice.

Why should I be sorry for not joining in? I thought. The man is certifiable, and that's a fact. We drove in a dull silence as far as Shepherds Bush, where I decided it was time to make peace. I pointed. 'That's where the West London group was based. Death Gulch, they called it. A demolition crew was at work, slicing into the remaining houses. 'They ran a food co-op on that estate by the flyover, I remember.' I pointed again to the skinny towering blocks on the other side of the road.

Matt chuckled. 'A food co-op, indeed.'

'And a press, too, like we did. What's wrong with food co-ops, anyway? It was pretty popular, as I remember it.'

Matt gave me a wry look. 'Straight up, June – you libertarians played at politics, don't you think? Revolution next Wednesday, and all that . . . Don't you think it was all a bit neurotic?'

His voice was like a nudge. Aquiesce, it said. I bristled. 'I disagree. Naive, perhaps – isolated, definitely. But we weren't *playing*.'

'No?'

'*No*.'

'You could have fooled me.'

I turned on him angrily. 'I wish I'd never said anything about it now. I just thought that you shared some of those politics, that's all . . . For Christ's sake, look at what we *did* . . . the evictions we fought, the things we shoved under the Council's nose, there was so much, I can't remember the half of it. All that energy we were putting out – into the Women's Centre, into the paper – and you mean to say it can all be written off as some sort of collective neurosis?' Exasperation made me inarticulate, and I burst out: 'Bugger the motives, anyway. It doesn't matter in the end about the motives... it's the *act* that counts.'

'Aha. Sparks fly.' Matt inclined his head, conceding just a little. 'Okay, okay.' He smiled grimly at the road ahead. 'I was draft-dodging myself, at the time...'

'Oh. Pardon *me*. I forget you're halfway American. I also forget that Americans are so patronising about other people's struggles.'

'I wasn't *struggling*, as you put it. Just staying out of the army. Surviving, okay?'

'Christ!' The blatant one-upmanship took my breath away.

After a while he turned and grinned at me. 'Touchy, you Scots.' He drummed his fingers lightly on the steering wheel. 'But seriously, June, whatever did it change?'

'In what respect?' My voice was icy.

'In any respect, sweetie, but specially *you*. Community action, collectivism, feminism – did you ever get what you needed? Did it improve your life any? Forgive me, but according to what you've told me, I would say not.'

'What happened or didn't happen to me can't be laid at the door of the political ideas I had.'

Matt changed lanes with a casual spin of the wheel. 'Sure about that?'

Besieged, I hung on to my seat-belt. 'What do you *expect* me to say when you bulldoze me like that? "Yes, dear, anything you say, dear"? God, sometimes I wish you'd go to therapy or something. You really wear me out.'

Matt laughed. 'Oh yeah? I don't notice that it helped you a whole lot, this therapy trip.'

'I'm not going to go on arguing. It's not a discussion, it's a dog fight.'

'Okay, okay, I read you. But just don't try to hive me off

like that.' He shook his head. 'Therapy! Honestly, what a cheek.'

In bed that night I dreamed of Vi before her easel. She was vibrant, concentrated. She was painting a portrait of Phil, who had just returned from Vietnam. His face was half destroyed, flayed by napalm. Vi's brushes, so fervently wielded, spattered paint on the floor, and down there on her knees my mother wiped and wiped at the stains, tutting savagely.

32

Phil was able to send only a limited number of letters from prison, and when, early in the New Year, I received one, I didn't pass it around, as was customary, but read selected excerpts to Jed instead.

Dear June,
Pity you couldn't make it on a visit – but it was nice to see Vi anyway. Thought I'd write one or two letters to individuals, rather than to ALL. Not so much of a strain, and more fun. I was heartened by the increasing togetherness of your letters, and by Vi saying there was something in the air about a job on *Womanright*? Sounds like a good idea . . .

The next paragraph was obviously for Jed, so I read it out to him:

In a September issue of the Sunday Telegraph I found this gem:
'There is evidence that the Windsor Free Festival attracted unwanted "organisers" who were happy to provide the basically well-behaved young pop fans with anti-establishment materials. An "underground" Press group churned out a daily newsheet and a stream of instructions and advice notices' etc. etc. Hey-ho, Jed . . .

Thank you for sending in Simone de Beauvoir's *Force of Circumstance* and Sartre's *Iron in the Soul*. Stunned by de Beauvoir's honesty – her ability to 'cast a cold eye on life, on death'. Throughout her journals there are moments when she says things like: 'Work had become meaningless. I no longer felt human. There was no way I could act which could affect anything.' As the massacres in Algeria mounted and she and the others of 'Les Temps Modernes' became entrenched against the Gaullists, and also the Communists, she felt more and more of an exile, more and more isolated against a collective national brutality and folly. This was her point of greatest despair. Of course, this is still where we live. But it seems to me that she turned to, in fact always moved among, other intellectuals and artists. A statue by Giacometti, for instance, provided the impulse to get her working again at one point... It seems to me that we live in that valley where we struggle to act in a way which will affect things for the better, thus we can't know in advance what will be required of us. This is a risky business, for we need to be able to recognise ourselves as well. De Beauvoir could point to her books – the concretisation of years of thought and experience and daily labour. What have *we* got to set against the defeats of our times? I know this is the source of a lot of my anxiety. I find Brunet, the Communist Party militant in *Iron in the Soul*, for whom the other soldiers in the Stalag are just so much material to work on, repugnant. I will always fight against Leninist mechanics-of-the-soul. But Mathieu, the philosopher trapped in individualist bids for freedom, shows no way either.

Faced with these problems of locating ourselves in the overall struggle I think some of us lapse into the 'Candomblé' or Ghost-Dance syndrome. I'll explain. In Brazil the shanty-town urban proletariat have a religious ceremony which gives each of them a chance to transcend the shit they live in – a chance to achieve a sort of ecstatic trance. Psychically it's as essential as their subsistence rations... Don't you think we sometimes identify ourselves as a colonised group within our own country, make of our hardships the justification for the pursuit of any release, whether it be drugs, or whatever?

One point that De Beauvoir makes about her relationship with Sartre interested me a lot. She said that throughout their thirty years together, it was Sartre who gave the ideological leadership. Although dedicated to maintaining a highly critical relationship, she accepted this and saw it as destructive to challenge him there. Instead of fighting on every front thrown up by their mutual interests, almost for the sake of contrariness, she saw it as a matter of recognising his leadership (in the case of ideology) as one of their differences. Thus it was Sartre who told her she must examine the economic and cultural differences between men and women if she wanted to understand her childhood, and this led to *The Second Sex*. Tricky one, this. Obviously there are few men around who have anything like Sartre's qualifications to give anyone an ideological lead, but I have felt, among our circle (ellipse, more like!) that a lot of energy is destroyed because the women, almost dogmatically, as an article of faith in the Women's Movement, are concerned to fight everything posed by the men every inch of the way.

When I read this section, I snorted with annoyance, and drew Jed's attention to it. Jed looked troubled, and said uncertainly: 'Yes, he's pushing it a bit.'

I read on:

Anyway I've found the winter between us really hellish, hating the indifferent/sadistic rigidity towards you I've felt trapped in. But then the other night you crept into my dreams, and there was a hint of the old warmth. I was surprised and relieved.

Love, Phil.

Prompted by Phil's letter to admit that he found it hard to get through the days without some kind of drug, Jed did seem to take note of my objections, and began to limit his consumption. His temper, though, was not so easily controlled, and his outbursts frightened me. I began to long for Phil to return and move into the house next door, not for my own sake, but rather to give Jed the stability he seemed to lack.

More conscious, now, of the effect of his rages, Jed took to removing himself from the house until they abated. The front door would slam, and from the window I would see him head for the dirt path which skirted the grass in the middle of the square. Round and round he would march under the bare branches of the trees, hands in pockets, kicking out at pebbles, and always, as I watched, there was the fear that one day – today, tomorrow, next week – he would go further afield, and would not come back. Marooned in anxiety, I waited for him, pacing like a tethered animal.

One day, at the window of the pale pink room, I detected a small change in myself. Jed was a distant figure hunched on the swings at the far end of the square. I went to the centre of the room. I stood still. My agitation became a restlessness. There was something I needed, something I was searching for, but it was not Jed. I couldn't put my finger on it. At last, fetching an exercise book from Andrew's room, I sat down in the armchair facing the window, and I wrote. I wrote about the dust on Jed's shoes, and the eerie brilliance of the light on the wet branches. I wrote of the north, of its dwarf oaks and burnt heather, of subjugation and punishment. And it was oddly comforting to sit there and let the language flow freely from me. When I had finished, a poem lay on the page before me, and I sat quite still, satisfied.

Looking back now, I realise that it was my letters to Phil which laid the first ground.

At first, I'd had no idea what to write to him about. I no longer worked on *Hard Times*, and put in only an occasional appearance at the Women's Centre. I steered clear of most demonstrations. I knew, anyway, that politics would be more than adequately dealt with in the others' letters. But what else was Phil interested in? I realised that I didn't know. I pictured him in his tiled cell; I pictured a mean barred window, a dull view over rooftops, and I wondered: what will he want to hear about?

After a while, by accident or instinct, I began to write about the open air, about the sweep of a ploughed field with violet water lying in its furrows. I described the sights and smells of trips I'd made with Vi to the country, or to see Jed at the Free Festival: the frosty light of a low moon over Windsor Great Park, the burning yellow of lichen on a hawthorn branch. The images pelted out. I wrote also of people, of the teenage couple who were married at midnight by Druids, of the ageing anarchist who, crazed by acid, marched round the encampment with a Union Jack over his shoulder, denouncing lechery, emptying drowsy lovers from their sleeping bags in the first light of dawn.

Sentence by sentence, I led Phil through the fleeting experiences of life as it went on and was lived outside his cell. And as I wrote, the language – which had refused to brake or harness the fearful stampede of feelings – took me by the hand and, seducing me by music and pictures, led me back out towards the world.

When Jed returned that afternoon he found me sitting there, still with the exercise book on my lap, staring out of the window. I had all but forgotten him. Interrupted, I turned and smiled at him, and he looked at me in surprise.

'I think I should have a go at the *Womanright* job, after all,' I said, and he nodded, but when I added that I had just written a poem, he looked at me warily.

That spring, Saigon fell to the NLF, and there was rejoicing in our circle. Phil arrived home in the middle of it, beardless, with his red hair drastically short. On the train he had downed three vodka-and-limes one after the other, and he peered at the assembled company as if through a mist.

33

Morning. A greenish light through the curtains, the room as if underwater. Shapes of lime tree branches moving against the window. On the desk, my typewriter sat in its place draped with

Matt's shirt. Beside it, the contents of Matt's bag were strewn around: two books, a hash tin, tobacco, Kleenex, biros. When I moved to get up, my head was heavy, my legs reluctant. Matt stirred and looked at me from under sleep-reddened eyelids.

'What's happening?'

'Morning, unfortunately, so steel yourself.' I opened the curtains and let in the dry white light. 'Tea. I'll make tea.'

'What's the hurry?' he asked, when I returned with the mugs.

'Well, I've got to start work.' I stretched across the bed to set the tea down beside him, and handed him a digestive biscuit. He grunted and pulled me down on top of him. The biscuit crumbled into the sheets.

'Give me a kiss.'

I kissed him, a small squeaking kiss on the brow, and started to withdraw. He loosed his grip immediately and turned his head away. My heart sank. 'I *have* to.'

'Not already, you don't have to.'

'Yes I do, but you can stay in bed. You don't have to hurry.'

'Cigarette, please.' Come on, come on, his hand gestured. I threw him the packet and dressed hurriedly. Then I took a deep breath and began to clear his things off the desk.

Behind me, I heard the sigh. 'Really clearing me out, aren't you?'

I tried to smile. 'I know, I'm flapping about my schedule.'

'What's the panic? What have you got on?'

My mind went blank. Challenged, I was suddenly unable to account for myself. 'Lots of things,' I said vaguely.

'Better get on then, if it's so important.' He picked up the *Observer* Colour Supplement and began to read. I stood at the desk for a moment, struggling with myself. The litter of his things on the desk was like an invasion; I knew that I couldn't work with him here, no matter how much I wanted to. I took a step into the centre of the room.

'I'm sorry, but I need to work here on my own. It's my office, you see, as well as my bedroom.'

Matt put down the magazine and shook his head. 'Okay,' he said in a long-suffering voice. Puritan, his face said, compulsive. I looked at him lying there among the crumbs, and felt hopelessly in the wrong, and suddenly hated him bitterly. I controlled myself with an effort.

'It's not that I like doing it. It just has to be done, that's all . . . and it takes *discipline* to sit down and work out exactly what has to be got underway first, and . . . '

'Patronising, aren't we,' he snapped. 'You talk to me in that tone . . . you think I don't work, or something?'

I grabbed at the straw. 'Okay, so how about a bit of solidarity when *I* have to?'

'I'm not stopping you, how am I stopping you?'

'I can't when you're . . . well, still here. I need to be alone.' I tried to speak firmly but my mouth quivered, betraying me.

'Listen to it! "I vant to be alone" . . . You really do believe in rationing, don't you. God, you're so half-arsed, I can't believe it.' Matt stumbled across the room, picking up discarded underpants and trousers as he went.

I tried pleading with him. 'Please stop making me feel guilty.' It should have been so simple. Coffee for two, toast, a kiss at parting. 'Work well.' 'And you.'

With his clothes under his arm Matt flounced out to the bathroom.

Sorry, sorry, sorry. Sorry I want to work, sorry I want to be alone, sorry I don't come. It would be carved on my heart when they opened me up; I could hear the surgeon tutting in annoyance at the mutilation.

Sorry Vi.

Matt returned fully dressed and muttering. 'Your work, your work . . . what about mine, I say? I wonder if you rate it at all. You certainly don't enquire about it a lot.'

'Don't I?' I said, disconcerted.

He shrugged. 'Not a lot.'

'There's only so much I can help you with,' I said. 'My hands are always so full these days.'

'Who's asking for help?' Matt said crossly. 'Just *recognise* me, that's all I want. He pointed first at me, then at himself.

'Two-way thing, June, not a closed circuit.' He paused by the mirror to check his hair. 'Reciprocity, okay?' His reflection admonished me.

'Point taken.'

He turned and wagged his finger at me. 'My, duckie, you are a one,' he piped, and having had the last word, withdrew peacefully enough.

I sat down at my desk with a sigh of relief. In the garden opposite a bald man was tying roses on to a green trellis, while his wife sat in a deckchair reading a magazine. They didn't appear to be talking. It looked tranquil. I picked at my nails. Piled all my hair on top of my head and screwed it into a knot. Chewed a pencil until it cracked in two, then wiped the desk clean of splinters of wood and lead. Patience, I thought: the rough with the smooth.

I worked badly all day, so that by evening I was well behind with the abominable *Book of Statistics*. To make things worse, Andrew came home from school and wandered in and out of my room, a small, hopeful face hovering on the outskirts of my consciousness, trying to attract my attention without actually asking for it. Even if I'd been capable of dreaming up a game to play with him, I would have grudged the time, and in the end heard myself saying irritably that *surely*, in that room bursting with toys and comic books and battleship games, he could find something to occupy him. Most children would have argued back, would have pestered – and in a way that would have been easier to take – but not Andrew. With no protest other than a shamed, disconsolate shrug, he removed himself. After the door had shut quietly behind him I stood up and threw a cup against the wall. The cup bounced back but did not break. I hadn't even written a poem for weeks.

While the coffee dregs dried on the wall, I came to a decision. If the next days were to be spent at *Womanright*, and the evenings given over to finishing the freelance work and being in the house for Andrew, then I could manage everything, meet the copy-editing deadline. Afterwards, with a clear conscience, I could deal with considerations of love and poetry.

34

'Afterwards', however, was not a concept Matt took kindly to. At the end of the week I called him, and his phone rang for a long time before he picked it up.

'Yes?' his voice said curtly, and then, 'Oh, it's you. The Queen Bee herself.'

'Listen, I can come over later. Tom's babysitting, and I've *almost* cracked the work . . . '

'Oh, can you?'

My spirits sank at his tone.

'The consort deeply regrets, ma'am, that he can't jump to her command today. He's too busy getting his own head together.'

I stared into the phone. It was the rap over the knuckles again. 'What's wrong with you?' I said, rebelling.

'Nothing's wrong with *me*, sweetie. It's what's wrong with you that's fucking us up.'

I held on to my temper. 'You're angry because I haven't been round.'

A laugh. 'Ha. No, I'm not *angry*. My guts are twisted out of my stomach and round my neck and I'm bleeding to death, that's all. *Sweetie*.'

'You could have come here,' I pointed out. 'I told you late evening was okay for me.'

'What?' Matt shouted, 'To your smelly house and your perpetual adolescents with their shitty little politics? No thank *you*. You're such a bag of nerves when you're there, it's not worth it.'

I slammed the receiver down. Who on *earth* did he think he was dealing with? I stood there wringing my hands, quite stunned by the ferocity of it all, and as if in a dream I watched the Rawlplugs which moored the phone to the wall loosen and sag, and a fine powder of plaster dust trickle down the wall. I only just caught the phone as it fell. Seconds later it rang in my hands.

'Don't hang up on me, June. It hurts.'

'The phone fell off the wall,' I said.

A chortle. 'That's what you get for hanging up on me. God's on my side.'

A silence, while he waited for my answering laugh, and I withheld it.

'Look, June, I'm just strung out and needing and aching for you, and you're not there.'

The phone crackled, interference as someone else tried to get a line. Momentarily another voice broke in.

'Crossed line,' I said, 'put the phone down and start again.'

'Thanks for nothing,' the phantom voice replied testily, and then Matt was there again, distorted by static. 'I'm sorry,' he said, as though from outer space, 'just come round as you said, okay?'

'I can't face any scenes, Matt. I'm too tired. And worried, too.'

'No scenes. Cross my heart. Just come. *Please.*'

The flat smelled of kippers, or kit-e-cat, I wasn't sure which. Matt didn't turn the television off when I came in, and merely raised an eyebrow in greeting. He was sitting on the sofa with his knees up to his chin and his arms boxing them in; he looked stoned. I sat down in the rocker and watched him watching television. Rough blond hair with fingers combing it, making it stick up; two pimples on his cheek, new among the old scars. The mouth full and red, but at this moment hanging open rather stupidly. A filmstar, I thought, feeling suddenly chilled, a doped-up starlet on an off day: if I ever really needed this guy I'd be in trouble. 'Can't we turn that down?'

Matt stretched out and turned the volume knob, but the picture remained, grey sea and destroyers and action men in woolly caps. 'So,' he said heavily, 'what's the worry?' His eyes returned to the TV.

'Work,' I mumbled, fingering my buttons. I hadn't taken my coat off yet, and he hadn't even noticed. 'And money. And Andrew. The usual... They want me to do full time at *Womanright* while Andrea's in the States,' I added, straining to get through to this deaf person.

'Going to do it, then?' he asked absently.

'I ought to. Really, I can't afford not to.'

'Do it, then. All power to your elbow.'

End of conversation. On the television, waves tossed and the ship's deck rolled, and the commander narrowed his eyes, giving soundless orders. To Matt, evidently, everything was quite straightforward. I stood up and took my coat off. 'I worry about Andrew,' I announced to the room. 'Sometimes I think I should never have been a mother at all.' I had Matt's attention at last. He looked up at me, fully engaged now.

'But he's a great little fellow, isn't he?'

I took a deep breath and heard the words rush out. 'But I never know whether he'd rather be with his father, or what he's *thinking* or needing or . . .' And then I was crying, chest heaving, nose streaming. 'I feel so inadequate all the time,' I wailed. Guilty and more guilty. I didn't know there was so much guilt in the world. 'I don't *do* things with him . . .' I don't even like him enough. Don't say it, don't even think it. Call yourself a mother? The whole truth was going to burst out now, dumped in his lap like an ill baby.

'Christ!' Matt sat up straight. 'Don't just stand there, come and hug.' He pulled my head down on to his chest. His mohair sweater was warm, and tickled.

'See what I'm really like,' I muttered.

'You do get yourself in a state, don't you?' He stroked the hair back from my forehead. 'But you have got a lot on your plate, I guess . . .'

Honeyed words. I let the tears trickle. 'It was our honeymoon, before, but now everything's different, isn't it? I'm not free, you see.'

Matt rocked me. 'I suppose Andrew's on the quiet side,' he said thoughtfully. 'But so are you . . . he looks fine to me, really.'

'He talks in riddles,' I persisted, 'he talks in TV jargon. And he loves useless facts and figures and football . . . *football*. What do *I* know about football? I mean, how can I get close to him, with all that in the way?' Matt grunted under me, and shifted my head a little. He's watching television again, I thought with sudden sharp rage. I sat up and gripped his arm; I wasn't finished yet, and I wouldn't rest until he had heard the worst. 'Sometimes the gap is intolerable. I get so *bored*, I swear I could *murder* him!'

A pat on the shoulder. 'Take it easy. So you get pissed off with him. That's normal, isn't it?'

'Is it? Is it? It feels pathological to me.'

Matt began to rub my back, a soothing, burping motion. 'Hey, I thought you feminists had all that mother stuff sewn up. Where's your politics, girl? It isn't all your own personal *fault*, you know.'

'Oh, maybe not,' I sighed, nonplussed. The argument was sound, wholesome as cod-liver oil, yet I was choking on it. It's irrational to bear a grudge, I thought, just because he seems to have all the answers. I laid my head down again and listened to the solid masculine thud of his heart. I was suddenly very weary, tired of all the debates that rattled in my head, tired of puzzling, tired of being in charge. Just let me sleep, I thought, leave me in peace. Outside the french windows, leaves swished in the wind. On top of the stereo the cat sneezed minutely, spraying a small quantity of spit. Just let me be safe.

Matt was moving, dislodging me. 'Up you get. Coffee time.' Distant commands from the bridge. His hands were heaving me up.

I blinked sleepily at him. 'I've had it.'

'Guess what? I'll make the coffee, then.' He sounded disgruntled.

Water splashed in the kitchen sink, and after a moment Matt called through, 'I saw your old mate in Camden Market today.'

'What mate?'

'Vi, dummy. With a barrowload of make-up on and some Irishman in tow. A painter from her past, she said.' He appeared in the doorway with cups. 'Did you hear me?'

I was wide awake now: so much for peace and quiet. 'How was she?'

'Fine, just fine. Why worry?' He held out a cup of coffee. 'It's sugared. Sweets for my sweet . . . Now look, I know you're beating yourself up about Vi, too.'

I shook my head stubbornly, and Matt gave an exasperated sigh.

'I wish you'd just forget it, because she wouldn't waste a worry on you, girl.'

'Lay off.'

A cunning expression flitted across Matt's face. 'You think I'm kidding? Want me to tell you what she used to say about you?'

'Just drop the subject,' I cried. 'I don't want to know. You know damn all about it.'

He laughed coarsely. 'Me? You tell *me* I don't know about Vi?

My mind's eye conjured up an image of Vi, not the taut, resolute Vi of the unfinished room, but a white-skinned body spread across a bed, and a red mouth burrowing into her, and her black hair moving on the pillow like snakes.

'I'll deal with it myself, if you don't mind,' I said icily.

Matt pouted. 'Oh. I get it. Another subject censored. Let me see, what can we talk about now?' He put a finger to his chin. 'Not Vi, not *Womanright*, not the sisters . . . And *no* phoning in the day. You like your own way, June, you surely do.'

Recant, recant. I set my jaw. 'Otherwise, we just fight.' Matt retreated to the far end of the sofa and sulked. 'It's true, you know it is.'

In answer he shook his fist at me. I knew I had won, but after we had gazed at the TV screen for a while, at ads for Philishave Floating Heads to adapt to every face and Rotary Blades designed to get close to you, my victory began to feel very empty. There was one infallible way of drawing him back towards me, and I used it. As my toes massaged him, his face broke into an unwilling smile. 'Shit, man,' he said to the silent newsreader, 'the punch this granite lady packs.' He got up and turned the TV off. 'Okay. You win, this time. We can always watch TV later.'

Giggling, he held out a cup of tea. 'It's a burning question these days, I believe – the fate of the ejaculate . . . 10 cc equals 300 calories. Better watch your waistline.' He closed his eyes and fell back on the pillows; small feathers of down flew up and floated. 'I died,' he said, 'that time, I was gone.'

Surrender, he'd said. As if it were a question of mere will. The smoke from my cigarette curled upwards and hung in plumes over the bed. Beside me he lay quiet and content, breathing deeply. His shoulder glistened, skin so smooth and healthy I could have devoured it. Curve of backbone; the long line of his arm draped along his side. His hand lay loosely, palm up, fingers open, as if he had given everything away. How abandoned he was in love, how prodigal. Yet underneath, the personality fluctuating, flickering, like the ever-changing ads on the screen.

Matt sniggered. 'I'm hypnotised by your ash.'

All this time he had been watching me covertly, and I hadn't noticed the long grey column gathering.

'There are chess players who do that. Kind of psychological terrorism. Did you hear about the guy who stuck a teeny thin wire up his cigar? To hold the ash on, get it?'

I laughed, seeing the two men facing each other: severe suits, grave faces, the reverence of the onlookers.

'. . . So the other guy gets absolutely transfixed waiting for the ash to fall off – five inches of it, imagine, and it never budges. How's that for psyching out?'

I laughed and laughed. Suddenly it seemed the most hilarious thing in the world.

Matt's face lit up. 'I make you happy, yes?' He tickled. 'Do I, old mope? Do I?'

Happy happy happy. No one else comes near.

My grandmother bounced me on her knee and I shrieked with pleasure.

'Bells on her fingers and bells on her toes, She shall have music wherever she goes.'

Why must I push him away, distance him? 'You do,' I gasped, as he romped around me. Wriggling free, I spoke impulsively. 'Come to see *Grease* with me and the boys. They'd love it if you came.'

'Ha. What's this, a yen for hot-crotch superstars?'

'Well?' I prodded him. 'Will you?'

He narrowed his eyes. 'Okay, doll,' he said, in Brooklyn-Italian, 'You wanna play families? Okay, I play.'

35

Some days later, Vi contacted me. On the phone I sensed her straining towards me, needing something. 'We don't have to talk about Matt,' she assured me quickly. 'There's no reason for him to monopolise all our conversations.' She was in the pub beside the Tube, could I meet her there? I put my head round Marie's door to tell her where I was going, and hurried up the street, taking a short cut through the park. On the tennis courts the last matches of the day were being fought out as the sun sank, and the skin of the players turned to gold under my eyes. When I broke into a run, crisp cylinders of bark shed by the plane trees crunched underfoot.

The interior of the pub was dark red. The drinkers at the bar were lit by rose-shaded lamps, and mirrored, so that their eyes sparkled, and the bloom of summer tans glowed. Commuters reluctant to let go of their after-work bonhomie clung together in groups which gave off sporadic bursts of laughter. There was an atmosphere of tremulous anticipation, of intercepted glances, and exchanges coded in hands, coded in cigarettes. Vi was waiting alone at a small table in an alcove, half-hidden by a red velvet drape. She was staring into a glass of tomato juice with a look of suppressed panic. Relief showed on her face when I approached.

'My class ended early,' she said breathlessly. 'The model fainted. I think she got her period or something.'

She waved away my offer of a whisky, saying that she never had been a drinker, really, and when I came back from the bar with mine she took her bag off the table, shifted the ashtray, made space for me and my drink and my cigarettes: a small, touching fuss which I hadn't expected. 'So,' I said, 'a drawing class?'

'I'm going to do a day class too – when I cut my work down to four days . . . ' She caught her bottom lip between her teeth.

'Can you do that?'

'They seem agreeable.'

I held up my glass to congratulate her. 'You're really getting things together.'

She drummed her fingers on the table, and shook her head: a disclaimer. Then she flushed. 'I hope so. It's about time.' A quick, questing look. 'Sometimes you *have* to take yourself by the scruff of the neck, don't you?'

I watched her hand move across the furry brown material of her cardigan, touching and tweaking at the long hairs, and I had a sudden image of lifting her up, a doll-sized Vi, and shaking her out like a dusty teddy-bear, and setting her down at her easel. 'I'm really glad,' I said, nodding and smiling. She is taking herself seriously at last, I thought. Without knowing why, I felt relieved, as if a weight had lifted off my shoulders. She had been painting self-portraits, she told me, nudes mainly, in which the torso floated, misty and formless, under the dark commanding head; try as she might to give the body substance, the face dominated: angular, brittle, alarming her. As she talked, her eyes flickered round the red room, and there was a hurt, faraway expression in them. 'It does make me feel like a freak,' she said.

I hurried to respond. 'So you are, in a sense . . . but you're not alone in that.'

Her glance was swift, weighing me up. It was still too soon. I let the smile die slowly on my lips. At the next table, a blond woman nibbled a maraschino cherry with controlled greed. Her companion said a word to her, and she cupped her chin in her hand and leaned towards him, smiling up at him through her lashes. Her hand strayed to the back of her neck in a coquettish gesture, smoothing the stray hairs. I turned back to Vi. 'There are worse things than the work ethic. For women, anyway.'

Vi wrinkled her nose. 'What you mean is . . . there's more to life than relationships with men.'

I stirred ice cubes around in my glass and edged deeper into the alcove, so that the tasselled border of the velvet curtain blotted out the animated, flirtatious crowd. 'That too,' I conceded. 'The snake-pit.'

Her eyes followed my every move. 'He's getting at you,' she said, and I tensed.

'Really, we don't have to talk about it. I knew what I was taking on, after all.'

'Jesus, that sternness of yours!'

'He calls it depressive, actually.'

'He's the depressive one,' she said, rather too briskly. Her hands fiddled with her hair, parting it into two bunches, tucking the bunches tidily away inside the collar of her cardigan, and a silence fell between us. On the jukebox they were playing 'Girl Talk', and Vi's lips moved to the words. 'Don't come any closer, don't come any nearer . . .' Then she drained her glass and stared at me defiantly. 'I told him everything, you see. All about your past. The very worst I could think of.' She took a breath. 'Oh, and more,' she went on, glancing nervously at me. 'Much more. When I ran out of things, I made them up.' Her eyes drifted, and a look of wonder crossed her face, as if something strange had just entered the bar, a giant, or a snake charmer, or a woman with three breasts. 'I never knew I had so much imagination. It was so *easy*.'

Dipping my finger in my whisky, I traced wet shapes on the surface of the table. Circles, stars, stars within circles.

'Don't you think I'm hateful, then?'

I lifted my hand. Yes. No. Fair exchange. 'I suspected as

much, to be honest.' All things considered, it was a relief to think that Vi, too, had done her worst.

Vi rushed on. 'I had to do it. This picture he has of you. The eyes like deep wells, and so on. The bloody feminine archetype. You know what he's like – the yang and the yin . . . '

'I know, I know.'

'Stereotype, more like,' Vi said angrily.

I tipped the ice into my mouth and sucked it slowly.

'So you're not furious with me?'

'I'm not furious with you, no.' I got up from my chair. 'Do you want a whisky now?'

Spite flared suddenly in Vi's face. 'After all,' she said, 'you did win the prize, didn't you?' I stood frozen, with my purse in my hand, and then she was shamefaced, apologising. 'Maybe I will have that whisky, after all.'

Forcing my way in to the bar, I caught the eye of a girl with a pony tail and rouged cheeks who stood, sad and irritable-looking, on the fringes of a group of men, an appendage in her carefully modish clothes and silver boots. She moved to let me past, and I signalled my thanks, but then her face closed. After-image of a brooch, a brave peacock brooch shimmering at the neck of her shirt. When I returned to the table Vi was chewing the ball of her thumb. 'I tell you, I can really sicken myself,' she said.

I pulled her hand away from her mouth. 'Look at the mess your fingers are in! This one's bleeding, even.' Vi allowed me to examine the new wounds around her fingernails, and the scars on her knuckles where she had scratched and picked. On her cheeks were two bright spots of colour, pinker than the rouge on the ponytail girl.

'I know. I take everything out on them.' The man at the next table was glancing over, eyeing our clasped hands, while his female companion was pretending not to notice. Vi raised her voice. 'All my *nastiness* . . . all my *evil*.' She crossed her eyes, an abominable effect, which made me laugh and the man drop cigar ash in his beer.

'You should go on the stage. You'd make a good Wicked Witch of the West.'

Vi took an experimental sip of whisky. 'Black-haired women are always the baddies, have you noticed? It's a conspiracy.'

'But the Snow Queen,' I joked, 'she was fair, wasn't she? And pure ice, a monster of calculation.'

Vi gave me a wry look, and a bleak feeling crept over me. Across the table, Vi was dark and vivid against the rich drapes, her skin smooth as a pebble, her colours rose and gold. I watched her drink her whisky; she drank steadily, puckering her mouth after each swallow. 'But to me, you're nearer it,' I said, floundering, 'if there is such a thing . . . the feminine, I mean. You know – emotional, and . . . sparky.'

Her mouth twitched. 'Spare me. Vivacious. I know.' She puffed on her cigarette and held her hand to her throat, coughing a little. 'It's all show. I'm just a tart, you see. I get done up. I flirt. I pick people up. It doesn't *mean* anything.' Her voice was harsh.

I hesitated. 'I had the impression that you were withdrawing from the fray a little . . . '

'Ah. Well, that's the impression you were meant to get.' She frowned. 'I'm such a liar, really.'

I sat back, perplexed. One step forward, two steps back.

Vi tugged grimly at her fringe. 'Look, just remember that *I* suffer too. No matter how many jolly noises come out of me, I can suffer every bit as well as you.'

'Did I say you didn't?'

She studied the small damaged fists resting on the table. Stains of charcoal, all the dirt of the drawing class. 'Oh, you know. Vi's so shallow. Surface. Bright as a button. No one wants to know the rest.'

I searched for assurances, but found a memory instead. At Windsor Free Festival she had danced on the grass, shouting and punching at the air. Flying hair, flying earrings; the heavy body transformed. On the stage, five men banged guitars and sang of gun barrels, while Vi cupped her hands round her mouth and yelled back at them: she'd rather have a real man than a gun up her, thank you very much! And on the grass the soft-faced boys and girls looked up at her dolefully: Jeez, what a hassle, man. I'd wanted so much to join in, to dance and shout with her, instead I hung back beside Jed, and envied her. I gazed at her now, feeling more and more confused. 'But who wants to suffer?' Did she think I made a virtue of it?

'It's a question of being real or unreal,' she said. For a while we argued obstinately about adversity, and whether it forged character, until finally, by attending more to her hesitations and the counterpoint of gestures than to what she said, I began to glimpse what she was after. I sensed that it wasn't, after all, a confession, or a catalogue of victories and defeats, or even a definite truth of what had happened between us. Rather, it was something simpler, some magic spell that would allow her to wind down like a clockwork toy, to stop prancing and waving her arms and clashing her brass cymbals. If I recognised her pain, would she then be able to accept it herself? I thought not. It couldn't be as easy as that. But meanwhile she sat opposite me, wanting this thing. And in the face of that, my scruples seemed mean and stubborn.

I saw myself, years before, sitting across the fireplace from my mother, sitting stiff as a stake in the armchair that had been my father's. Around us, the good bone china and the sausage rolls left over from the funeral feast. My mother brushed crumbs from the lap of her black suit, and sighed faintly, and touched the marcasite brooch on her lapel. The minutes stretched out, while I sat with my lips shut tight on my grief, which could not be portioned out or shared, which was all I had. My mother's need pressed. Yes, she was bereft; yes, she was lonely as the grave – but what was I? What had I been all those years? And so now, sitting in the firelight, it was my face which would forbid, my arms which would withhold. When at last my mother stood up to go to her empty bed, I saw her look at me with fear in her eyes.

Vi was waiting, with her knuckles in her mouth. Rash, she was, to want this of me, to put herself in my hands. Deluded, even. I shivered, and took the hurdle at a rush. I said merely: 'I know what you must have been through.' The words themselves were meaningless, anodyne: a dozen other phrases would have served as well. Yet afterwards, something had changed. I saw it in the way Vi's face cleared and softened, and I felt it in myself, too, but there it was like a loosening and a falling away, as if moss on a roof, dislodged, had slithered and rolled down the smooth slates.

Vi took her fingers out of her mouth, and looked at them, and smiled. 'Sorry. I forgot.' And she folded her hands together on the table, nodding.

We talked quietly for a while, of more ordinary things. Jed, Phil, a vote-rigging scandal in the local Labour Party which *Hard Times* had scooped. Jed had been accepted for a degree course at the local Polytechnic, Vi said. 'He always did want to be a Marxist intellectual, really,' she said with a grin.

When the bell rang for closing time, there was a stir in the main bar, and shouting. I pulled aside the velvet drape in time to see the ponytail girl push through the crowd and vanish out of the door. Meanwhile, the group near the bar had parted to reveal a man in a desolate, scarecrow stance. Beer dripped from his hands; it was in his eyes, in his hair. His face was scarlet. Keeping their distance, his friends commiserated. Embarrassed looks: you're better off without her, mate.

'Good for her,' Vi muttered, and wiped her mouth. Her hand left a charcoal smear. Around us the red room dimmed, and the barman cried for glasses. 'I was thinking,' said Vi, as she stepped out from behind the velvet curtain, 'remember that day in Reuben's room – you know, when I had to lift you? When you said . . . or he said . . . that I had to? Thinking back, I must have been so angry. Me having to take *your* weight, and you being the baby. I must have wanted it so much for myself . . . You know – to be looked after?'

We parted in the forecourt of the Tube.

'You will come and see the portraits?' she asked.

'I will.'

With a wave, she was gone into the station.

Walking home through the park, the stars were very bright, and there was an edge of winter in the air. Suddenly, compared to Vi, Matt seemed like a clumsy cat-burglar, breaking and entering. Wavering loyalties. It was a vertiginous feeling.

That night I dreamed that Vi and I danced together; Vi in cascading white skirts, and I narrower, in black. As we whirled, Jed in a white dinner jacket tried to butt in and, refused, whispered: 'You're like two stars twinkling away together.' And Vi stuck out her tongue and said: 'Ah, fairytales.'

36

Zac and Andrew's primary school was a low modern building with wide windows decorated winter and summer by children's cutouts: flowers or fruits, snowmen or Easter eggs, depending on the season. At the start of the campaign which Andrew had so confidently committed me to, the theme was witches, in preparation for Hallowe'en. The inaugural meeting was long, noisy and purposeful, and I left it with a fistful of statistics on education cuts, a draft letter of protest to the local education authority, and a tense headache. Andrew and Zac walked home beside me, gossiping about whose mother was at the meeting, and what so and so's dad looked like and how Darren Dukes had farted in the middle of Miss Anderson's speech. They carried big sheets of white card, sticks, and magic markers from the school store cupboard, to make placards.

'Let's think up slogans when we get in,' said Andrew, kicking up storms of leaves in the gutter.

'Aren't we going to the pictures?' Zac frowned.

Ankle deep in leaves, Andrew rubbed his nose. 'Oh yeah. I forgot.'

'D'you think they'll throw us out of the Town Hall when we go? Will they?' Zac's eyes gleamed with excitement.

'It has been known.' I smiled. 'Depends what we do.'

'Have you? Been chucked out? Marie has, hasn't she?'

'Oh sure,' I said, nonchalant, 'quite a few times.' Andrew turned and stared with unconcealed admiration. 'It's nothing to worry about,' I added. 'They'd look pretty bad if they used brute force on a bunch of mothers and kids, wouldn't they?'

'Maybe we'll get on telly.'

'I doubt it. Maybe when the campaign takes off. But we have to contact the local papers first.'

Zac nodded seriously, taking it all in. Later, no doubt, he would show Marie how much he knew about politics, but for the moment, like Andrew, he was pleased as punch that I had been the one delegated to deal with publicity; as we left the hall I'd heard them muttering to each other, making ready to boast at school tomorrow. For of course, having resolved to do the very minimum, I'd ended up by taking on a lot. Maggie Anderson, recognising a kindred spirit, had simply homed in. It had been impossible to refuse.

'Teachers are certainly a different kettle of fish nowadays,' I said to Zac, thinking of the Deputy Head's magenta hair and the staunchly militant badges on her lapel. 'We used to be so scared of ours.'

'But you got that strap thing in Scotland, didn't you?' Zac said knowledgeably.

'Actually, me and Marshall are having a *men's* group,' Matt slurred into the phone, 'and hitting a bottle of Dutch gin – so I can't.' He snickered. 'By the way, Marshall informs me that you and the delightful Violet are reconciled, n'est-ce pas? Nice work, old girl.'

I was astounded. 'But you promised to go.'

'Oh, I did? Well, sorry . . . but unlike you I don't get off on nostalgia. Nor on the revolting gyrations of Travolta. Really, I'm surprised at you!'

Feeling angry and foolish, I argued back. I'd already told the boys he was coming, I said, they were looking forward to it.

'Hang on.' Mutters and bursts of laughter came from the receiver. When Matt's voice came back it was chillier. 'Look here, June, it's stupid. You know what I think of this dating business. I do think it's terribly teenage, don't you?'

'It just depends how much you want to see me, doesn't it?'

'Oh Christ . . . let's just *be* together, can't we? Let's go away somewhere together.'

'Like where, exactly?'

'Well, you must have some friends with cottages.'

'*I* must?'

'Among the well-heeled sisters, no? What about that little dacha you used to plot the dictatorship of the proletariat in?'

He wants me to parry now, to retaliate, I thought – then he'll really go to town. 'I really can't discuss this. The kids are waiting.' Sour, sour voice. The disappointment was crushing.

'Oh shit,' Matt groaned.

'Why can't you fit in with me,' I cried, 'just for once!'

No answer, only a re-run of the muffled giggles and consultations. 'Sorry,' he said at last, 'Marshall keeps acting out these heart-rending Oedipal traumas . . . give *up*, Marshall, you wank-tank, you're so *absurd*.' A peal of laughter. 'I'm sorry, darling, I can't control him . . . '

I recoiled. 'Right. I'm going.'

'Oh, come on, it's not a crime to be drunk and incapable once in a while, is it?'

'I said goodbye.'

'Wait, wait . . . I may be completely out of it now, but remember – the cottage idea – I'm really serious about that. Okay?'

It was the same cinema Matt and Vi and I had gone to after the carnival but this time the queue stretched halfway round the block.

'We won't get in,' Andrew said stoically. Zac's mouth quivered.

'Shut up!' I said, 'it's too early to be pessimistic.' Too young as well, I thought. Andrew responded by hunching his shoulders and sealing his lips tight. Crossing my fingers inside my pocket I drew myself up and pronounced like an oracle: 'We'll get in.' Two pairs of eyes fixed on me, daring to hope. I slipped my hand into Andrew's pocket and held his small diffident one, and in this way we waited, shuffling forward when the queue shuffled, not speaking in case some spell should break and all the luck spill out on the pavement. We edged along, shivering a little in the October night, until we reached the bright lights of the foyer, and finally the cash desk, where, before some uniformed arm could bar the way, I slapped the money down. Andrew let out a gusty sigh. The sweat of fear shone on his forehead.

'Victory!' he whooped, clasping his arms above his head, when the cashier threw the tickets on the counter and we were safely in. Begging me for change I couldn't afford, the boys ran to buy popcorn and Pepsi-Cola, while I waited in the centre of the foyer and watched couples climb the mirrored stairs arm in arm. Now that Andrew and Zac were happy I was free to taste my own disappointment. I sucked in my cheeks and rolled it around my tongue until the boys, reappearing, tugged me towards the stairs, and slowly, like an aniseed ball, it dissolved.

37

The other players on Parliament Hill tennis courts wore their whites as if they had been born in them; their tennis balls were new, their spare racquets snug in presses, and though they sweated, they did not *purple*.

At the beginning of the match, my knees trembled, my hand was slippery on the racquet handle. I felt both doomed to fail, and furiously determined to win: familiar symptoms of playing with a lover. So while Matt danced, laughing, round the court, his grasshopper legs covering distance easily, all thought of strategy flew out of my head, and I dashed untidily from baseline to net to tramlines, cursing at every shot missed. On the adjacent court, two tanned Germans knocked up without effort. Matt won 6-3, 6-2, 6-4.

'You're okay, when you relax,' he encouraged. 'Great potential. All you need is practice – get some spin on the ball, some control.'

I wiped my face on a T-shirt. My hands were scarlet, my breath came raggedly.

'Too many fags.'

'Too much pen-pushing,' I replied, with difficulty.

As we strolled back to the flat, Matt slipped his arm round my waist. 'We'll do lots of walking in the country, won't we? We'll get lots of exercise.' His face radiated contentment. His bare brown leg brushed my red one; the skin was damp and hot, and the touch of it made me forget to feel ugly. If it could always be like this, I thought.

'It isn't great walking country. Too flat, really. But there are forests, and flint mines, and the sea not too far away.'

'No ghouls and ghosties from your interesting past? And on Hallowe'en as well.'

'What could come near with my knight at my side?' I said, putting aside thoughts of the white room.

Matt sighed. 'It was good of your mate Mike,' he said, apparently without sarcasm. He swung his racquet back and executed a perfect slice. 'Marshall's giving me the car Thursday, so if the weather only holds . . . '

We chattered and we planned; Matt was like a five year old, brimming with hopes, all his expectations pinned on this one brief weekend. A tremor passed through me, at the generosity of it, and the danger, and I reached up and touched his cheek.

Matt stopped in the middle of the pedestrian crossing. 'Let me look at you.'

Thursday. Something stirred at the back of my mind. It was the school demonstration! How could I have overlooked it? My hand flew to my mouth. 'I can't. Not on Thursday.'

'You're kidding me.'

'I have to be at the Town Hall on Friday. I can't get out of it.' I hardly dared look at Matt. 'I'm sorry, but we'll have to go Friday afternoon.'

Matt's face buckled with misery. 'You swindler,' he said, 'you little swindler.'

Traffic moved towards us. There was going to be a scene now, I could see that. 'We can't hang about here. Please,

Matt.'

'Three or four days! You promised me that. And now you're going to wriggle out of it?' A car hooted, and then another. Waving two fingers at the nearest driver, Matt strode to the kerb. 'Cancel it! You can do that, at least.'

'Friday, we can go Friday, idiot!'

'Just get out of it, or you can kiss your trip goodbye.' He turned and walked on fast, so that I had to run at his heel, hating it, hating him for humiliating me.

'Don't order me around!' I shouted.

He stopped dead. 'Just when, tell me, are you going to make any commitment to me? Eh? Unzip your lip and *answer* me.'

I balled my fist, thumbs tucked in, the way my father taught me. It's not true about red, I thought, you see black, and sparkling things. 'What do you *want?* What more do you want?' Then I hit him. He staggered a little, then recovered and held the racquet in front of his chest like a shield. 'So what did *you* do for this trip? You got the car,' I yelled, 'you actually got the car. Miracles! And while we're at it, when are you going to grow up and stop throwing your *poisonous* tantrums!' My voice was a distant roar.

'Tantrums?' he snapped. 'Oh sure. Who slams the phone down, then? And would you mind not bellowing so loud? I have to live in this street, you know.'

Automatically my mouth closed, and I glanced around.

'Come now,' he said, steering me by the arm, 'let's do our arguing in private.'

The argument continued in the bathroom. I stood with my back against the sink, preparing my statement. Ever since that night with Vi I'd been mulling it over: long enough to convince myself I had a just case. 'Wait till you're at the cottage,' Mike had advised. 'It'll be easier to talk things over there.' But Matt's behaviour had pre-empted that. Water rushed, and the Ascot heater ignited with a small explosion. He will not have it all his own way, I thought vengefully.

'You must take my life into account,' I said, 'or else it's just no good.'

Matt tipped pine essence into the bath and stirred the

water into green whirlpools. 'Demands, eh?'

'Yes. Non-negotiable ones.'

His lips drew back. 'Well, you don't say. Orders are orders and must be obeyed without question at all times? That's you all over. One big whine for nurture and support.' His hands clutched the edge of the bath; in the background, the Ascot roared. 'Well, *Ms* Guthrie, don't bother coming to me for that stuff. You get that from the sisters, don't you, isn't that what it's all about? You and Vi? And what do *I* get? Crumbs, bloody leavings, rationed out like sheep shits!'

I shrank back against the sink and watched him rave. Bitter, bitter words.

' "Nurture and support",' he spat; 'you make me throw up, the lot of you.'

I gauged the distance to the door. 'Is that your last word, then?'

Matt went pale. 'No, I didn't mean . . .'

'Well, you said it.' Stony. 'As from now, I know the limits on our relationship. And *you* set them.'

He held out his hands. 'Please . . .'

'Watch the bath, it'll run over.'

We looked at each other, aghast.

Dinner was poor: neither of us had the heart to cook properly. I pushed slushy brussel sprouts around on my plate and thought of nothing, wanted nothing. When I dropped my knife on the floor Matt put it back on the table with exaggerated care. He leaned towards me with a woebegone smile.

'We'll still have the weekend, won't we, badger?'

I looked down at my plate. He was wooing, wheedling: it was pathetic. 'Why not? Now that we know where we stand.' I felt hard and clear, all the soft parts cleaned out, excised in a neat piece of surgery. Matt took my hand in his. He really believes he's forgiven, I thought.

In bed, there was still the fragrance of skin, the same flashpoint. Seeing my lips soften and part, Matt smiled. *He thinks he has won*. I let him kindle me, but then I turned away from him, and saying nothing, explaining nothing, I began to masturbate. I did it avidly, unrepentantly, for what did it matter now if I was greedy or obstreperous, or damaged his self-esteem? I too could be every bit as nasty as he was, could grab what I wanted, ignore other people's needs: oh yes, I could do that, now I was past caring. I only grabbed for him, blindly, when I felt myself coming, and he held me as I tensed and cried out, and he breathed, Oh baby, in my ear, and his body echoed my contractions, rippling like a small boat caught in the wash of a larger one.

38

'Bless you,' the contributor kept saying, as my sneezes scrambled our telephone conversation.

When I put the receiver down, Jude laughed. 'What a sight. Why don't you just give up?'

'What about the headlines?' I said through my handkerchief.

'We'll do them. No *problem*.'

'Yes,' said Clara, pulling her shawl round her shoulders, 'otherwise I'm bound to catch it.'

I was putting on my jacket when Mike came over. 'Good weekend,' she murmured, and Jude looked up from her desk, all ears. 'Aren't you going away with your romance? How exciting . . . is it your Hampstead Heathcliff?' she said in a stage whisper. 'News travels fast.'

Mike and I looked at each other and laughed. 'Actually I'm off to a school demo. Business before pleasure.'

Jude flapped her hand. 'Boring,' she grinned.

Mike handed me the keys. 'Take it easy. Let him look after you a little.'

On the steps of the Town Hall there were some thirty parents, mostly mothers, and fifty children arranged in rows. Andrew was among them, standing in line behind a placard which said: Save Our Teacher. When I went up to him he looked at me suspiciously. 'Are you crying again?'

'No, nitwit, my eyes are streaming. It's a cold, or 'flu, or something.'

'Phil's here,' he said, pointing. I spotted him at the bottom of the steps; he was leaning on his bicycle and had a camera case slung over his shoulder. Maggie Anderson came up the steps to lead the children's chants, so I followed the other parents into the foyer of the Town Hall. Inside, councillors were being lobbied and arguments argued with much verve and a fair number of threats from some of the mothers. The marble-floored hall echoed with swear-words and the yells of bored toddlers, and the councillors argued back in low voices, as if trying to instil in the angry parents a reasonable respect for their surroundings. I moved from group to group taking notes, while outside the children chanted: 'No, no, she won't go.'

After I had filled several pages I went outside to find Phil. He was standing straight-legged, with his feet astride; his corduroy trousers bagged around his knees. He held a sheaf of *Hard Times* across his belly, and he looked care-worn. When he saw me his face brightened and he said in a singsong voice: 'Latest issue. Your local socialist paper. Hot off the presses.' I smiled, and he cleared his throat. 'Andrew and Zac seem to be enjoying their new role as militants, don't you think?'

They were standing together now, posing for photos, and as the photographer hopped from step to step, taking them from various angles, the grins were stiffening on their faces. I tapped my notebook. 'Will the middle of next week be okay for your copy date?'

Phil inclined his head, then, smoothing his eyebrow lightly with one finger, he said: 'I was thinking of having a cup of tea?' When I didn't reply immediately he gazed around, blinking in the sunlight. There were new wrinkles round his eyes. 'It's rather beautiful, this Indian summer,' he said.

I looked at my watch without seeing the time. 'I'm in a bit of a rush, actually. I'm off to the cottage at four.'

'Ah, pity.' His face was inscrutable. 'You must be feeling brave,' he added. Surprised by such an acknowledgement, I waited, hoping that he would say more. On the steps of the Town Hall the noise was dying down. People were leaving the lobby, collecting prams and children; at the foot of the steps, Maggie Anderson was piling up placards.

'Well, I'd better get the boys.'

Phil sighed and folded up his newspapers. 'Knocking off time, then.' He slipped them inside his sweater and zipped up his jacket. 'Thanks, by the way,' he said, climbing on to his bicycle, 'for the article, I mean.' And he pedalled away across the forecourt.

'I'll bring it over next week,' I called after him. 'Say Wednesday?'

He waved his assent, and the bike wobbled.

39

Matt was waiting in the car at the front gate. 'I've got all the food in the back,' he said, '*and* wine.' He looked proud of himself.

'I wish I was coming,' Andrew said dejectedly. I patted his shoulder in consolation.

In the car, I sat with a rug tucked round my knees and allowed myself to be ferried out of London. There were black bullocks in the Essex fields, a late harvest. Exhausted by the Town Hall, I sucked boiled sweets and watched the landscape blearily, until the sun sank, and ahead of us the tall fir woods began.

Not even my cold affected Matt's good humour. On the dark flint-strewn track through the forest he performed dare-devil stunts, swerving the car from side to side, skidding round potholes. When the cottage appeared in the headlights he cried out gaily.

'It's a gingerbread house. So where's the witch, that's what I want to know?'

Catching his mood, I laughed. 'She lives down the well, of course.'

'There's a well?'

'Oh yes. Everything. Except mod cons. You need to be a good boy scout here.'

My teeth chattered as I stepped out into the night air. I fumbled with the rusted lock on the cottage door, then, inside, moving fast to keep warm, I piled paper, twigs, logs on the fire. It caught first time, and Matt complimented me. I sat down in an armchair and listed the tasks that still had to be done. Checking the water barrel, unpacking the food, bringing a mattress down from the attic, chopping, peeling, cooking. Matt gazed around with an air of helplessness.

'I see what you mean about boy scouts.'

I shut my eyes for a moment, feeling dizzy. Had he forgotten that I was ill? I let my arms dangle over the side of the chair. My feet flopped sideways: a rag doll.

'I'm afraid you'll have to do the dinner. I seem to have had it.'

'Oh?'

I waited for him to ask why. 'If you bring me the potatoes, and a candle, I'll peel them in here.' I was weary. Fluids bubbled in my head. The fire twittered strangely in the unusual quiet.

He shrugged. 'Okay.'

Yes, he did try. I have to give him that. He heaved the mattress single-handed and without complaint, carried everything in from the car, rooted for candles in the dark kitchen. Yet all the time he was bustling, I was apprehensive. It was as if I expected to be told off for slacking, for asking too many favours.

When he returned his shadow preceded him, and I jumped.

'You're right about the attic,' he said, warming his hands at the fire, 'it's as cold as the grave up there.'

'It's Hallowe'en. Don't spook me.'

In the unsteady light of the candle I set about peeling the potatoes. I peeled the first one in a long continuous strip which dangled from my knife down into the dirty water in the bowl.

It was an old trick of country girls. On Hallowe'en you lit a candle by your mirror, peeled an apple without breaking the peel.

'Throw it over your shoulder and you'll see the man you'll marry.' Rona had almost teased me into it once, but at the last moment I backed out. Girls' stuff, I sneered, and who wants to marry? Shaking her head at my heresies, Rona went ahead. Afterwards, she was very quiet, and refused to joke about it.

From the kitchen came the sound of Matt slicing vegetables, a cost sound. 'We should have a turnip lantern,' I called.

Matt put his head round the door. In the candlelight his eyes were cavernous. 'Turnip's off, dear.'

We were folding up the sofa to make space for the mattress when something which had been lodged behind a cushion fluttered out. It was a Polaroid photo of Sherry, naked apart from a pair of unlaced plimsolls. Half in light, half in shade, she was carrying a big blackened kettle towards the well. An appendix scar was a thin crescent of white across her belly.

'This is where they escape to,' I said sadly.

Matt took the photo and held it to the light. 'Well. Such goings on, I don't know.'

'I'll take it.' I held out my hand. 'Her husband comes here too.'

'So?'

'So I'll return it to Mike.'

Smiling, he held the photograph out of reach. 'Let *me*.'

Suddenly I was angry again, and mistrustful. 'Don't play silly buggers!'

'Steady on. It's yours. Here.' He put his arm round me. 'Don't take things so *seriously.*' The words seemed to come from far off, sibilant and whispery. 'Just shows what you think of me,' he grumbled.

I tucked the photo away in my bag and tried to smile. Perhaps I had over-reacted. It was the effect of illness, probably. The distorting factor. I felt my forehead. It was hot. I was feverish, Matt was trying to look after me: nothing else made any sense. I sat down on the mattress. 'I must have a temperature.'

Matt finished the cooking alone, and served me eventually with a lamb chop which was bloody in the middle, and very bright orange carrots. As I ate, everything resonated. My teeth clicking, my throat swallowing. Twigs collapsed into the fire with the crump of faraway bombs, and the flames hissed, insinuating. The springs of the armchair in which Matt sat eating made a hollow music.

'So how are you doing?' he asked after a while.

I sank deeper into the pillows. 'Ill,' I said truthfully, 'quite ill.'

A startled look crossed his face. 'No, I said – how am *I* doing? Do I get promotion to sister?'

In the night my sleep was dank with sweat and dreams. I dreamed that a Sister shook me awake, saying: 'Mum's here,' and so she was, her hair a bright flame in the salt-white room. Spreading a napkin on the bed to guard against crumbs, she brought out a roll, and whispered that it was scrambled egg, in case they weren't feeding me right. Touched by her concern, I picked it up, but when I opened my mouth to bite I saw that it was full of worms.

40

And so it is time to go to the market, bumping in the car along the track through narrow corridors of trees. Matt cries out at a flash of antlers in the thorny dark undergrowth, and I wonder suddenly if I haven't judged him too harshly. That awful vulnerability of his, the jealousies. How can I, of all people, condemn him for those? When I too have been unhinged by the city and its separations?

The market is in the village square, a cluster of stalls with awnings around the red sandstone of the Corn Exchange. At a second-hand pottery stall, where earthenware jars are warm in the sun, we buy each other glass bottles roughened by the sea – amber for him, green for me. My legs are heavy and rubbery, weakened by the night's fever. Matt takes this with equanimity; he even offers his arm, and as we stroll together eating rum fudge, I can almost convince myself that we are in harmony. Simply a young couple in love, buying cauliflowers and oranges: probably something sophisticated in the city. The eyes of the stallholders testify to it, the whole village witnesses it. The village girls in their clothes which lag two years behind the fashion look on enviously. And it's good to forget, for a while, to drift along with linked arms in the hazy sun of Indian summer, and believe that this is the whole truth of the affair.

A charmed life, I repeat to myself dreamily. Back at the car, Matt takes a cloth from the dashboard and wipes the windscreen clear of fly blots.

'Please mum,' he simpers, 'can we go to the seaside now?'

There's plenty of time. The treats of the day have not yet run out.

We drive due north, along straight roads bordered by wind-twisted pines through which we glimpse now and again a red barn, the square tower of a church, the grey hangars of a USAF base in which bombers skulk, shark-like and silvery.

While we are driving it's easy enough to suspend decisions. I keep up a running commentary – here is a yellow school with its chimney on fire, here under the hedge a clump of red hens sunning themselves, and there a scarecrow, and there above the kale field a single magpie, for sorrow . . . Mile by mile, Matt's responses grow more reluctant. The car slows. Ahead is a tractor and trailer, from which dung-damp straw trails and falls in wisps on to the road. We crawl at ten miles an hour.

Matt looks gloomily at the tractor, and at me.

'Is this what you call relating?'

Having felt it coming, I am prepared.

'Being together – isn't that what you wanted?' To soften the words, I lay my hand on his shoulder. 'If we can just be peaceful together, for a little while . . . '

Matt shrugs, but looks slightly mollified. His hair ruffles in a draught from the window. He wrinkles his nose at the manure smells.

At the coast, a barricade of dunes thatched with wattle fencing holds back the sea. Fine white sand fills our shoes as we clamber down to the beach. It stretches for miles: flat, greyish, fringed with a line of beach huts which the owners have painted in improbable colours. Yellow with purple, red with salmon pink, greens of all shades. The sea glitters.

Matt turns up his jacket collar. 'You shouldn't be afraid of going in deep,' he says into the wind, 'not when I love you . . . ' He purses his lips. 'If only you'd open up about this sex . . . ' But the wind steals the rest of his words, and he frowns, and shivers.

We walk the high water mark, among tousled seaweed and bone-white flints and driftwood pale as Matt's hair. Up on the dunes sheep stop in their tracks as we pass, rocking apprehensively.

'The tide's coming in.'

Matt watches me watching the waves.

'What is it you have to defend?'

I stare mutely at the sea, hunching against the wind. Think, suddenly, of the tales my grandmother told me of our martyrs. Two stakes in the Firth, and two Margarets, mother and daughter. Covenanters. The tide seeping across the mudflats, filling pools, slapping at rocks. The air smelling of salt and herring. Small noises like bubbles bursting as lugworms cast up their spiral heaps on the wet sand. The tide rises, freezing water laps at the base of the stakes, at the hems of the women's gowns, at their calves, their thighs. From the sand dunes men and ministers cry *Recant*! The younger Margaret shakes her head fiercely. The wooden stake to which she is tied feels strangely safe and solid in the whirling water. On the shore the men wait in the marram grass for the screams which never come. They stamp their feet to keep warm. Their boots are careless, crushing oystercatchers' eggs.

I can almost envy them, those proud Margarets. They knew that their cause was just; they could concentrate all the forces of their will on resistance.

Matt takes my arm and turns me to face him. 'It's for your sake, too, dummy. It's yourself you're denying, in the end.'

My mother handed me a roll full of worms.

I take a step back. 'Denying myself, defending myself – I wish you'd make up your mind.'

Matt throws up his arms in exasperation.

'Anyway,' I add, 'we've been through this before. And we agreed it wasn't the time . . . '

'It's *never* the time!' he says angrily. 'When will it be the time?'

On the sand at my feet there are flints, white and calcified on the outside, with dark, gleaming centres. The sand blows at a breath, but the flints are dense, compressed under heat, harder than glass. I stand my ground, feeling mulish, mean, yes, but I cannot help it, he should know better than to drive me into a corner.

'Oh, have it your own way,' he mutters, and strides off down the slope of the beach towards the sea. His shoulders move, his hands, he looks as if he is talking to the empty air, arguing. I bend down and fill my pockets with flints.

Down by the waves Matt eats half an orange, turning the pith inside out like a child does, to get at the last of the flesh. When I join him he is bent over, studying shellfish on a rock, wondering what kind they are, limpets or barnacles. I tell him that barnacles are the tiny jagged ones; when you get keel-hauled, barnacles are what they drag you across.

A wave rattling with small stones rushes at Matt's shoes, and he jumps back. 'I do envy your country lore. We city boys are such wimps.' He looks at me sideways, holds two fingers up behind his head. 'Peace?'

'Peace.'

He grins. 'Nasty way to go, keel-hauling. Worse than walking the plank, by a considerable margin.'

Heading inland again, we drive past greened fences and ash woods, their trunks a vivid lime colour against the rust-red of dead bracken.

'Further to our discussion, dear heart,' Matt says, 'I remembered something, on the beach. I told you I used to live in Detroit, didn't I? Well, it was when I was a kid. Highland Park, it was called. The houses were wooden – mock-ranch and mock-Tudor and mock everything else under the sun. Our house had stained glass doors, with rainbows on, and these lilies, what are they called? Sort of trumpet shaped.'

'Arum lilies?'

'Yeah, funeral things. Anyway, I'm standing outside these doors, and I can see my ma and pa and my brothers. They're sitting in the kitchen, and they're all colours from the stained glass – red and yellow and purple, jawing away like crazy. And it strikes me something important is going down, so naturally I want to get in on it.'

He glances across at me for a second. His hand rotates in the air, as if turning a door handle.

'But the door was locked!'

His eyes widen, there is shock on his face.

'And then?'

'I waved them to open up, but they wouldn't. They were laughing.' He strikes the steering wheel with the flat of his hand. 'They looked so . . . wicked. Their faces kind of floated . . . ' He shakes his head. 'And so I put my fist through the glass! Just like that.'

I'm touched by the bewilderment on his face. 'And you say you'd forgotten all this?' He so rarely speaks of his family, it's strange, it's as if he'd really prefer to be a foundling or an orphan.

'Yes, how could I have forgotten it? Jesus, there was blood everywhere.'

'Back to daddy Freud,' I say, with a sudden frantic hope that this time he will see the shadows as his own, will take them back. I've grown so tired of hearing that he has no problems in life, at least none that a proper relationship wouldn't solve. I glance sidelong at his dreaming face, hold my breath, wait for him to draw the conclusions.

'Even my ma – now why she wouldn't let me in, it beats me.'

The favourite, I think: he was his mother's favourite.

'How could I have forgotten it?' he says again, wonderingly.

'Do you have scars?'

He holds up first one wrist, then the other. 'They faded, I guess.'

I wait, but the subject seems to be closed. Matt begins to hum softly: 'Jesus Christ, Superstar, who are you, what do they say you are . . . ' After a moment's hesitation, I say: 'It's good that you told me.'

'Yeah?'

'I mean, I don't want to be the glass you have to put your fist through.'

'Aha.' His face closes. 'Instant-shrink. More to her than meets the eye.' He is ironic, sparring again. I think of a Chinese game we played once. It was a game of bluff. Stone blunts scissors, scissors cut paper, paper wraps stone.

One, two, three, our fists banged on the mattress.

Stone, mine. Stone, his: two clenched fists.

And again. Stone: stone.

Then two fingers outstretched. Scissors: scissors.

No winners. It was uncanny. I raised my fist of stone in a

salute.

'Matched.'

He wrapped his open hand around it. 'Paper,' he grinned.

The village pub is flat-fronted, a whitewashed building squeezed against a narrow pavement in the main street. Saturday night, and the street is empty, windswept. Inside there are benches like pews, with high wooden backs. At the bar, two farm labourers play a tranquil game of shove ha'penny. The barmaid eyes Matt admiringly, and hurries to serve him.

The brandy warms and anaesthetises. I lean back on the padded bench and watch other people come into the bar. There are two young couples in good Saturday clothes who greet each other but don't sit together. One of the girls wears an engagement ring, the other is married and pregnant, with her first child, otherwise presumably, she wouldn't be out. The four faces are so alike that they might be siblings or cousins – the same broad cheeks and pink skin, the hair all shades of blond, from mustard yellow to a pale mealy colour like the sand on the shore. They speak with country quietness, moving their lips only a little, so that it's impossible to eavesdrop on them.

Compared to them, Matt looks thin, subtle, exiled. When he sees me appraising him he frowns and says reproachfully: 'Care to join me in the here and now? That is, if you've fully recovered.' He wipes a milky froth of beer from his mouth, studies my face with the truculent attention of a lip-reader, and I look away. Remembering hurts. Not so long ago I would have sworn that he could hear my dreams. Not so long ago he was claiming me on the basis of . . . what? What was natural, wordless, exuberant? . . . but claiming me, anyway, I'd never felt so claimed. And so it's hard not to feel, now, that he has gone back on that promise.

'Tell me, then,' he says, 'what's the verdict?'

'Verdict?'

'Come on, I know I've been on trial all day.'

'Must you stir it?'

Matt thumps his beer glass down. 'So this is your idea of a good time,' he snaps. He stares round the bar with a look of indignation, a look which withers and distorts like the splintered mirror of the Snow Queen, a look that sucks me in against my will. Until I can see nothing here but shabbiness: the bar lights pink as butchers' windows, to make the meat look fresh; the young men oafish and inbred; the girls prinked out with an inane vanity.

I fight back sullenly. 'What's wrong with just sitting?'

'Well, you're not exactly a rave to be with . . . all day, this clinging to me, then pushing me away.' His sniff is self-pitying. 'I feel like a bloody yo-yo.'

'Thanks a million.' I sip brandy, steadying myself.

Matt's eyes fill with angry tears. 'I mean, with all your sexual problems and depressions and whatnot, you're hardly a laugh a minute!'

Straight to the heart of the matter. I wonder how long he has been holding this back. I think of the nursing, the caretaking, the caresses: all fraudulent, then, the product of a terrible restraint.

'Quite a heavy little number, in fact,' he adds.

'And you?' I say, trying not to shout, 'you're a lightweight?' I reach for a cigarette, but Matt catches my wrist, and then I do shout, horribly loud and hysterical in that soft-spoken place: Stop controlling me! My arm jerks and sweeps Matt's glass off the table. The shove ha'penny players turn and stare hard. Beer dribbles over the table, the floor. The barmaid frowns across the bar.

'Do you have a cloth or something?' Matt gets up and goes over to her. I watch how winningly he smiles. Little boy lost, so vague, so eager to make amends.

Her face softens. 'Happens every day, dear.'

When Matt sits down again with a fresh glass of beer his angelic smile still hovers, and I'm entirely in the wrong. 'Just remember,' I hiss at him, 'it takes two to make a problem.'

'Well, I'm glad you've admitted *that* at last.' He nods to one of the players who has winked at him, and says to me out of the side of his mouth: 'Everybody knows how difficult *you* are.'

'Everybody knows, everybody knows – *who* knows?'

'Oh, Vi, the sisters – who else?' Before I can react his hand is on my arm, restraining me. 'Look, I've been at my wits' end trying to understand you . . . and if you won't help me, I have to look elsewhere . . . ' His face floats, a mask of concern. 'It's the way you clam up on me – I have to do *something.*'

My head is suddenly hot and fogged with panic. I grip the edge of the seat, and see Matt as Vi saw him – the spider in his web of telephone wires, that hateful portrait. I see the room slide sideways to cast me off, and there he is, waiting to catch me, the one who prised me loose in the first place. The magician, grinning, proud of his sleight of hand. 'You mean you talked to people behind my back?'

He shrugs. 'I don't see there's anything to get melodramatic about.'

Coins click across the polished gaming board. The barmaid giggles with a customer at the hatch of the public bar. He's lying. Any other conclusion is unthinkable. 'I don't believe you. You have nothing but contempt for my friends.'

'Your *what?*'

Turning, I meet a blue stare of pure vindictiveness. How ugly he is when cornered. How ugly his tricks. Ugly as sin. The icy, startled thoughts jab at me. I can't bear to look at him. His hand walks down my arm, pounces on my hand, encloses it. 'Seriously, love, all I want is to *engage* with you. I'm only digging for the real June, and Jesus, for that I need all the help I can get.'

'You're *mad.*' I try to drag my hand away, but he has it pinned down. Sweat breaks out on my forehead. 'I'm sick,' I say, shivering, 'I want to go home.'

He gives a short, gasping laugh. 'Sick? So am I. Sick of *you*.

I can speak and speak till my words run out, I think, and he'll just cover my hand with his, and block up my mouth with his, and round and round we'll go, locked, mechanical, demented. '*Please*,' I beg, as the nausea rises, 'I need to.'

'Ho, so we're back to that old whine, are we? You and your *needs*. All the same, you lot . . . ' His voice soars to a mocking falsetto. "What about my *needs*?" you say, "What about my needs?" . . . Well, what about my *knees*, I say, what about my knee-ees?' He ends on a high, squealing singsong note, and throws his head back. 'Christ!'

Tears well up, impotent, childish. 'I'm sick and I need to go back now . . . ' I listen to the stupid persistent pleading, to the girl's voice which surely can't be mine, for haven't I always known better than to throw myself on anyone's mercy? The voice goes on, tinny, infantile, expecting protection where there is none . . . the nausea ebbs and flows. I look Matt in the eye. 'That's it,' I say. 'The end. I'm not seeing you any more, understand?'

Matt's finger stabs at the air. 'Bullshit you aren't! You don't pack me off just like that. I'm not one of your men-against-sexism weeds, your *camp-followers* . . . ' He looks at me triumphantly. 'You see, you can't just decide on your own, wanker. No way.'

The girl cannot contradict, her mind is hobbled, dreaming; if she tries to run the mud sucks at her feet and all her force can propel her only inches. Think clearly now, choose only words which can't be snatched up and twisted, words which will cut us both free.

'There never are any guarantees that things will work out . . . I'm saying . . . I'm admitting to myself . . . that they haven't. And if one of us thinks that, it's over, don't you see that?'

'Don't talk to me as if I was six. Really, who *would* put up with you?' He is sneering, but his face is grey, parched-looking.

'Face it, then,' I urge, desperate now. Does he not see the damage we do to each other? '*Don't* put up with me. Put an end to it!'

Suddenly he's on his feet, pulling on his jacket. 'Are you coming, then?' As if nothing remarkable had passed between us. His face is blank, his voice only faintly impatient. 'I'm driving you back. Isn't that what you wanted?' And automatically I am standing up, following him to the door.

Inside the car it's frosty; our breath steams. Not a word from Matt, not a protest, but the silence is still frightening, for I've never known him to give in so easily. And even silence, after all, can be turned to his advantage, can obliterate what went before. But he will not get away with it, I'm determined about that.

'If you think you can keep me against my will, you must be mad.'

Matt's profile is frozen, haughty. 'I'm not going to waste my time arguing with you.'

'Which means you agree?'

'Which means I've had it up to *here*.' His voice is prim, scornful. I see that for the moment I am the small girl who has erred and must be brought back into line.

'Good. So you won't grudge me my freedom.'

'Freedom,' he cries, wrestling with the gearstick. 'You don't know the meaning of the word. Freedom for what? To say no? To run away?' He finds the gear, and calms down a little. 'I'm telling you, one day you've got to learn how to say yes.'

'And you're going to teach me, I suppose?' *If you're man enough*. The taunts rise to my lips, I'm brimming with them, a regular harpy.

He swipes sideways at me, clipping my shoulder. 'You're really pushing it,' he mutters.

Now it's my turn to sneer. 'Is that some kind of threat?' *I dare you, I dare you*. Now that I've forfeited all rights to Matt's protection, the abuse burns in me, and I'm an adolescent again, a boasting boy itching for a fight. I'm panting a little, my mouth puffs out clouds of steam in the cold air. It's Matt who has brought me to this, who has backed me into a corner, and I hate him for it, but at the same time I'm oddly thrilled and askew; the jubilation rages in me. But now something else, suddenly: a smothering, aberrant desire which has no place here, which the boy would stamp out ruthlessly if he could. I turn my head away, hiding, feeling the beginnings of disgust. For how Matt would crow if he knew how even in hating him, I want him; what a meal he would make of it. I breathe on the frosted window and melt a hole big enough to see through; soon, almost instantly, I'm collected again. All of this will have to be examined some day, but not now, not in enemy territory. Truths are luxuries reserved for peace-time: this is one lesson I've learned from Matt. We are driving down a tunnel of darkness at the end of which the moon glints, and somewhere under the black skirts of the trees is the cottage, and in the cottage is the white room. The logic of it has been there, of course, from the beginning.

'You'll freeze up there,' Matt says angrily. He still can't believe that I'm serious.

'No.' I unlock the cupboard in the kitchen and find two paraffin stoves, one without a wick, and a box of candles. Without saying goodnight, I carry everything upstairs.

In the room, little has changed. A crimson and brown rug hangs on the wall, obscuring a place where in the old days the plaster was spongy and flaking. There's a dusty oblong on the floor where Matt removed one mattress. The other is in the place I remember – against the wall which faces the deep-silled window. Under the window, an iron-hooped chest where sheets and blankets are stored. Behind the bed, at knee height, there's a square alcove in the wall, with a candle in an old-fashioned blue enamel holder.

Tugging at the wick of the paraffin heater, I think of Vi. Sometimes you have to take yourself by the scruff of the neck, she said. I shiver. To do that you need allies, helpers, and I'm alone here.

Cobwebs. It's such a square room, like a white cube. Vi likes me, Mike likes me, Andrew likes me. I repeat the words to myself like a litany.

I undress quickly down to my socks and underwear, and sneeze at the first encounter with the cold sheets. Through the floorboards I can hear twigs crackling on the fire downstairs, a safe, warm, tempting sound, and I lie rigid, listening, envying

Matt, and thinking: how foolish; I'm ill, I should make more allowances for myself. I look at the door. It is white too, made of tongue and groove boards, with a heavy metal latch. I look at it, but I know that it would be easier to fly to the moon than to cross the room and open it. There is no escape there, only the same flecked and hissing darkness. Either way, I will dive and go down, whether he propels me or my own weight takes me. Neither way is safe. But if I wish to nose deeply for my own shadows, or lie still as a newt on a stone, will he allow this? Has he ever allowed this? No, he must be there, I must go down only as far as he can follow me with his eye, must bring back gifts in my teeth, can keep nothing for myself. Better to go alone.

The candle flickers in its holder, and small insects sizzle in the hot wax. The blue of the enamel holder intensifies.

One thing I've learnt is that qualitative changes in the colours and sounds of things signal the entrance of the underlying. Reds and greens sparkle, blues burn, sibilants overrule other sounds. All you have to do is look and listen. It would comfort me to think that it was merely a question of frequency, of wave-length, quite explicable by science. I'd like to believe that someone has the answers.

I didn't flee from here without good reason, that much is certain.

The height, that is the other thing: the cold crystalline leap and soar, the ghostly ticking of mind and will.

The air inside the white room whispers with illness. Mine. June's. In the four corners of the room her voice is imprinted, a nervous high twittering. And inevitably, the room becomes dangerous.

There is only myself, raging mind in the immovable echoing night. Jed has turned away, or perhaps I have pushed him away, and for comfort I am touching myself. (Natural enough, I suppose, to seek the centre there, to stake a claim.) With one forefinger and thumb I twist and twirl at the wiry hairs, but that little mountain of mine which is both plump and bony feels like nothing of mine. Keeping my elbow away from Jed – who has been denied – I work and work away at it, too determined at first, too abrasive. Change the angle, shift in the mattress, alter the speed and the friction. It's possible of course that Jed may still be awake, but he has seen a woman masturbate before and in any case I am past caring.

Outside in the wood, the hoot of an owl. Downstairs, Matt moves in the mattress. He'll be smoking, watching the fire, waiting for me to weaken. I must breathe slowly, loosen the bonds around the chest.

Stroking and pummelling, the charge builds. I suck in deep breaths, for the fear has leaked in and is adding electricity, almost too much: it is like a mixing of atoms, a confusion of incompatible chemicals. I see myself prickle with a strange glow like the aura of the candle flame, an alarming blue shimmer, and I want suddenly to wake Jed and say: look what you would have risked, entering. I watch it wreathe my arms, and think of cats, these cats painted by schizophrenics, animals whose fur is a glistening frizz which can shock your fingertips. Rubbing with my thumb, I hook a finger inside and tickle firmly, as if at the yielding place behind a cat's ear, and my fingers collect pure static. The current leaps, crossing ridges. And all the time I am moving higher. Some way below, Jed is very small, and still shrinking, and it occurs to me that I am in no way anchored by him, and I see at once that it is a challenge, a challenge issued not to Jed, but only to those worthy of it.

I rose and rose, then, as the cold moon climbs: I was beating hard, to reach the top. The risk was the icy-blue place up there, just ahead, I was nearing it . . . don't turn, I told myself. On and on, I propelled myself.

The electricity bolted through, spinning me of course. I convulsed once or twice, and then I was dropping, drifting to earth, no longer weighed by the useless tumescence of flesh and feeling, but clean and clear, my head burnt empty as a scraped egg . . .

Smell of paraffin from the stove. Weight of blankets. My face is wet. It isn't fair, it isn't fair at all. That place. It was nothingness. They say its existence is purely theoretical, but they're wrong. For when I descended I carried it back with me into the whitewashed room and the low bed.

I was so excited. There had been punishment, yes, but I had taken it bravely. I had travelled, and I had returned, and with the return I felt nothing, needed nothing; I was light and whirring, like a moth. I shook Jed to wake him, to tell him that at last it was over: the clinging girl was banished for ever, and I was free again, and worthy.

Jed jerked his head up and the draught guttered the candle. His long brown hair had streaked red furrows along his cheek. His eyes were bloodshot.

'What?' he said, and I shrank a little. 'What?' He dragged strands of hair out of his mouth and cried at me: 'What are you saying now?' And then, rolling over, turning his back, he muttered to the wall: 'Oh God. Sweet Jesus.'

Disturbed, I kissed his shoulder and asked if he was all right. And again I tried to tell him my news, several times and in several ways – first reassuringly, then urgently, then cheerfully. But still he resisted, and in the end burrowed his head under the pillow to obliterate my voice.

I placed the flat of my hand between his shoulder-blades and let it rest there, waiting for him to calm. After his groaning had been going on for some time I realised that he was crying, and I was astonished that he should cry now, of all times, when there was no longer any need for tears. I stroked him once, tenderly, making a circle with my hand, and wondered how to make him understand that it was a time, instead, of heroes, a time for welcomes and celebrations.

Suddenly Jed threw off the pillow and turned on me with a stare like a wild man's. Tears clung to the bristles on his chin. His teeth glittered in the candlelight...

'Ah yes. Autonomy,' Reuben said, when I first mentioned my stay up there among the angels. 'But what about dependency?'

But on whom, I thought, stranded in that consulting room, belonging nowhere: who will contain it? I told him that I did not know the meaning of pity. 'I broke my mother's favourite vase,' I warned, 'it was china. I stamped it into the floor.'

'Don't worry about me,' he replied. 'I don't break so easily. I am elastic. I bounce back.'

The crimes that I listed! Against mothers, children, dolls. Crimes of robbery, of breaking and entering.

He linked his arms behind his head, and flexed his muscles, and smiled. 'You still haven't convinced me of how very *bad* you are.'

'No,' I argued, 'it's you who hasn't convinced me that I'm *not*.'

Oh, certainly I was mad. The girl knew it, too, learned as much from Jed's uncomprehending stare, and fled to Phil's arms hoping to find herself. That girl soft as an oyster who has lodged in me since, and whom I have grudged. The girl to whom Matt signalled. She is curled now in a ball in the centre of the bed, hugging herself, thinking of warmth, thinking of Andrew. His bedtime. Mutterings on the stairs, snatches of comic-strip conversation: Asterix and Spiderman, funnymen and supermen. The hands rinsed briefly under the tap and the dirt wiped off on the towel. Squeak of bedsprings. Sssh. Goodnight. Goodnight.

Cobwebs flutter and droop in the corners of the window frame.

As for Matt. Well. He knows another desperate character when he sees one. He knows, too, how to punish; truly, we were meant for each other.

Cynical, I'm being cynical. A perceptible change. Inch by inch, I am tearing away from him.

Think of good things, the good things Reuben told me I must learn to take in. Perhaps I just need more time. But then, how much time does it take? (Goodnight, goodnight.)

When I sleep, I dream of one of those toys, Kelly Dolls, they call them, which are round and weighted at the bottom, so that if you push them they may swing over but always right themselves again. This one is life-size, though, the image of my father, and something has gone very wrong with it. It simply will keep falling over. Phil and I stand with our arms round its ample waist, and with our combined strength we try to prop it up, even after we realise that this toy-father is, after all, quite dead.

41

Morning. Sunday bells in the distance. Today we will go back.

Downstairs, the kitchen table rolls with yesterday's purchases. All through breakfast Matt slashes at me with his words. I can eat nothing, but drink coffee and listen, licking honey from a knife.

Outside, it continues, until finally in the sycamore grove beside the cottage I put my hands over my ears and scream at him to stop. He pays no attention; I see his mouth working and working, fanatical, and hit out at him. He floors me with one kick.

He looks very big standing above me, with his feet crushing the clover heads. I curl up on the ground beside the well. Not a word, not a word. Stone blunts scissors.

He watches my face, and goes white, blank.

Under me, frost-crisped leaves, dank leaves, crinkled cases of beech nuts. 'Out. I want out.'

I get up and walk towards the cottage with my back as straight as any gladiator. There's so much to be done before we leave: sweeping, and clearing out the ashes, and the rugs have to be shaken; the cottage must be left spick and span, the way Mike left it for us. But first, I remove the axe from the woodpile where Matt has left it, and lock it away with the paraffin heater in the cupboard.

After a while Matt joins me. He takes instructions meekly. I feel his eyes on me.

When we have finished, he pleads: 'Come with me. Just for a minute.'

I look at my watch. 'It's time to go.'

'Look, I know you're angry with me. Just come with me while I wash . . . throw a bucket of water at me or something.'

I follow him to the well. He pulls off his clothes and

stands naked on the wet grass.

When I loose the rope to let the bucket hurtle down into the water the axle spins and the trestle shudders crazily. A yellow leaf drops from the sycamore branch, flutters down on to Matt's bare shoulder, rests there tenderly. Down below, the bucket hits the surface of the water with a smash. I begin to wind it in. Watching me, Matt winks and pumps up his muscles: a Charles Atlas pose.

'You will throw it at me, won't you?'

I nod. Certainly I'll play, if games will get me out of here.

The water hits him full in the face, making him jump back. He shudders with the cold, courts me with terrible faces. 'Better?' he says, 'Do you feel better now?'

'Slightly,' I lie, but evidently he believes me, for as he rubs himself with the towel he is smiling.

The bare body with its curves and hollows confronts me, sun-dappled. I look at him severely. Severe, severing, I am severing the bonds. My heart twists.

'Shouldn't you put your clothes back on?' I look at him, the brilliant flaring surface of him, one last time.

The motorway is grey and long. I sit with my arms folded tightly, protecting the soft parts.

The tide of words begins again. I answer absently, playing for time. Suddenly he brakes, flings the wheel round, stops short on the hard shoulder. Behind us a Volkswagen swerves, blaring its horn.

'What are you going to do?'

'About what?'

His arm slides along the back of my seat. 'Relationships. Another relationship.'

I edge away from him. He knows the weak spots. A woman alone. But that is no longer any concern of his. 'Nothing,' I say, keeping all expression out of my voice.

'But who else would put up with you?'

'That's my worry.'

He hugs the steering wheel, and rests his head on his arms. 'But how will you manage?' he says miserably. 'I mean, how will you get what you need?'

I stare at him, startled by his tone. There are *tears* in his eyes.

'I'm your chance for life,' he says, and his voice breaks. 'Some things you just know in your gut . . . '

'How do I know how I'll manage?' I answer helplessly.

He wipes his eyes on his sleeve. His pupils are stretched wide, black, despairing. 'But what about me?' His vision pummels at me; I have no protection against this mischief. He's shivering, I can't bear it. A dangerous groaning sound comes from him. 'I'll always love *you*,' he says.

I cover my ears and shout; he must stop, I can barely take responsibility for myself, can't he see that, is he blind and deaf?

'I have one child already, damn you!'

Scissors cut the cord: a clean cut, sterile.

His head snaps back. His fist trembles in the air. 'You're a murderer, you know that? A murderer!'

The words echo. Crimes against passion. For a long moment I watch the colours pass over his face. He can beat and beat at me with his little boy's fists, I think coldly, but I am not his glass to be smashed through.

'If you don't drive on, I'm getting out.'

He chokes with rage, and shouts back at me that I am gutless, despicable. 'So this is your idea of life, liberty and the pursuit of happiness?' he snarls. 'You prefer your rotten fantasies to the real thing.'

I put my hand on the door handle. 'Maybe. Maybe you do, too. Maybe we just weren't the people we expected each other to be.'

'Always got your slimy escape routes, haven't you?' he mutters. 'Christ, what movie do you think you're in?' But he starts the car.

It's dark and starry when we arrive at the house, and the city air smells of fireworks. Matt turns the ignition off and we sit for a moment in silence. Now everything has been said and done, I think.

'Do you want me to come in?' he asks.

'No.' I gather my belongings together. The flints I collected for Andrew clank together in their plastic bag. 'No.'

'You threw it all away, you lousy bitch,' he cries, as I close the car door.

Upstairs I take the flints from the bag and arrange them on my dressing table, end to end, in a long chain. Outside, they are white as the bones of dead heroes; inside, spangled dark hearts.

When I sleep, I dream that I bear a child which Matt doesn't want, which no one in the big collective house wants – there are already too many children, they say, and not enough space. There are no cards or congratulations for the baby girl, and, sensing she's unwelcome, she squalls and rages a lot. It's all I can do to hide the noise from the others. I have to keep her tucked away in a filing cabinet in my bedroom, with scraps of doll's bedclothes to cover her and hardly a corner in the cupboard for her nappies. For the Ostermilk and bottles I clear a space on my dressing table between the mirror and the make-up jars. And gradually, very gradually, the tiny wrinkled thing grows plump and obstreperous, and laughs, and throws leaflets into the air.

At eight o'clock I wake with my thumb still in my mouth. Andrew stands at the end of my bed, coughing politely. I sit up and sneeze hard.

'I heard you come back last night,' he says, 'but you didn't look in.' Even in the greenish half-light I can see that his face is flushed. He coughs again, a real, rough cough this time.

'You're not well.'

'I must have caught your cold.' He plays with the cord of his dressing gown. 'Did you have a good time?'

I hesitate, about to lie, then shake my head.

'No, actually I didn't.'

He clears his throat.' 'I don't think I feel like going to school.' He watches his bare toe trace patterns on the rug.

'I don't think I feel like going to work, either.'

He looks up eagerly, and both of us laugh.

'Welcome to the sick-bay,' I say, and draw the quilt aside.

Book
Tokens
Give them
the pleasure of choosing
Book Tokens can be bought
and exchanged at most
bookshops